What people are saying about

Into Sh

Not your traditional high fantasy.

Has all the traditional elements – an uncertain hero, loyal companions, a magical item that puts the world at risk, a perilous quest, a powerful adversary – and Morgan Daimler turns these elements all on their heads.

And it works. Beautifully.

Into Shadow is an adventure that will surprise and delight you.

Catherine Kane, author of *The Land That Lies Between* and *Swans of War*

Morgan Daimler leaves an indelible mark in modern literature, using the power of high fantasy as a means of raising awareness of pressing issues that humanity must confront. *Into Shadows* revolutionizes the genre by redefining the hero archetype and the social norms surrounding marriage and gender identity. Daimler masterfully brings together vibrant and complex characters. Dramatic situations lend themselves to subtle humor, and the suspense continues, until the very last page. *Into Shadows* stands out as an excellent book, equally entertaining and educational.

Daniela Simina, *Where Fairies Meet: Parallels between Irish and Romanian Fairy Traditions*

What a delightful adventure! A rich, well-crafted world, intriguing adventure that kept me guessing throughout, and great action to keep me riveted to the page. I highly recommend this to anyone who wants to escape into another world.

Christy Nicholas, author of *The Druid's Brooch* series

Morgan Daimler is something rare, an author without comparison. I always feel when reading my work that it's easy to see which authors influenced my work, but their writing is so unique, so fresh, that I cannot think of another author to compare them to. They present normal flawed people in a fantasy setting in a way that I never knew I needed. This book is for everyone who thought they were too old, too weak, too impaired to be a hero. It shows us that all we need to be heroic is the love of others and the determination not to let evil stand. I finished this book with a tinge of sadness that the tale was over, but I will take with me so much joy, and the memory of the phrase "Don't try to lessen yourself to keep me comfortable." A lesson I think we could all learn.

Ian Power, author of *The Other* series

With well-written characters and a richly detailed world that stays with you long after you bid your farewell to the last page, *Into Shadow* is the kind of book that lures you in and keeps you hooked.

Catherine Heath, author of *Elves, Witches & Gods*

Into Shadow is a refreshing look at the outsider's experience of grief and sheer determination towards life. So many of us have dragons to slay, but in the process, we must fight not to lose ourselves also. Muireann's experiences really spoke to me, and I was absorbed into her colourful world just like the many wonderful characters who cross her path.

Tara D. W. Tine, author of *Flight of Fire*

Into Shadow

The Tallan Chronicles

Into Shadow

The Tallan Chronicles

Morgan Daimler

COSMIC EGG
BOOKS

Winchester, UK
Washington, USA

JOHN HUNT PUBLISHING

First published by Cosmic Egg Books, 2023
Cosmic Egg Books is an imprint of John Hunt Publishing Ltd., 3 East St., Alresford,
Hampshire SO24 9EE, UK
office@jhpbooks.net
www.johnhuntpublishing.com
www.cosmicegg-books.com

For distributor details and how to order please visit the 'Ordering' section on our website.

ISBN: 978 1 80341 218 4
978 1 80341 219 1 (ebook)
Library of Congress Control Number: 2022934752

Design: Stuart Davies

UK: Printed and bound by CPI Group (UK) Ltd, Croydon, CR0 4YY
US: Printed and bound by Thomson-Shore, 7300 West Joy Road, Dexter, MI 48130

We operate a distinctive and ethical publishing philosophy in
all areas of our business, from our global network of authors to
production and worldwide distribution.

Contents

For everyone who ever thought they couldn't be the epic hero because they weren't thin, able bodied and young. This one's for all the fat, queer, middle-aged people out there who want to be the fantasy hero too.
And for Mel, the Calla to my Muireann (except for the dragon part).

With thanks to my beta readers, Aleja, Ashley, Mara, Máire, Tom and Tricia

Note to readers: Muireann is pronounced roughly 'mwir-ehn'

Chapter 1

The Dragon

The slightest tinge of sulphur was in the air and Muireann knew she was getting close to her destination, although how close she wasn't sure. She'd spent the last winter reading extensively about dragons to prepare for this but reading about it and experiencing it were vastly different things, and in her case was limited by the resources she could lay hands on. Still, she slowed her pace a bit, shifting the strap that held the quiver against her hip, pushing a stray lock of copper-coloured hair behind her ear, adjusted her glasses, and glanced nervously around the newly greening spring woods. The trees hadn't started to thin yet and there was no sign of anything burned – hopefully that meant she was still far enough from the dragon's lair that it couldn't sense her. This was another area that her books had proved less than ideal in, because there were several different types of dragons and every author seemed to have their own opinions and ideas, which were all always expressed as certainties. It was confusing but she was sure she'd gotten the most important things straight anyway.

Not that it matters really, Muireann thought to herself, edging slowly forward, *I'm not going to walk away from this anyway, but as long as I take the dragon out with me, that's alright.* It was a morbid train of thought and yet perversely it was exactly that thought which had kept her going for the last six months. Since the dragon had moved his hunting range west. Since her husband's farm had been attacked, just as winter was closing in and the sheep had all been brought to the farm pasture. Since she had emerged from the rubble of her home, the only survivor; her husband dead in the sheep field, her four beautiful children killed by falling rubble.

1

They'd thought they were safe, although looking back later Muireann had seen the hubris in that. Who could possibly be safe from a dragon? But Edren had been confident they were close enough to town – the closest farm, actually – and would be spared while the farms further away would see their livestock taken. And, of course, until then it had mostly only been livestock taken, she could think of less than a half dozen farms burned or razed to the ground in the 20 years the dragon had made its home on the slopes of Mount Lassen. But who could really predict dragons? They did what they pleased and the warriors and knights who tried to kill them were memorialised in song for a winter, then forgotten.

Honestly Muireann had also thought trying to kill a dragon was hubris, and she recognised the irony that she was throwing her life away at it now. But in the first grief-soaked weeks after the attack she had sat at the graves and promised her children that she would try. Not for her husband, who had been a solid, dependable man but for whom she had no great affection, but for them, her children, who had never made it free of the ruin of their house. Even now after so many months of careful preparation she guessed she had, at best, a fifty per cent chance of doing the dragon any harm at all, but she was committed to trying.

She paused where the trees thinned, giving way suddenly to clear dry ground opening up before the cave in the cliff face where the dragon lived.

This is so ridiculous, she thought, moving her heavy braid over her shoulder before taking the bow and stringing it, testing the tension. *I'm a scribe not a warrior.* Anyone who saw her would have laughed or tried to talk her out of what she was doing. Muireann, farmwife and town-scribe, mother; plump from a job that meant mostly sitting down, with heavy glasses over a pair of weak, green eyes, wearing pants borrowed from her brother that bagged around her ankles and a farmwife's heavy work dress, she was not the picture of a hero in anyone's mind.

But Muireann had spent the last half-year practicing constantly with the bow, until she was skilled enough to shoot an acorn off a tree or take down a small bird on the wing. Obsessively practising and obsessively reading everything she could find about dragons. Her brother had thought it best to leave her to work things out on her own; he hadn't seen the hardened resolve, only the sadness. No matter how ridiculous she looked, she was as ready, or more so, than any of the knights who had tried this same thing before her. They, of course, had all failed, attacking the dragon with brute force and the usual range of human weapons, and dying quickly in flame and ash.

She had a plan, though, one she thought no one had tried before, at least as far as she had been able to find. In her research she'd come across a note, scribbled in the margins of an elvish treatise on dragons, which mentioned a flower which she suspected was poisonous to them. It wasn't certain that it was, but the note mentioned that there were several accounts of northern snow dragons seeming to avoid areas where this plant grew, and the scribe had suggested it was because of the plant. Muireann had taken that idea further and formulated a theory that it was poisonous to them or could be if prepared properly. A bit more research and she'd tracked down the name of the plant in her own language, Snow Cup, and learned it was extremely rare but not completely unknown, and better that it might, possibly, be found in the foothills where she lived. It flowered near midwinter and only for a week, so she'd been worried that she wouldn't be able to find it in time and would have to try again after waiting a full year more, but luck had been with her the fifth day she went looking. On midwinter eve she'd hiked into the hills and run into a woodsman – he had of course cautioned her about being out in such conditions – who had recognised her description of the flower. He had directed her to a small patch of the plants growing close under an ancient yew tree and she'd fallen to her knees there and wept as she gathered them.

Making the poison to coat the arrowheads had been easy after that, just a matter of learning how to properly distil the flowers and preserve the resulting liquid. She had plenty of books that discussed such things, and no one even questioned why she was making a salve from a strange plant or why she wouldn't let anyone else touch it – not because it was any danger to humans but because she thought it too precious to waste. Even if she couldn't be sure it would work it was by far her best chance; dragons were notoriously hard to kill, impervious to almost all weapons, to the usual common run of poisons, to all magic. In the few previous cases where a dragon had been killed the circumstances were exceptional and nearly impossible to replicate.

If she could have she'd have gone after the dragon right then, but common wisdom held that most dragons in areas such as hers with snowy winters sealed themselves into their caves to hibernate in the coldest months. Only the two far northern snow dragons stayed active throughout the heavy winter. Muireann didn't know for certain that it was true all other dragons hid away in winter – so much about dragons was pure speculation – but it seemed logical to her since otherwise wouldn't the great heroes and knights just wait and attack the dragon while it was resting in the winter, rather than fighting it when it was awake in the warmer months? And certainly no one saw that fearsome glittering red form in the skies in the winter, once the snow started to fly. So, she was patient and waited until spring, until she heard a rumour of another dragon attack a few villages north of her own. And then she'd gotten her poisoned salve and her arrows and her bow and walked off into the woods, without a word to anyone.

Taking a deep steadying breath, flinching at the stench in the air, she pulled an arrow, coated the arrowhead carefully in her poisoned salve and readied herself. She raised the bow, stepping slowly out of the cover of trees. The birds had fallen silent long ago and nothing moved here except a slight breeze in the young leaves. It was unnerving and Muireann could hear her pulse hammering in her ears. Across a wide expanse of raw, dry earth the cliffside rose up like a wall. The dragon had carved its cave into this once solid surface but after two decades of use the stone was smooth without any sign of claw marks. Although it looked small in the immense cliffside the cave mouth itself was enormous, a gaping darkness in the lighter reddish stone. A faint haze of smoke drifted from the dim interior of the entrance obscuring whatever was inside, and Muireann swallowed hard, fighting to hold the bow steady.

The truth was she'd never actually seen the dragon before, except high in the sky overhead. The day of the attack she'd been inside, in her root cellar organising supplies for the cold months to come and had only heard the terrible roaring and crashing. Being in the cellar had saved her when the house had come down above but it also meant that she didn't know many things for sure, including the size of the dragon, its speed and most importantly where its eyes were on its head. Her books had been little help as every illustration she'd found had depicted slightly different versions of dragons and it was impossible to guess the truth of the one she was facing. The greatest flaw in her plan was this uncertainty because everything depended on her being able to hit her target, near the eye, quickly. Well, and the not-insignificant chance she'd freeze and fail to even get a single arrow off at all.

She stepped further into the barren expanse, her footsteps loud in the thick silence. She hadn't made it more than a dozen feet when the smoke at the entrance suddenly shifted and billowed, parting as the dragon's head emerged into the afternoon light. Muireann did indeed freeze instinctively at the sight, watching in atavistic terror as the dragon stretched itself up like a cat woken from a nap. The head was easily bigger than any wagon she'd ever seen, no she realised as it moved forward out of the cave, as large as a small house. The scales that covered the dragon from nose tip to tail tip and armoured it against weapons sparkled in the sunlight, a dizzying spill of ruby fire. For one hysterical moment Muireann wondered if the entire animal was burning inside, if that was possible, and then the dragon saw her, its reptilian orange-red eyes narrowing.

With no more warning than that it charged, the massive bulk of it moving lightning fast towards her. Her mind went blank, but her arms came up and aimed, reflexively after so many months of daily practice. When the dragon was almost upon her, she locked eyes with it and fired, her tiny arrow speeding to its target.

The dragon jerked its head sharply to the side, away from Muireann. Before she could react – before she could think – the animal's front leg was lashing out at her, swatting as if she were a mosquito. She saw a blur of shining red coming at her as fast as one of her own arrows.

Muireann's body lurched backwards instinctively, the dragon's claw catching the side of her face. In the moment it touched her a jolt went through her, her whole body spasming painfully. She felt, for an instant, like a wine-skin that was being overfilled, as if she would burst from the terrible pressure.

Then, everything went dark.

* * *

Muireann woke to a blur of blue above her, shivering on the cold ground. At first she couldn't understand what was happening or where she was, but slowly the memory of the gigantic red dragon lunging forward at her came back. She shivered harder, not from cold this time but from fear, her hands scrabbling at the ground around her trying to find her glasses. She was aware enough to realise they must have been knocked off, either by the dragon or when she fell, but without them she couldn't see anything further than a few inches from her face except as a blur of colour. It was unnerving to be on the ground, blind, and unsure where the dragon was or what had happened after she was knocked out.

Finally her fingers grazed the familiar shape and feel of her glasses, and she pulled them to her, newly terrified that they were damaged. Facing a dragon was a nightmare but being out in the wilderness unable to see well enough to survive – possibly with a very angry dragon still around – was a greater one. Luckily the lenses and frame were in about the same state they'd been in before, and she pulled them on with a sense of relief that equalled her earlier panic. The world immediately came back into focus, although she rather wished it hadn't.

A few feet from where she was lying the heavily scaled forearm of the dragon was extended, large as a tree trunk. She remembered, then, the feeling of the dragon's claw hitting her face and in renewed panic reached up and began feeling around her left cheek. Her fingers came away sticky with blood but even when she pushed as hard as she dared she couldn't feel any injury. There was no pain, which she might have put down to shock from the situation, but the lack of pain and lack of any tangible injury despite the blood confused her. After a moment sitting there with one hand pressed to her cheek, staring at the huge red limb, she let out a long shaky breath. The dragon lay completely still and after another cautious moment she clambered awkwardly to her feet, her whole body aching, and moved cautiously towards the animal.

Once she was standing she could see the entire dragon stretched out, as if it had fallen mid-leap. It was so utterly still that she started to dare to hope that she'd succeeded, that despite the odds she'd actually killed it. With growing courage, she stepped closer and reached out to touch it; it was warmer than she'd expected, and she jerked back immediately before reminding herself that it had probably been quite a bit hotter than most animals before and would be slow to cool. She reached out again and ran her hand along its scales; they varied in size from comparable to a knight's shield down to dinner plates and joined together seamlessly. They were as smooth as a stone pulled from the water, soft and almost sensuous under her fingers. She didn't know what she'd expected but it wasn't that. She marvelled at the scales themselves, which fit together perfectly and formed an impervious armour. It was easy to understand, seeing it this closely, why dragons were so impossible to kill.

Well, Muireann thought to herself, suddenly giddy *not impossible. I proved that. Oh, no one will ever believe me!* She fought back a giggle, the emotions of the day and the sheer surrealness of the situation overwhelming her. Taking another deep breath, almost unaware now of the stench of sulphur, she moved forward along the front limb, admiring the deep red claws, each longer than she was tall. Remembering that one of those claws had hit her, or at least grazed her, she shuddered and touched her face again, her previous giddiness dissolving as the reality of the situation started to sink in. *How am I still alive?* she wondered, moving slowly around towards the animal's head. *How was I not impaled or skewered or something else fatal? No one is that lucky.*

The dragon's head was twisted away from her, the neck in such an unnatural position she would have guessed it was dead even if she wasn't sure already. She followed the curving neck around until she reached that giant head, truly so large she felt like a mouse trying to study a human. It was hard to believe that something that huge could exist when she was used to thinking of cows and bears as big animals. She paused a few feet away from the head, staring at the huge open eye which stared back, lifeless, at her. It was half open, a dark orangish red with a vertical black pupil. It was beautiful even in death, as the rest of the dragon was, as if the whole being had been sculpted from red jewels and molten metal.

Barely visible jutting from the corner of the dragon's eye, where all her books said that the main eyelid joined with a second clear eyelid, Muireann saw her arrow. Or at least the fletching of it, as most of the arrow was buried in that one, small, vulnerable spot. The area around the arrow was a shockingly dull grey, as if all the colours had been pulled from it, and she had no doubt that was the work of her poison.

I didn't know it would work so fast, she thought, her emotions swinging into grief. Seeing it dead now it seemed a terrible waste to have killed the dragon. *It's just an animal. It wasn't malicious, it was just doing what dragons do, looking for food. Gods! Dragons are purely magical creatures, like unicorns, and perishingly rare. And now thanks to me there's one less in the world. Because of me.* Her vision blurred as she started to cry, mourning what she'd done. It hadn't brought her children back, it hadn't even let her join them. It had just destroyed something rare and beautiful, no matter how deadly that something was.

She stood there next to the dead dragon and cried for a long time, until she felt as if her body had been drained of tears and she'd made some kind of tentative peace with what she'd done. As much as she regretted it, she knew there was no undoing it. *But I will never tell anyone how I did it*, she thought with the same determination that had set her on her course to kill it in the first place. *If I tell people how I did this then others will try the same thing, all those knights and heroes trying to make a name for themselves, and people seeking treasure, and people who just hate dragons and see them as monsters.* She winced and reached a hand out to caress the scales again. *If anything is a monster here it's me. It only killed for food or by accident because of its size, but I killed it just to kill it.* Deep down she knew that wasn't entirely true, that her reason had been to keep anyone else from suffering the grief that had nearly broken her, but standing there looking at the dragon, magnificent even in death, all she could do was marvel at it and mourn its loss.

Shaking herself out of her reverie Muireann turned and looked around the clearing, unsure what to do now. She hadn't thought there would *be* a now and hadn't had any plan beyond confronting the dragon. She didn't even have any food packed to get her through the hike back to her village.

With no clear direction she walked slowly back around the dragon's outstretched forelimb and then started walking along the length of its body. The entire creature was so massive it was hard for her to really comprehend it; it reminded her somewhat of the time one of the great whales had washed up, dead, on shore and everyone had hiked out to see it. It just seemed too large to be real. It lay like a glittering red hill, the wing on that side partially unfurled as it relaxed in death. She walked under it, between the bulk of the body and the cover of the curled wing, craning her head up. The joint of the wing was perhaps twenty feet above her head on the dragon's shoulder and the wing itself, even folded, extended over an area that her village square could have easily fit in. The sun was blocked out and without thinking she wandered closer to where the wing met the ground, reaching out to touch it. She had assumed that dragon wings would be something like a bat's wings, like skin stretched between bones, but she quickly realised that wasn't so. The dragon's wing was covered in tiny scales, each no bigger than one of Muireann's fingernails.

Pulling herself away from the mesmerising tiny scales she walked further down its body, seeing that its back legs were stretched out behind it and its tail extended back into the cave. Overcome with a morbid curiosity she decided to see how long its tail was, to try to get some sense of the length of the animal. She thought perhaps she could make some good come from what she'd done by writing a thorough description of the animal, to add to the existing material about dragons which was often based on observations of living animals from distance.

She should have anticipated how large the cave would be to fit the dragon's bulk but somehow stepping into the enormous space was still a shock. At first all she could do was gape upwards at the roof and walls, which had been worn or melted smooth like the entrance. Finally she tore her eyes away and looked down, noting the packed earth of the cave's floor and the clutter of material pushed to the edges. Stepping closer to one wall she tried to identify some of the flotsam packed in there but it was impossible to make sense of it all: gold (of course), spears and swords, armour, bones, metal wheel rims, platters, iron hoops, jewels and jewellery...she realised it was all shiny or had been once before it tarnished or rusted. *It's like a magpie,* she thought fascinated, *filling its nest, or cave anyway, with any shiny thing it finds.*

Stepping back again she moved further into the dim interior walking along the extended tail. The space seemed to go on endlessly, growing darker as it went further into the mountain side. Muireann could hear running water as well as the slow dripping of water from somewhere ahead, the sounds running together. Even though she knew the dragon was dead it was unnerving, the stillness and slow sound of water and the growing darkness. She started to back up and tripped over a helmet, falling gracelessly to the ground and swearing.

Before she could pick herself back up a voice called from the darkness above her. 'Hello? Is anyone there?'

She froze, shocked, then cleared her throat. 'Ah, yes. I'm here. Where are you?'

'I'm up here,' the voice replied, agitated. 'Hurry and help me get down before it comes back.'

Muireann squinted, searching the walls around her until she noticed the opening about thirty feet up. 'Give me a minute to find something to help get you down. And, ah, you don't have to worry about it coming back. It's dead.'

'What!' the shout echoed in the space and Muireann winced. 'How can it be dead?'

'That's a long story,' Muireann shouted back, picking through the debris on the ground looking for anything that might be useful. 'I'll tell you later but let's focus on getting you down first. Is anyone else up there with you?'

'Not anyone alive,' the voice responded, grim now. 'It's got a bit of a cache of food up here and I'm unlucky enough to be one of its saved-for-later bits.'

Grimacing again Muireann moved aside what looked like a door, covered in brass fittings, and an almost completely intact glass window before finding a heavy iron hook attached to a length of equally heavy rope. She suspected it was a ship's anchor, but it didn't look like any that she'd seen before. 'Hang on. I think I found something that can help. Are you hurt?'

'Just a bad knock on the head.'

'If I throw you up a rope can you climb down?'

Her question was met by silence for almost a minute then finally. 'I think so. There's nowhere in here to tie a rope but I... have an idea.'

Since the stranger had mentioned being in with corpses Muireann really didn't want to ask for any details about this idea. Instead, she worked to get the rope untied from the anchor and retied to a smaller metal crosspiece whose original use she couldn't figure out. It was enough to give a bit of weight to the end of the rope, though, and she knew she'd need that to throw it where she wanted and give the stranger time to catch it.

For the next half hour Muireann stood and tried tossing the rope, over and over again. Sometimes she missed entirely. Sometimes the rope would just start to disappear into the black space of the smaller cave then fall back. Her arms burned with the effort and sweat dripped off her face, but she kept trying, ignoring the encouraging words and suggestions being shouted at her, which were only a distraction. Just when she thought her arms and back couldn't take any more efforts, the rope disappeared into the space with a metallic clang, the crosspiece hitting against stone inside, than went taut in her hands. Above her the stranger gave out an excited cry, pulling at the rope as they did whatever they needed to do to secure it on their end.

Muireann, for her part, looked around frantically for a place to anchor her end of the rope and finally, afraid her new friend was about to try climbing out when there was nothing holding it but herself, jogged over to the dragon's tail and hastily tied it off to one of the smooth spines that protruded regularly down the animal's back. Not sure that was enough to anchor it she also stood and held it as well, slightly terrified that she'd gone to all this trouble only to have the stranger plunge thirty feet to the ground if the rope slipped.

She was facing the dragon when the tension on the rope shifted, the coarse material pulling against her hands. She put her shoulder into it, trying to keep it steady as it fought her like a living thing. And then it went slack.

'Thank you, I can't tell you how grateful I am to be out of that mess,' the stranger said from somewhere behind her, the voice much happier than before.

Muireann let go of the rope and turned to face the person she'd just helped.

It turned out that the voice belonged to a high elf and for a moment Muireann was rendered speechless. She had known a few elves in her life, was even friends with a river elf who sold books in the closest town, but she'd never met one of the reclusive, powerful high elves who ruled her world before. She was about the same height as Muireann, perhaps five-and-a-half feet, so that the two women stood eye to eye. The woman's skin was a rich golden brown, her hair fell to her waist in a mass of bright scarlet red, and her eyes were black. Her gently pointed ears would have made her elven heritage plain if the faint aura of magic around her hadn't. She was well muscled and sturdy, clearly a fighter even without a blade strapped to her side, and she carried herself with the pride that Muireann would expect from one of the elves who ruled across the kingdoms. She was wearing heavy canvas pants, knee-high leather boots, a fine dark blue linen shirt and a heavy leather belt. The clothes were bloody, ripped and worse for wear but had clearly been good quality when they were new.

Feeling suddenly awkward in her second-hand pants and homespun wool, she said, 'Hello, I'm Muireann.'

The elf smiled and nodded. 'Hi. I'm Callavealysia, but you can call me Calla.'

'Oh, ah, alright. Calla.'

The elf nodded again, staring past Muireann at the clearly deceased dragon. 'So Muiri, tell me the story of how this happened.'

She opened her mouth to object to the nickname, then shut it, deciding it was better than what she'd heard during her childhood. After a silence that was too long and an impatient gesture from Calla she mumbled. 'Well, I killed it.'

'You killed it? How?' Calla said, sounding curious but not shocked. Muireann was oddly grateful for that, as she knew she didn't present the picture of someone who would be out slaying dragons.

'Ah, right,' she mumbled, trying to think of how to explain what she'd done without giving too much away. 'Well, I, ah, shot it. In the eye.'

'And that killed it?' Calla did sound sceptical now, no doubt well aware that such an insignificant wound shouldn't have brought down the magical creature.

Feigning nonchalance, Muireann shrugged. 'I can show you the arrow if you want. It's still in place, where it struck.'

Calla looked thoughtful, then nodded again. 'I would like to see it yes, if only so I can tell this story properly later.'

Shrugging slightly Muireann led the other woman out and around to the dragon's head, gesturing broadly towards the shaft sticking out of the corner of its eye.

Calla glanced at the quiver still hanging from Muireann's hip, then back to the dragon. 'That is your arrow, and the dragon is definitely dead. I must admit I wouldn't have believed it if I hadn't seen it myself but as you say, you killed it with an arrow in the eye.'

Muireann waited for Calla to comment on the strange discolouring around the eye, not sure what she'd say to explain it, but the elf didn't say anything. Instead, she moved with an agility that the human could only envy and started climbing up the animal's head. The sight of the elf easily scaling the smooth surface drove any questions from Muireann's mind and she simply stood and watched, starting to understand why people found elves so intimidating. Calla disappeared from sight just over the dragon's eye ridge and Muireann moved back trying to see what she was doing.

Before she could get a better view, Calla was already sliding back down, landing easily on her feet. *That looked like fun,* Muireann thought, oddly envious. She couldn't remember the last time she'd done anything purely for fun. Then the elf was walking over to her, one hand thrust out. Without thinking Muireann put her own hand out and Calla dropped a large, flat, crystal into her hand. Muireann stared at it in fascination; it looked somewhat like an opal but was dark red and the colours were subtly shifting in it, like slow moving flames. She stared at it for a moment, mesmerised by the coruscating shades of crimson. It was slightly warmer than her skin, not uncomfortably so but noticeably. She looked up, meeting Calla's eyes. 'Why did you give me this?'

Calla's bright red eyebrows rose towards her hairline. 'It's the Dragon Stone. You killed the dragon, it should be yours.'

Muireann looked back at the jewel, recognising it as soon

as Calla named it, her mouth going dry. She had read about Dragon Stones and heard stories but had never seen one or even dreamed of holding one. They weren't properly stones, of course, but something more like horn or scale, a natural substance formed by the dragon, between its eyes, which contained, according to popular wisdom, the dragon's essence. Muireann doubted this was literally true as the stones were not reputed to have any particular magical qualities, but she suspected the real value of the stone was in its rarity. Until that day there had only been three of the distinctive Dragon Stones in the world; they were considered priceless and held by the wealthiest families, including the imperial family. As surreal as it had been to see the dragon dead after she'd first woken up, seeing the glittering Dragon Stone in her hand was even more so. *I'm just a simple village scribe,* Muireann thought, watching the colours move languidly across the stone's surface. *My only claim to fame is that I can read and write better than anyone else in the village. It's madness to be standing here holding this as if it belongs to me.*

Unnerved at all the implications, Muireann tried to hand the stone back to Calla. 'Here, you take it.'

The elf put her hands up, stepping quickly away. 'Absolutely not. You saved my life, I'm not going to rob you now.'

'You aren't robbing me. I'm giving it to you.'

'It belongs to you.'

'No,' Muireann insisted. 'It belongs to a hero or warrior or, or someone great. One of the great families.'

'You are a hero,' Calla said, as simply as if she were commenting on the fair weather.

'I am *not* a hero,' Muireann said, shifting uncomfortably.

Calla rolled her eyes. 'You killed a dragon.'

'Well, I...no...I mean *yes* I did, but...' she trailed off flustered.

'You don't think killing a dragon is heroic, Muiri? Because I'm fairly certain it's the best definition of a hero. That's why all those fools keep throwing their lives away trying to accomplish it,' the high elf's words dripped with amusement and Muireann felt herself blushing.

'I realise that, but I didn't...I wasn't trying to be a hero,' she mumbled, not wanting to admit that she hadn't thought she'd walk away from the attempt.

'If the only people who were heroes were the ones that were trying to be, then we'd all be in a lot of trouble.'

It was Muireann's turn to roll her eyes. Seeing her rebellious expression Calla went on. 'It's yours, Muiri, by right. Yours and only yours. You should keep it, because it belongs to you, but if that isn't enough reason then keep it because if you don't take it then whoever comes along and finds the dragon next will, and they will undoubtedly claim they were the ones who killed it.'

I don't care if they do, Muireann thought, but her fingers closed around the stone anyway. 'You really believe people will come and try to claim credit for this?'

'Of course,' Calla said, making a face. 'Sooner or later people will realise the dragon isn't around and they will get the courage to come and see if it is still here or has moved its territory. And when they do, they'll find whatever is left of it and take what they can including credit for its death. Come to think of it, we should head to Verell from here, it's the closest decent-sized town, and start spreading the word ourselves about what happened.'

'We?' Muireann said, amused at the high elf's easy presumption.

'Yes, we,' Calla said, smirking. 'Whoever you have waiting for you back home can manage without you for a little while longer and we need to celebrate.'

'I don't have anyone waiting for me,' Muireann said, far more subdued now. She wasn't at all eager to explain any of this to her brother who she knew would be absolutely horrified at her reckless actions. Never mind when the rest of her family found out. 'And I don't know that I want to celebrate killing the dragon.'

Calla gave her an odd look, before wrapping one arm around the other woman's shoulders. 'Well, I want to celebrate not being eaten. And I want to celebrate with you, my new friend, since you are the one who rescued me from that horrible fate. Besides, if you don't spread the true story then there will be a dozen charlatans running around within a month claiming they did it, getting people to pay them outrageous sums and running off with the money.'

'I'm not sure,' Muireann said, still hesitant.

'Think of it as a public service – we tell the truth and you keep people from being defrauded and as well you give people a real hero to look up to,' Calla said. 'We can find a good inn and eat, drink and make merry to celebrate being alive, and share our tale.'

Muireann felt a small smile pulling at her lips despite her sour mood. It was hard to resist the elf's cheerful attitude and enthusiasm. 'I'm no real hero, but what did you have in mind for how we'd manage this?'

'We can take more than enough treasure from the dragon's hoard to live our lives in comfort for quite a while,' Calla said, walking back towards the cave and pulling Muireann along with her. 'And certainly, enough to stay in the best inn in Verell for as long as we like and really enjoy ourselves.'

Muireann couldn't deny the idea had a certain appeal, especially as she'd never stayed in anything but the cheapest inn on the rare occasions she'd travelled far enough to merit an inn at all. Still, she hesitated a bit at the idea of taking anything from the cave. 'Isn't it wrong to steal from this place?'

Calla laughed, the sound ringing merrily through the air. 'We are hardly stealing from a dead dragon, and as to that everything here was stolen in the first place. Besides, as I already mentioned people will descend on this place in droves once word gets out and they will strip the cave bare. We deserve to take what we can more than they do, you killed it after all, and it owes me some compensation for killing the merchants I was travelling with and so rudely saving me for a later meal.'

Muireann nodded slowly, admitting that what Calla said made sense. They stepped back into the cave and Calla immediately moved to the nearest pile of flotsam, somehow finding several pieces of still serviceable cloth among the chaos. Getting the idea Muireann moved to another section nearby and did the same, scavenging a heavy sack, leather bag – she suspected it had been a messenger's bag which was confirmed when she dumped it out and an assortment of scrolls rolled across the floor – as well as a square section of canvas that she thought she could use as rough bag if she pulled up the corners and tied them. Carrying these she started scrounging through the piles, sorting out all the coins, jewellery and gems she could find. She was surprised by how much of that there was given the look of the piles but eventually realised that the smaller pieces, which were her targets, had mostly settled near the bottom underneath the bigger things, like armour and wagon parts.

She had filled the sack and messenger's bag, refusing to let herself stop to think about how much wealth she was actually dealing with, and was starting to toss things onto the canvas when Calla called her over. Muireann could see that the elf had made as much progress as she had, with several bulging bags and sacks at her feet.

'Here let me see the Dragon Stone for a moment,' Calla said, her expression thoughtful. Curious and hoping the elf would take it and keep it, Muireann pulled it from her belt pouch and handed it over. She could see that Calla was holding a pendant, the gold chain swinging freely. It was a pretty piece, Muireann had to admit, a delicate filigree around a flat sapphire. Calla held the Dragon Stone up to the sapphire, making a thoughtful noise to herself.

The elf's deft fingers worked for a moment and then the sapphire popped free, falling with a sharp sound to the ground. Muireann frowned, wondering why Calla had ruined the pendant, but before she could ask, the elf's motives became plain as she carefully worked the similarly-sized Dragon Stone into the filigreed setting. She pushed at the metal for a few more minutes, making sure the gold was bent back into place as well as she could manage and that the stone was secure. Finally, she presented it back to Muireann, looking well pleased with herself.

'There you go, my friend friend.' She smiled cheerfully at Muireann who stood and stared at the pendant silently. When she didn't reach to take it, Calla slipped the chain over Muireann's head, letting the stone fall so that it rested in the centre of her chest.

'Thank you,' Muireann said reflexively, not sure how she really felt about it. The weight of the Dragon Stone felt heavier than it should and, suddenly self-conscious, Muireann reached up and slipped it into the neck of her dress so that it lay against her skin.

Watching the movement Calla frowned again. 'The first thing we're going to do when we get back to civilisation is buy some new clothes. For both of us.'

Although she was unsure how they'd become a duo in the space of an afternoon, Muireann smiled at Calla's words. 'Truly? That's the first thing you want to do? I'd have guessed a good meal and a long bath.'

'Oh, we'll get to that as well, but there's no point to a bath if we just have to put these rags back on. And how can I enjoy a good meal like this?'

Muireann snorted, not trying to hide her amusement. Somehow Calla was exactly what she'd anticipated in a high elf and also nothing like she'd have guessed. 'This is my best wool dress.'

'Was your best you mean,' Calla said, smiling back. 'It looks a lot better than anyone would expect knowing you fought a dragon, but it has definitely seen its best days.'

Muireann looked down at the dress, now covered in dirt and blood, several long tears in the left arm. The blood and tears reminded her of the blood on her face when she woke up and her brief levity quickly evaporated. She reached up to touch her cheek again then said. 'Calla, can I ask you something a bit odd?'

'Sure, Muiri, I enjoy odd.'

'Is there a cut or wound on my face?' she asked, turning her head so that the elf could inspect the area she knew had to have been hurt by the dragon. As quick as the events had happened, she did remember the claw coming at her, the pain, and the blood when she woke up.

Calla leaned forward then reached out and gently inspected the side of the other woman's face. Finally, she pulled back, shrugging slightly. 'There's dried blood in your hair and some on your face but no sign of any wound.'

Muireann was truly shocked by the words, even though a part of her had almost expected them. 'There's nothing? Nothing at all?'

The elf shrugged again, obviously curious at the human's reaction. 'Nothing but that old scar. I'm sure there's an interesting story with that.'

Old scar? Muireann thought, confused. She didn't have any scars, anywhere. She'd broken an arm as a child, falling from a tree one of her brothers had dared her to climb, but other than that she'd mostly been the sort of child who sat and read books. Even the dragon attack on her farm had left her with nothing more than scrapes and bruises, sheltered as she was in the cellar. She opened her mouth to press Calla for more details then stopped, nodding and turning back to finish gathering treasure. What could she say really? She wasn't sure herself what had happened and as much as she'd taken an immediate liking to the high elf, she had to remind herself that they'd only known each other for a very short time. She didn't want Calla to think she was making up stories for attention or worse that she wasn't in touch with reality. She wanted the other woman to like her.

She moved a bit away from Calla who had already resumed her own hunting and started looking through more debris. She'd already found enough that she was getting picky, trying to choose what looked like the best rather than just any gold or jewels she could find. She'd added a handful of coins, several elaborate necklaces, and what looked like a crown to her last pile when something caught her eye. It shone faintly in the dim light of the cave's interior, partially hidden under a shield and some decaying pieces of wood. She moved the other junk aside to reveal a thick, flat green stone, slightly larger than an acorn.

It looks a bit like an emerald but not exactly, Muireann thought, as she scooped up the crystal.

The world went black. And then she started seeing flashes of scenes, like a dream but moving quickly from one to the next. Darkness. Fire. A heavily built castle with a man standing on the walls, clad in dark clothes, the green gem in his hand; below him an entire army writhing on the ground, blood flowing like water across the hard earth. Fire. A large town, the people running, screaming, then falling silently to the ground. Stillness. Darkness. Fire. An army marching across a plain, stopping, blue fire lashing out then dissipating, a green mist overcoming them; they fell screaming, bleeding from their eyes, ears, mouths...

Calla reached for her hand, and she twisted away, snarling, a possessive urge to protect the gem filling her. Lightning fast, Calla moved and knocked the crystal from her hand; Muireann felt a jolt of pain in her wrist, quickly gone, and an instant later the strange visions and violence left her.

'Are you alright?' Calla asked, anxious and obviously

worried.

She looked at Calla in shock then down at her empty hand, back at the elf, then at the green stone now resting several feet away on the floor. The knowledge of what it really was flooded through her. 'Oh no. Oh *no*, this is so bad.'

'What is? What just happened?' Calla asked, stepping away from the crystal. 'You picked up that stone and then froze. I was worried you were having some kind of fit.'

'It's...I'm not sure I can pronounce the name,' Muireann fretted, wiping her hands on her skirt. 'It's a weapon, an old magical weapon from the first civilisation, from the Aldovanan.'

Calla's gaze sharpened. 'That's impossible, all the magical weapons from the Aldovanan were destroyed in the First War, when they annihilated themselves.'

'Not all of them,' Muireann said, frowning. 'The High Temple in Verstla is supposed to have one of their magical relics, a healing crystal. And the elves have two of them, a healing crystal and one that shows the threads of the future.'

Calla grimaced. 'Those aren't weapons, though, not even the Foreseeing Stone. All the *weapons* were destroyed.'

'Not this one,' Muireann whispered, more afraid now than when she was facing down the dragon. 'The dragon must have stolen it – oh!'

'What?' Calla said, looking unnerved now.

'The dragon...' she turned to look at the shining body. 'This was Murjergalan. The Great Red One. But that's impossible – it lives in the south-east, at the edge of the territory between Harnsben and Vreal. That's...thousands of miles or more from here.'

'Muiri, you need to take a deep breath and calm down,' Calla said, reaching out and gripping the human woman's shoulder. 'Slow down and explain what you are talking about. How do you know the dragon's name?'

Muireann did as she'd been told and took a long breath

before answering. 'Dragons are extremely rare creatures, as you know. They say that there were twenty of them created when the world was born, embodiments of pure magic. Seventeen still live...ah...' she paused to glance at the corpse and made a face. 'Well, sixteen of them now, I suppose. Anyway. They are immortal, except in the rare circumstances where they are killed. The ones still living have been alive forever, since the birth of the world. We have many conflicting stories about them, but mostly they are avoided, people don't live where dragons are, because they are so difficult to kill. The only reason there's so many settlements near this one is that it arrived 20 years ago, and people are too stubborn to move when it mostly only takes livestock.'

'Right, I know all this,' Calla said impatiently.

'Well, what we do know about dragons is mostly bits and pieces of information in legends and stories. When I was studying dragons to...before I came here today...I read anything and everything I could find on them. And that included a very old children's book, and that book had a story in it about a red dragon named Murjergalan who killed one of the most powerful mages of the Aldovanan. The dragon lived in what is now the border of Harnsben and Vreal and was blocking some military route the mage needed for the war, something like that, and he set out to kill it using this weapon, this magical weapon. But instead, the dragon killed *him*, and don't you see? Everyone assumed the weapon was destroyed when the mage died but the dragon must have taken it the way it takes all the shiny things it finds.'

'So, you killed the dragon who has been guarding a weapon of unfathomable destructive magical power for the last 10,000 years?' Calla said.

Muireann took another slow deep breath. 'I seem to have, yes. And touching that stone, it's like it shows you everything you could do with it, how it could be used, and it was horrific,

Calla. Just utter death to everyone it was used against.'

She shuddered and wiped her hands against her dress again. Now that the stone's spell over her was broken she was horrified at the visions she'd seen.

'Why wasn't the dragon affected by it?' Calla asked, frowning at the stone on the floor.

'I can't be sure but…Maybe it's because dragons are animals, and aren't intelligent enough to direct magic, beyond breathing fire. Maybe it's because the stone's magic was too different from Murjergalan's. Although I'd guess that it's most likely because dragons are purely magical beings. They can't be killed by magic and probably can't be affected by it either. That was the mistake the mage made, assuming his weapon was powerful enough to do what other magic couldn't.'

'Hmm,' Calla said thoughtfully. 'Sounds like the arrogance of the Aldovanan alright.'

'It's that arrogance that led them to destroy themselves,' Muireann agreed. It was well worn old history, the stories of the first civilisation in the First Age that had grown so powerful and so fluent with magic that they had utterly destroyed themselves with infighting and civil wars. 'But that's not the point here. The point is that for whatever reason the dragon wasn't affected by the stone and has kept it for all this time, but since the dragon had it no one who could wield it could get to it.'

'Until now.'

They both glanced down at the stone. Sighing, Muireann said. 'We can't just leave it here. If anyone finds it they could, no they will, unleash absolute devastation using it.'

Calla frowned, for once looking utterly serious. 'And anyone who finds it will use it from what you've said. No, that can't be allowed to happen. We haven't had a major war since the empire was established in my great grandparents' time.'

She was talking about events that had occurred more than two thousand years ago as if they were far more recent history and Muireann was suddenly reminded about one of the main differences between elves and humans – humans lived at the utmost a hundred years, but elves usually saw at least a thousand. It seemed jarring to hear the founding of the ruling empire discussed that way, even for Muireann who had some casual acquaintance with elves and had experienced their odd way of talking about time before. *Then again,* Muireann thought, *if dragons were capable of higher thought, they'd probably feel much the same way about all civilisation, compared to their own lives which stretched back to the very beginnings.* It was an odd thought, and she wasn't sure why it had popped into her head. *I'm just feeling guilty about Murjergalan's death,* she thought uneasily, pushing the idea away. She cleared her throat into the thickening silence. 'So, what do we do now?'

Calla sighed heavily. 'We can't leave it here for anyone to find. I suppose the only thing for it is to bring it with us.'

'Are you mad?' Muireann retorted, although she had to admit a part of her wanted to keep the stone with them, although she didn't know exactly why.

'Possibly,' Calla shot back, grinning again. 'Definitely if you ask my family. But my sanity aside I don't see that we have any other option. We can't leave it here. Hiding it is as much of a risk as leaving it anywhere else, because who knows what ill chance might work against us? And I assume we can't destroy it, or you'd already have suggested that.'

Muireann shook her head slowly, feeling the warmth of the Dragon Stone heavy against her heart. 'If there is a way, I don't know of it. The other Aldovanan weapons were destroyed by each other, in great battles as far as the stories go. This one was assumed to have been destroyed in the dragon fire that killed the mage wielding it, but obviously dragon fire doesn't damage it any.'

'Obviously,' Calla agreed drily. 'Can it be destroyed with any magic that does exist in our age?'

Muireann hesitated, then shook her head. 'I don't know. The only other relics that survived are obviously more helpful, and I don't know any stories of anyone trying to destroy them. Most if not all the old Aldovanan magic and the knowledge of it was lost long ago.'

'Mmmm,' Calla agreed. 'It's passed out of even elven memory, not that I'm any expert in magic. So, you don't have any ideas about destroying it?'

'Not off the top of my head, no,' Muireann said, biting her lip.

'Well, you found a way to kill an immortal dragon, perhaps you can sort this problem out as well.'

Muireann almost snapped back that killing the dragon was different, but she stopped herself, looking slowly over at the red dragon's body. She nodded thoughtfully. 'I researched everything I could find on dragons, I suppose I could take the same approach here, research everything I can find on the Aldovanan and their magical weapons. It's a place to start anyway.'

Calla nodded decisively, as if the decision had been made. 'Then let's find a safe way to transport this – I think I saw a lady's compact mirror in this mess that is big enough to fit the stone in it – we can scoop it into that and seal it shut. Then we get everything we are taking together and head for Verell to spread word of your heroic deed and enjoy some of this gold.'

Muireann nodded, her mind already on what references she might be able to find for this new project. 'There's a bookseller in Verell who may have useful texts.'

Calla rolled her eyes. 'Fine, but priorities. First new clothes, then a good meal and bed, then we can find your bookseller.'

'How exactly are the two of us supposed to carry all of this out of here anyway? Even one bag is too heavy to carry far.'

'No worries, Muiri,' Calla said confidently. 'I found a handcart that was almost entirely intact. We can repair it easily and take turns pulling it.'

'We'll be a target for bandits of course,' Muireann couldn't resist pointing out. 'The two of us pulling a cart laden with treasure. It's a bit conspicuous.'

Calla laughed. 'I have a plan for that as well. We'll cover the bags with more fabric we scrounge up in here, make it look like we're ragmen – or women as it were – selling old cloth. We certainly look the part right now and there's enough of that sort on the main trade routes and in cities no one will look twice at us. Once we're in the town we find a banker to exchange the coins and open an account for you and a jeweller for the gems and jewellery.'

'I doubt there will be a jeweller in Verell that can take so much as this.'

Calla shrugged, obviously not worried about it. 'Then we keep what we can't sell until we get to a bigger city. And don't worry about our safety, I already found a very good sword in this mess, and you have your bow. If you can take down a dragon with it, you can certainly handle highwaymen.'

Muireann must have looked dubious at that because Calla went on. 'And once we are better outfitted if it comes to it, we can hire a sell-sword to guard us as well.'

'A mercenary?' Muireann said, not liking that idea at all even though her knowledge of mercenaries mostly came from books and stories of great battles.

'I'm a mercenary you know,' Calla pointed out. 'Or at least I was. With this turn of luck I won't have to sell my sword for a while, and we can live comfortably. Just think of it, Muiri, travelling the world, seeing all the great cities, eating the best food…'

'Lugging around a deadly magic weapon,' Muireann said, although she was already excited about the picture Calla was painting.

'Why do you think we'll be travelling? It's the perfect way

to do your research without arousing any suspicion. We travel about and you can see all the great libraries and if you happen to look at books on the Aldovanan while we're there, who will know?'

Muireann found herself nodding, a smile spreading across her face. 'That sounds...fun.'

'Oh, it will be,' Calla said, smiling back. 'I didn't barely avoid death by dragon not to have some fun now and you, Muireann Dragonslayer, definitely deserve to celebrate. Why I'd wager we won't have to buy our own dinner or drinks for months just telling this story – minus the magical death crystal part, of course.'

'I'm not sure I like that name,' Muireann said hesitantly.

'Dragonslayer?' Calla shrugged one shoulder, already turning away to retrieve the compact she'd mentioned to secure the crystal. 'What were you called before?'

Muireann blushed. 'Muireann of Gorseview. It's my home village.'

'Meh,' Calla said, distracted for a moment getting the crystal into the compact, careful to avoid touching it, and using her strength to bend the metal so it wouldn't open. 'It's not a bad name but it hardly fits a woman who killed a dragon and rescued an elven mercenary from certain death.'

'You're very dramatic, you know that?' Muireann said, fighting back a giggle. Calla tossed her the compact and Muireann quickly shoved it into her belt pouch.

'Admit it, that's one of the things you like about me,' the high elf said, still grinning impishly.

'You know something, it is,' Muireann agreed, finding herself unable to deny the strong kinship she felt with Calla. 'It really is.'

'Of course it is,' Calla said, as if Muireann was just being sensible. 'Now I think we've gotten the most valuable things here, and more importantly I doubt we can carry any more, so help me get this cart fixed and we can be on our way to adventure and fine living.'

Muireann moved to help pull the cart out from where it was jammed up against the wall, already starting to wonder what adventure would be like. One way or another she knew she could never go back to her old life, and she realised she didn't really want to. *Maybe,* she thought tentatively as the two women set about repairing the cart, *maybe this is exactly the new beginning I need.*

Chapter 2

On the Road to Adventure

Muireann and Calla travelled for three days, alternating between pulling the heavy cart along deer trails through the woods and using the roads that wound their way through the foothills around the small mountain the dragon had called home. At Calla's urging Muireann hid her quiver and bow in with the old pieces of cloth they'd salvaged from the dragon, where she could reach them if she needed to but without them being obvious. Calla had hidden the sword she'd found in the dragon's hoard the same way, creating the illusion of two poor women heading towards Verell to sell rags. Muireann had been nervous at first about being so vulnerable but as Calla had predicted the few people they met along the way took them for indigent women selling scraps and avoided them with obvious distaste. In the past this would have bothered Muireann, but between the obvious safety it provided them – they were no targets for robbery the way they looked – and the infectious happiness of Calla, who regaled her with tales of the high elf's previous experiences on the road, Muireann found herself enjoying the journey.

At night they camped in whatever clearing they could find, cooking the small game Muireann hunted then sleeping under the cart, now with their weapons close at hand. It was rougher living than Muireann was used to but somehow Calla made it all seem like some grand game. Calla had an undeniable way of lightening the tedium with jokes, stories, and winding conversations. By the second day Muireann felt as close to the elf as she ever had to anyone back in her village; for her part Calla seemed to have adopted the human and always spoke of what they would do together in the future, as if they were unquestionably a team. Muireann liked it.

When they reached the outskirts of Verell she couldn't deny she was excited to see what would happen next. The smell of the sea was strong here, as Verell sat along the western coast, and she relaxed at the familiar tang of salt air. The Dragon Stone still hung heavy against her chest and the green stone was a constant presence in the pouch at her belt, but despite it all for the first time in a long time Muireann felt hopeful.

The road was wider and busier this close to town and when the walls were in sight, Calla, who was pulling the cart, moved off to the side where they could rest for a moment and talk in relative privacy. Muireann leaned against the small cart, stretching her back, glad for the rest.

'Now we need a change in strategy,' Calla said cheerfully. 'We can hardly expect to go into any of the shops or talk to the bankers looking like this.'

Curious about what she was thinking, Muireann nodded. It was true that after two days on the road their clothes, which had been the worse for wear to start with because of the dragon, were in a decidedly sorry state. On the other hand, they were dragging around a ridiculous amount of gold and jewels, and they could hardly just leave it sitting anywhere unattended. Even looking like a rag cart the chances were too high someone would get curious and poke into it.

'What I propose is this,' Calla said. 'We find a quiet alley near to one of the shops and one of us takes a few of the coins and goes in and buys a pair of better dresses. It doesn't really matter what as long as they fit decently well and look better than what we're wearing now.'

'That won't be difficult,' Muireann said, pulling at the hem of her torn dress.

'Right. Then we take the cart as near to the bankers' as we can manage, preferably behind the guildhouse, and we change into the better dresses. Then one stays with the cart and the other goes in and asks for the guildmaster.'

'Will there be a guildmaster here, do you think?' Muireann asked.

Calla shrugged. 'There will be someone in charge. We just need the highest-ranking person. And we bring them out – actually it may be best if you do this part so if they question you or say the story isn't believable you can show them the Dragon Stone. Anyone who sees it will recognise it for what it is. We don't need them thinking we are trying to rob them.'

'I see,' Muireann said, resigned. 'And then I bring them out and they can have the cart brought in and we deal with them from there.'

'They get a ten per cent trade commission for converting everything so they should be more than willing to assist us,' Calla said, with her usual confidence. 'It will mean a small fortune for them. I have an account with the guild already and they can open one for you, so we will have a place to deposit most of the money.'

It all seemed a bit convoluted and silly to Muireann, but she knew Calla was sure it would work. They couldn't wheel the cart in directly without getting a lot of attention and having half the town know they had so much wealth – even assuming the guards let them in the door pushing the unwieldy cart. They couldn't risk leaving it alone in town nor stand outside and ask a banker to come out...although that last thought gave Muireann an idea. 'Calla, we have a decent number of modern coins that don't need to be changed. Why don't we find an inn close to the bankers' hall and get a room there? We can move the bags up from the cart without anyone needing to know what's in them, bathe, dress, make ourselves more presentable and send a message to the guildhall requesting a meeting. It would make the process smoother at least.'

'Hmm,' Calla made a thoughtful noise, staring pensively at the town gates. 'Alright. It will be easier to deal with them if we don't look quite so much like we've been sleeping under a cart for several days.'

Muireann smiled, relieved and desperately looking forward to that bath. With a plan in place the two women headed for the gates of Verell, but Muireann found the heavy load less difficult to manage with their goal so close at hand.

Despite the changes Muireann had suggested the first thing they did was stop near a dress shop, the kind that sold pre-sewn and second-hand dresses as well as made to order, and Calla stood guard next to the cart while Muireann went in. She was nearly shown right back out, given the state of her clothes, but managed to convince the woman who owned the shop that she and her friend had some trouble on the road to explain the tears and dirt. Showing the woman a handful of gold probably didn't hurt either; perhaps a risk given that the duo were trying to avoid attention, but at that point Muireann would have given it all to the woman, despite the outrageous amount, just for something clean to wear.

Having convinced the owner that she could afford to buy everything in the store she found herself receiving very solicitous attention. It was embarrassing but Muireann supposed better than being thrown out. Trying to get the errand done as fast as possible, and aware of Calla waiting outside, she was quick to choose the first dresses that seemed serviceable. Luckily her experience with her children had made her very good at estimating fit by eye, and she was confident that what she'd gotten would work for their purposes. She overpaid, and knew she had overpaid, but she was too eager to get back out again with the cloth bundled in her arms to care.

Once she'd re-joined Calla the two women wandered until they found the bankers' guildhall and then a bit further down the street a very nice looking inn. They bribed the stable boy with a silver coin to let them change clothes in the relative privacy of a stall in the barn behind the inn; they'd never be allowed in the place looking as they did.

Standing in the fresh straw and gratefully pulling off her old clothes Muireann mused aloud. 'It's a pity that everyone is so quick to judge by how a person looks and what they are wearing.'

'Perhaps,' Calla agreed, waiting her turn in the aisle. 'But you can tell a lot about a person by how they dress and comport themselves.'

'Perhaps,' Muireann agreed, smiling as she slipped the new second-hand dress on, pulling it into place. It wasn't ideal but would work well enough for the time being. 'But look at us, for example. We are nothing at all what our appearance would make people believe. Even if we didn't have what we do, couldn't afford new clothes, does dirt and ripped clothing make us bad people?'

'No, of course not,' Calla agreed. 'It's foolish to assume a person's quality is reflected by their looks. I've known many very rich looking people who were rat bastards that I wouldn't trust at my back in any circumstances.'

'You just said you can tell a lot about a person by their clothes,' Muireann pointed out, pushing her feet back into her old shoes.

'And so you can,' Calla said. 'But a lot isn't everything and you shouldn't make any final judgements or assume a person's *character* based on such.'

Muireann hummed slightly in response, wishing somehow that it could be simpler, that the quality of clothes didn't immediately get a person judged. She shook her head, pushing the thoughts away, and quickly tied her belt around her waist, slipping the pouch which hung from it through the slit in the skirt so that it hung safely away from any pickpockets. Or safer at least; she was sure a skilled pickpocket could still find a way to get the pouch even secured as it was. Patting the slight bulge beneath her skirt, to reassure herself that she still had both the metal compact which held the green stone and the gold coins she'd put in there, she moved out of the stall allowing Calla to take her turn changing.

'Ugh, why would you get me an orange dress?' the high elf groaned as she changed, her tone teasing. 'I look like a pile of autumn leaves that's grown legs.'

Muireann giggled at the image. 'I just grabbed the first two things that looked like they'd fit. Do you think I want to be wearing pink? With my skin tone and hair?'

Calla laughed, throwing her old clothes out for Muireann to add to the pile on the cart. 'Fair enough. Well at least we shall look ridiculous together.'

'And we may look ridiculous, but we won't have an issue getting a room.'

'Not unless the innkeeper has fashion standards,' Calla said, emerging from the stall. 'Then we may still be in trouble.'

Muireann smothered a giggle, feeling more like a teenager than she had when she actually was one. 'Alright, well, you have the most experience renting rooms and dealing with innkeepers. I'll stay here with the cart, and you get us a room.'

Calla nodded and headed off, leaving Muireann alone in the small stable. She sat on the end of the cart, peering around curiously at the stalls. The stable boy was at the far end of the structure mucking out a stall with its occupant, a glossy chestnut mare, tied out in the aisle. The horse watched Muireann with the same interest that the woman studied her with and Muireann found herself smiling again. Even the thought of how much her children would have enjoyed this had they been there didn't make her feel sad. Instead, she found herself imagining their various reactions with a sense of nostalgia.

'Come on, Muireann, let's start moving this inside,' Calla said, appearing next to her.

Muireann slid off the cart and started moving aside rags, quickly grabbing her bow and quiver then shouldering the heavy leather messenger bag and the larger makeshift canvas bag. Calla was also grabbing bags, carrying more for her part than Muireann could manage, but there was just too much for the two of them to bring in at once. Realising that, Calla turned towards the stable boy. 'Ey! Your name is Kevill right? Well, Kevill how would you like to earn another coin by helping us carry our bags up to our room?'

The young man – probably 14 or 15 Muireann guessed – hopped eagerly out of the stall he'd been cleaning, dodging around the mare and jogging up to them. 'Sure, Miss. What do you need help with?'

Calla gestured at the remaining bags, which the boy picked up with a surprised grunt. 'What do you have in here, rocks?'

Muireann, perhaps inspired by several days of Calla's company, quipped back. 'Something like that. We've come to Verell to trade our 'rocks' for something easier to spend.'

Calla snorted loudly and nodded. 'That's right. Hard to use 'rocks' to pay for things.'

The boy looked puzzled and a bit put out at what was obviously an inside joke, but his mood improved considerably when they reached the room the innkeeper had assigned to them and Calla gave him a silver coin for his help as she'd promised. The youth swiftly shoved the coin into his pocket. 'Anything else you ladies need help with just call for me and I'll handle it for you.'

'Thank you, Kevill,' Muireann said, closing the door as politely as she could manage without making it look like she was trying to get rid of him. Which she was. She turned to Calla as soon as the door was closed. 'That wasn't very wise you know. He'll spread word that we have money.'

Calla shrugged, moving around to inspect the room. 'There's no avoiding that now and he deserved something for helping us. Once we meet with the guildmaster and get these coins and jewels changed and put on account, I doubt an hour will pass before everyone knows we have some wealth. That's part of why it's essential we start spreading the story of the dragon. I can defend us against most threats and you're amazing with that bow, but I don't exactly want us to end up in gaol for fighting or worse with all of our possessions confiscated and run out of town.'

'Yes,' Muireann agreed, wondering if that was even possible. 'Let's not do that.'

Calla looked amused. 'Once people know you killed a dragon they'll give you – us – some respect and we'll be safer.'

Uncomfortable with the idea, Muireann turned away, leaving the assorted sacks of treasure in a corner. 'Which bed do you want?'

The high elf shrugged. 'It doesn't matter to me. I'm used to sleeping rough on the road.'

'Says the woman who has spent days waxing poetic about a good bed and a good meal,' Muireann teased. 'Alright then, I'll take the little bed by the window, and you can take the bigger one near the fireplace.'

'If that pleases you,' Calla said, stretching out across the larger bed.

'What will please me is a nice warm bath and getting all of this mess off,' Muireann said.

Calla waved an indolent hand towards a door at the back of the room. 'This is the best room this inn has. We have a private bath just through there and they have a mage on staff so there's as much hot water as you'd like.'

Perking up at this Muireann moved towards the door, eager to see this bath and test the water. Calla stopped her just before she got to her goal. 'When you're done I'll have a turn and then we can get that meeting at the bankers' guild – actually now that I think of it, I'll send a messenger while you bathe and try to arrange it for early this afternoon.'

Muireann nodded. 'Alright. That makes the most sense I

suppose since we have a lot to accomplish today.'

With that she moved through the door, leaving Calla to sort out the details. Studying the bathing room she had to admit that Calla was right; this was surely the best room in the inn. The smaller adjoined room was divided by a wall down the middle: to the right was a toilet and sink, to the left was a large iron bathtub, a low seat with several towels piled at one end and an ornate mirror on the wall. Above the bath were several pipes with levers, which Muireann was vaguely familiar with. She hadn't seen such a nice indoor bath since she was young, but it didn't seem too far removed from what had been in use twenty years ago.

Moving to the bath she studied the levers for a moment until she found the one that controlled the hot water, pressing it up. She was rewarded by a flow of water into the tub and a cloud of steam, proving that the water was indeed hot. It was tempting to just use the hot water but the steam did give her some pause and so she spent a few minutes playing with the levers to mix in some cold water until the temperature was what she wanted. Humming cheerfully, she slipped out of her dress, tossing the pink garment onto the seat. She quickly added her underthings to the pile, ran her fingers through her tangled hair and eased into the water. Her glasses she kept on, careful not to splash the lenses.

Muireann had always enjoyed bathing, even without such a fancy bath to do it in. After washing her hair and getting the road dirt off herself she drained the bathtub and refilled it, laying back so she could soak in the hot water. It was a luxurious experience, eclipsing even the moderate luxury she'd grown up with as a merchant's daughter and a far cry from what she'd had as a farmer's wife, and she wouldn't deny to herself that she could get used to it. She had a feeling somehow that travelling with Calla she was going to get used to it one way or another anyway as the high elf definitely appreciated the finer things in life. It was a bit strange to already be thinking of Calla as a permanent part of her life, but she supposed that the experience with the dragon had been a unique bonding event, and it wasn't like she had anything much to go back to otherwise.

Eventually she dragged herself out of the bath, not wanting to leave the warm water but starting to feel selfish. Calla deserved a turn as well after all. She dried herself off with a towel, combed her hair as best she could with her fingers, and dressed again. She had started to leave when she suddenly remembered the mirror, now thoroughly fogged from the bath. She stepped up to it and used the towel to wipe off a section, leaning forward to examine her face. Across her left cheek and up to her temple was a distinct scar, the white line of it like a pale slash across her face. Fascinated Muireann reached up and ran her fingers along the length, from chin to hairline.

I definitely didn't have this before the dragon, she thought, realising the scar ran under the arm of her glasses. *But it looks old, years old at least, and fully healed. How is that possible?* Muireann shifted uneasily, fingers still obsessively tracing the scar. It was jarring for her to see it, where nothing had been before. The only thing she could think was that in the moment when she'd blacked out the dragon's outstretched claw must have struck her, but she didn't remember it happening. It would explain the blood on her face when she'd woken up although she had no idea how it had healed so quickly. Still unnerved and uneasy at the implications Muireann shook herself slightly and backed away from the mirror.

It doesn't really matter, she told herself, not entirely able to believe her own words. *One scar doesn't make a difference. And so few people ever kill dragons, who knows what the wider effects of that might be?* She pushed that thought away, swallowing hard and suddenly afraid the mark was a sign of some divine repercussion for what she'd done. She wasn't a very religious person, but she had been raised with the same ingrained respect for the gods who had created the world as anyone else. *Maybe I'll try to go to a temple and make an offering,* she thought, hanging the towel to dry and heading out of the room. It wasn't much but even thinking of such a small action made her feel better.

* * *

The rest of the day passed in a blur, beginning with their meeting with the bankers' guild. That went better than Muireann had feared and she only had to show the Dragon Stone once at the start of the meeting for their story to be taken without questions. The guildmaster sent some of his people to bring their bags to the guild hall and then they spent several hours counting out the items the two had taken and dividing them evenly. The guild was able to take all of it, even the jewellery, because there wasn't a jewellers guild in Verell. As Calla had said the bankers took ten per cent of the total as a commission on the trade to modern coins and for setting Muireann up with an account; the account was essential given the amount they were dealing with, and Calla didn't want Muireann to feel as if she was claiming everything by putting it into her own account. She insisted it all be split fairly between them. The bulk of it would be stored in a guild vault but each account could be magically accessed at any bankers' guild hall. This meant they could keep out what they might reasonably need and withdraw anything else when they wished without worrying about carrying everything on themselves or storing it in one fixed location. Muireann was given a ring with a magical seal on it which would allow her to prove her identity at each hall to access her account; Calla already had a simple ring but was given a newer, fancier one because she hadn't previously had a vault, only a small account on record.

The total amount they put on deposit was a number that Muireann could barely conceive of – Calla had been underestimating when she'd said they could live comfortably for a while on it. Muireann guessed that even the long-lived elf would never have to work again in her life if she didn't want to. It was dizzying and felt unreal to Muireann, who was used to living on modest means.

When they left the bankers Calla dragged them from shop to shop gleefully equipping them as she felt necessary. Nothing too extravagant, hopefully nothing that would mark them out as prosperous enough to be worth robbing despite their weapons, but certainly the best quality that Muireann had owned since her childhood. Like waking up after killing the dragon the entire experience seemed surreal to her, both exciting and also dreamlike, but it was difficult not to be infected by Calla's enthusiasm. It was fun, more fun than Muireann had had in a long time, and there was a giddy freedom in being able to simply buy what she liked without worrying about the cost; she could see the appeal of Calla's plan. By the time they headed back to the inn they were staying at, arms weighed down with new clothes, boots and weaponry, Muireann felt like an entirely new person. They still had the green crystal to deal with, but everything seemed far less grim.

The two women changed into some of their new clothing before heading down to the inn's common room for dinner. Muireann felt a bit awkward in the pants, tight-sleeved tunic and leather corset that had replaced the loose farm dresses she was used to wearing, but Calla was right that for an archer tight sleeves and a corset were much more functional than a loose dress. If she was going to live the life of an adventurer she may as well look the part.

Sitting down by the hearth they ordered the best the inn had to offer, a rich stew with fresh baked bread and glasses of blackberry-mead. Muireann by this time was just as excited as Calla to sit down and enjoy the food, having had more than enough wild cooked rabbit since leaving the dragon's cave. The stew was thick and delicious, the mead sweet, and Muireann couldn't remember the last time she'd had such a good day. She smiled at her new friend suddenly, unexpectedly grateful for everything that had happened since she'd walked into the dragon's cave. 'I'm sorry your merchants were killed, Calla, but I'm glad we met each other.'

'As am I,' the high elf said, returning the smile. 'And not just because you saved me from a very unpleasant death. You're a good person, Muiri, and a good friend. I think we will have many grand adventures together.'

Muireann flushed slightly at what seemed an unwarranted compliment, but she was decidedly pleased by it anyway. 'You know what? I think so as well.'

'If you don't mind my asking,' Calla said, taking a long grateful drink from her mead, 'how exactly did a farmwife end up taking on a dragon? So, I can tell the story properly later.'

Muireann sighed. 'I don't know that I want you saying that part of the story to be honest, even if I agree that telling the rest is necessary.'

Calla was silent for a minute, both women eating their stew, before going on. 'Would you mind at least telling me then? I won't repeat it if you'd rather I didn't.'

Muireann hesitated, then set down her spoon. 'I suppose I should. You're my friend and you deserve to know the whole of it as much as anyone does. Besides if we need to pass through Gorseview or go to Strandview people there will know and tell you, and I wouldn't trust their versions.'

'Gorseview, Strandview,' Calla laughed softly. 'Your people aren't much for creative naming, are they?'

Muireann smiled slightly, teasing her new friend right back. 'Given that half of high elven cities are named some variation of "shining height" I'm not sure you have any room to talk.'

Calla snorted and nodded. 'Fair enough and accurate too. Alright so neither of us comes from creative people.' The elf hesitated then shrugged slightly. 'I would like to know what led you to the dragon, if you're willing to talk about it.'

'It's not much of a story, really,' Muireann said, but went on as her fingers traced the woodgrain of the table. 'I was married to a sheep farmer. We lived just outside the village proper, and I was less of a farmwife than I should have been, if the truth is told. I spent much of my time in the village acting as a scribe for the mayor and council, that sort of thing.'

'No offence to you, Muiri, but I'm surprised your husband tolerated that. Most men I've met want their wives at home caring for them. Which if you're wondering is why I'm not married – I haven't the temperament for that nonsense or for being settled.'

Muireann made a face in return. 'Well Edren might have complained about it but...I made him feel more important, you see? I wasn't born in Gorseview, I was from Strandview and my family – my father – was a merchant.'

'He married up then?'

'Basically, yes, and he knew it. Most people in the village are literate, of course, but I'd had real schooling and I can read and write better than anyone there, and in several languages besides. So, when the mayor was asking me for help, of course Edren was honoured and when it became something of a daily task for me, he hired a girl to help around our house.'

Muireann stopped, her mind as always going back to the circumstances of that awful day that had lined up to leave her the sole survivor of her family. Her voice softened, her eyes fixing, unseeing, on the fire in the hearth nearby. 'It's funny in a humourless way you know. I shouldn't have even been in the house that day, and if I hadn't been, Annie and Brook wouldn't have been either. But it was getting cold, and Brook had been feverish – she was my youngest – and I couldn't bring her with me to the council house and didn't want to leave her. Annie was to be married the next spring – this spring – and should have been in the village working at the baker's, because she was working in exchange for special food for her wedding, but she stayed home to help me. Anyway, I'm making too much of this tale. It's just that we wouldn't usually have been there, but we were, we all were, except Edren who was out in the fields with the flock. And I'd left the children by the hearth and gone down to the cellar to check our supplies for the winter, to see if we needed to trade for anything before the weather really turned....and then the dragon attacked.'

'I'm sorry,' Calla said when Muireann fell silent, sounding as if she genuinely shared in the human woman's grief. 'I lost my closest friend when the dragon attacked the traders we were guarding. He was a mercenary, like me, and we'd worked together for years.'

'I'm sorry, Calla, I didn't realise,' Muireann said, wincing in sympathy and understanding a little better why Calla seemed so intent on their friendship.

Calla sighed. 'We always knew we might die on the roads, it can be dangerous work. I never expected there'd be a dragon involved though. But enough of that, it's time for your story now not mine.'

Muireann shrugged. 'I didn't see what happened obviously, but I was told later by neighbours that Edren died in the field when the dragon first attacked, and in its landing it struck the house. It was destroyed of course – you saw the size of that dragon. They told me the children were all still near the hearth. They died when the house came down. And when I realised that I was the only one left...I decided that killing the dragon would somehow right things. It didn't, by the way. But that was why I did it.'

'I can understand,' Calla said solemnly. 'Losing your whole family like that, I'm not sure how you move past it. You must miss them terribly.'

'I miss the children,' Muireann said, tears filling her eyes as they always did when she thought of them. Her two daughters, one sixteen, the other three, and her sons, clever sweet boys of ten and six. She'd hoped that her older son, Edrik, would follow in her footsteps and be a scribe as well, he'd shown real talent for it even at his young age. That was all lost now.

'Not your husband?' Calla said tentatively, interrupting Muireann's morose train of thought, obviously too curious to let the matter rest.

'Not really,' Muireann admitted. 'It may sound harsh to say it, but the truth is we got on well enough, but didn't love each other. It was an arranged marriage and we both just made the best of it over the years.'

Seeing Calla's expression, Muireann went on. 'My father and Edren's father knew each other from the years they served together in Lord Arvain's guard. When my mother decided I needed to be married off or I'd end up shaming the family as a spinster, well I think they all felt a farm would be good for me. Get my nose out of books.'

Calla nodded thoughtfully. 'I forgot the lord here compels all men to service in his guard or army.'

'It's mostly a bit of a joke around here to be honest,' Muireann said, regaining some of her good mood. 'He's a very pompous sort is Lord Arvain, and he likes to present the appearance of an impressive force, but they're none of them well trained and their equipment is more for show than use.'

'Is it true he only compels men to serve?' Calla sked, moving the subject to less depressing things.

'It's true,' Muireann said. 'He's pompous *and* old fashioned.'

'I'd use another word for it,' Calla said, rolling her eyes. 'I can't believe there's still anyone around who thinks women can't fight. Even the elves allow women in the army, and we aren't known for being quick to change or for being forward thinking.'

The young men at the table near theirs had fallen silent and

Muireann realised that it might be wiser to continue discussing the local lord's flaws in private. Not everyone appreciated such criticism and while she suspected Calla would relish a good bar fight Muireann was not in the mood to duck mugs and hide under a table. She cleared her throat. 'Yes, well, anyway. My point was just that it was an arranged marriage. Obviously women can do anything men can do.'

'Perhaps more since you killed the dragon where all the men before you failed,' Calla said, raising her mug in a toast.

They were interrupted by one of the young men at the other table, now staring fixedly at Muireann and making no effort to pretend he hadn't been listening to them talk. He was muscular, dressed in simple clothes but with the demeanour of someone used to demanding respect. His military-short hair was brown, his eyes - narrow and mean - a sky blue, his skin fair but tanned as if he were outdoors a lot. If Muireann were to guess she'd assume he was some noble's son or perhaps a knight's squire. She also knew on sight that he was a bully; years of dealing with people like him had given her a keen sense for the subtle signs of a person who delighted in putting others down.

'*You* killed a dragon?' the teenager said loudly, his voice dripping scorn as only the young and absolutely certain could. 'You expect anyone with sense to believe that tripe?'

Muireann would have been happy to ignore him, but Calla was already speaking loudly, returning the scorn as only an elf could. 'Since you're obviously eavesdropping on our conversation it should be clear that she did. She rescued me from a great red dragon who had killed the merchants I was with.'

The entire common room had fallen silent, not even the sound of utensils on plates or people moving in chairs breaking the heavy silence. The young man glanced around quickly but the rapt audience only seemed to encourage him. 'I don't believe you. You can't seriously expect anyone to believe that fat old woman killed a dragon. What'd she do, bore it to death?'

There was some amused tittering from the crowd. Muireann had heard far worse from her peers growing up and his words didn't faze her, but Calla was incensed. She stood quickly, her chair scraping loudly across the floor. 'Who are you to criticise her? A boy who's done nothing more dangerous in his life than bully younger children.'

'How'd she kill it?' he pressed, sneering. The crowd had begun to murmur and move restlessly in their seats.

'She shot it with an arrow,' Calla replied with absolute confidence. Muireann squirmed a bit, uncomfortable at this turn but, of course, as far as Calla knew, and had seen with her own eyes, she was speaking the absolute truth.

'You expect us to believe that?' the young man said again, gesturing around the room as if everyone was on his side.

Calla turned to Muireann, expectantly. 'Show them.'

'Show us what?' the youth said, still sneering. 'Some poorly done sketch of an imagined dead dragon?'

Muireann ignored him but stood up, moving next to Calla. Without a word she pulled the pendant with the Dragon Stone from her tunic. Silence consumed the common room for a second time, marred only by the slight shuffling of people leaning in to get a better look at something they had heard about all their lives but never seen. For just a moment the young man's face softened with awe as he studied the stone swinging below Muireann's fingers, the red colours drifting lazily across the surface. Then his expression hardened again. 'However you got that, it wasn't by killing a dragon.'

'That's the only way to get one,' Muireann said, finally speaking. 'I'm sure it's obvious we didn't rob one of the Great Families and if we had we'd hardly have made it this far without the entire empire knowing.'

'Besides,' Calla interjected, 'of the existing stones none are red the way this one is. That proves our words, and that it came from a red dragon – I'm sure you all have heard of the red dragon who lived by the mountain just north of here? Well, Muireann has put an end to it. I saw its corpse with my own eyes.'

The crowd was murmuring again but in excitement now and Muireann relaxed. Whether or not the young man backed down the crowd was on their side and she knew that would be a deciding factor. Perhaps sensing as much the youth hesitated, but he was either too stubborn or too proud to give up. 'Then I challenge you to a duel.'

'Excuse me?' Muireann said, too shocked to think of anything clever to respond with.

He straightened a bit, as if her surprise encouraged him. 'Certainly, you know what a duel is, *mighty dragon slayer*? If – when – I win, I'll take the stone and I can say I defeated the one who killed the red dragon.'

Calla hissed in anger, but Muireann couldn't hold back a laugh. The young man flushed, the crowd falling still again, their eyes tracking between the woman and the young man. Muireann shook her head, slipping the stone back into her top. 'I won't fight you.'

'You must,' the man insisted. 'I challenged you, in front of witnesses. If you refuse to fight you are a coward.'

'I killed a dragon,' Muireann said, struggling not to laugh again. 'I don't think anyone would believe I'm a coward. But be serious! You're what, eighteen, nineteen?'

The youth glanced around, blushing harder. 'I'm nearly twenty and have trained with a sword for many years.'

'You're nineteen,' Muireann repeated drily. 'Barely a few years older than my oldest child would've been. I'm old enough to be your mother. I have no training with a sword – if you want a duel with bows to see who can shoot the best I might consider it – but as it is what honour could there be for you in saying you took the stone from an unarmed woman old enough to have birthed you? It would be nothing less than robbery.'

Several people in the crowd laughed at that while a few others frowned and glared at the young man as if he'd insulted their own mothers. Muireann went on before the boy could gather his thoughts. 'If you want to prove yourself you won't do it by bullying strange women trying to have a quiet meal in an inn. Go out and do something worth bragging about yourself. Earn a reputation that you deserve to be praised for – even if I was good with a sword and you defeated me and took the stone what would that prove anyway? You still wouldn't be the one who defeated the dragon, you'd just be the one who had a lucky day and won a prize. It proves nothing. And this rashness will get you killed, or worse. No, go and find your own glory, don't try to steal someone else's.'

The young man looked like he still wanted to fight but a quick look at the hostile faces turned towards him made it clear that he'd get no support if he tried it. Muttering to himself he turned and stormed out, most of the other young men following him. Muireann couldn't help but notice the one who didn't, a youth of about the same age as the first: dusky skinned, with tight-curling, black hair cut military-short like the others, who lingered near the door. Before she could think too much about that, several townsfolk were approaching their table. An older man spoke up for the group. 'We'd be very grateful, strangers, if you'd tell us the tale of the dragon's death.'

Calla relaxed, smiling at the now friendly crowd and rested a hip against their table, settling in. 'Fair enough a request and a great tale it is too. Let me tell you then of Muireann Dragonslayer and how I was rescued from certain death...'

Muireann rolled her eyes at her new surname, already accepting that she was stuck with it, and sat back down to finish her meal while Calla regaled the mesmerised room with their story. Muireann couldn't deny that the elf had a definite way with words and talent for turning any tale into an epic.

For her part, though, she felt that living it once was enough and she didn't need to hear it again, especially told with Calla's dramatic flair.

As Calla had predicted before when vowing to spread the story, they did indeed get a free meal and drinks from it, and Muireann had to grudgingly admit that it was nice. Foolish perhaps since they could easily afford the price but for once in her life Muireann felt admired and it was a good feeling, especially after the young man's taunting earlier. When the story had been told once another group approached and soon Calla was making the rounds of the room, repeating the tale, leaving Muireann to eat and relax alone.

Eventually the crowd began to thin, Calla returning to the table as the night wore on, the two women enjoying their mead as the room quieted down. It was then that Muireann noticed the young man again, the one who had stayed back when the others had left. Before she could look away her eyes locked with his, green to brown, and he moved quickly across the room.

Catching her frown Calla asked. 'What's wrong?' but the youth was already at their table.

'Good evening, ladies,' the young man started, clearly nervous. He was tall, at least six inches taller than Muireann and Calla, and had the lanky look of a young man who hasn't quite reached adulthood yet.

Muireann, who was in no mood for another confrontation, frowned harder. 'I'm no lady. And we were just about to retire for the night.'

'Wait! Please,' he said quickly, sliding into an empty chair next to them.

'I don't think we invited you to join us,' Calla said, predictably looking more amused than annoyed. She had been in fine spirits since the almost-duel.

'I'm sorry, you didn't, of course, but I was hoping that you'd be willing to speak to me.'

'About what exactly?' Muireann asked, fighting a yawn and wishing for the inn's comfortable bed.

'About training,' he said, then went on when both women gave him puzzled looks. 'I was hoping I could be your squire.'

'I don't need a squire,' Calla said, smirking.

Muireann shot her friend an annoyed look. 'We aren't knights.'

'That too,' Calla murmured, still smirking.

'Well, no perhaps not,' he agreed, pushing forward despite their clear lack of enthusiasm. 'But I could train with you.'

'As you heard earlier, I don't use a sword,' Muireann said, sighing. 'And I doubt you're looking to uproot your life for some archery training.'

He flushed but didn't waiver. 'No, but I could travel with you.' He turned to Calla. 'You use a sword, if nothing else I could spar with you, help you practise.'

'You don't even know where we're going or what our plans are,' Muireann said before Calla could answer.

Calla looked between them, then shrugged and drained her mead cup. 'I'll leave this to you, Muiri. Whatever you decide about him I'm alright with.'

Muireann turned to her in surprise as the elf stood and stretched. 'Where are you going?'

Calla smiled wolfishly. 'I'm not nearly ready to sleep yet and that trader over there is handsome and lonely. I'm going to go see if he'd like some company tonight.'

Muireann sighed again, this time at getting stuck handling a situation entirely out of her experience while Calla went off to have fun. Resigned she turned back to the young man. 'Why do you want to do this?'

'Truthfully, for the experience,' he said, leaning forward earnestly. 'I just finished my two years with the Lord's Guard, and I wanted to make a career of it. But when I mentioned that to one of the knights, he said I needed to get out and travel, live a bit, before committing to a life guarding the walls of the keep. Those were his exact words. And the more I thought about it the more I realised he was right. I want to be a warrior, maybe a knight one day, but I've never seen more of the world than here and the Lord's Keep. I want more than that.'

'So, join a mercenary company,' Muireann said, trying not to sigh once more. 'Join a merchant's guard. Travel to the capital city and petition for knight training with the royal guard.'

'I'd thought of all those things, but I don't even have the experience to know which would be the best one for me,' he said. 'I heard you and your friend tonight, and I realised that what I really need is to travel and live. And it seems to me that whatever you are doing, wherever you are going, if I go with you, I can figure out where I need most to be.'

Muireann closed her eyes, knowing she should turn him down cold but also undeniably swayed by his words. She thought of her own life, decided at eighteen for her when her parents declared she'd wed. Of her oldest daughter who had been absolutely certain at sixteen that marriage was what she wanted. Of her two sons, years younger than this man, who would never grow old enough to worry about these things. 'You realise you might get yourself killed travelling with us.'

He nodded, looking serious. 'I know that. Nothing in life is certain except death. But I can die in bed of an illness or drown in a flood or any of a dozen other things I've lost friends to over the years just as easily as die fighting.'

'Perhaps not just as easily,' she pointed out.

He shrugged. 'Perhaps not, but it can still happen. Like they teach in the temple, "all people meet the fate the gods write for them". Whatever my fate is won't be changed either seeking it out or running from it.'

Muireann grimaced, hating that particular belief but not in the mood for a religious debate. She rubbed one hand across her face, tired, pushing her glasses back up on her nose. And she remembered Calla's words about considering hiring a mercenary to travel with them in case anyone tried to rob them. 'How much did you make in the Lord's Guard?'

He straightened up before answering. 'Three silver pieces a week, because I was helping train the younger recruits and was sparring with the knights. I'm proficient with a bow, crossbow and polearms, and am considered fairly skilled with a sword. The short sword that is, but I was trying to learn longsword as well.'

All of that meant very little to Muireann, whose only experience with weaponry besides her own bow was what she'd read in books over the years. Still, the young man was obviously proud of his accomplishments and she guessed that he had put in a lot of extra work with the intent of applying for knight training later. Or perhaps he had overheard her criticising the lack of training in Arvain's guard earlier and wanted to reassure her that he was useful. 'What's your name?'

'Tash,' he said.

'Alright, Tash,' Muireann said, hoping she wasn't making a poor choice. 'We'll hire you on as a guard then. One gold piece a week in pay.'

His mouth fell open, then he stammered. 'That's far too much my lady, that's a fortune—'

She held up her hand to stop him. 'I told you before I'm not a lady. You can call me Muireann. My friend is Calla. And it may be a lot but as I said you may get yourself killed travelling with us. We're planning to journey to several of the main cities so I can conduct some research at the libraries. But there's no telling what may happen on the road, what trouble we may run into, or where our journey may end up taking us. If you want to come along then I'm going to pay you for it, more than what you made walking the walls of the keep. And if you are set on becoming a knight, you'll need money to petition an order and pay for your training.'

'Yes, my la…ah Muireann,' Tash said, sounding dazzled.

She sighed, suddenly feeling the gulf of years between them. 'Do you have a room in town or are you staying at the keep?'

'I had been living at the keep, of course, but was released from duty several weeks ago,' Tash said. 'I've been renting a room in Verell since then, but usually I walk the five miles out to the keep every day to spar with the knights and train.'

'I'm tired and turning in for the night,' Muireann said, hoping she didn't sound rude but just too tired to care much. 'If you want to meet us here tomorrow morning after breakfast and accompany us on our errands around town – I warn you they will probably be boring – you are welcome to. Otherwise, if you need to go and give any notice with the knights that you are leaving, meet us here tomorrow night for dinner and by then we should have a better idea of how long we are staying in Verell and where we are heading next. We'll start paying you based on when you start working.'

'I'll meet you in the morning,' he said, looking so delighted that Muireann half expected him to be waiting in the same seat when they came down for breakfast.

A quick glance around the room showed that Calla and the trader she'd gone off to flirt with had both disappeared. Hoping they hadn't disappeared to her shared room she stood up and extended a hand to Tash. 'Good night to you then and I'll see you tomorrow.'

He shook her hand, his grip firm, then turned and left, to Muireann's great relief. Feeling exhausted after all the events of her first day in Verell she headed up to her room to get some much-needed sleep.

Chapter 3

The Selkie

The next morning Muireann rose before Calla, who had returned to their shared room some time late in the night. Not wanting to wake the elf but too restless to stay in bed, no matter how comfortable it truly was, Muireann got up as quietly as she could and dressed, pulling on a new pair of pants and tunic from the pile of clothes they'd purchased the day before, and eased her feet into the stiff new boots Calla had insisted would be more useful than her old work shoes.

She slipped from the room and down the quiet hall of the inn, realising that it was early enough that the whole place seemed to still be sleeping. The common room was deserted but she could hear someone moving in the inn's kitchen, no doubt starting the morning meal. She hesitated a moment, then let herself out the front door deciding to take a walk to the shore. She had always loved the ocean and thought it would be nice to walk near the waves and watch the fishing boats heading out for the day.

The sun had barely cleared the horizon behind her and there was a chill in the air making her wish she'd worn a cloak, but the walk was pleasant nonetheless. She walked down to the main town docks and watched the boats casting off for a bit then grew restless again and started walking south, enjoying the tang of salt in the air and the crashing of the waves on the sand. After walking aimlessly for a bit she found a road that paralleled the water and wandered along that.

She hadn't gone more than a half mile from the docks when she noticed someone standing up ahead, just off the road. For a moment she debated turning back but even without her bow to defend herself she wasn't too worried; this close to town and with the fishermen on the docks and nearby in boats she could call for help if she needed to. Resolved she continued on but as she drew closer she realised the man wasn't alone, although it was difficult to understand exactly what she was seeing at first.

She stopped within a few yards of the strangers but it took Muireann a moment to make sense of the bizarre tableau. Just off the ocean side of the road a young man was standing over a woman. The man, who looked like any of the young farmers Muireann had known back home, was clutching some kind of bundled fur in his hands, his brows furrowed and his expression threatening. The young woman was, as far as Muireann could see, naked and crouched down in among the seagrass that grew to the edge of the road.

Hearing Muireann approach the woman turned and met her eyes, long brown hair a web across her features so that all Muireann could clearly see were her dark, pleading eyes. The man ignored her entirely.

'What's going on here?' Muireann asked, doubting it was anything good.

'Move along, woman,' the man said dismissively, shifting the fur in his hands as if he thought the naked woman might grab for it. 'She belongs to me now and she knows it.'

Everything clicked into place instantly for Muireann. The young woman must be a selkie, one of the seal-folk who lived in the sea but could remove their seal skin and become human-seeming on land. Muireann had never seen one so close, but she had grown up near enough to the shore that she had often seen them in seal form playing in the waves, and a handful of times from a distance dancing in their human forms on the shore. Selkies could be fierce fighters but would also help fishermen and they generally lived in harmony with local human communities. It wasn't unheard of for a human and selkie to marry although, as with any such mixed species union, any children would either be wholly selkie or wholly human. Every few generations, however, it happened that an enterprising young man would find and steal one of the sealskins when its wearer was on land, trapping the selkie away from her kin; although by ancient law this bound the selkie to the human these situations always caused problems between the two communities and at least where Muireann had grown up was strictly forbidden. She could only guess as bold as this man was being that it either wasn't illegal here or he was desperate enough that he didn't care.

'Give her back her seal skin,' Muireann said, wishing that Calla was there. If this came to blows, she didn't know what she'd do. She wasn't a fighter.

'Stay out of this, stranger,' the young man snarled, clutching the sealskin tighter in his fists. 'This is no business of yours.'

'You are making it my business, trying to force this girl to go with you when she clearly doesn't want to,' Muireann said, stepping between the man and the cowering selkie who was still looking at the woman with pleading eyes.

The man freed one hand long enough to shove Muireann back, his fingers poking hard into her shoulder. 'I said it's none of your business. I found a selkie wife and I'm going to keep her.'

'I won't be a good match for you. I told you,' the selkie interjected, her voice as soft as her eyes. 'I can't be what you want me to be.'

'You *will* be what I want because I have your sealskin,' the man shot back, his face twisting. 'Those are the rules.'

The selkie sobbed quietly, and Muireann's temper snapped. She had always thought of herself as a patient person, always gentle with her children and soft spoken to neighbours, but seeing the ugliness in the young man's expression and thinking of too many times she'd seen one person bully another she acted reflexively. Her hand balled into a fist and she punched the arrogant youth right in the face.

He fell like a stone, straight to the ground, and Muireann stood there stunned for a moment as much that she'd actually hit him as that she'd knocked him out. Finally, she reached down and scooped up the sealskin, which was softer than anything she'd ever held in her whole life, turning to hand it back to the selkie who was still crouched down as if expecting a blow. Seeing Muireann with the sealskin she stood slowly, her expression cautious.

The seal woman could have passed for any of the local fisher-folk; her skin was tanned light brown, her hair dark as fresh turned earth, matching her eyes exactly. She stood just over five feet tall, looking up slightly at the taller human woman. Seal-like even in human form, her body was all rounded curves and soft flesh, although she didn't look delicate. In short, from Muireann's point of view, she was gorgeous. Feeling awkward Muireann held the sealskin out towards the other woman. When she didn't immediately take it, Muireann said. 'Here. It's yours I'm giving it back to you.'

'Why?' the selkie whispered, still unmoving. Her dark eyes now darting between Muireann and the unconscious man.

'Because it's yours,' Muireann repeated calmly, trying to look anywhere but at the beautiful woman.

Slowly the selkie reached out to take the sealskin, pulling the soft folds against her chest with an almost audible sigh of relief. Muireann had fully expected the other woman to turn and leave immediately but she didn't. Instead, she regarded the human woman thoughtfully before saying. 'You saved me.'

Muireann was quick to shake her head, remembering the way the townsfolk stared at her when Calla regaled them with stories of Muireann rescuing her from the dragon. The look in the selkie's eyes was a bit too close to awe. 'I didn't save you, exactly. I was just trying to help because you obviously didn't want to go with him.'

'He had my skin,' the selkie said sadly, as if it still pained her to think of it. 'I would have had to go with him. I'm powerless without it.'

'Well now you have it back, so you don't have to go with him or anyone else,' Muireann said, still unsure why they were discussing this.

The selkie looked down at the sealskin then back up at Muireann. 'Why did you give this back to me?'

Muireann shrugged, ready to turn and start walking away herself. Instead, she kept up the conversation. 'Because it's yours. It belongs with you. What he was doing was wrong and I couldn't just stand by and watch it happening.'

The selkie seemed to think about that for a minute, the two women standing and regarding each other with the waves crashing relentlessly in the background. When she spoke again her voice was more confident, as if she'd come to a decision. 'My name is Lee.'

'I'm Muireann.'

Lee nodded slightly, then wrapped the sealskin around her shoulders like a cape. 'Muireann…it means sea bright. I like that.'

Muireann smiled. 'I've always liked my name as well, and the sea too for what that's worth.'

The selkie returned the smile. 'It's worth a lot to me, but I suppose that's stating the obvious.'

Her smile faltered after she spoke, and her expression grew serious. 'I feel rude being so blunt but none of this is what I thought it would be. It all feels so different from what I expected.'

Seeing Muireann's confusion Lee rushed on. 'Not you. You're amazing. I'm so glad I met you, and you seem very kind for a human.'

'I don't think I understand,' Muireann said slowly, trying to sort out what the selkie was really saying.

Lee squirmed slightly, looking down at the sand. 'I came on land because I wanted to live here for a time. To experience the world-on-shore while I can. I hid my sealskin, planning to find some shore clothes and pass as human. I thought I'd hidden my sealskin very well but when that awful man stole it, I thought I'd made a poor choice and should have stayed in the sea or at least kept my sealskin with me even though that would mark me as a selkie. Then you came and...and...I still want to see what life is like here and I want to stay with you. And you seem kind and...' she trailed off, throwing a shy look at Muireann, '...and I like you even if I don't know you well. I had thought when you fought him and took my skin that maybe you meant to keep me.'

Muireann shook her head quickly. 'I'd never force anyone to be with me like that. It's wrong.'

Lee blushed. 'I was afraid when it was him. I know how to fight and have done so many times against different dangers, but the magic of the sealskin has its rules, as you seem to know, and I was powerless to get it back. But I want to stay with you. If you don't want me to I'll understand but even if you aren't looking for a wife, I can still be helpful to you.'

Muireann stared at the selkie, starting to realise that there was more going on than she'd thought. She did know, as anyone growing up by the sea would, that there were rules that selkies were compelled to follow when it came to their sealskins and she realised that in all the stories she'd never heard of a human giving a skin back, only of selkies who found their own skins again and fled. Seeing the look in the other woman's eyes she had a sudden sinking feeling that she'd misstepped in handling the situation, that she should have let Lee retrieve her own sealskin. She cleared her throat nervously. 'Well, I...that is, I'm flattered. And I like you too, but I wouldn't want you to stay with me because you were compelled to. Free will is very important to me, that's why I did what I did.'

'I am choosing this freely though,' Lee said, her hands running over the smooth fur of the sealskin. 'You returned my skin. I can leave whenever I want. But I don't want to leave, I want to stay with you.'

Muireann felt herself sweating despite the chill air. This situation was entirely outside her experience, and she had no idea how best to handle it. Lee seemed nice, and Muireann couldn't deny she was attracted to her, an attraction that seemed to be mutual, but she was worried that she had triggered some ancient magic related to the sealskin and that Lee's feelings weren't real. Having been subjected to an unwanted marriage herself she would never inflict that on another person. But if it was magic, she didn't know what would happen if she simply refused and sent Lee away. As much as she didn't want the selkie bound to her unwillingly she also didn't want the other woman pining to death because she was rejected. 'I'm just not sure,' Muireann stuttered nervously. 'if this is a good idea. If it's what's best for you. For either of us.'

'You don't want a wife then,' Lee murmured to herself, looking sad again. 'Even so, would you consider letting me stay with you for a time? I can be helpful, I can clean or cook or mend things. I'm a fairly good hunter, at least of small game—'

Muireann cut into the woman's speech, shaking her head. 'Lee, please, you don't need to convince me of your value. I already think you're amazing.'

A bit hyperbolic perhaps, but the words slipped out before Muireann could really think about them. Lee looked hopeful, stepping closer to the human woman. 'Do you want a wife? Because I am yours if you will have me.'

Starting to feel slightly hysterical Muireann replied. 'Wouldn't you rather have a nice selkie husband? Or a fisherman? I don't live here, I'm only visiting, and I'm – my friends and I – are travelling right now. We aren't staying here for long.'

Lee shook her head emphatically, reaching out to grasp Muireann's arm. 'I don't like men, not for bedding anyway. I tried to tell him that, but he wouldn't listen. We'd have been a bad match. But you are beautiful and strong and kind and if you'll have me, I will make you a good wife. I will go where you go. I'd like to see more of the world, anyway, more than just what's under the waves.'

On the ground the unconscious man groaned and started to stir. Muireann stepped back not wanting to be there when he woke up – she really wasn't in the mood for an actual fist fight and doubted she'd be as lucky a second time. 'We should go before he wakes.'

'We?' Lee smiled. 'Then you will have me?'

Flustered and more focused on the man she'd knocked out who was definitely starting to wake up now, Muireann hastily said. 'Alright, if that's what you want, but—'

Lee cut her off before she could finish, pulling Muireann close and kissing her deeply. When she pulled back, she said. 'Oh! I'm so happy! You'll see, you won't regret this, I'll be an excellent wife...'

The young man groaned again and rolled over, grimacing as he stared blearily around. Muireann, still blushing from the kiss, grabbed the selkie's shoulder and gently pushed the other woman to start walking towards the town. 'Fine, yes. We can talk about that later. Let's get moving now, back to Verell.'

They walked hand in hand for a way, quickly until Muireann was sure the young man wasn't going to chase after them, then a bit slower. Glancing sideways at the selkie still clad only in the sealskin she'd wrapped around herself Muireann finally broke the silence. 'We'll have to stop and get you some clothes. Er, some clothes like people in town wear. Not that your sealskin isn't very nice, but while people here may be used to selkies coming in to barter for supplies people further inland don't usually walk around naked and I don't want anyone ill-treating you or trying to steal your sealskin while we travel.'

Lee nodded seriously, clutching the fur tighter. 'I understand about human clothes. As to my sealskin, it can't be stolen from me while I'm touching it, if anyone tries to grab it while I have it on, even like this, they won't be able to take it.'

'That's actually very reassuring to know,' Muireann said, relaxing slightly. She already had the green stone to worry about losing, she didn't relish the idea of constantly having to guard the sealskin as well. As they reached the edge of town, Muireann leading them towards one of the clothing shops a few blocks from the inn she was staying at – praying it was open even though it was early – Muireann decided she may as well finish what she'd wanted to say earlier. 'Lee, I know you want to stay with me right now, but I want you to know that if you change your mind at any time and want to leave, you don't need my permission or anything like that. You're free to do as you will.'

Lee squeezed her hand, smiling at her in a way that made Muireann's heart skip. 'That's how I know I made a good choice with you. You have a good heart and care about my well-being and happiness. What more could I want?'

I'm too cynical for these romantic notions, Muireann thought, using her free hand to push her glasses up on her nose. 'Well, I just want you to know that I don't and won't control you. You are your own person. And if you meet someone else you are attracted to or find you have feelings for, I don't want you to think you're stuck with me.'

Lee giggled. 'How can you worry so much about this when I chose to go with you? You're being silly. But just so you know, wives we may be, but I don't expect to own you either. If I find another I want to tryst with I will feel free to, and if you want to lay with other people I won't be upset – just don't throw me aside. If we choose to part later then so be it, but for now, and by custom for the next year and a day, we are wed.'

Lee missed Muireann's look of shock, too busy staring at the buildings around her as they walked. 'We are?'

'Mmmhmm,' the selkie murmured peering curiously at a blacksmith's shop. 'By the laws of my people at least. Are yours so different then? Isn't it simply that two people declare themselves wed and then it is so?'

For the second time Muireann realised she may have erred in how she was dealing with Lee. *I must find a good book on selkie customs, or who knows how much more of a mess of this I'm going to make,* she thought, swallowing hard before saying. 'No, with my people it's a bit more complicated than that. The couple would make public vows and the community acknowledges them as wed.'

Lee stopped, pulling Muireann to a halt with her. 'Do you not consider us wed then? Must we do something more for your people to acknowledge it?'

Seeing how upset Lee was getting Muireann immediately answered without thinking. 'No, of course not, it's fine. If it's how your people do things, then it's fine.'

Relieved Lee leaned over and kissed her again, smiling happily. 'Oh good. I wouldn't want to do anything wrong with you or offend your people. I don't know very much about the shore-people to be honest.'

'I can teach you,' Muireann responded automatically, keenly aware that she was in over her head and also realising that her attraction to Lee was definitely compounding the issue. She'd had several female lovers over the years, and she knew that under different circumstances she'd have been perfectly happy to add the selkie to those memories; but those had all been fairly short, passing flings focused on simple physical pleasure, not anything like actual involved relationships. She'd been married at the time to Edren, and it had just seemed easier to keep anything else superficial, even if she knew most married people preferred a few constant lovers whom they could rely on as both lovers and friends. Muireann had never had many friends in the village, if she were being honest with herself. But she was drawn to the selkie on a deeper level and that meant that she wanted to keep her happy and, more, that she wanted Lee to like her. So instead of questioning what Lee was saying or trying to convince her they weren't married after knowing each other for less than an hour, she found herself agreeing with all of Lee's assertions. Still, she was worried that all of this was happening too quickly, and while she could accept Calla's friendship which had also happened quickly that seemed as much from inertia on Muireann's part and natural inclination on Calla's. 'Umm, Lee? You wanting to go with me and being married and all of this, it isn't because I did something, so you had to, right?'

The selkie looked at her, puzzled. 'What do you mean?'

'I just don't know much about selkie customs or how the sealskins work and if you feel like you have to go with me because I gave your sealskin back—'

'Oh no, of course not,' Lee interrupted. 'If you'd stolen it, of course I'd be compelled but you didn't. I want to go with you and be your wife. You said you wanted that as well, don't you?'

'Well, yes,' Muireann stammered, then repeated. 'I just want to be sure you're doing this of your own free will.'

Lee pulled Muireann to a stop again, her pretty face distraught. 'Muireann, I chose to go with you. You protected me when I needed it, and now we can protect each other. We'll be safer together. And I find you very attractive. Isn't that all a good basis for a marriage?'

'I suppose it is,' Muireann agreed, still feeling like everything was happening too quickly. 'Just...I mean is it always like this with your people? So quick to marry?'

'Of course,' Lee said. 'Why wait? Besides if we don't suit each other in a year we can part. I think we suit each other very well though.'

Muireann nodded, thinking that every teenager in her village would prefer the seal-folk approach to marriage. 'Well then, let's find you some shore-folk clothes.'

At least they were able to find a dressmaker that had opened early and outfit Lee with the necessary clothes. Muireann encouraged the selkie to choose whatever she liked, insisting only that she include some smallclothes that the selkie wasn't familiar with. She quickly gathered that Lee hadn't ever worn clothes before, as the selkies didn't, and patiently explained what various things were for and how one would normally wear them. Unsurprisingly Lee's sense of fashion was eclectic and eccentric, and they left the shop with her wearing a loose blue dress without corset or belt, her sealskin draped around her shoulders like a fur wrap. She refused stockings or pants but eventually agreed to a pair of silk slippers. Muireann carried several more dresses, all in bright colours and all loose fitting, as well as several more pairs of slippers. She didn't think they'd last long but the selkie refused any of the more rigid or tight footwear outright and Muireann didn't want her to hurt her feet walking barefoot everywhere.

When they walked into the inn Calla and Tash were sitting together at a table in the nearly empty common room, and Muireann spared a moment to curse her luck that Tash had come so early even though she'd expected it. She'd hoped to have a chance to talk to Calla alone first. The young man was dressed in leather armour over canvas pants and a linen shirt, a sword strapped to his side. When Muireann and Lee walked in the two were deep in a discussion, but they stopped and turned at the sound of the door closing.

Muireann led Lee over, wiping her hands nervously on her tunic. This was really a lot to deal with before breakfast.

'This, ah, this is Lee,' Muireann said awkwardly, trying to ignore Calla's puzzled look. 'She's...ah...she's...'

'I'm her wife,' the selkie volunteered cheerfully.

Muireann saw Calla's eyes widen slightly and the way that Tash immediately looked at the selkie's seal fur. She could feel her cheeks reddening. 'She's not, I mean she is my wife, yes, but not because I made her do it. She still has her sealskin.'

Lee cocked her head to one side, looking slightly annoyed. 'Is this going to be what everyone assumes? I'm starting to feel like I'm the one who trapped you the way you explain it!'

'Oh no, Lee,' Muireann said, flustered. 'No, I just...most people are used to selkies who aren't wives because they want to be. I just didn't want my friends thinking the wrong thing.'

'Muiri, you are the absolute last person I would ever assume had stolen a seal bride,' Calla said, looking deeply amused at the very idea.

Tash cleared his throat slightly, nodded at the selkie, and said. 'Good to meet you, Lee. I'm Tash. I'll be travelling with you all.'

Lee smiled at the young human, but Muireann didn't miss the way she adjusted the sealskin, pulling it tighter around her shoulders. 'Nice to meet you, Tash.'

'And this is Calla,' Muireann said, introducing the high elf who nodded thoughtfully at the selkie.

'I'm the one Muireann saved from the dragon,' Calla said.

'A dragon!' Lee gasped, eyes going wide. 'Muireann, you saved her from a dragon?'

Now everyone was looking at Muireann strangely, although for a very different reason. The human woman squirmed under the scrutiny. 'Ah yes. I'll tell you all about it later.'

'No,' Calla cut in. 'I will. Muireann doesn't have any flair for storytelling, and I do particularly enjoy telling this one.'

Muireann was saved from replying when one of the serving girls arrived with two platters of simple breakfast fare: cooked eggs, sausage and toasted bread. Calla stood, gesturing for Lee to take her seat before turning to the waitress. 'Excuse me, Anna, was it? Can we get two more plates of food, please? Lee, Tash, you eat while Muireann and I go have a quick chat about supplies. We'll be back directly.'

With that Calla grabbed Muireann's arm and pulled her across the room and up the stairs, without waiting for either of the others to reply.

As soon as they were up the stairs where Tash and Lee couldn't see them, Calla stopped and said quietly. 'Are you sure this is a good idea, Muiri?'

'Which part?' Muireann asked, blushing.

'The part where we gained two new travel companions in the space of a day. How far can we trust them if it comes to our other project? And what happens while we are travelling? That isn't likely to be a very safe endeavour you know.'

Muireann rolled her eyes. 'You are so melodramatic, Calla. Tash is a warrior and you told me it was up to me if we let him travel with us – and that we might want to consider hiring an additional guard. Well, he is that, isn't he? And Lee...that's a long story, but she says she can fight too, we'll just need to get a weapon she can wield.'

'Mmmhmm,' Calla said, looking amused. 'I would really love to hear this long story about how you went for a morning walk and came back with a wife. A selkie wife no less, although obviously not the traditional way.'

'I would never,' Muireann snapped, genuinely offended. 'No, I found her with this man, and he had stolen her sealskin. And I just, er, got it back for her.'

'Just?'

'Well, I punched him,' Muireann admitted, flushing. 'And knocked him out and then took the fur back—'

'You knocked someone out with one punch?' Calla said, looking genuinely impressed. 'Muiri, you've been holding out on me! I didn't think you had such violence in you.'

'Don't tease me, it's not funny,' Muireann snapped, still embarrassed.

'I'm not teasing, I'm all in favour of knocking bullies down – or out as the case may be. I just assumed after last night that you were the sort that would rather avoid a fight than seek one out,' Calla said innocently.

'I am!'

'Says the woman who gained a seal wife by feat of arms.'

'Well, I wasn't trying to,' Muireann protested weakly.

'Then why not send her back to the sea?' Calla asked logically.

'I don't know if I can,' Muireann admitted. 'There's very old magic tied into sealskins and the taking of them and I *didn't* take hers, but I did take it *from* him and that seems to also be a thing although I don't know what I did. There's no stories about this. And she says she's my wife now and she wants to stay with me. I...I do like her. I mean I don't know her well yet, but I find her attractive and sweet, and I want to know her better and...'

Calla held up both hands, struggling not to laugh. 'Slow down, slow down. I think I understand what happened, at least the broad strokes. And I assume you aren't against the idea of having her as a wife?'

Muireann blushed scarlet, not wanting to admit how very not opposed to the idea she was, even to Calla, who she trusted more than anyone else.

'Right,' Calla said, still looking extremely amused. 'Don't worry, Muiri, I'm the last one to criticise you or your choice of bed mates – or wives – and I appreciate that you didn't lock me out last night. And that you aren't taking the chance to tease me for spending the night with a trader.'

'I wouldn't,' Muireann said, relaxing slightly. 'It's none of my business who you bed.'

'Then you are far kinder than most mercenaries who would not let me live it down. Warriors see traders and merchants as soft-living folk and there's usually a strict unspoken rule about not bedding them. But I get a few glasses of good mead in me, and I don't care so much about that and a lot about a handsome face and some good company.'

'My parents are merchants,' Muireann reminded her.

'And I like you anyway,' Calla shot back, smirking in her usual way. 'Alright well, here we are then. You and I still have our other problem to deal with and now we have a hired sword with us and a selkie. What sort of weapon do you think she'll be good with?'

'I don't know, I didn't think to ask.'

'We'll ask over breakfast then. Do you think we should tell them about our special project?'

'No,' Muireann said quickly, glancing nervously around the empty hallway. 'I think we'd be better off not telling anyone unless we absolutely have to. As they say, it's not a secret once three people know it.'

'As you will,' Calla agreed. 'Our original plan to visit bookshops and libraries researching the Aldovanan holds then?'

'Yes,' Muireann said firmly. 'I still think it's our best approach to handling this. If we can find out something about the nature of the magic they were using we at least have a place to start in deciding how to destroy it or unmake it.'

'Alright then,' Calla agreed, shrugging. 'Let's get our breakfast and get on with our day.'

The two headed down to re-join the pair eating at the table, unaware of the figure lurking down the hall who slipped back towards the servant's stairs, taking a different less obvious route downstairs.

* * *

Later that morning the group, led by Muireann, headed to the bookshop she'd thought might be helpful. Lee was now equipped with a very deadly looking spear. The selkie had explained that she had used something similar before and that it was a common weapon among her people. She also had a long knife at her waist, swinging from a loose cord she was using as a belt, which Muireann didn't doubt she could use with deadly efficiency. Honestly, Muireann felt bad for anyone who assumed the selkie was helpless or weak; barring the magic of the sealskin that wouldn't let her harm those who stole it, she seemed more than capable of defending herself.

They were getting more than a few strange looks as they walked through town, between Tash's armour, Lee's short spear and Calla, who had equipped herself with several swords and as many knives as she could strap on. Muireann felt like a duck among hens walking with them, especially since she'd left her bow in their room seeing no need to drag it around town, and was carrying only the leather messenger bag she'd taken from the dragon. Emptied of treasure she'd decided it was a serviceable bag to use for her own personal items, including the books she hoped to find that day.

Doing her best to ignore the looks and whispers, Muireann led the way into The Last Page, a bookshop that her friend Reyleth had often spoken highly of. She trusted his opinion and while she didn't expect to find exactly what they needed here she hoped she'd find a place to start looking.

Stepping into the shop she was greeted with the beloved smell of old paper and leather and she felt herself relaxing. Ever since she was small she'd delighted in such shops, begging her parents for spending money and using all of it on whatever books she could get. Even though she'd never been in this bookstore before it was so similar to ones she knew that it still felt like coming home. After the strange experiences of the past few days there was something deeply reassuring in being back in her own element.

There was a young man sitting behind the counter; he peered curiously at the group as they entered but Muireann ignored him, heading off into the rows of shelves to start hunting. Her plan was immediately side-tracked, though, by Lee who joined her peering curiously at all the books. 'Is there one here on the customs of your people? I'd like to read it.'

Muireann caught herself before she could ask if Lee could read, realising that was rude and also that the selkie wouldn't have asked about a book if she couldn't read it. Instead, she smiled and led Lee through the shelves until they found a small section of treatises on local customs. A few minutes of digging and Muireann managed to find one that wasn't either terribly out of date or focused on the nobility. She handed it to Lee. 'This one should do nicely. Why don't you get started on it and see what you think, and I'll pay for it with my others when I'm done?'

Lee nodded happily and opened the book, letting Muireann slip away to begin her own search. Or try to. She'd no sooner found what she thought was the correct section – shelves with books that seemed focused on history – when Tash appeared next to her. The young man cleared his throat awkwardly. 'So, Muireann, you're a bit of an expert with books, aren't you?'

Turning to the younger man she was about to tell him she was busy when she caught sight of his eyes, sincere and uncertain. She sighed. 'I was the scribe for the town I lived in and have more than a passing knowledge of libraries and bookstores, if that's what you mean.'

Relief flooded his face and he smiled. 'Yes. I was hoping you could help me, you see Alain – he, ah, he's my friend, a knight, well he's my friend who is a knight – anyway. He's the one who told me I should travel and get some experience before committing to a career with Arvain's guard. And he said it would be good for me to learn more about the things that knights know.'

Muireann blinked at that stammering, awkward explanation. 'The things that knights know?'

Tash shifted from foot to foot looking uncomfortable. 'Manners, and about the nobility, and strategy. History. Those things.'

Muireann stared at him for a minute, slowly realising that he had no idea exactly how much study he was talking about. She repressed a sigh. 'Alright. That's years' worth of material. Let's start with this, I assume you can read?'

'Yes, although I'm slow at it,' Tash admitted. 'I've always been better with active things – I pick up weapons training very quickly. But I'm willing to work at it. Oh! And I'm very good with numbers. My instructors have always praised my skill with maths, and I can do figures in my head faster than anyone else.'

Muireann nodded, considering what he'd said. With a glance at the books she'd wanted to look at, she led Tash through the shelves until they found several books she thought would suit his purposes: one on the basics of strategy in war, one on the various orders of knights in the empire, and one covering manners and customs throughout the nine kingdoms. He looked daunted at the growing pile, so she reached out and gave his shoulder a reassuring pat. 'I know it looks like a lot, but this should get you started on all the things you mentioned, I think. If any of it is confusing or difficult for you just come and ask me and we can talk through it.'

He smiled shyly at her, holding the books against his chest. 'Thank you, Muireann. I know I'm already asking a lot of you, of both you and Calla, but I don't want to squander this opportunity or waste any of my time. Alain said it's very difficult to become a knight and I know I may not have it in me to go so far, but even if I go with the Lord's guard, I'd want to be a captain one day and I'm already behind in the studies that are required for it.'

'If you want to be a knight then set that as your goal and do what you can to accomplish it,' Muireann said, thinking of the dragon. 'Many things can seem impossible to accomplish at the start, but we get there through innumerable small steps.'

He smiled, looking more relaxed. 'You would know the truth of that if anyone would I suppose.'

She blushed, hating the way her fair, freckled skin always betrayed her embarrassment, and it was his turn to be reassuring. 'Truly, Muireann I can't thank you enough for everything. I know we haven't known each other for long but giving me a chance to travel with you as a guard, helping me find these books, I genuinely appreciate it.'

She gave his shoulder another pat. 'It's nothing, Tash, truly. And I meant it about helping you study. I used to help the children in my village with their schooling sometimes, when the regular teacher was ill or busy on her farm, and I'd be happy to help you when you need it. Honestly, I'm likely to be less than useful on the road and it will make me feel like I'm contributing more than wild game for meals.'

He laughed at that, his mood obviously much improved. 'I'll teach you how to camp properly and I can even teach you to fight with a short sword if you'd like. We can say it's a trade for your instruction.'

She returned his happy smile. 'Consider it a deal then. For now, though, I need to go and look for the books I came here for.'

With a nod at the young man, Muireann turned and headed into the shelves once again, returning to the section she'd noted earlier. She'd pulled a couple of books and returned them as unsuitable and was just starting to look through a third when a hand landed on her shoulder. She turned to see Calla standing next to her. This time she did sigh aloud. 'Please don't tell me you need my help finding a book.'

Calla looked surprised, then laughed. 'Well I'm not opposed to some well written pornography if you think they have any in here. Keeps those long nights on the road interesting. But no, I just wanted to see how your search was progressing.'

Despite her frustration Muireann laughed, unable to resist Calla's irrepressible personality. 'I'm sure they do have some actually – even a town like Verell which isn't so very large has enough scholars to make it worth it for the bookseller to stock that sort of, er, literature.'

'Really? Scholars? I wouldn't have guessed.'

'Oh certainly. They read it, they write it, it's its own sort of business,' Muireann said, giggling.

'You have no idea how much I want to ask you how you know all of this,' Calla said, looking absolutely intrigued. 'So remind me to do so later. For now, though, any luck finding anything useful? We've been in here for a bit and it's after lunch already.'

Muireann shook her head, frowning. 'I haven't had any time to look, truth be told. Not really. I've been helping everyone else find books they need.'

'Muiri, seriously, you know how much I like you but priorities,' Calla said, her friendly tone taking the sting out of her words. 'They can ask the bookseller if they need help. We're here on a mission and you need to focus.'

'I know, and I am now,' Muireann said, embarrassed that she'd just naturally put her own work aside to help everyone. 'Listen, Calla, if you're hungry why don't you and the others go get something to eat? I'll be here for a while yet and I'm not ready for lunch.'

Calla hesitated, her eyes roaming the packed interior of the small bookshop. 'I am hungry, but I don't want to leave you alone.'

'Why?'

'We're strangers in a strange town,' Calla said, shrugging one shoulder casually although her eyes were still sharp. 'People know we have wealth and after last night that you may have killed a dragon but can't use a sword.'

Muireann felt herself flushing again. 'I was only being honest. And I'd think it's obvious I don't use a blade since I don't carry one.'

'All to my point,' Calla said. 'After the incident with that man last night I'm not eager to risk you getting into another fight when I'm not around to help.'

'I went out by myself this morning,' Muireann couldn't resist pointing out.

'While I was asleep and didn't know you were going,' Calla replied, and Muireann couldn't quite tell if she were teasing as usual or serious. 'And look how that ended.'

'It ended fine considering I knocked that man out when I needed to.'

'You were lucky, and still you came back with a wife which we both know isn't what you set out looking for.'

'Calla!'

'Fine, I'm just saying,' the elf protested, holding up a hand. 'For a scribe and farmwife you manage to find a lot of trouble.'

'I found you,' Muireann said, giving the high elf a pointed look.

'Well now you're just making my point for me,' Calla shot back, smirking. 'Come with us and get some food and we can come back afterwards.'

Muireann stubbornly shook her head. 'This isn't going to take me so very long if I could just focus on it and not be interrupted every few minutes.'

Calla sighed, still scanning the shop restlessly. 'Alright. I'll take Lee with me and get some lunch and leave Tash with you. He's good enough with that sword to handle any trouble you might wander into—'

'In a book store?' Muireann interrupted, snorting.

'—and when I get back, he can go eat,' Calla continued, ignoring the interruption. 'Or if you're done then you can both eat.'

Muireann sighed, a bit more melodramatically than she'd intended. 'I can't talk you out of this, can I?'

'Definitely not.'

'Alright then, do as you will. I'm going to see what I can find here.'

Finally left alone and hoping no one else was going to ask her for book advice Muireann got back to the business of searching for anything that might lead them to clues about the weapon they'd found, or about the principles behind Aldovanan magic. It was a frustrating search; most of the books were dry histories of the First Age or its empire that discussed particular people, places and battles but without the details that Muireann needed. The ones that had more details were almost always speculation or thinly veiled fiction. After searching until her neck started to ache the best Muireann had found was a slim text that proposed some theories about the nature of Aldovanan magic. It was far less than she'd hoped for although realistically she'd known it wasn't likely to be easy to find the resources she needed.

Resigned she left that section, stopping to grab a blank journal so she could record her observations of the dragon and take notes on the Aldovanan, before ducking quickly into a cluttered area near the back of the store where she suspected she'd find the other thing she was looking for. Her guess was correct and within minutes she'd located the books Calla had jokingly been asking about. She had no idea if the high elf had been at all serious but had decided that since she'd helped everyone else find books, she'd get one for her friend as well. At the least it lightened her mood considerably.

Carrying the books, she headed to the front of the shop where all three of the others were waiting with various degrees of impatience written across their faces, having regathered as the afternoon wore on. Muireann tried not to wince, realising she'd been in the shop for several hours. She paid for the book and journal she'd found, the book she'd suggested for Lee and a small book of illustrated erotic tales she'd decided to get for Calla as a surprise and the group left.

She stopped in the street just outside the shop, pulling the book for Calla from her bag. Somehow managing to keep a straight face, even to look grave, she handed the little red leather-bound book to the high elf. 'Here, Calla, I got you a gift.'

'A gift?' the elf said, looking surprised and pleased. Then she opened the book, the very vivid illustration on the page she turned to making its contents clear. 'Oh my...'

Calla started giggling, biting her lip as she flipped through to look at several other pages. Tash, curious, leaned over to see as well, then immediately turned away, so flustered that Muireann almost felt bad for him, even if she was sure he'd seen or at least heard about worse living in the barracks as a soldier. Lee also leaned in, her face curious and slightly confused but not at all outraged. The very calmness of the way she studied the drawings made Muireann wonder if she thought them tame and she reminded herself again that she needed to find a book on selkie customs and culture, which the store she'd just left hadn't had.

'Oh, this is just delightful,' Calla said, looking like she meant it. With a final quick look at another page, she stowed the book in the bag at her waist, hanging just in front of her left side sword. Muireann was happy that the elf liked the gift; she'd been fairly confident that she would, but it was nice to see her belief confirmed.

Tash was still staring fixedly at the milliner across the street, so Muireann gently elbowed him. 'I'm sorry if we embarrassed you.'

'I'm not embarrassed,' he lied. 'I just didn't expect such bawdiness from ladies of your status.'

'We aren't ladies,' Muireann and Calla said together, then both started giggling.

Taking pity on him Muireann gestured for the group to start walking before heading down the street herself. 'So, I didn't find what I needed there, and I doubt Verell has any booksellers with a better selection although we may as well check them all anyway.'

'What do you propose?' Calla asked, moving briskly down the street so that the others were forced to walk quickly to keep up.

'I have a friend, an old friend, in Strandview,' Muireann said, shifting the bag she was carrying against her hip. 'He has a bookstore as well, and more than that he's a mage and has a good knowledge of magic and magic theory.'

Calla gave her a sharp look over her shoulder and Muireann quickly went on. 'Which is what I'm researching. Magical theory of the Aldovanan. Anyway, I think he can help us and if he can't directly, he may know which of the great libraries would be our best bet.'

'Are we to head to one of the great cities then?' Tash asked, perking up noticeably at the prospect. The great cities were few across the empire, usually but not strictly the capitals of the individual kingdoms, and were known as centres of culture and art, as well as intrigue if you believed all the rumours.

Calla nodded. 'We'll go wherever we need to for Muiri's research. Even to Gold Spire, if it comes to that.'

Calla didn't sound thrilled at the prospect of heading to the imperial capital, and neither was Muireann. 'I hope it won't come to that. We'll head to Strandview first, maybe in a few days once we've checked all the shops here, and hope we find some answers there.'

'You don't want to see the capital of the empire?' Tash said, obviously a bit disappointed.

Muireann made a face at him. 'It's a two-week journey journey, at best, to Mistlen which would be our next goal if Strandview isn't enough. Mistlen's library is renowned by scholars throughout Lanal, through all of the empire even. If that fails us and we have to go to Gold Spire that's more than a month further and through the central mountains as well.'

Calla looked grim. 'It's a dangerous journey, especially this time of year. With the spring rains come flooding in the mountains and foothills, and it's much worse in the central mountains than here. It's dangerous enough that traders usually go all the way south to Port Vres and sail from there rather than risk the trade roads, at least until early summer.'

Muireann nodded. 'I trust Calla to know all the best roads and routes to take. She has years of experience guarding traders.'

Tash nodded as well, resigned. 'We could go towards Port Vres ourselves and south of the mountains.'

'We could,' Muireann agreed. 'but I'd still rather not have to. At best it would double our time travelling to go so far around.'

'Well, it may not come to that at all and if it does it may be we'll be well into summer by then and the roads between Mistlen and Gold Spire a better option,' Calla said, frowning. 'For my part I think we have many options of places to search in Lanal before we contemplate leaving for another kingdom, never mind the capital.'

Lee was watching the conversation unfold in fascinated silence, and Muireann spared a moment to reach out and grab her hand, squeezing it to let her know she wasn't being ignored. The selkie smiled and squeezed back, her fingers soft.

'Come on, let's cut through here,' Calla said, turning into an alley. 'This will get us back to the inn faster.'

'Sounds fine to me,' Muireann agreed. 'I missed lunch and am more than ready for dinner now.'

Later Muireann would think it was sheer luck that it was Calla who stepped into the alley first; with her years of experience guarding travelling merchants she recognised the ambush for what it was moments before it began. Those few seconds were critical in allowing her to respond while the men leaping out of the shadows around them still thought they had the advantage of surprise.

By the time Muireann realised what was happening Calla had already drawn both her swords and was swinging at the man closest to her. Their attackers – about a half dozen of them, all men as far as Muireann could tell – were dressed in nondescript clothing, with hoods pulled low over their faces to obscure their identity. All she could tell about them was they shared a similar, stocky build and were fighting with long, thin blades.

Calla leapt into action, fighting fiercely in the small space. Tash had drawn his sword moments after Calla and waded into the fray without hesitation. Lee, for her part, pulled Muireann behind her before levelling the short spear, using it to good effect to hold off the swordsmen who had a shorter reach.

Muireann watched the violence helplessly; without her bow she had no way to aid the others. Calla had wounded one man, who staggered back out of the action, and was deftly parrying two others. Tash was engaged in a fierce duel with a third. The remaining two harried Lee, trying to get in under the spear's sharp point but the selkie was too fast. Only once did the fighter on their left succeed in ducking and stabbing forward when Lee was dealing with his partner; Muireann seeing the blade coming at the selkie's side tried to do the only thing she could think of and threw her heavy leather bag between them. She felt a sharp burning pain in her arm, for just an instant, then Lee was swinging around, catching the man in the face with the shaft of the spear. Blood sprayed as his nose broke under the blow and he staggered back, dropping his sword. Behind him one of the other men yelled something Muireann couldn't quite make out and in the next moment the fighter on their right had dodged around to grab both the fallen sword and the semiconscious man Lee had hit. He turned to run, and Lee jabbed him in the shoulder, drawing blood, but he didn't slow down. The other men who had attacked them were retreating as well, disappearing back into the depths of the winding alley that they'd emerged from.

It was all over in a matter of minutes, before the noise of the fight could start to draw curious passers-by.

In the aftermath, the silence as sudden as the attack had been, Muireann was left reeling, standing against a wall close by Lee. Calla backed up slowly, gesturing with her chin for Tash to follow, pushing them all back the way they'd come until they were on the busier main street. Only then did she relax her guard and slowly sheath her swords. Seeing that Tash did the same and after another moment Lee set the spear butt against the ground and started examining the blade.

'You're bleeding,' Calla said, her voice sharp with worry. It took Muireann a few seconds to realise the high elf was talking to her and by then Calla had crossed over to her and grabbed her arm. Tash and Lee crowded around as well, watching as Calla moved aside the ripped fabric of Muireann's sleeve.

Her arm underneath was whole and uninjured.

Calla frowned. 'I don't understand.'

Muireann felt the hair go up on the back of her neck remembering the flash of pain, but resolutely shoved it away, looking for a rational explanation. 'I'm fine. My sleeve was torn in the fight. I don't think the blood's mine, it must be from when Lee broke that man's nose.'

'You blooded one of them?' Calla said, turning to the selkie. 'That's impressive. You really are good with that spear.'

Lee smiled in obvious pride. 'I've hunted with spears since I was young and fought more than once with them against humans who thought selkies would make easy targets to steal from or drive off.'

'Good for you,' Calla grunted, eyeing the selkie with new respect. 'I take back my concern that you'd be useless to us in a fight.' Before Lee could respond to that Calla was turning to Muireann again. 'I'm sorry I suggested that shortcut. I should have known better. Now that the whole town knows we have money we'll have to be more careful and on our guard.'

'You think they meant to rob us?' Muireann asked, uncomfortable with the idea although she couldn't quite say why.

'I'd guess as much yes,' Calla said. 'Unless you think it was personal, revenge perhaps for refusing to fight last night?'

'It wasn't Bren and the others,' Tash cut in, anxious. 'I won't deny such a low thing is something he might do, if he were embarrassed enough about being shamed at the inn, but they all trained with me in the guard and I know their fighting styles. Those men had a very different way of fighting than we use.'

'Hmmm,' Calla said, her eyes narrowing. 'That's true now that you mention it. They fought like southerners.'

'Southerners? Like from Harnsben or Vreal? Where the dragon was from?' Muireann asked, unnerved at the thought of any connection there. Something about that resonated with her, though, in a way that the idea of simple robbery didn't.

Calla shook her head slowly. 'Not so far east as that. I was thinking more like Donlach. They have a particular style of fighting there that uses thinner blades, like those men had, and focuses on stabbing rather than slashing.'

Glancing around at the people walking near them Calla turned and started walking back towards the inn again. 'I'll have to give that some thought. I've run into gangs of thieves in Port Vres that fought like those men and used a similar strategy, but I can't imagine why any group like that would be here. Port Vres is almost four hundred miles away – Port Gray north of us is nearly a hundred, so even if they'd arrived on one of the cargo ships, why would they have come all the way down here? Verell is no city to support a group like that robbing people, even with the travellers and traders who pass through.'

'It doesn't make much sense,' Tash agreed, frowning.

'It doesn't,' Muireann said unhappily, fussing with the tear in her sleeve to distract herself. 'But I don't see how we'll ever know their motives. They fled and we're leaving town soon enough.'

The others all nodded, and the conversation moved to other

things as they walked.

They returned to the inn along a slower route, and it was clear to Muireann by the way the subjects of discussion shifted to supplies for their upcoming journey that the others were already putting the fight from their minds. Even though she'd been quick to say they'd never find answers, something about the incident nagged at her and she couldn't quite make herself believe it was thieves as Calla had suggested. Nonetheless even she let her worry go when they entered the common room and found that a travelling bard was staying the night and paying for her room by entertaining. She was a mountain elf, her skin a deep brown, her eyes and hair black, her voice a stunning alto that filled the room with tales and songs she'd learned in her travels. She accompanied herself while singing on a delicately carved lute occasionally switched for a well-worn but fine hand drum. She was richly dressed in silk and velvet and Muireann knew just from that she was a high-ranked bard and a very rare treat for the folk of Verell, which was certainly why the common room was packed to the beams with townsfolk as well as travellers staying at the inn.

After a short wait, during which Muireann stored her bag and Lee's spear up in their room, the group was able to get a table in a corner with a good view of the performer. Muireann had no doubt that Calla had bribed someone for the prime spot and she was glad of it. It had been a long time since she'd experienced live music beyond what her humble village could offer at fairs and celebrations, and longer since she'd heard anyone as skilled as this bard.

Tash stayed through dinner enjoying the bard's songs and stories as much as the rest of the room. Muireann appreciated the company, both his and Lee's, since Calla wandered off at intervals to talk to other people in the room, including the bard when she was taking short breaks. Muireann admired the elf's boldness but was glad she had other company and wasn't left alone at the table half the night. As it was she was able to relax and talk with both her new friends until she felt as if she knew them well enough to be comfortable travelling the roads with them. As the evening wore on Tash took his leave, heading to his own rented room after agreeing to meet the group again in the morning. It was getting late enough that Muireann started to think of heading up to the room she and Calla shared – she supposed that they shared with Lee now as well – but the other two didn't seem ready to retire yet.

Seeing Tash leave, though, Calla causally returned from yet another chat with the bard, her eyes locking with Muireann's. While Lee was staring, engrossed, at the bard who had begun a long traditional ballad, the high elf crowded in next to Muireann.

Calla leaned close, her bright red hair forming a curtain between them and the rest of the room. She kept her voice low. 'I've made a new friend in the bard. I'm going to keep her company this evening and give her the long version of our tale. She wants to make a song of it, and if I'm lucky wants more from me than just the story. I won't be back until late again which will give you and Lee some private time.'

Muireann blushed, embarrassed both at the thought of a song about her killing the dragon and of Calla avoiding their room so she could be alone with Lee. Even if she wanted to be alone with Lee and desperately hoped the selkie felt the same way. Before she could say anything Calla went on. 'We need to switch beds though. That small bed won't fit two people and I'm not so selfish as to make you try. So, you take the bigger bed and I'll take the smaller one. And tomorrow we can talk to the innkeeper about getting different rooms.'

'Alright,' Muireann agreed, her face still hot. Despite all the talk of seal wives she hadn't thought too much about how this night might go. She didn't want to get her hopes up but also couldn't help hoping.

Smiling as always, Calla nodded and headed towards the common room's small bar. Muireann turned to Lee, watching her watch the singer until she finished. She reached out and gently touched the other woman's shoulder. 'Lee, I'm going to head up to bed now, you can stay here if you want to keep listening to the music.'

Lee's dark eyes widened, and she quickly shook her head. 'No, I want to go with you. I want to be with you.'

Still feeling nervous and afraid to read too much into that, Muireann led her away from the thinning crowd, up to the small room they were staying in. She found herself talking to fill the silence. 'This is our room. Mine and Calla's and of course yours now. I put your new things up here earlier. And your spear. Over there. There are two beds, I was using the smaller one, but Calla offered to switch with me, with us I mean. And this, ah, this is our bed. That is if you want to share a bed...'

Lee laughed, reaching out to caress Muireann's cheek. She shivered at the light touch. 'Of course I want to share a bed with you. I told you I wanted to be your wife, I'd hope I have a place in your bed. If you want me there, that is.'

Muireann licked her lips, then nodded, speechless. Smiling, the selkie stepped away and quickly slipped out of her loose dress and underwear, then carefully hid her sealskin between the wall and the bedframe, her body lit by the moonlight coming through the window. Muireann thought it was one of the most beautiful sights she'd ever seen. When she didn't follow suit and undress Lee hesitated, her eyes searching Muireann's in the dimness. 'Do you not want me?'

'I do,' Muireann whispered, trying not to look away. 'I'm just...it's been a while since I...'

Lee's smile returned, softer now but not unkind. 'Don't worry, I'll go slowly with you. I've been thinking about this all day.'

'So have I,' Muireann admitted.

Lee stepped closer, reaching out and taking Muireann's hand, then pulling her slowly towards the bed they would share.

And soon enough Muireann forgot what she'd been so nervous about.

Chapter 4

An Old Friend

They stayed in Verell for a full week, but oddly the final morning reminded Muireann of the first she'd spent in the town, a blur of almost surreal shopping. Calla knew exactly what to buy and where to get it for travelling but she seemed intent on equipping them for a journey of far more than the three days it would take to get to Strandview. Also, it was clear that given an unlimited budget she was going to buy only the best quality she could find. Muireann went along with her suggestions, agreeing to everything from the high-quality canvas tents and travel bedding to the new boots and cloaks Calla insisted would be essential. She only put her foot down when Calla suggested they buy horses; while that would speed their journey and make it easier to carry everything Muireann knew it would also cause a lot of complications for them as well. She doubted Lee knew how to ride and knew that a new rider on such a trip was a risk in itself, and horses would mean even more supplies as well as additional camp chores.

The group set off just before noon, walking north out of Verell along the coast to avoid the more difficult mountainous terrain to the east. Each of the four carried a large, bulky pack, heavy enough that Muireann was starting to regret arguing against horses. The other three didn't seem bothered by the extra weight, Tash being used to it from his training and Calla and Lee being stronger by nature than any human, but Muireann was already anticipating aching muscles and blisters later.

When they stopped for the night, setting up camp just as the sun started to set, Tash was true to his earlier promise and showed Muireann how to pitch her tent and safely set up the fire pit. She had intended to try to hunt for some rabbits as soon as the basic chores were done, so they could have a hot dinner, but just as the fire was really catching Lee emerged from the woods carrying several grouse, the birds already gutted but not defeathered. Tash smiled warmly at the sight. 'Excellent! We will eat well tonight. I'll get some sticks to spit them on and we can roast them with some of the salt and garlic we packed.'

He hurried into the woods and Muireann couldn't resist smiling at his enthusiasm. She stood and walked over to Lee. 'They are wonderful looking birds.'

The selkie preened under the praise. 'Thank you. I told you I am quite a good hunter, and truth be told while I appreciate that you all enjoy a varied diet, I prefer meat, and fresh is better.'

Muireann nodded, taking the birds from Lee and heading closer to the shoreline side of camp to remove the feathers. She hadn't thought about it, but she supposed seals did survive on fish and sea animals so it made sense the seal woman would prefer a similar diet. She made a mental note to stock up on dried meat and jerky next time they needed to travel, so Lee could eat what she liked if they failed to get any fresh game.

She crouched down in a cluster of rocks and started pulling feathers with abandon, letting the wind take them away from camp. Lee watched curiously for a few minutes then asked. 'Why are you doing that?'

'Hmmm? Oh, we always take the feathers off before cooking them.'

'Interesting,' Lee murmured, leaning closer. Muireann felt heat rising to her face as the selkie's breath tickled her cheek. 'We don't. We cover them in mud and bake them under the coals of a fire. It's quite good.'

'It's sounds good, maybe we can try that next time since I already started doing it this way,' Muireann agreed, making quick work of the birds. She'd had plenty of experience with the chickens they'd kept on the farm. 'I hope you like them spit roasted as well, since you caught them.'

'I'm sure I will,' Lee said. 'It's fun to try new things, and I miss the taste of salt.'

Heading back to the fire where Tash was already waiting with several sharpened sticks, Muireann made another mental note to buy more salt. Calla was sitting down near the flames, sharpening one of her swords, the rhythmic sound of the whetstone sliding along the blade soothing in the thickening shadows.

Muireann handed the now de-feathered birds to Tash, who had returned with the spits to roast them and sat back to let him take over cooking the grouse. Besides her brief experience on the road after the dragon, she'd never camped before – the other times she'd travelled it had been by wagon on the trade roads and she'd slept in the wagon at night – and never travelled in a group like this before either. Looking around at the oddly domestic scene she found herself smiling, happier than she had been in a very long time.

*　*　*

Travel the next day brought them close to Gorseview, and Muireann could feel herself tensing up with every hour that passed. When they reached the large crossroads a few miles south of town she went west on the ocean-side road while Calla started to turn onto the road that would have led them to Muireann's previous home village. Lee and Tash hesitated in their wake, unsure who to follow. Muireann ignored them and forged ahead until Calla noticed and ran to catch her with the others trailing more slowly behind.

'Hey, Muiri, what are you doing?'

'Walking,' Muireann replied, refusing to stop.

'Yes, I see that,' Calla said drily, matching Muireann's strides to walk next to her. 'But why this way? We can go to Gorseview and sleep under a roof tonight.'

Muireann sighed and shifted the weight of the heavy pack against her shoulders. 'There's no inn at Gorseview, the village is too small. There's a tavern that sometimes lets travellers stay overnight in the common room, but we'd be more comfortable in our tents – most traders that pass by camp at one of the sites outside town.'

Calla frowned. 'I'd rather sleep near a hearth, even if it's in a common room, than camp if I have the choice. Besides wouldn't you like to see your friends? Visit your brother?'

Muireann shook her head quickly. 'Truthfully no. If we stop in or pass through Gorseview you may as well plan on staying at least a week. I doubt we'll get free any sooner, especially if we mention the dragon.'

Calla lowered her voice so the others wouldn't overhear as easily. 'Don't you want to let your brother know you're safe? You said you left with no warning, he must be worried.'

Muireann made a face then shook her head. 'He doesn't worry, he gets annoyed, and I don't need a lecture about how irresponsible and selfish I am.'

'Ahhh,' Calla said slowly, then nodded. 'Yes. I see. Lead on, my friend, and you can show us where this campsite is.'

Muireann nodded briskly, continuing on as fast as her aching feet would allow. After another minute or so of walking Calla said, her voice still low, 'Won't it be awkward seeing your parents in Strandview then?'

'We won't be,' she said, shrugging which turned into adjusting the pack on her shoulders. 'I grew up in Strandview, but my parents moved to Port Gray years ago. They don't come back down here, not ever. Not even for the funerals.'

'Ah,' Calla said again. 'Yes, I do understand. I also find my family to be…complicated. And if our situations were reversed, I wouldn't relish seeing them again, truth be told.'

'They didn't approve of you becoming a mercenary?'

Lee and Tash had caught up with them at this point but were

silent, letting the two women talk. Calla sighed, looking out towards the sea. 'They don't know I'm a mercenary. They had a very set idea of what they wanted my life to be, and I didn't agree with it, so I left. I've been on my own since, earning a living through my own skill and intelligence.'

'And doing a great job of it,' Muireann said, smiling at her friend to try to lighten the mood.

'Well at least until the dragon,' Calla said, smirking.

'Oh, I disagree,' Muireann said quickly, 'since that situation worked out to give you enough money to live on as comfortably as you like for even your long life.'

Calla laughed, then shrugged. 'True enough I suppose, although I have you to credit for giving me the chance to walk out of that cave at all.'

'But walk out you did,' Muireann reminded her. 'Anyway, we're both walking paths that are very different from what our families would want for us now, so we have that in common.'

'Me as well,' Tash said, surprising everyone. Looking slightly embarrassed he went on. 'My father is a healer and my mother a mage. They both thought I'd follow one or the other of them, but I hated always being stuck inside with their dry books. I was thrilled when I was old enough to serve my two years with Lord Arvain and...well...when I decided to make a career of it, they were very unhappy. It's a dangerous life and that's not what they wanted for me. And even though mageskill in humans is so rare I think my mother had set her heart on my inheriting hers and following her, so she was disappointed that I didn't even try.'

'Aren't mages and healers the same thing?' Lee said, sounding genuinely puzzled.

Tash looked surprised then shook his head. 'Not for humans, no, although I understand other species like elves can work many kinds of magic. I suppose they have the time to learn all the different methods. And as it happens my father isn't a magical healer, he uses herbs and physical means.'

'Ahh,' Lee said thoughtfully.

'I often forget that human magic is so specialised,' Calla said. 'But you are likely right, Tash, that it has to do with lifespan and also perhaps innate ability. Not that I'm putting humans down, I'm not, but magical ability does seem rarer among humans compared to other species.'

'It seems so,' Tash said, shrugging. 'My parents seemed to think if I tried, I'd show some ability, but I never wanted to try. I was playing with wooden swords as soon as I was old enough to hold things, much to their dismay.'

'But you're being true to yourself,' Calla said, smiling at the young human. 'That's what we all must do.'

'Yes,' Lee said, her voice subdued, her eyes fixed on the sea. 'We all must.'

'Are you alright, Lee?' Muireann asked, worried about the sadness she could see plainly in the selkie. 'Do you want us to go closer to the water so you could—'

'No!' Lee cut in quickly, then with less urgency. 'No. I wanted to come onto the land and experience life here. I'm fine. And I don't want to be away from you if you need me for anything. I just meant that Calla is right, we must all be true to ourselves if we want to find any happiness in life.'

Muireann almost pushed, wanting to know if anything was bothering Lee, but decided it was too public to ask what might be very personal questions. And she also realised that it could simply be that Lee's choice to voluntarily live on land for a little while, though not so different from Tash's desire to experience more of life before settling down into a career, might be seen as odd by her people. Like the other three she could be feeling as if her choices were at odds with her family and that could be a subject she wasn't ready to discuss yet. With a reassuring smile at the selkie she let the matter drop and the group continued on towards the campsite in silence.

* * *

Although they'd only been together as a group for a short time they quickly fell into a routine, which Muireann quite liked. The four of them worked well together, taking turns with the various camp chores and trading stories. In the evenings after dinner Muireann would help Tash with his studies while Lee read her book quietly to herself and Calla went through weapons drills. When Tash had enough of Muireann's instruction he'd join Calla in her practice, the two sparring together. Lee and Muireann would sit and talk into the night, watching the other two fight, or Muireann would make notes about the dragon and her research in her book, until it grew late enough that the fire was put out and they all sought their beds. It was a routine that Muireann felt she could easily get used to, and she started to understand why Calla enjoyed travelling so much.

After camping to the west of Gorseview they rose the next morning, a heavy late frost covering the ground and a hard chill in the air, and packed up camp for the final leg of their journey. Calla chatted as they walked, talking about the various things they could do in Strandview, which she had passed through on occasion but apparently never had time to stop in. Muireann listened with half an ear, her own mind torn between excitement at seeing Reyleth again and nervousness at returning to the town she'd been born in. She hadn't set foot in Strandview in more than five years, and the town held as many good memoires as bad.

They were walking through an area of thick scrub brush when the attack came, a group of people in heavy dark cloaks appearing from the bushes without warning. Unlike in Verell this time Calla wasn't anticipating an ambush and they were all caught off guard. Nonetheless the elf drew her blades quickly and charged at their attackers. Tash was close behind along with Lee who brandished her spear as before, using it both to stab at the cloaked figures and to strike them with the shaft. Muireann for her part quickly pulled an arrow from the quiver at her waist and drew back, aiming at the closest enemy, a woman coming towards her with a sword, but hesitated. She had never shot a person before, only animals, and it felt wrong to aim at one now even if the person in question was swinging a sword at her.

Muireann's decision was made for her when the woman with the sword swiped at her face and Muireann reflexively dodged back, tripped and released the arrow. It struck the cloaked woman in the side; she screamed and fell back, disappearing into the brush. Muireann swallowed hard but drew another arrow, knocking it and looking for another target. She'd barely got the bow back up when something struck her on the side of the head, and she fell.

By some ill chance her glasses went flying, and she found herself on the ground unable to see anything but a blur of colours. Panic bloomed in her chest. She heard voices shouting around her, Lee and Calla both calling her name, but in her panic all she could think to do was try to find her glasses. Reaching out across the ground her fingers brushed the familiar frames and she hastily pulled them back on, relieved as the world came back into focus. Heart still pounding furiously she rolled over, grabbing for her bow, only to see the last of their attackers fleeing down the path. Blood gleamed on the blades of her friends, but there were no bodies on the ground. She scrambled to her feet, scooping up her bow and the arrow which she'd dropped, her hands shaking in the aftermath of the fight.

Lee was at her side a moment later, eyes wide and concerned. 'How badly are you hurt? Do you need to sit?'

Muireann looked at her in real surprise, having almost forgotten about the blow that knocked her down to begin with. Calla and Tash crowded around as well, swords still out and on alert. She put the arrow back in the quiver with the others, glad she had a decent supply, and reached up with her free hand to feel the side of her head but found nothing. Puzzled she shrugged and shook her head. 'I'm fine. It doesn't even ache. I think it was just a glancing blow, but I was already off balance and fell.'

'Are you certain you're alright?' Lee pressed, worried.

'I'm embarrassed more than anything,' Muireann admitted. 'You all keep praising me as this heroic dragon slayer and our first real fight where I have my bow and I trip and fall on my butt.'

Calla snorted. 'You did kill a dragon and you are a hero no matter how much you hate me saying so. And I saw you shoot one of those highwaymen before you were knocked down – and as to *that* it's fortunate you did fall or that blow may have ended you and then where would we all be?'

'You're always so melodramatic,' Muireann complained, still running her hands over her head to check it.

'That may be so – and once again let me remind you that you love me for it – but it's still true. I've seen more than one person struck hard on the head who never rose again,' the elf said, shrugging before starting to clean her blade.

'Is everyone else alright?' Muireann asked. 'No one was injured?'

Tash shook his head, his whole demeanour sombre. 'None of us were touched, although we inflicted wounds enough on them.'

'I almost felt bad to be honest,' Calla admitted. 'We were clearly the superior fighters, and it was not a fair fight at all. I don't think we did them any mortal harm, though, only minor injuries. That's usually enough to drive robbers off. They won't throw their lives away for a few purses from travellers.'

'Do you really believe they were highwaymen?' Tash asked, mirroring Calla and cleaning his own sword before sheathing it.

'What else?' Calla said, sighing. 'I admit I wouldn't expect robbers like that, so organised and in such numbers, on this small road and this early in the season, but I've seen stranger things.'

'Isn't it odd,' Muireann mused, 'that we've been attacked twice in a week?'

Tash frowned slightly, shifting the sheathed sword at his hip, his hand lingering near the hilt. Lee watched the conversation in silence, close by Muireann's side. Calla hesitated then shook her head. 'I don't think so. Everyone in Verell knew we had money, if not how much still that it was enough to spend like we had no worries. I expected something to come of that or even from the confrontation in the inn. And it's early for robbers on the road but if the year has been difficult, crops poor or bad fishing, that will force people to such.'

Muireann nodded, feeling only somewhat reassured. 'I trust you to know about these things.'

'In truth,' Calla admitted, 'I might be suspicious but the men who attacked us the other day used rapiers and had a distinct fighting style. This lot was as motley as they come, barring only the similar cloaks; they had different types of swords, different fighting styles – all the hallmarks of a group of desperate people that have banded together for a common purpose on the roads.'

'Rather like us then except with different motives,' Muireann joked, and even Tash cracked a smile at that.

'Very different motives,' he said, 'unless there's something you haven't told me.'

Calla laughed. 'I've only known you a few days, there's plenty I haven't told you yet but give me time and you'll tire of my stories. And rest assured none of them involve a secret plan to rob anyone.'

'That is reassuring,' he said, smiling.

'Alright,' Muireann cut in, frowning at the underbrush around them. 'Do you think it's safe to proceed then?'

'I'd guess they've fled for good, but we should still be on our guard until we reach open terrain,' Calla said. As they turned and resumed their journey, she set her hand lightly on the hilt of one of her swords. The others followed suit, Muireann keeping an arrow in one hand as she walked.

Lee stayed close and spoke as they walked, keeping her voice low. 'Are you certain you are alright?'

Muireann smiled at her new wife. 'I am, truly, but thank you for being so concerned.'

'Of course,' Lee said, then. 'Is it always this dangerous being on land?'

'Not usually, although I suppose we do get used to certain things,' Muireann said, thinking as they walked. 'When the dragon was alive, we knew it would attack some of the farms during the year to take livestock and that occasionally, perhaps once every several years, a person might be hurt or even killed. But it's such a persistent risk that you become accustomed to it and stop really worrying about it. Like the great storms that come once a decade or so.'

'Hmm,' Lee said, then nodded. 'I suppose that's true in the sea as well. There's always some risk from the sharp-toothed whales and in the summer from sharks and coming on land from humans. Even in the sea sometimes young seal-folk will get caught in fishermen's nets and drown.'

'Life isn't a very safe endeavour,' Muireann agreed, then added, worried again that Lee was regretting her decision, 'If you aren't happy here—'

'No!' Lee interrupted immediately, reaching out to grasp Muireann's shoulder. 'I am. It isn't exactly what I expected but not in a bad way. I'm glad I'm here and I want to stay with you.'

'I just want to make sure you know you can tell me if you are feeling sad or homesick. Or change your mind. This journey may not end in Strandview, there's a good chance we'll at least have to go as far as Mistlen and that's quite a bit inland. You'd be out of sight and scent of the sea by weeks and weeks of walking.'

Lee straightened her shoulders. 'I know. I understand it may be difficult and I promise you that I will tell you if I start to pine for the waves. But I can swim in freshwater as well, even if it's not the same, and this world is so big – I want to be able to look back when I am older and say I've seen more of it than the shoreline my people claim.'

'I can understand that,' Muireann said, meaning it. 'I think you and Tash have a lot in common actually, wanting to see the world before settling down in it.'

'And you don't feel that way?'

'I just want some answers,' Muireann said, turning her gaze to the north-east, where she knew Strandview waited. 'And I hope we may find some, or the start of some, soon.'

* * *

They arrived in the town, bigger than Muireann's village but smaller than Verell, just before sunset. She knew the others were tired, although after that one incident on the road the journey had been quiet, and they wanted to get settled in one of the inns that Strandview boasted, but Muireann was anxious to see Reyleth. Now that they were in town even the heavy weight of the travel pack wasn't enough to slow her steps.

'Just let me stop in for a moment,' she said, steering them through the streets towards Rey's shop. 'If I can at least let him know what we need he can give it some thought and make suggestions or have some ideas ready for us to start looking up references tomorrow.'

'This must be a very good old friend that you're so intent on seeing him immediately,' Calla teased.

Muireann blushed, hating the way her complexion always gave her away. 'I've known him almost my entire life, since he opened his shop when I was a teenager. He's a skilled mage and very knowledgeable in magic and exactly the person we need to talk to about this. The Aldovanan are a personal interest of his, he's done a lot of research on them himself.'

'Mmmmhmmmm,' Calla said, dragging the sounds out and arching an eyebrow. 'Purely for research purposes. Can't wait until morning. Sure.'

Muireann glanced nervously at Lee, not wanting to make the selkie uncomfortable. She didn't seem perturbed but still Muireann felt the need to be reassuring. 'It was never anything like that. He's just a good friend.'

'Sure,' Calla repeated, still smirking.

'Calla!'

'What? I'm agreeing with you,' the high elf said innocently.

Muireann rolled her eyes but let the matter drop, leading them on until the familiar sign for The Bound Ink came into sight. It hung, gold and black lettering on light blue, above the door to the little bookshop that sat tucked between an apothecary and magical supply shop. The three stores formed a sort of unofficial mage's section of town, being the only three that catered to magic users, although the apothecary and bookshop had other customers as well. Muireann's mother had been unhappy when she'd first started frequenting the place, as much because she feared her daughter would decide to be a mage – the only thing she viewed as worse than being a spinster – as that she didn't like elves and thought Reyleth wasn't the sort of person Muireann should hang around with. But Rey's shop was the best in town and carried the sorts of obscure texts that Muireann loved, and which other bookshops didn't bother with, so she'd developed a habit of visiting whenever she had any spending money. She and Reyleth had quickly become friends and after she'd moved they'd kept up a correspondence. He even sent her books sometimes, something that had saved her when life on the farm and in the small village had seemed oppressively restricted.

Reyleth had come to the funerals the previous autumn, but that whole experience was a grief-soaked blur in her mind. She remembered that he'd been there, but not a word that they'd exchanged or even how long he'd stayed. Besides that, it had been five years since she'd seen him and she felt suddenly nervous. She knew he was very intelligent and, more than that, clever and she'd have to be careful to ask her questions just the right way or he'd grow suspicious. And she didn't know if she could outright lie to him if he pressed her on things she didn't want him to ask about. Reaching the door she pushed the worries away, too proud to let the others see her hesitate after she'd made such a fuss about coming straight to the bookshop.

The inside of the store was exactly as she remembered it, cluttered and haphazardly crammed with shelves of different types and sizes. Somehow Rey managed to fit more books in his small shop than the larger store in Verell had, and she felt a smile tugging at her lips at the thought. His assistant, a tall, thin human about Muireann's own age, stood nearby restocking a shelf. Pol had been a fixture in the store since Muireann had still lived in the town and except for the fact that his hair was thinning, he looked much the same as he always had: dusky skin, over six feet tall but thin as a reed, clad in dark pants and shirt covered by a leather apron liberally smattered in ink stains. He had always reminded Muireann of a heron.

When she and her group walked in, he looked up and then smiled. 'Well hello, stranger! You're a pleasant surprise today.'

'Hello, Pol,' Muireann said. 'It's always good to see you. I was hoping Reyleth might be in?'

'He's at the back counter,' he smiled at her and nodded at the others. 'Why don't you leave your packs by the door? I'll keep an eye on them for you.'

Before Muireann could agree, the others were already dropping theirs to the floor. Tash said. 'I'll stay here.'

'As will I,' Lee added, then seeing Muireann's worried look. 'I still haven't finished the other book you've found me, and this place is rather crowded. I can stay here with Tash and guard the door.'

'Alright then,' Muireann agreed, feeling oddly as if Lee was intentionally trying to give her space while she was visiting her friend. Part of her appreciated it but another part was nervous about it; Edren would never have been so understanding, in fact had always hovered around her on the few occasions she'd visited Reyleth when they were married.

Leaving Pol, Tash and Lee by the door, she and Calla walked back through the store. They found Reyleth huddled over the counter in the back, transcribing something from a very old looking book onto a fresh paper. Muireann took a moment to simply admire him, appreciating his beauty as she always did. Like all river elves his skin was the white of fresh snow with the faintest hint of blue tinging it. His hair was such a dark blue-green many people mistook it for black; it had always remined Muireann of a grackle's feathers. He was wearing the same thing he always seemed to be wearing when she saw him, dark pants and a linen shirt, the white of the shirt looking pale yellow against his blueish-white skin. Sensing their presence he looked up, those familiar dark blue eyes met hers and a wide smile spread across his face. 'Muireann! I'm delighted to see you again. You wouldn't believe the strange rumours I've been hearing lately.'

She fought not to grimace even as Calla slightly behind her snorted loudly. 'Hello, Reyleth. I'm afraid to admit that some of the rumours might be true.'

He gave her an amused, conspiratorial look. 'So you did kill a dragon then?'

She fought to keep her face neutral, stepping up until she was standing against the opposite side of the counter, the wooden plank all that separated them. 'I did.'

'Wait, what?' he gaped at her, all the teasing gone from his voice.

'I did kill a dragon,' she repeated, feeling her cheeks warming. Flustered as he continued to stare open mouthed at her she pulled Calla's gift from under her shirt, letting the Dragon Stone swing from her fingers. 'I really did.'

He reached out but stopped just short of touching the faintly glowing stone. Finally, he pulled his hand back slowly, rallying his usual good humour to cover his shock. 'Well if anyone could pull off the impossible it would be you.'

She blushed harder. 'Don't tease me, Rey.'

'I'm not teasing you at all,' he said, his voice gentle. 'You underestimate yourself, Muireann, you always have.'

Stepping up next to her, Calla cleared her throat loudly and Muireann tried not to laugh at the utter lack of subtlety. 'Reyleth, this is my friend, Callavealysia. I told her that you were the best one for us to talk to about magical theory texts.'

'Call me Calla,' the high elf said, sizing up the river elf coolly. 'Muiri has told me a lot about you.'

Rey looked uncertainly from Muireann to Calla. 'Hello, Calla. Your pardon but you don't seem to be a mage.'

'I'm not,' Calla said casually. 'But we are researching magic relating to enchanted objects. That sort of thing.'

Muireann could see the confusion on Rey's face although she doubted someone who didn't know him well would pick up on it. They'd been friends long enough, though, that Muireann noticed the slight tension in his mouth and narrowing of his eyes, and she knew she should intercede before he asked any questions they couldn't easily answer. She turned to Calla. 'Why don't you get Lee and Tash and go find us rooms at the Dancing Tide – it's the best inn in all of Strandview, you'll like it, I think. Take a left out of the shop and then turn right at the end of this street and you'll see it.'

Rey's puzzlement deepened at that, but Calla perked up immediately. 'Certainly. Hopefully it's better than the last one we stayed at. That was nice enough but not as nice as it could have been.'

'You seemed to like that bard well enough,' Muireann couldn't resist saying.

Calla sighed appreciatively. 'I did indeed. I doubt there will be anyone nearly as appealing here, though, although don't worry, I will do my best to find out.' She nodded politely at Reyleth then said to Muireann. 'We'll bring your things along with us and meet you in their common room when you're done here.'

The group left as abruptly as they'd entered, Muireann relaxing in the now quiet shop. She'd spent a lot of time here when she lived in Strandview, and it was the one place she always made sure to visit whenever she was in town. It felt like coming home far more than visiting her parents would have. Where they stood in the back they were mostly hidden from Pol, still filing away new books, and she could at least imagine they had some privacy.

Her silent contemplation of the interior was interrupted by Reyleth moving lithely around the counter to her side. He was slightly taller than she and she turned and looked up into his face as he drew closer. Wordlessly he reached out and traced the scar on her left cheek, frowning. 'What happened?'

She grimaced, annoyed that she hadn't anticipated his reaction to the scar, then reached up and took his hand in hers, moving it away from her face and squeezing it before letting it go. 'I killed a dragon.'

'Not so very long ago though. Rumours of it have only just reached here and no one has the story straight,' he said with his eyes still on the scar.

'Calla will be sure that the whole town knows the story before nightfall, don't worry.' Muireann said, trying for humour. When he didn't immediately say anything, she went on, answering his question. 'When I killed the dragon, before it died, its claw caught me just there. It left that scar. I can't explain why it looks so healed and so old when it's new, maybe it's some magic from the dragon, I don't know.'

Reyleth frowned, looking troubled. 'I've never heard of such a thing before, and dragon magic is usually destructive, not healing.'

She shrugged. 'As I said, I don't know. It doesn't pain me at all – most of the time I forget it's there – and it was as healed as this when I first realised it was there at all. We are here trying to research some of the old magics, though, so maybe I'll run across an answer to that as well.'

'Yes, about this "we"...'

She smiled, knowing he must be desperately curious about the odd group she was travelling with. She'd never been the sort to have many friends at all, and before now Reyleth would have qualified as the most interesting of them. 'Calla was in the dragon's cave – she'll tell you all about that as well – she'd been working as a guard for some traders when they were attacked. We've been travelling together since and we've become fast friends.'

'I'm surprised you would say so, given how slow you usually are to trust people,' he said, still giving her a searching look.

'True, but it's been a very strange time and a dragon tends to bond people. And Calla seems to have set her mind to us being friends and she is very strong willed. Anyway, there's also Tash, he's a young human we hired as a guard while we travel.'

'You hired a guard?' he asked. Muireann as always admired the way he could pack so many layers of question into a few simple words.

'We took what we could from the dragon's hoard so we can afford a guard,' she said, shrugging.

His gaze sharpened, worried now. 'Please tell me you aren't carrying all of that around with you, or you need far more than one guard.'

'No, of course not. We lodged it with the bankers' guild in

Verell.'

He visibly relaxed, nodding. 'Ah yes, of course. Wise choice.'

'Right,' she agreed. 'And we're also travelling with a selkie, Lee, you'll meet her later. She's, ah, she's, my wife.'

She was already blushing, stumbling over the words and anticipating his teasing her, but his genuine shock caught her off guard. 'Your wife? You remarried already? I thought...isn't it the custom here to wait at least a year before remarrying, to honour the dead?'

'It is the custom, yes,' she stammered. 'But you know there wasn't any love between me and Edren and the situation with Lee was unexpected.'

'You unexpectedly married someone?' he said, with a ghost of his usual humour.

'I kind of saved her from a man who had stolen her sealskin,' Muireann admitted, feeling like she was making it sound much more dramatic than it actually was. 'And I gave her back her sealskin and she said we were married.'

Rey looked deeply unhappy at her words, but nodded. 'Yes, I have heard of such, although it's rarely done that way.'

'You've heard of selkies marrying that way? I hadn't ever heard or read a single story that mentioned it,' she said, oddly annoyed that he knew this when she didn't.

He still looked unhappy when he spoke. 'River Elves and the sea-folk don't have the best relationship, historically, but we do know something about each other's cultures for all of that. Selkies will sometimes marry based on trials by combat where a suitor proves their worth by fighting for their desired mate. I'd imagine that was close enough to the situation you stumbled into.'

'Close enough,' Muireann agreed, thinking of what had happened.

'If you didn't intend it that way you are within your rights to refuse the marriage,' he started until she held up a hand.

'I've already accepted it, at least for the next year, which Lee said is the traditional term,' she said, as firmly as she could manage. She knew she was committed to Lee at this point, no matter how quickly it had happened. 'On that subject, though, among other things I was hoping to find here I don't suppose you have a book on selkie culture, do you?'

He hesitated a moment, still looking unhappy but then nodded. 'I have something that will do for that, yes. What else were you looking for?'

'Anything that you have about the Aldovanan, especially their magic,' she said, immediately feeling that she'd been too blunt. It was funny; she'd always enjoyed their word games before but seeing him now she couldn't seem to focus enough to be at all clever.

He looked around the store thoughtfully. 'You know that's a passionate interest of mine so I have several, but it would help if you could narrow down what you are looking for.'

She hesitated, unsure how much to say, especially as she didn't seem up to her usual level of banter with him today. Finally, she settled for misdirection. 'I'm not sure exactly. As Calla said we're looking at their magic around enchantments but to be honest I don't know if that's even the right focus. So, at this point I'm casting a wide net.'

He sighed, frowning around the rows of books. 'Let me give it some thought then. I'm sure you already know that there isn't very much solid information on their magic at all to begin with, but there are hints in some of the history books and there have been some promising theories developed, especially by several of the elven scholars.'

'And as you certainly remember I do read several elven dialects,' she said, teasing him since he was the one who had helped her learn them, 'and so I could use those books as well.'

He smiled. 'It's reassuring to know you haven't forgotten everything I taught you.'

'Not everything,' she agreed. 'Alright, well I should go meet the others before they worry I've fallen into a stack of books and gotten lost.'

He glanced around the empty store. 'I'll go with you.'

'Are you sure?' she said, surprised. He usually had to be prised out of his shop and she could only think of a few previous instances where he'd left voluntarily with her. 'I don't want to take you away from anything important.'

'This is nothing that can't wait, and Pol can close up tonight,' he said firmly, leading her towards the door. 'I'd like to hear the full story of the dragon and get to know these new friends of yours better.'

'Fair enough, and Calla tells the story better than I do,' Muireann agreed, trying not to look as pleased as she felt. 'You can join us for dinner then and we can catch you up on everything.'

He stopped by the door to let Pol know where he was going and then the two of them headed into the deepening twilight. Muireann felt more relaxed than she had in a long time and she was glad that she'd decided to go straight to see him even if it meant the others might tease her for it later. Only as the silence stretched between them as they walked did she start to feel nervous, afraid of the pointless small talk she knew Rey hated but wanting to rebuild that sense of closeness she'd always felt around him; at least she had until today. It was hard to pinpoint what had changed.

She was still struggling to think of something to say when a half dozen cloaked figures appeared from the narrow alley between two buildings. She barely had time to register what was happening when the closest person swung his sword at her head.

Reyleth grabbed Muireann's arm and pulled her back sharply, the blade swinging by her face so closely that she could feel the displaced air as it went by. She staggered back, off balance, and overcompensated, ducking forward, which saved her from the second attempted sword strike. Unlike the first time, this time she did have her bow but no time to ready it. In desperation she pulled an arrow, thinking she could at least use it to stab with and it would have more reach than the small dagger she kept at her belt.

Reyleth chanted, the words sharp and clipped, and a moment later, before their attackers realised what was happening, the cloaked figures were all thrown back and off their feet. The magic didn't affect Muireann at all, she assumed because she was still physically touching Reyleth when he cast it. Their attackers scrambled to their feet and ran, disappearing back into the narrow alley. Down the street Muireann could hear several people calling out in concern, asking what was going on.

'Blast it,' Muireann hissed, flustered, her heart still racing at the sudden violence. 'That's the second time today.'

'What?' Reyleth said, his voice low, his hand still on her arm. 'No don't tell me here. The town guard will be here any moment. Keep walking, quickly.'

'Will we be in trouble?' she asked, guessing the answer from his hurry.

'I will be. You know it's illegal to use magic against another person in the town limits.'

'It was self-defence!'

'Yes, and I'd argue as much when I was brought before the magistrate,' he said, as they walked quickly around the corner onto the street that the Dancing Tide was on. 'But I don't fancy the time in gaol until then.'

'I wouldn't let that happen.'

'What would you be able to do for me, Muireann?' he said sadly. 'You know how things are here.'

She clamped her mouth into a hard line, because she did know but she'd forgotten in the years she'd lived in Gorseview. Her little village didn't have an official guard, and the worst trouble that tended to happen was the occasional drunken fist fight at a harvest celebration. It was easy to romanticise Strandview in her memory and forget the bad parts, including the overzealous guard.

The Dancing Tide wasn't that far from the shop, and although Muireann had never stayed there herself it was said to be the best inn in town and many of the locals liked to eat dinner there when they could afford to. Muireann had always wanted to see for herself, but her mother had seen it as a frivolous indulgence, even more than books, so she'd never had the chance. She couldn't deny the prospect of finally taking a meal in the common room was more exciting than it should have been, enough to almost put the incident on the street out of her mind. Almost.

The common room was as busy as Muireann had expected, filled with locals and inn patrons. It only took her a moment to locate her friends sitting in a back corner and she hurried over to the group, Reyleth in tow. She slid into a seat next to Lee, pulling Rey down into the seat next to her. The other three weren't eating yet but had ordered drinks and were lounging back in their seats relaxing when Muireann arrived. Muireann took a deep breath, feeling slightly better when she saw they were all fine, but after quickly introducing Reyleth to everyone she asked anyway. 'Are you all alright? Nothing happened after we parted?'

The others all look confused but shook their heads, Tash speaking for them. 'We're fine. Came straight here and got rooms, then came down here to wait for you.'

'What's wrong?' Calla asked, her voice sharp, correctly guessing from Muireann's strained face and question that they'd had trouble.

'We were attacked on the street,' Muireann admitted. 'We're both fine but only because Reyleth scared them off with a spell.'

Lee slid her hand into Muireann's, her face worried; Muireann tried to squeeze her fingers reassuringly, starting to feel like she was overreacting now that she was somewhere safe. It had been a close call but not that close after all and no one had been hurt.

'I shouldn't have left you alone,' Calla said, shaking her

'It's fine, Calla, really, there was no way to predict this would happen,' Muireann cut in. 'And thanks to Reyleth, they ran off quickly enough.'

'What did you do exactly?' Tash asked, then looking a bit embarrassed, 'I'm sorry, I don't mean that the way it sounded. I grew up around mages and am curious what spell you used.'

Reyleth nodded, accepting the explanation. 'It's a basic chant, keyed into one of my rings, that creates a temporary displacement of the air.'

'Could you repeat that again using smaller words?' Calla said, rolling her eyes.

Rey frowned at her, but it was Tash who answered. 'It's a simple spell that creates something like a sudden gust of wind that knocks everyone around the mage off their feet.'

'Exactly,' Reyleth agreed.

'Interesting,' Calla said, her voice more thoughtful now. 'Maybe you're more than just a simple shopkeeper?'

Reyleth flushed, the colour bright on his white cheeks. 'I'm a shopkeeper who knows that people assume shopkeepers have money and that sometimes we're targeted for robbery because of that. If you are a mercenary then you must know that most offensive spells take time to prepare, so obviously having one set up for emergency use is a wise course.'

'You don't have physical weapons you can use? Not even one of those staffs so many mages favour?' Calla managed to tread a fine line between sounding disbelieving and sounding disinterested. Muireann admired it, in a way.

He sighed. 'I am fairly good with a sword or daggers, but the town guard frowns on mages carrying weapons through the streets. They believe we are already dangerous enough without any extra weaponry.'

'Because you can do magic?' Lee asked, sounding genuinely curious.

Muireann had expected Rey to give a short answer, but he didn't. 'There is a small community of mages here because they believe that this particular location is a natural source of arcane power, which it may indeed be, and so the town guard feels there are too many of us and that we pose a potential threat. And mages in general are often seen as immoral, amoral and less than law abiding. So, they watch us more closely than others and have certain laws that only apply to us.'

Calla looked like she very much wanted to say something to that, but Rey turned to Muireann and went on before she could get a word in.

'Why are they targeting you?' Rey said, his worry a subtle tone in his voice.

'We don't know why we keep being attacked,' she said, making a face at the table's surface.

'I meant you personally,' he clarified, earning a sharp look from Calla.

'There's no sign Muireann is the specific target,' the high elf said, as if the matter was closed.

Reyleth didn't agree, nor was he intimidated by Calla's firm dismissal. 'She was attacked tonight, and you were not.'

'True but we were all attacked the other times and there was no indication they were after her in particular,' Calla said. 'Tonight was almost certainly because we three stayed together and she was alone. Well alone except for you.'

Muireann saw the insult register on Rey's face and quickly interceded. 'I'm lucky Reyleth was with me, or it wouldn't have ended so well. As it is, though, the better question may be why are we, collectively, being attacked like this? It can't be coincidence.'

'No,' Calla agreed. 'Coincidences don't run into threes, for certain. But I'm still puzzled why the first two groups were so different. This attack tonight, were the people cloaked, or using rapiers, or something else entirely?'

'Cloaked,' Muireann said without hesitation. 'The same as this morning, dark cloaks and no clear organisation. Their attack felt haphazard.'

'Hmmm,' Calla said thoughtfully. 'So perhaps the first incident, the one in Verell, was just thieves trying to rob us because of rumours we had wealth. But today, two attempts by what seems to be the same group. What do you think, Tash?'

The young man startled slightly, obviously not having expected to be asked for his opinion although he had been listening intently. 'Well. This is outside my experience of course but...if I had to offer a theory...I'd guess that either the group this morning is stubborn or angry over the injuries we dealt them, and perhaps followed us here, or were coming here anyway and saw Muireann alone – that is without the rest of us – and thought to get revenge.'

Calla nodded slowly. 'That is certainly possible. I won't deny I've gone after a person later when an earlier fight didn't fall out my way. Lee, what do you think?'

The selkie, who had scooted over close to Muireann and was still holding her hand under the table, looked solemn. 'I don't pretend to understand exactly how your society works, and my impression of humans prior to this may not have been ideal. But what everyone is saying seems to be sensible. We should be on our guard now and if we are fortunate there will be no more attacks, but if there are we shall hopefully not be caught off guard.'

Their conversation was interrupted by the arrival of several town guard at their table. The guards looked unhappy and next to her Reyleth tensed. Muireann remembered what he'd said after the attackers fled and, thinking quickly, looked up at the closest guard with what she hoped was an adequately innocent expression. 'Oh, I'm so glad you're here, sir!'

He was stocky, tanned, with light brown hair, and wearing expensive leather armour. The badge of the town guard, polished until it gleamed, hung pinned to his shoulder. At her words the man's hazel eyes went wide, his mouth under his heavy moustache twitching noticeably. 'Excuse me, ma'am?'

'You're here about the message we sent, aren't you?' Muireann said, every eye at the table now fixed on her. 'To the guard post? About being attacked on the street a few minutes ago? I didn't expect you to get here so quickly and I must admit that I appreciate how seriously you're taking this incident.'

'Ah,' the man stammered, his eyes going from Reyleth to Muireann then around the table. 'Yes. Of course, we take all incidents seriously here, ma'am. But I'm not sure what message you mean—'

'We sent a messenger, a boy,' Muireann cut in, waving her hand trying to do her best imitation of her mother. 'I don't know. You know what I mean, young boy, looked like he could run fast enough. Paid him a copper to carry a message to you about how we were just *viciously* attacked in the street. I thought Strandview was more law abiding than that, and I was told that there were laws against people using magic against others here but clearly that isn't so when a woman can't even walk two blocks here without being set on by thieves.'

The group of guards looked absolutely baffled now, their presumptive leader most of all. 'Yes, well, er, ma'am, we do our best you understand but nowhere is completely free of all crime, you understand, and ah, that is, we had wanted to talk to the elf here, as he's a mage—'

'Oh, excellent idea,' Muireann cut in, still channelling her mother. 'Reyleth was absolutely my *savoir* tonight and he witnessed the entire thing. I'm certain if he hadn't been escorting me to meet my friends here, I'd have lost my life and my gold, instead of just getting a terrible fright. Everyone warned me not to come to such a small town – no offence intended – but where else can we find a decent inn between here and civilisation? But I shudder to think if Reyleth hadn't been with me how badly it would have gone.'

'Ah, yes, ma'am,' he mumbled, having lost all control of the situation. 'I'm sure he was

helpful—' 'Oh, he certainly was! I know what you're going to say, sir, that I never should have been walking around without my hired guard here,' she gestured at Tash, as always wearing his leather armour and looking the part of a personal guard despite his bemused expression. 'But I didn't expect I'd need an armed guard to walk a few blocks in what is supposed to be a *civilised* town. I won't make that mistake again, I assure you.'

'Yes, ah, yes,' the guard said, at a loss for words by this point.

'Well, I appreciate you coming all the way out here to check on me and I trust that you'll do your utmost to investigate and find out who those ruffians were and make sure they don't attack any other honest citizens,' Muireann said, waving dismissively. 'But I have had quite a fright tonight and I think I need some wine now. If you have any more questions, I'm certain they can wait until tomorrow.'

'Ah,' the man said, already starting to back up. 'Yes. Fine then. Have a nice night, ma'am.'

She grabbed Calla's glass and pretended to take a large draught from it, almost spilling the contents across her face in her attempt at melodrama. The guard turned and summarily fled the building.

Her three travel companions stared at her in open mouthed shock. Reyleth, for his part, laughed quietly. 'I never thought all those impressions you used to do of your mother were that convincing, but that, that was like having Lady Cynna here in person. Absolutely terrifying.'

'Thank you,' Muireann said, wiping mead from her face with her sleeve, flushed with success. 'And didn't I tell you I'd protect you if there was trouble with the guard?'

'You did,' he said, smiling softly. 'and I retract my earlier doubts that you could do so.'

'If that's what your mother is like then I fully understand why you don't want to go visit her,' Calla said, sounding slightly awed. 'That performance was worthy of any of the Grand Theatres.'

Muireann giggled at the thought but was flattered. 'Well, moving on anyway. It doesn't seem like we have any way to get answers about this group unless they attack again, and the guard here will be of no help, as you may have gathered.'

'The group may not attack again,' Calla said. 'It's not a coincidence, surely, but it could still just be ill luck. However, to be safe we'll stay in groups while we're here, at least two together at any time.'

Tash nodded. 'That seems reasonable.'

Reyleth was frowning, though, looking troubled. 'Reasonable perhaps but not ideal, especially as Muireann isn't martially skilled.'

'She excellent with a bow,' Lee said, defensive for her wife's sake.

Rey looked at Muireann in surprise and she, predictably, blushed. 'I've done a lot of training since, well since the dragon attacked last year. I'm fairly skilled with a bow now.'

'Skilled enough to kill a dragon with it,' Calla said proudly.

Reyleth blinked slowly at that. 'Yes, I still have not heard this story, perhaps you would enlighten me?'

'Gladly,' Calla said. Before she could start, though, the serving boy arrived to take their meal order. He started with Lee, who asked for fish.

'I'm sorry, miss,' the boy said. 'The catch was poor today and we've served all we had.'

Lee was thoroughly nonplussed by this at first. The others ordered their food, and the boy eventually came back around to her. Hesitating slightly, she said. 'Can I order chicken?'

'Certainly miss, we have a roast chicken with fresh spring greens—'

'No greens, please,' Lee cut in. 'Just chicken.'

The boy blinked slowly, then nodded. 'Alright, just chicken. No sauce then?'

'No, just chicken,' Lee repeated, then added. 'But if you could give me some salt with it?'

'Salt?' the boy repeated, looking confused.

'Just bring a small bowl of salt for her please,' Muireann said, sure that he'd never served a selkie before.

He blanched. 'A bowl miss? A whole bowl?'

'A *small* bowl, yes,' Muireann said patiently. 'I'll pay whatever the cost is.'

He visibly swallowed, eyes wide at the idea of anyone ordering a whole bowl of expensive salt, but nodded. 'Yes, miss. As you will, miss.'

Calla had watched this exchange impatiently and as soon as the boy left, she plunged into her version of the dragon's death. The food arrived and the group ate while Calla told a very dramatic but mostly factual version of Muireann's fight with the dragon and her rescue of the high elf, then their journey to Verell. Muireann tried not to watch Lee dipping her roast chicken in salt, the human woman's mouth puckering at the thought of it.

Calla was winding down about the same time the meal was being cleared away, having interspersed telling the tale and eating. Muireann had to admit the rumours about the Dancing Tide's food were well founded; even the simple bread and stew she'd ordered was delicious. Watching Calla finish her plate, laden with apple roasted pork, seasonal vegetables and some of the same fresh bread Muireann had got; she wished she'd ordered that instead of staying with the common room staple she'd chosen.

Reyleth sat next to her throughout the meal nodding occasionally during Calla's story but not interrupting or asking any questions. It made Muireann nervous because he was the only one who might guess that her plan to take on the dragon hadn't had any exit strategy, something everyone else seemed to ignore or not realise. When it was done, though, he just looked thoughtful for a while then said. 'And now you are researching Aldovanan magic.'

Muireann's heart fluttered at the unexpected question, now fearing that he had somehow guessed their true purpose. But she only nodded and said as calmly as she could. 'Yes...I have a Dragon Stone now as you know, and the others are all relics of the Aldovanan's time. It seemed like a good place to begin investigating.'

It wasn't exactly a lie, she tried to comfort herself, *because I didn't actually say that was why we were researching it.* But the thought felt hollow. She didn't like deceiving any of her friends and especially Reyleth. With the others she could justify withholding the information about the green crystal because knowing about it could put them in danger, but she knew that not telling Rey meant he couldn't really help her research it and that if he found out it would show her lack of trust in him. But she and Calla had agreed to keep the stone a secret and she was more afraid of telling him the truth and word getting out somehow about what they carried than of hurting his feelings by not telling him.

He pushed the last of the food around his plate, looking troubled. 'I don't think I have anything in my shop, or even my private collection, that might help.'

She squirmed in her seat, trying to hint at what they really needed without giving away too much. 'Well, I don't expect to find much about the stones specifically. At this point I'm casting a wide net and looking for anything about the Aldovanan mages, their magic, that sort of thing.'

She knew he was suspicious now and prayed he wouldn't press for more details in front of everyone else, but he just said. 'Alright then. I don't have much that isn't pure speculation or little better than children's stories, but I can pull a few references for you.'

Calla had been listening intently and caught Muireann's eye. 'Perhaps we should see what books we can buy here and head to Mistlen. The library there will undoubtedly have more, and there's no point wasting time here if we're going to have to make the journey through the mountains.'

Tash frowned at that. 'Even I know it's a bad season to cross the Red Mountains.'

'Perhaps,' Calla agreed. 'But we'll lose more time heading north towards Port Gray to avoid them. If we take the northern trade pass, we can save ourselves at least several days, and it will still take two weeks or more to reach Mistlen.'

'A few days doesn't sound so bad compared to being caught in a flash flood,' Tash said.

'Are the mountains so dangerous then?' Lee asked, her eyes darting uncertainly between the other two.

'Not in summer,' Muireann said. She'd never crossed the Red Mountains herself, but she'd heard enough from traders and merchants passing through to have some sense of the way the seasons affected travel. 'But they're impassable in winter and spring can be dangerous with the runoff from the snow and flash floods from storms.'

'Traders won't take the mountain pass for another month, until the weather settles,' Tash added.

'True but we are neither traders nor merchants, who are burdened with carts and heavy wagons,' Calla pointed out calmly. 'We should be able to make it through the pass in two days instead of the three it takes them and then it's only another ten days or so to Mistlen.'

The others fell silent, considering what she'd said, although none of them looked happy at the idea. Into that contemplative silence Reyleth spoke, his voice firm. 'I'm going with you.'

They all turned to look at him and he went on, defiant now. 'It's a dangerous journey and you will find a mage a useful addition to your ranks. Besides that, if the rivers are in flood from the snow melt or there's a sudden flood from rainfall, who better to have with you than a river elf? And moreover, I can help Muireann with her research. Besides the Great Library, the elven markets and bookstores in Mistlen may also have helpful resources. I have been there in my youth and have some familiarity with them. I could help by looking there while she checks the library.'

'I'm convinced,' Calla said, looking amused at his impromptu speech. 'and it's fine by me. Muireann?'

'Of course,' she said too quickly, then tried to cover it by clearing her throat. She turned to her left. 'Lee?'

The selkie looked surprised to have been consulted. 'I have no love of the river-folk but what he says is true enough, and it does seem wise to have a mage with us. If we're set upon by an enemy using magic, we should be able to fight back in kind, and elven mages can heal.'

'Tash?' Calla asked, turning to the young human.

'I think it's a good idea,' he said simply.

'It's settled then,' Calla said, nodding. 'You're in if you're set on it.'

'I'm in,' Reyleth said. 'I'll arrange for Pol to handle the shop while I travel. He's done as much before when I needed to be away for a time. I'll pack what books I think might be useful and we can go through them as we travel.'

'Pack your sword as well,' Calla said archly, earning an annoyed frown from Rey.

'Of course,' he snapped. 'I'll bring what weapons I have as well as what spell ingredients seem likely to be useful.'

'I'll be glad to have you with us,' Tash said, obviously trying to sooth the mage. Muireann appreciated that, knowing that he and Lee would likely be at odds if only because their peoples didn't have a history of getting along and he and Calla seemed to strike off each other like flint and steel. She wasn't sure what she'd do if the entire group was hard towards him.

Rey spared a grateful look at the young human. 'Thank you for saying so. I will make sure I pull my own weight.'

Calla looked like she was going to respond to that with another jab until she caught the look Muireann was shooting her, instead she stood and rolled her shoulders. 'Well, then, we seem as set on a plan as we're going to get. Reyleth can meet us here in the morning and we'll resupply then head for the mountain pass. As for now I suggest you all get some rest.'

'And what will you be doing, oh storyteller?' Muireann asked, suspecting she already knew.

'Telling our story around the common room, of course,' Calla said cheerfully. 'And then I suspect the same thing you will be doing although that will depend on whether I can find anyone worth bedding in this place, given its lack of gorgeous elven bards.'

Muireann laughed along with the others, although she knew she was blushing. The teasing was fairly tame, not even enough to make Tash uncomfortable, but she didn't dare look at either Lee or Reyleth to see their reaction to Calla's jibe. She felt uncomfortable sitting between her current wife and her long-time friend who, if she were totally honest, it was probably pretty clear to everyone she had deeper feelings for. Edren had certainly always suspected as much, and he wasn't usually a jealous man. Still, she managed a half-hearted 'Have fun' as the high elf sauntered off.

Yawning, Tash stood as well, prompting the entire group to get up. He nodded slightly to the others then headed up towards his room. With an awkward wave to Reyleth, Muireann started to head towards the stairs as well, with Lee close by her side.

'Muireann, wait a moment,' Rey called, and she slowed then nodded at Lee to go ahead to their shared room.

The selkie leaned over and kissed her, then said softly, 'I'll be waiting for you. We're in the second room on the left.'

Muireann nodded. 'I'll be right up.'

Lee smiled slightly. 'Take your time, I'm not going anywhere.'

Rey watched the selkie go up the stairs until Muireann reached out and gently touched his arm. 'Rey?'

'Yes, sorry,' he murmured before moving into a quiet corner of the room. She trailed behind, curious what this was all about. 'There's something I wanted to do if it's alright with you, and I think now is better than later, in case there is any more violence.'

'I rather hope there won't be,' she said, making a face at him.

'Ideally perhaps but – and I don't say this with any judgement or expectation you will reveal anything to me – but there is clearly more going on here than you are telling me.'

'Rey—' she started, but he cut in quickly.

'It's alright, Muireann. I trust you and I don't think you would conceal anything from me unless you felt there was no choice.'

'I would tell you if I could,' she admitted, 'but it could put you in danger.'

He nodded, solemn, then. 'That aside, I was hoping you would let me enchant your glasses for you.'

'Enchant them how?'

'I have a spell, a minor enchantment, which would prevent them from being damaged or broken,' he said.

She felt tears pricking her eyes at the thoughtfulness of it. 'I...yes. Please. I would really appreciate that.'

He visibly relaxed, as if he had feared she might be angry at his offer. 'I've been thinking since the fight in the street, and I know you can't see without them. If we are to travel so far, especially through the mountains, it seems the safest course to be sure your glasses can't be damaged.'

'You don't have to convince me,' she said, reaching up and taking them off to hand to him. It made her anxious not to have them on, the dim room reduced to a smudge of dark colours with Rey a blur of bluish white closer by. She couldn't see what he was doing but she heard him chanting softly, his voice low and intense, and felt that odd tingling rush of active magic. Then he was taking her hand and carefully putting the glasses on her palm. She opened the arms, the well-worn silver smooth under her fingers, and slid them back on, undeniably relieved as the world came back into focus.

Reyleth looked as relieved as Muireann felt, although still somewhat uncomfortable. 'I hope you don't judge me too harshly for not offering before. I only learned this bit of magic a few years ago and I hadn't seen you since, except at the funerals which was hardly the time for that. I had thought I would suggest it the next time I saw you...'

'Reyleth I would never be upset that you didn't offer to do anything for me,' she said quickly. 'I don't take your magic for granted, and I consider this a great gift – come to that I'm just glad it's something that you can do now and that you were willing to do for me.'

His eyes searched hers as if he were looking for something more in her face than what her words were telling him. Whether he found it or not he finally nodded. 'I'll let you go to your rest then and meet you here in the morning. After breakfast if that suits, I'll need to talk to Pol and gather my books and other things for the journey.'

'Have a good night.'

He nodded again, then turned swiftly and hurried from the room. Muireann shook herself, pushing away any worry that he was having second thoughts about going with them – she selfishly wanted him to go, even if she was baffled that he'd volunteered – and headed up to her room. It was easy to find with Lee's direction and she slipped quietly into what was probably one of the nicest inn rooms she'd ever been in; nicer even than their room in Verell. Lee was waiting for her and she went to the selkie without hesitation.

* * *

Later, as they lay together just on the ragged edge of sleep, Lee pulled Muireann closer, cuddling with her under the sealskin. 'You like him, don't you?'

'Who?' Muireann murmured sleepily, her fingers caressing the soft fur.

'The elf, Reyleth.'

That drove thoughts of sleep away. 'He's my friend.'

'Yes, but I mean you want to bed him.'

Muireann bit her lip, not wanting to offend Lee. 'I can't deny he's attractive but I'm with you. I don't want you to feel like I'm choosing him over you. I am happy with you, with us.'

'It's alright,' Lee said, snuggling her head against Muireann's shoulder. 'I don't mind if you do.'

'Are you sure?' Muireann pressed, knowing they had discussed this but still concerned that what was between them was too nascent to risk adding a third person in as a factor.

'Of course,' Lee reassured her. 'We already talked about this and agreed we'd each be free to pursue others if we wanted as well, and I can see the way you look at him.'

'It won't change anything between us,' Muireann said, relieved that Lee didn't mind her being interested in someone else.

'It will,' Lee said, her voice calm. 'But not in a bad way. Just don't forget who your wife is.'

'How could I?' Muireann said, smiling into the darkness. She'd only known Lee a week and she was still thoroughly infatuated with her. She wouldn't risk what they had, new as it was, for what might only be wishful thinking on her part towards Reyleth. But if Lee didn't mind then she thought she'd at least try to talk to him about it, if she could get up the courage. Between the recent dragon related tragedies she'd suffered and the strange attacks over the last few days she felt like even the risk of terribly embarrassing herself was worth it if it meant at least knowing how he felt.

The two women settled down to sleep, the sound of the fire crackling in the hearth of their room a gentle counterpoint to their breathing.

Chapter 5

Through the Mountains

It took two days of walking to reach the mountain pass, a narrow road that wove into the foothills between two mountains in the Red Mountain range. This was the northern-most pass and the least popular; the other three main trade roads through the mountains were longer but passed through mountain elf settlements or near dwarven outposts which offered both added safety as well as trade opportunities. This pass, though, was in an unsettled area and while it was shorter being further north, it was also snowed in the latest in the spring and earliest in the autumn – and up until very recently had been home to a dragon. Most passing this far north would avoid the mountains altogether and head to Port Gray then follow the coast south rather than risk the uncertainty of the pass, the risk of the dragon and the famously mercurial weather.

As they entered the pass Muireann stared up at the two mountains looming above them, pulling her heavy wool cloak tighter around her shoulders. To the south was the other side of the same mountain the dragon had called home and it was strange to her to think that its body lay just over the jagged rocks. It was a constant reminder to her of the things she had set in motion with her reckless desire to seek revenge, and the mountain's presence felt more and more like judgement rather than stone. To the north was Far Peak, named because it was the northern-most mountain in the range; it rose a third again higher than its neighbour and even now it still had snow heavy on its upper slopes. The road they walked gradually rose through the foothills into the mountains proper, the ground growing rockier and more difficult as they went. The mountain rocks had a distinct red coloration like ochre, which had given the mountain range its name. The trees thinned as the road went further into the hills and the familiar oaks, birch and beech gave way to pine and fir.

They stopped at mid-day to eat and rest, the group scattering slightly across a small open area along the trail. Muireann made sure Lee was comfortable and eating some of the dried fish they'd packed, but she was too restless to sit herself. Instead, she wandered aimlessly around the space and a bit ahead on the trail, eating her hard bread and cheese as she walked. She passed Tash and Reyleth who were sitting eating together and talking quietly, then turned a small bend in the road, walking around a looming boulder. Turning back, she realised that she could no longer see any hint of the coast on the horizon; they were entirely surrounded by open rock and evergreens. Disconcerted she started ripping up what was left of her bread and throwing it off the path, quickly gaining a flock of small birds who gobbled up the crumbs. Watching them cavort and chirp and eat cheered her up slightly.

'You shouldn't waste that,' Calla's voice behind her startled Muireann so that she jerked around, sending the little birds flying every which way.

'Oh, hey, Calla,' she greeted her friend, trying to sound nonchalant despite such an obvious overreaction. The high elf was lounging against one of the rock outcroppings just behind her, hands casually resting on her hips. As used to Calla's flair for everything as she was, Muireann had to admit that the high elf had style; she was wearing fine leather knee boots, sturdy canvas pants, a loose linen shirt under a tighter leather corslet, with leather gauntlets on her wrists and her swords strapped to her sides. Her long, bright red hair was pulled back into a tight bun. She looked every inch a successful adventurer. Muireann resisted the urge to look down at her own clothes, which Calla had helped her pick out, which she still felt slightly uncomfortable in. A lifetime in drab skirts and earth-toned dresses was hard to put aside, no matter how much more comfortable she was now in pants, corset and a tunic, in deep jewel tones she liked and had chosen herself. Even the dark leather boots, comfortable and utilitarian as they were, served as a reminder of how far she'd come from the scribe and farmwife of a few weeks ago. Only the weight of her quiver at her hip, her glasses against her nose and the heavy copper braid laying against her back felt familiar, as if some of the old Muireann was still there underneath the flash Calla had layered on.

'You should eat all of your lunch, Muiri,' the high elf continued, her voice serious despite the casual posture. 'We have at least five days walking before we'll reach another village, and some of that is hard walking. You'll need your strength.'

Muireann sighed. 'I know. I'm just feeling a bit...untethered at the moment.'

'Anything you want to talk about?'

She shrugged. 'I was just standing here thinking I can't see the ocean and I've never been anywhere that I couldn't hear or smell or see the ocean or sea birds. It's even stranger for Lee, I'm sure, but when I talk with her about it she always sounds so positive, like it's a grand adventure. I just feel...a bit lost. I've never been this far from home before.'

Calla nodded slowly. 'You eat while we talk. I can understand how you feel, I think. It's been a few hundred years since I started travelling but I do remember that feeling when I first began. I wanted more from life than what my family had planned for me but back then I wasn't sure what exactly more was. Just that I needed to actually live my life. The first job I took, guarding a merchant caravan, I was excited but also afraid because everything was so new and strange. I knew I was good with a sword, but would I be good enough? Would I get used to being on the road? Would I make friends?'

'I can't picture you not having friends,' Muireann said, smiling slightly as she dutifully ate some more of her food under Calla's watchful eyes. 'You're so outgoing.'

'Lots of practice,' the elf said, shrugging. 'It's like a game to me and has been for a long time. I don't think I have very many friends – not people I'd truly call a friend, that I'd trust at my back in the worst situation. There's you now and maybe a few others. But it's much easier to have people that I am friendly to and who are friendly to me than to have real friends.'

'That I understand,' Muireann said. 'I've never really had many friends myself. Growing up, well as you may have guessed from my pretending to be my mother the other night, she isn't the sort of woman who people find endearing. And I was a quiet child, I'd rather have been reading than socialising. After I married, nothing really changed because I was an outsider in the village, even after one of my brothers moved there as well. Reyleth is my friend, of course, and has been for a long time, and you and I are friends now, and there's Lee and I'm starting to think of Tash as a friend. This is probably the most friends I've ever had, now that I'm thinking of it.'

Calla nodded, her expression unusually solemn, then her usual smirk took over. 'Speaking of Reyleth, any interesting history there?'

'No,' said Muireann, squirming slightly. 'And since we're speaking of Reyleth, would you mind telling me what you have against him?'

'What do you mean?' Calla asked, head tilting curiously to one side. 'I don't have anything against him.'

'Are you sure? You seem to criticise him a lot,' Muireann said, carefully. She wanted to know but she also didn't want to offend Calla by asking.

The high elf sighed. 'He's just very young and very...stuffy. Typical mage in that way I suppose. It would be good for him to lighten up a bit. Or a lot to be honest. So, I may tease him more than the others but it's only for his own good, so he'll stop taking everything so seriously. Of course, you could help that as well since he's your, ah, "friend" as you say. A little more *friendship* on a regular basis would probably do wonders for his mood.'

Muireann blushed at the implication. 'We really are just friends. We've been friends since I was a teenager.'

'If you say so,' Calla said, with a look that made her disbelief plain.

'Calla! I'd tell you if we'd ever been more than that, but we haven't.'

'Do you want to be?' the high elf pressed. 'Because he's very obviously in love with you.'

'He is not!' Muireann sputtered.

'He is,' Calla said, raising an eyebrow. 'He's young for an elf – I'm guessing around 200? – and he's as subtle as a rock to the head. Not his fault you don't really learn subtlety until you're into your third century, but still...he dropped everything with no notice, left his shop and hared off on this journey without any idea how long it would take, just to follow you. That's more than friendship. I've seen the way he looks at you, which also isn't subtle, and that's more than friendship too. And if you don't mind my saying so it seems clear you feel more than that towards him as well.'

Muireann groaned. 'How is it so obvious? Lee guessed as much already as well.'

Calla did look troubled by that. 'Lee, I had almost forgotten that was more than just sharing a warm bed. Hmmm. Having a wife could complicate things – I'm sorry I was teasing you, if this is an awkward situation for you.'

'It's awkward that apparently everyone can see how I feel so plainly,' Muireann said. 'But as to Lee, we talked about this the day we met – well not literally this – we talked about being open to having other partners besides each other. And she's already told me she's fine with me also having a relationship with Reyleth if I wanted to.'

'Do you want to?' Calla said. 'And for what it's worth as much as you are oblivious to his feelings towards you, I'd guess he has no idea how you feel either.'

Muireann groaned again. 'I'm not sure if that's better or worse than the alternative.'

'Which brings us back to the important question – do you want to pursue him? As short as that pursuit would likely be before it involved nudity and sweat.'

'Calla!' Muireann said, but she couldn't restrain a laugh at her friend's words.

'Muiri, for what it's worth I think you should. Regret is a hard thing to live with,' Calla said, more seriously. 'It may give Tash fits, I think he's from one of those minor religious groups that encourages monogamy and frowns on anything overtly sexual, but then again maybe not, he's awfully open minded for someone who's barely seen two decades and hasn't experienced very many other cultures. And either way he'll get used to it – it may even be good for him since he'll see a lot of different ways to approach relationships in Mistlen. Or really anywhere outside whatever group he grew up in, since monogamy is so uncommon. Obviously, I don't care and if Lee said it was alright...I think you should do it.'

'I'll think about it,' Muireann prevaricated, dusting the crumbs off her hands. 'For now, let's get back to the others and get moving.'

Calla looked amused, seeing through her attempted change of subject, but nodded and straightened up, pushing away from the stone she was leaning against. 'Yes, we have a way to go before we make camp.'

* * *

Muireann waited until the group naturally started to spread out as they walked and then carefully manoeuvred so she was walking with Reyleth, a bit behind the others. She knew that there was a chance she was about to make a fool of herself, but between Calla's encouragement and Lee's approval she'd decided to risk it. She'd spent the time between talking to Calla and this moment rehearsing what she'd say, different ways to work around to the subject, although she wasn't sure, even still, if she should discuss how she felt first or stick to talking about the physical attraction she had long had towards him. Neither approach seemed ideal, the first overly romantic and the second decidedly not. But she'd already faced a dragon so admitting her feelings or attraction to him wouldn't be harder than that. She hoped.

She glanced at him out of the corner of her eye, still getting used to the change in him between the bookshop owner she'd always known and this new adventuring Reyleth. His dark hair was pulled back into a serviceable braid, much more neatly done than her own perpetually messy one. His shoes, casual dark pants and loose shirt had been traded in for boots similar to Calla's, dark grey leggings and a sturdy blue tunic. He wore a long sword at his hip and his belt had several serviceable looking pouches hanging from it, no doubt filled with things he needed for his magic. Muireann didn't know very much about elven magecraft, which differed from human magecraft in several important ways, but she did know that any mage of any species would need certain supplies for some spells including various herbs, resins and stones. He wore a dark blue cloak over everything and carried a pack with his other supplies, just like everyone else. Walking next to him Muireann felt like a child playing at going on an adventure in comparison, but then all of the others made her feel that way, seemingly so much more competent at every aspect of what they were doing than she felt.

Shaking the thoughts aside she tried to push forward with what she wanted to talk about before she either lost her nerve or was interrupted.

'Rey,' she started, trying to think of the best way to ease into it. 'Can I talk to you about something?'

'Certainly,' he agreed, aimable as always. 'Is this about the Aldovanan? Because you know I'm always willing to discuss my favourite topic, but it would help if you could be a bit more precise in what you are looking for relating to them. As much as you can be, of course, under the circumstances.'

'No,' she said quickly, then, 'Well yes that too, but first there's something else I wanted to say. I'm not sure what you're going to think of it, but I think I need to say it one way or another. Although whatever you say about it, I'll understand.'

'Go on then,' he said, his expression politely curious.

'I'm in love with you,' Muireann blurted out, far less tactfully than she'd intended as all of her rehearsed options flew out of her mind. 'I've wanted to be with you for almost 20 years.'

Reyleth looked startled then smiled softly. 'As have I, with you. But you wed so young, and I knew your husband wouldn't approve of it.'

'No, he wouldn't have, he was always very...rigid...about the idea of my taking another man to my bed,' Muireann agreed, feeling giddy that he was also attracted to her, or had been. She'd always felt something between them but once her parents sent her off to be married that had changed, and of course she'd rarely been able to see Reyleth afterwards, keeping in touch mostly through letters. Edren may have enjoyed her status as town scribe, but he hadn't wanted her travelling days away to Strandview, especially without him, and he'd always made his dislike of Reyleth plain. She'd had some casual female lovers over the years, as Edren had, and neither begrudged the other those dalliances, but Reyleth was across a hard line for Edren and Muireann had tried to respect that. Beyond the simple jealousy that might be expected given that he'd likely guessed how she felt about him, Edren had been a good man but he had a particular dislike for elves. It was a prejudice that sadly ran deep in some humans, who were less than pleased to be under the rule of the High Elven Empire. She wasn't sure he'd ever have accepted her taking a male lover but especially not an elf and definitely never Reyleth. Accepting that had been one of the many compromises of her first marriage. Pushing the thoughts away she continued. 'But things are different now.'

He regarded her with such a carefully neutral expression that she grew nervous. She'd been hopeful when he'd said he had wanted her too, but she was realistic – he was an elf, and she wasn't. He looked the same as when they'd first met, and she very much didn't. She would understand if he was about to gently tell her that he'd rather they stay friends, even if it wasn't what she'd hoped for.

They walked in silence for a minute, until he said. 'Yet you are already wed again. I seem to have missed my opportunity, such as it was, to ask for your hand myself.'

Hope bloomed in Muireann again at his words. 'I am married again it's true, and if you wanted – want – to marry me, then that's something we'd have to discuss later, if Lee and I part, or if we decided we wanted a co-marriage. But marriage isn't the only option for us, unless you are set on that.'

'I had planned to ask you when your mourning period had ended,' he confessed, looking away. 'But I'm not set on it if you think there's another option.'

'Lee isn't Edren,' Muireann said, slightly stunned at what he'd just said about his plans. She'd never had any idea he felt so strongly. 'She doesn't mind if she isn't the only one I spend my time with or the only one in my bed and she doesn't care if I bed men as well as women. We've already talked about it, and she knows how I feel about you, or, well she guessed. But we did talk about it, and she is in favour of us being together if we both want, and provided of course I stay with her as well.'

He turned his thoughtful look to the trees around them, Muireann's nerves screaming at his seeming hesitancy. 'Selkies and river elves aren't known for getting along particularly well. And, I hope I don't offend you saying this, but I have no interest in her.'

'Oh no, that's fine. Good I mean. She's not interested in you either,' Muireann rushed to reassure him, stumbling over her words. 'I don't want you to feel pressured, though, or awkward about this. If you'd rather not act on any of it, I really will understand and it won't ruin our friendship. I'm not eighteen anymore and you...are still you.'

'You are still yourself as well, Muireann,' he said, reaching out and taking her hand. 'It's true that I'll live another eight hundred years easily and you won't, but I don't care about that. None of us know how much time we have and for all of this worry I could be killed before your natural life span is over.'

'I don't want to think about that,' Muireann said quietly, feeling the fresh burn of grief in her chest. 'I've already lost too many people I love.'

He squeezed her hand. 'If there's one thing that living among humans has taught me it's that we must seize joy when we can. It is far too rare and fleeting.'

'So, you're saying...?'

'That I would very much like to be your lover,' he said so sincerely that she couldn't even make a joke of his words to relieve her own nervousness.

'Even though I'm not young anymore and—'

'Muireann, I don't care about any of that,' he interrupted her, anticipating the self-depreciating speech before she could really get going with it. 'I care for you, and I want to be with you for however much time we may have.'

She couldn't stop the grin that stretched across her face, and she didn't try too hard. 'Good. Good. That's what I want too.'

They fell into a companionable silence after that, Muireann still nervous about how exactly she'd find a way to balance such different people in her life, but even having the opportunity to try gave her hope. She'd lost so much the year before that she was willing to take a chance on happiness now, even if it was a fleeting or hard to maintain happiness.

It was late in the day, with twilight closing in, when Calla finally called a halt to set up camp. Muireann was more than ready to stop and by the looks of them so were Tash and Lee who quickly dropped their packs, but Reyleth frowned at the location Calla was indicating. 'This is too close to that stream.'

Calla made a dismissive gesture. 'This is an old campsite that's been used many times before. It's as safe as anywhere else we'll find.'

Rey frowned harder and shook his head. 'It may be safe enough in summer but not in spring. It's still too much of a risk. You can see the marks in the soil and stone where the water rises when this area floods. There's rain in the air and even if it passes us over, if it strikes higher and releases any of the snow packs it could easily trigger a flash flood.'

Muireann looked from Rey to Calla. 'I think we should listen to him. He is a river elf after all, he knows water and rivers in a way we don't. And there's no harm in camping higher if nothing happens.'

She watched annoyance and frustration chase themselves around Calla's face before finally settling into resignation. 'Alright, so be it then. Where do you suggest we camp, mage?'

Muireann knew that Calla's refusal to acknowledge Reyleth by name was intentional and feared she'd be hearing it more in the future if the two disagreed often on things like this, but to her credit Calla was listening to him, no matter how much ill grace she was doing it with. For his part Reyleth looked as if he had expected more of a fight and hesitated before looking around at the deepening shadows, brush and boulders that surrounded them. Lee and Tash both picked up their packs without a word, waiting to see where the elf would lead them.

After a minute studying the terrain Reyleth moved off the

trail and up a slope, deeper into the rocky area. The others did their best to follow, Muireann and Tash slipping and sliding on the loose soil and rocks they couldn't see well in the growing dark. They walked for several minutes more until he called a halt in a small cluster of trees. The ground looked inhospitable even in the shadows, but the trees were close enough and overhung the space in a way that would offer some extra protection if it did rain. Calla took her time examining the site then finally said grudgingly. 'We can make this work. We'll only be able to set up two tents here; Tash you can share mine and Muireann and Lee can take the mage.'

Muireann tried not to wince at that, knowing it was logical but also bound to be at least a somewhat tense night for her, literally stuck between her wife and someone she'd just confessed her feelings to. Circumstances and agreement notwithstanding, she wasn't sure how she'd manage that. At least not so quickly.

Calla was going on, oblivious to – or intentionally ignoring – Muireann's obvious discomfort. 'Muireann and I can start getting the tents set up. Tash, you can prepare a fire pit in the centre of this clearing; be extra careful to clear the ground completely. Reyleth can gather firewood. Lee, if you'd be willing to hunt for us tonight?'

'Of course,' the selkie said, perking up at the suggestion. She set down her pack and disappeared into the brush with her spear before anyone could say anything else.

Tash nodded, all business, and immediately set about clearing the old pine needles and branches from the middle of the clearing in a wide circle. Reyleth, for his part, looked more than slightly put out at being assigned a menial chore, something that Muireann often did as the least experienced person in camp, but didn't argue and disappeared into the woods around them. With a tired sigh Muireann dropped her own pack and started helping Calla set up the two tents; thanks to Calla's spending spree in Verell, they were the largest and finest making Tash's perfectly serviceable smaller second-hand canvas tent and Rey's slightly larger plain tent look drab and utilitarian in comparison. Muireann didn't personally care which tents they used since as far as she was concerned a tent was a tent and as long as the roof didn't leak and there wasn't a draft it was fine by her. Calla had far higher standards.

The two women made short work of the set-up, having enough practice at it to do it almost without thinking now. By the time they were done Tash's fire circle was finished as well and stocked with firewood courtesy of Reyleth who was crouched down using his magic to create a flame far faster than any of the others could have done with flint and tinder. Muireann lugged her pack, then Lee's and finally Reyleth's into their tent, then came back out to stand by the now crackling fire. It was colder in the mountains, and she found herself hoping if they did get bad weather it would be rain and not snow, which wasn't entirely out of the question for that time of year. Walking the next day in slushy snow would not be pleasant.

'Is that a goat?' Tash's shocked voice broke through her contemplation of the weather, and she turned with the others to stare at Lee, who was returning with what did indeed look quite a bit like a goat.

'Is that what it is?' the selkie asked, dropping the cleaned animal down by the fire. Muireann could only gape at what was by far the largest game Lee had brought back so far.

Calla crouched down to inspect the animal more closely. 'It's a wild goat! However did you manage to catch it? They're notoriously hard to hunt.'

Lee beamed with pride at the implied compliment. 'It was quick but not as fast as fish in the water, and I think I can see better than it could in the dark. I thought with five of us to feed it would be better to get large game rather than many small animals.'

'Good idea,' Tash said, still looking impressed.

'I can help,' Reyleth volunteered suddenly. 'Goat is a tough meat, but I have a few spells that can make it easier to cook and chew.'

'I'd make some sassy comment about your magecraft being more useful than I expected,' Calla said. 'but that really does sound wonderful and I'm hungry.'

Muireann watched Rey's face twitch as he tried to decide whether to be insulted or pleased by the comment before he settled on sarcasm. 'As long as my help with the cooking pleases you, Tinairi, then my presence is certainly not wasted.'

Muireann's eyes went wide at the honorific, an elvish term that meant roughly 'high lady' and was usually reserved for nobility. She looked at Calla, waiting for the inevitable return shot. The high elf arched her eyebrows and stretched languidly. 'I'm not sure I'd agree but I'm sure Muireann would – or will soon enough – although not for your cooking or mage skill.'

'That's enough of that,' Muireann cut in, sputtering. Implying Reyleth's only use was in her bed was definitely something that might annoy him, but he could just as easily try to turn the quip around to his favour and she really didn't want to hear it. 'You two are worse than my boys were for arguing. Calla, go relax while we get this cooked. Lee, Reyleth, I'll help you.'

'And I'll keep watch, since we're bound to attract predators,' Tash volunteered.

'Fortunately, there aren't many worth worrying about much out here,' Calla said. 'No bears or wolves in this area and no great cats either. Foxes, wild dogs, weasels and possibly smaller wild cats, nothing that could be more than annoying to us. That at least is one advantage to this particular road.'

She nodded at Muireann, ignoring Reyleth entirely. 'I think I'm going to go read some of that book you got me. Let me know when dinner's ready?'

'Of course,' Muireann quickly agreed, glad that at least the bickering had stopped. She was already nervous about finding a way to balance having Lee and Reyleth both in her life; she didn't need the added stress of mediating between Calla and Reyleth all the time as well.

Luckily despite her concern Rey and Lee worked well together cooking, even if they were both being overly formal and polite to each other. As promised Rey worked several simple spells that turned the chewy, gamey wild goat into something comparable to the best slow-roasted goat Muireann had ever eaten, and the magic combined with the salt and basic spices they carried with them to improve their meals when they had fresh game made it as good as anything they'd have gotten in a town or city. Even Calla complimented it. It was certainly the best Muireann had ever had, so good that when the rain started as she was finishing eating it didn't dampen her spirits.

As the rain began to fall harder the group stored what was left of the goat to finish in the morning and then quickly put out the fire and sought their tents. It was not cold enough to snow but only just and the heavy rain had everyone shivering and rushing to finish and get to shelter. Inside the tent, Muireann changed into fresh clothes to sleep in and hurriedly crawled into the blankets she shared with Lee, the selkie draping her sealskin over them for added warmth against the damp chill. Rey put his bedding at Muireann's other side, lying so that he was almost as close to her as Lee was. Under other circumstances Muireann would have felt uncomfortable between the two, for different reasons, but as it was the cold was a good motivator for them all to care more about staying warm than anything else and, tired and full of good food as they were, they fell asleep quickly.

* * *

Muireann woke to thunder so loud it shook the tent around her, startling her awake. Next to her Lee mumbled something vaguely soothing, resting a hand across the human woman's waist before going back to sleep. Muireann lay awake, though, her heart pounding. On her other side Reyleth's voice was soft in the darkness. 'Do you hear the water?'

She focused past her own fear, listening intently. She could hear the rain, pounding down on the tent, trees and ground. There was more thunder, this time further away. And underneath it all a low rolling rumble. She frowned, trying to sort out the layers of sound. 'I hear something, besides the rain.'

'It's the water,' he said, voice still soft but more intense now. 'The stream has flooded and burst its banks.'

'Lucky we listened to you about our campsite then,' she said, shivering at the thought.

'Travelling tomorrow will be difficult,' he said. 'The road stays close by the stream for a way ahead, more than a mile at least.'

'How do you know that?' She moved, careful not to wake Lee, rolling over to face him even though she couldn't see him in the darkness, not even with her glasses which she had gotten into a habit of sleeping in.

'When I was gathering firewood last night I walked a bit down the road to get a sense of things. I was worried because that camp seems poorly placed, so close to the water. I'm sure in summer this area is probably dry, perhaps even prone to drought, but this time of year it's perfect for flooding, a natural low area between rocky inclines.'

'That makes sense,' she agreed. 'And explains why this route is considered too dangerous this time of year.'

'Indeed,' he agreed, his voice moving closer as if he was leaning in towards her, although she still couldn't see anything. 'But the more pressing issue is, if we cannot follow the road then we must perforce hike across higher ground, which may also be flooded in areas, and it will be dangerous going.'

'Are you worried it will slow us down too much?' she asked, trying to get to the heart of the matter.

'I'm worried that three of the five of us would be at high risk of drowning, should the water take anyone,' he said, his hand finding hers beneath the blankets.

'I wouldn't let anything happen to Muireann,' Lee said from her other side.

'I'm sorry, I didn't mean to wake you,' Muireann apologised, Rey's fingers tightening on hers.

'It's alright,' the selkie said. 'He's right that floods are more dangerous than many people credit. Even young selkies sometimes get into trouble with them, not the water but the mud and debris that go along with them.'

'I didn't think that would be an issue in the ocean,' Muireann said, fascinated.

'Young selkies sometimes go a bit inland,' Reyleth said, his voice neutral, 'but are wise enough to stay near water where they can flee any dangers more easily.'

'Mmmmmm,' Lee made a noncommittal noise. 'It's not the water of the flood that's a risk to us seal-folk but the other things that go with flooding.'

'That seems logical,' Muireann said. 'And you, Reyleth? How do your people deal with floods?'

He squeezed her hand again. 'No river elf can be drowned. The debris in the water presents a risk but every flood is different. I would also be concerned about the cold of it with both you and Tash and even Calla. This is snow-melt water as much as rain and anyone not meant for living in water will freeze quickly.'

'I hadn't thought of that,' Lee said, her voice subdued. 'Cold doesn't bother selkies, we are made for such. I didn't realize it was such an issue for humans.'

'Well, if it's as bad as all that then perhaps Calla will decide to stay in this camp tomorrow and see if the waters recede a bit. Otherwise, we'll just have to be extra careful.'

'Why is she the one making decisions?' Rey grumbled.

'She has the most experience on the roads and with all of

this in general,' Muireann pointed out, defending her friend. 'It makes sense for us to trust her judgement.'

'That is so,' Lee agreed, 'and she was wise enough to listen to you, Reyleth, when you advised a different camp site.'

'True,' he agreed, albeit reluctantly. 'I suppose we will have to wait and see what the morning brings.'

With that they settled back to try to sleep again, but Muireann found it hard to ignore the rumbling thunder and the incessant sound of rain and water. When she did sleep she woke again several times from dark dreams where she found herself alone as the tents were swept away or filled with water. She finally gave up and lay staring into the lightening darkness until the others began to stir around her. Once she was certain she wouldn't be waking anyone else up she squirmed free of the mass of shared blankets, careful to move Lee's sealskin back over the selkie, and stood.

Since she was already dressed she only had to slip on her boots and wrap her heavy cloak around her shoulders before slipping out into the early morning air. The rain wasn't as heavy as it had been through the night but it still fell and dripped off the branches around them. Muireann shivered as a cold drop hit her face and glasses, blurring everything on the left side so that she had to take the lenses off and try to wipe them dry on her tunic. The sun was up as far as she knew but it was difficult to tell; the sky was still dark with clouds. The wind was starting to pick up, adding its distinctive note to the symphony of rain and flood. It was, altogether, a miserable morning.

She hurried into the woods to find a spot she could use as a bathroom, shivering and wishing for the comfort of even the smallest inn. Camping while they travelled had a certain appeal to it in good weather, even when it was cold, but that appeal evaporated under bad conditions; she couldn't imagine how people did this all the time and realising that this was Calla's life as it had been Muireann's parents' when they were younger made her feel very sheltered and a bit selfish.

By the time she returned to the campsite the rest of the group was up, huddled around the remains of the previous night's fire. Calla gestured her over. 'We're trying to decide the best plan for today.'

'Do you think we should stay in camp until the storm passes?' Muireann asked, hoping she'd agree.

Calla shook her head. 'The weather is lessening and if we are lucky should clear soon.'

Rey didn't look happy, but he didn't argue. 'There is risk in any plan at this point. If we stay and the weather clears, then we may delay only to find ourselves caught in another storm. If we proceed and the weather worsens, we'll have to stop and make camp again, but that won't be ideal in this mess.'

'Whatever we do is a matter of choosing the best of bad options at this point,' Calla said, sighing. 'I had hoped we'd be able to get through the pass without any bad weather, and here we are directly in the middle and stuck in a storm. But there's nothing for it now but to make the best of a bad situation.'

'I think we should press on,' Tash said. 'It's a risk but there have been storms that lasted a week this time of year and I don't fancy sitting here huddled in our tents for that long waiting for sunshine.'

Lee nodded slowly. 'I am fine with whatever the group decides. This weather doesn't bother me but I understand it has its risks for you so I don't feel like I should be able to say go or stay.'

Muireann looked around the group then nodded reluctantly. 'I don't relish the idea of travelling in this, but I don't want to stay in the mountains longer than we have to either.'

Calla gave a short, decisive nod. 'Then let's eat and pack up. If our luck holds the weather will break by the time we're moving.'

'We can't take the road.' Muireann pointed out the obvious,

wanting to know if Calla had a plan.

'No, we'll have to make our own path as best we can until we find the road on higher ground. It weaves quite a bit through here, going along what was the easiest course for the heavy wagons.'

Reluctantly they all moved off, returning to the shelter of their tents to eat a cold breakfast of leftover goat. As soon as they'd all eaten they started breaking down their camp, anxious despite the drizzling rain to get moving. Calla turned to Reyleth as they prepared to leave the small clearing. 'Would you be willing to lead the way?'

Surprise flashed across his features, then he shrugged. 'If you prefer.'

'I know the road here well, but you know the water and off the road I trust you not to lead us into danger,' Calla said simply.

The river elf did not look pleased by this responsibility but started walking east, the others trailing single file behind him. Muireann hadn't appreciated how difficult breaking a trail would be nor how miserable it could be to hike through the rain. By midmorning her legs and back were burning from the constant need to step over and around obstacles and balance the weight of her pack as she traversed the slippery ground. The soil was loose and rocky so the water didn't absorb in it as she would have expected but pooled and ran off, creating innumerable small streams and puddles, and the trees that dared grow here added their gnarled roots to the mix, creating an uneven obstacle course. Her glasses were constantly getting wet, blurring her vision and adding another layer of difficulty to everything; she stumbled when she failed to see rocks or roots and she walked face first into several branches she couldn't see through the water on her lenses. The cold sank into her bones through even the heavy wool cloak until she started to dream longingly of warm hearth sides and then to doubt she'd ever be warm again.

It was, without a doubt, one of the worst experiences of her life.

She had slowly fallen to the back of the group, struggling to keep up, and was contemplating using her bow as a walking staff even though she knew she'd risk ruining it. But as the space between her and Lee, who was trying to stay with her, kept widening, she worried that she'd end up left behind and lost in the mountains. With that idea to motivate her she walked as fast as she could manage, slipping and sliding on the uneven terrain. The section of path they were taking was a narrow clear space of a dozen or so feet between a sharp drop-off – the roiling flood water a few feet below – and a sloping upward incline. They wove between scrub brush, stunted trees and various sized boulders. It felt precarious and reminded Muireann of exactly how dangerous what they were doing was.

When she fell she assumed in the instant it was happening that she'd finally, inevitably, lost her footing. It wasn't until she hit the ground and felt what could only be a knee against her hip that she realised she'd been pushed. She heard Lee shouting as the rain picked up again, felt a hand in her hair, and even through the cold- and exhaustion-induced daze had enough survival instinct kick in to start fighting back. Something stung her neck and then she had an arrow in her hand and was stabbing it back over her shoulder, fletching end first, at whoever was holding her down; there was a short scream, a spray of blood and the weight fell to the side pulling the arrow from her hand. Muireann scrambled up and back, the bulk of her travel pack hampering her movements, then Lee was there arriving spear first before the next person could attack. Muireann, through the blur of her wet glasses, saw several darkly clad figures. She watched, still trying to regain her feet, as Lee mercilessly skewered one man; he fell with a cry down the drop-off they had been walking next to, splashing loudly into the flood water and disappearing. In the next instant Tash was there, sword drawn, pushing past her, followed quickly by Calla and Reyleth. The area they stood in wasn't good for fighting, something the people who attacked them must have quickly realised because before Muireann could manage to get her numb fingers properly around her bow and get an arrow knocked, the fight was over.

Lee appeared at her side, reaching out to wipe at the blood on her hair, face and chest. 'How badly are you hurt?'

'I'm not,' Muireann said, putting the arrow back in the quiver and trying to make sense of the scene before her. The man Lee had killed was gone, taken by the water. The person who had knocked her down lay in a mass of cloak on the ground, her arrow jutting backwards out of his eye; her stomach turned at the sight of it. She'd never killed a person before and even knowing she'd had no choice didn't ease her conscience. Near his hand lay a long thin blade, the sort she recognised from the attack in Verell. A few feet away a cloaked woman lay stretched out, dead from what Muireann guessed was a sword wound, a similar weapon to the man's still clutched in her hand.

The others had gathered around Muireann, even as Lee kept searching for the source of the blood. She shivered, feeling water dripping down her shirt. She hoped it was water. Without thinking her fingers felt for the lump of the battered compact that held the green crystal, palpable through the leather of her belt pouch; feeling it was reassuring. She didn't know what they'd have done if it had gone into the water. She took a slow breath trying to calm herself. 'Truly I'm fine. I was knocked down, but beyond that I'm not hurt.'

'I saw him stab you,' Lee said, her hands running ceaselessly over Muireann as if to reassure herself the human was really alright.

Muireann shook her head, puzzled. 'He must have missed. He grabbed my hair and then I got an arrow in my hand and struck backwards with it, but I think my pack was in the way after he knocked me down.'

Muireann slid the heavy canvas bag off and quickly checked it over, pointing to a long slash down one side. 'You see, he hit the bag not me, at some point anyway. And then when I hit him, well this blood is all his, I think.'

Reyleth was hovering next to her as well, crowding the small space they stood in. She met his worried eyes, appreciating that he wasn't trying to push Lee out of the way although he obviously wanted to, and smiled. 'Truly I'm fine. I don't think I was hurt in the fall even, just a bit stunned.'

'Let's keep moving,' Calla said, her eyes roaming the trail behind them restlessly as the rain started coming down in sheets. 'Reyleth, you lead as before, but have your sword ready. Tash, you follow him, then Muireann, then Lee, and I'll bring up the rear.'

'Were they the same as the ones who attacked us in Verell?' Lee asked, obviously also having noted the swords.

'I don't think there's any way to be certain,' Calla said, frowning. 'But at this point given they were bearing rapiers and fought like Donlachians, I'd rather err on the side of caution and say yes. There are too many strange coincidences going on for us to discount any of them. If that lot have followed us this far, we should assume they'll keep on following us, even now that they've seen real causalities'

'We'll need to set a watch tonight,' Tash said, his voice grim.

'Yes, we'll set a schedule and take turns of it,' Calla said, frowning at the terrain around them. 'I think I remember a series of caves through here. If we can find a habitable one that would be the best place to camp tonight.'

'We won't be clear of the pass before nightfall?' Muireann asked, not wanting to admit how much she'd hoped they would be.

'No, we have perhaps another full day's journey from here,

so a half day tomorrow,' Calla said, sounding unhappy. 'On the road perhaps we could have made better time, even in this weather, but hiking through the wilds and dealing with this storm, not to mention that fight...honestly, I'm impressed we've made it as far as we have.'

Muireann nodded, resigned, and the group resumed their journey, this time with weapons at the ready. The rest of the afternoon managed to be worse than the morning had been, a long, endlessly cold and wet slog through the trees, the cacophony of the flood ever-present and the threat of another attack keeping everyone on edge. Whoever was pursuing them had melted back into the shadows yet again, though, and there was no sign of anyone around or behind them.

Late in the afternoon the lightning returned, flashing bright across the sky and filling the air with the roar of thunder which overcame even the noise of the water. As much as Calla might have wanted to cover more ground before they lost the light, she wasn't willing to risk travelling in a lightning storm and quickly called a halt. Rey volunteered to search the area for caves saying that he would be the fastest to go. Muireann wasn't sure if that was true or if he was just trying to prove he could help with more than just cooking, but either way he did manage to find a suitable space fairly quickly.

He led them to what looked like a narrow opening in the face of a particularly steep section of ground, but when Muireann eased through it she found it opened into a surprisingly large space, bigger than any of their individual tents. He'd already set up a small fire near the entrance, undoubtedly with magic, but even with that it was warmer than she'd expected, the air damp but not at all chilly. She thought it was pleasant, almost hot in comparison to outside, and removed her heavy wool cloak as she explored the area. She quickly discovered it wasn't a single cave but rather the opening into a series of passages that led deep into the rock face.

'How far back does this go?' she asked Reyleth, peering into the darkness that narrowed and extended out of sight.

'It leads to several tunnels. I explored them enough to be sure nothing is living here and they all dead end eventually.'

Calla grunted in what Muireann guessed was appreciation then dropped her pack to the ground. 'Let's get set up. We'll put our beds back along the walls past the fire. Tash, you take first watch, then Muireann, then Reyleth, Lee and then me. A few hours each and that way we can all get a decent amount of sleep.'

Muireann heaved a tired sigh but went over to set her pack down, wincing when she saw the rip along the side which she'd have to repair. She took off her quiver and set her bow down as well, knowing she'd have to take them up again soon but wanting at least a few moments without the quiver against her hip and needing to free both her hands. She started setting up her and Lee's bedding in what seemed a good spot, Lee helping her spread the various blankets out. She was unsurprised when Reyleth walked over to join them, setting his own bed next to the side Muireann slept on. She supposed she might as well get used to this arrangement, which seemed agreeable to both of the others, at least as long as she was between them.

'I found several hot springs deeper into this cave system,' Reyleth said when he was done. 'I already told Calla and Tash, because the water won't be ideal for drinking unless we cool it a bit first and don't mind the minerals, and there is a better option just outside. But...the water is pleasant, and I thought you might enjoy the chance to clean up and get warm again.'

'Oh yes, both of those things sound amazing!' Muireann said, wondering if she'd be able to wash her bloody tunic as well as bathe.

Lee hesitated, then shook her head. 'I'll pass, thank you.'

'Are you sure?' Muireann asked, too tired to hide her disappointment at Lee's lack of enthusiasm.

Lee glanced at Reyleth who was watching the two women with a neutral expression. She took Muireann's arm and pulled her a bit away then leaned in to speak so only she would hear.

'I don't like hot water,' Lee said, wrinkling her nose. 'It's unnatural.'

Muireann giggled. 'It's a hot spring. That's pretty natural.'

Lee pulled her closer, her fingers tracing the lines of Muireann's cheeks. 'You go and get cleaned up. I'll go hunting.'

'Is it safe for you to go out alone? In the storm?' Muireann asked, worried and cuddling closer to the selkie.

Lee smiled gently. 'I can see better in the dark than humans can, and so far those pursuing us seem to be entirely human. And as well with my spear I don't fear them, I have the reach of any sword and am faster than they are. And as to the storm, I am a selkie after all, we love such weather.'

'Just be careful, please,' Muireann said, kissing the selkie lightly. 'I don't want to lose you.'

Lee's smile widened. 'You won't. But it might be good for you to have some time alone with the elf.'

'Lee,' Muireann said, embarrassed. 'I don't want you worrying about that.'

'I don't mind and I'd much rather you do so away from me,' Lee said, snickering slightly at Muireann's blush. 'Besides, then I won't feel so selfish having you all to myself tonight and *he* will just have to accept that.'

'You're incorrigible.'

'I'm insatiable,' Lee corrected. 'When it comes to you at least. Now go have your fun and enjoy your unnaturally hot water, and I'll find us some food. Perhaps another goat if I can manage it and the elf can earn his keep by helping cook it.'

Despite her awkwardness at the entire conversation Muireann couldn't help but laugh at the idea; she doubted Rey would be happy to know that was what everyone appreciated about his magecraft. Even if her mouth watered a bit at the idea of another dinner like they'd had the other night.

Tash was already on watch, standing by the entrance to the cave as Lee left. The two nodded at each other and Muireann felt somewhat reassured that Tash knew the selkie was going out and could keep an eye out for her. Reyleth led Muireann back into the depths behind where they'd set up their things; as it grew too dark for her to see easily, she slowed. 'We should have brought a torch.'

'Ah, my apologies,' Rey murmured and a moment later conjured a small glowing ball of light which bobbed just above their heads. The rough stone passage in front of them was filled with a soft white light and Muireann continued forward with more confidence. She could smell the hot springs before they arrived at them, the air filling with the scent of minerals. Muireann had only been to such springs once before when she'd been very young and her parents had gone on a journey to the northern kingdom of Irna. It was a more heavily volcanic land and hot springs were common there, much to her childish delight. The chance to experience that again was enough to help her put the misery of the day out of her mind, at least for the moment.

They turned a corner in the passage and arrived at a wide shallow pool, steam rising from it in a languid cloud. Calla lounged in the water looking as relaxed as Muireann had ever seen her.

Muireann started to step closer but Reyleth took her hand and held her back. 'There are other pools as well. If you'd rather one that was deeper. Or more private.'

She correctly read the implication in his words, her heart fluttering slightly. She looked from Calla, still lying back against the stone with her eyes half closed, to Reyleth, who was watching her patiently. She thought of what Lee had said and of what her own heart was telling her. 'Private might be better.'

He smiled at that, a faint blush colouring his blueish-white cheeks and she smiled at the thought that for once she was the one making someone else blush. Wordlessly he led her further into the cave, Calla letting the opportunity to tease them pass by, although Muireann caught the exaggerated wink the high elf threw her way. And ignored it.

After a few more twists and turns and passing several other pools, they arrived at a more open area in the passage just before the tunnel dead-ended. The ground was mostly smooth except for a few rough outcroppings of stone, and the hot spring itself sat against the right-side wall, a carved-out area filled with steaming water. Muireann could see why Reyleth had preferred this one – while the first pool was acceptable in size and depth and the others had been similar, this one was ideal, as if it had been shaped intentionally. Of course, for all Muireann knew it had been although she didn't quite want to ask Rey if he'd done anything to it. The magical light he'd conjured bathed the space in a soft glow which reflected and refracted off the steam rising from the water, making the entire space feel otherworldly.

Entering the small chamber she moved close to the water's edge, admiring it, then backed up looking for a place to set her clothes. Finding an acceptable ledge she took off her boots and socks, enjoying the feel of the stone beneath her bare feet. There was something soothing even in that small sensation after days living rough on the road.

She slid out of her clothes, self-conscious but too excited at the prospect of the hot spring to let that stop her. After setting her pants and underthings with her shoes she held the stained tunic up critically, debating. 'Do you think I can wash this out or is it better to call it a lost cause?'

Reyleth came up next to her, his own clothes already neatly folded in a pile on one of the other rock outcroppings. 'I can repair it for you, if you'd like.'

'Truly? You have a spell for that?' Muireann asked, holding the soiled clothing out.

'A surprising amount of magecraft can be used for mundane things,' he said, taking the cloth from her and inspecting it himself. 'There are those of course who argue against using the power for anything that isn't grand and elaborate, but my teacher believed it was better to use one's skill regularly, even on minor things, to keep in practice.'

'I like how your teacher thinks then,' Muireann said, watching as he traced arcane symbols over the cloth. 'It seems like it would be better to use it as much as is possible – and safe – rather like weapons practice. I certainly couldn't have gotten so good with my bow without using it daily.'

'It's a similar theory, yes,' he agreed, handing her back the now spotless tunic.

'Thank you so much for that,' she said, admiring the work. 'It's almost new and I rather liked this one. It would have been a shame to see it ruined.'

'I like the way the dark green sets off your eyes,' Rey said, leaving her momentarily speechless. This wasn't the usual way they had spoken to each other over the years and while she liked it there was also something about it that threw her off balance.

She set her cleaned tunic with the rest of her clothes and then moved over to the pool of steaming water, inhaling the scent of minerals that laced the air. She left the Dragon Stone on, letting it hang on its gold chain, inexplicably reluctant to take it off. The green crystal was safely in its metal compact in her belt pouch, with her clothes.

Before she could climb into the water Reyleth stopped her with a hand on her wrist. 'Aren't you going to take off your glasses?'

'I can't see without them,' she said, looking away.

'You won't be able to see with them either,' he pointed out logically. 'The steam will fog the lenses. This isn't a warm bath in a tub.'

'I don't suppose you have a spell to keep them from fogging?'

He shook his head. 'I'm sorry I don't. If I can find one—'

'It's alright, don't worry about it. You've already done so much for me.'

'Take the glasses off, Muireann,' he said softly. 'They'll be useless in the hot spring anyway, and I know you've been sleeping in them. Let yourself relax, if only here.'

She hesitated, and he gently reached out, tracing a hand along her cheek. 'Do you trust me?'

'Yes,' she replied immediately.

'Then trust me to keep you safe here.'

She nodded slowly, reaching up to take the glasses off. He took them from her and she watched his blurry form move over to where she knew her clothes were before returning. He kissed her, a soft brush of lips, then stayed close enough that she could see his face. 'I won't let any harm come to you, Muireann.'

'I know.'

Together they walked to the pool, and he held her hand as she eased into the water. It was just on the comfortable side of hot and she couldn't restrain a small happy sound as her body relaxed into it. After the cold and the exertion of the day it was blissful. He climbed in next to her, hovering a few feet away, a blur of white and dark blue to her eyes. 'Is this alright?'

'Would you like to be closer?'

'Very much.'

'Then come here,' she said, holding her arms out to him, suddenly feeling brave. After everything that had happened in the last weeks and even just that day, she didn't want to miss any opportunity she might find for some happiness.

So she took the happiness she had found.

* * *

Later they lounged together in the pool, wrapped in each other's arms. Muireann knew they shouldn't linger too much longer;

Lee would be back soon if she wasn't already and they should help her cook. And Muireann also had to take her turn on watch after Tash and she needed to get ready before then. But despite all that the warm water was too relaxing and Reyleth's arms around her felt too good for her to hurry to leave.

'Muireann,' he said, his mouth close to her ear.

'Mmmm.'

'I love you.'

'I love you too, Rey,' she said, sighing. She supposed maybe they'd both known it for a long time, but hearing it out loud made it real to her.

'Are you certain that you must continue forward with this?' he said. 'There is far more danger than I expected you to be facing.'

'I know, there's more than I expected too,' she admitted. 'I wish we knew why these people keep attacking us.'

'Attacking you,' he pointed out, drawing her closer.

'I was the last person in line and the logical one to attack in that situation,' she said calmly. 'I really don't think I was being personally targeted.'

'Perhaps not, but I still don't like it.'

'I wouldn't have liked it if it was you knocked down and with a sword over your head,' Muireann admitted, turning towards him so that she could look in his eyes and actually see what she was looking at. Their faces hung inches apart in a way that felt far more intimate than what had just happened between them.

'You almost died,' he said softly, his face filled with pain. This close she couldn't avoid seeing it no matter how much she wanted to.

She reached up and cradled his face in her hands, leaning her forehead against his. 'But I didn't.'

'You could have.'

'But I didn't,' she said again. 'I don't know why these people keep attacking us but so far we have always come out alright, and at this point there's nothing for it but to keep going forward.'

'Do you think finding the answers you seek will stop the attacks?' he asked, his eyes searching hers.

'I can't answer that since I don't know why we're being attacked,' she pointed out. 'But I know that no matter what obstacles appear we must push forward.'

'It's that important?'

'It is.'

'It's worth your life?' he pressed.

'It is,' she repeated, watching the fear and pain cross his face.

'Nothing is worth that, Muireann,' he whispered.

She closed the small distance between them, kissing him, then pulled back. 'This is. I can't explain to you why it is, but you have to trust me, it is.'

'I do trust you,' he said, but he wasn't happy about it. She worried that if it came to choosing between her life or destroying the stone, he wouldn't be able to let her die, and she prayed to whatever god might be listening that it would never come to that. She could sacrifice herself if she had to, she knew she could, but she couldn't bear the thought of causing such pain to people who loved her, not to Reyleth or to Lee.

She kissed him again and then squirmed free of his arms, climbing out of the wonderfully hot water. 'As much as I'd love to stay here forever, I think it's time to get back and help with dinner.'

He stretched, then followed her out. She walked carefully across the open space to where she remembered their clothes being, finding her glasses by feel on the top of the pile of clothes. Once they were on the world came back into sharp focus and she set about redressing, pulling her clothes on even though she was still dripping from the hot spring. She enjoyed the warm air of the cave that meant she wasn't shivering even now, and selfishly wished they really could stay there forever. But her sense of responsibility was too well developed and with a final glance at the pool she turned and followed Reyleth as he led the way out, the little ball of light he'd conjured bobbing along above them like a loyal pet.

No one reacted when the two re-emerged into the main camp area of the cave, although Muireann thought even Tash had to at least suspect what they'd been doing given how long they'd been gone. Calla was sitting on her bedding, sharpening one of her daggers. Tash and Lee were near the fire, Tash still on guard and Lee preparing what looked like a deer. While it wasn't the goat Lee had aimed to get the venison was just as much of a treat and Muireann was glad to see it. They joined the two by the fire, and Rey wordlessly began working his magic on Lee's catch to turn it from rough camp fare into something much more appetising. Muireann was waiting to help with the actual cooking, so she walked over to join Tash where he stood guard closer to the entrance.

'Will we have time to do some studying tonight do you think?' he asked hopefully. She had been tutoring him every night since he had joined them except for the last night because of the storm.

She smiled at his eagerness, so different from the village children who were always happy to avoid a lesson. 'Certainly, if you'd like.'

'I would,' he said. 'It's funny, I never enjoyed studying before but now that I have a goal to work towards I find it all much more interesting. And we'd been discussing the founding of the empire and I realised how little of the actual history I know, mostly stories I was told as a child.'

'Mmmm,' she agreed. 'The real history is mostly in the elven works, because they are only a few generations out from the founding unlike the human texts that are scores and scores of lifetimes away from a living memory of it. Of course, the issue with the elven works is reading past the bias in them, since obviously it's their empire they are writing about.'

He nodded. 'It's all so interesting though. And then we can talk about the founding of the nine kingdoms, yes?'

'Definitely. You can't discuss the empire without talking about the nine kingdoms, and of course any good knight should know all of that.'

Tash looked pleased at her words and flattered that she had so much confidence in his chances of knighthood. 'Let me retrieve the cooking spices and we can get this deer roasted.'

'Wait a moment first,' Muireann said, realising she'd lingered in the hot spring longer than she'd thought. 'It's my turn on guard duty after you, and I need to retrieve my bow.'

She went to get her things, wishing she didn't have to eat dinner while on watch but not regretting what had delayed her. Lee followed her over to their area of the cave, pulled her into a hug and whispered in her ear. 'Did you take my advice?'

Muireann was sure her face must be scarlet but she kept her voice level when she answered. 'Yes.'

'Good,' Lee said. 'I wasn't sure because all I can smell on you is the water from the springs. But now he can't complain later that I'm keeping you all to myself.'

'Lee!'

'He can't. Unless you don't want me tonight?'

'I always want you, but we are in rather tight quarters here,' Muireann said, still blushing.

'So? What difference does that make?' Lee sounded genuinely puzzled, and Muireann wondered if this was another cultural difference between humans and selkies. The book she'd found on selkie culture hadn't mentioned that aspect of things.

'How about you and I sneak back further into the caves where we won't be keeping anyone else awake?' Muireann suggested.

'That seems fair,' Lee agreed, even though Muireann suspected she was only agreeing to keep Muireann happy.

She quickly attached her quiver to her belt and took up her bow as Lee went back to the fire to help cook. As Muireann moved to take Tash's place by the entrance she started to think that having two committed lovers was going to be more complicated than she'd realised, certainly more so than her past experience with casual lovers during her marriage. Still, she wouldn't give up Lee or what she'd found with Reyleth, and so long as they were both agreeable to the situation as well she supposed she'd find a way.

My life has become something so strange, she mused to herself, adjusting the quiver against her hip and pulling an arrow which she set loosely against the bow. *I really am a different person than I was a year ago, not even because I killed a dragon, but who would ever have thought I'd be journeying through the wilderness with a group of adventurers, fending off strange attackers, trying to help prevent a dangerous weapon from being unleashed on the world? With my new best friend the high elf, a future knight, a selkie wife and Reyleth.*

As she peered into the darkness, rain still lashing down furiously from the sky, she realised that she didn't regret any of it, though, no matter how odd her life had become. She did wish that these attacks would stop, or at least that they could understand why people kept going after them, but that aside she was happy enough with her life as it had become.

* * *

The next day dawned to yet another stormy sky. When Muireann pulled herself from her bed she found Tash and Lee still sleeping, and Calla and Reyleth standing by the cave entrance, talking. She wondered if they might decide to stay where they were for another day and found herself hoping that was so. She wasn't eager for yet another day of miserable hiking through the rain-soaked hills and this cave was so nice – not to mention the hot springs – that she would be happier to stay than face the weather.

She walked over to where the others were standing, shivering slightly in the loose pants and linen shirt she'd slept in as she drew closer to the cave entrance. 'Good morning.'

Calla nodded, her eyes on the area visible outside and Muireann remembered that she was on guard duty now. Reyleth smiled warmly at her. 'Good morning to you as well.'

'I'm surprised you're up already, Reyleth, since you had the mid-watch.'

He shrugged. 'I slept as much as I could but was restless when dawn came.'

'Have we a plan for the day?' she asked, peering out at the drizzle.

It was Calla's turn to shrug. 'The weather seems to be drying out, which is fortunate, although the water will still be high. I'm hopeful, though, that we can find the road again on higher ground, and we should be clear of the pass by mid-day at the latest.'

Rey nodded, looking troubled. 'It's tempting to stay here, this is a defensible position should those who follow us still be on our trail. But on the other hand the longer we linger here the easier for them to get ahead of us and set a true ambush or surround us, both of which could be worse for us.'

'I'm tempted to stay for the hot springs,' Calla said. 'A person could live in that pool, and I'd love to try. But even my hedonism has its limits and it's too dangerous not to press on. Once we clear the pass it's another full day of travel through unsettled land before we'll reach the first town. That's Harven. It's about the same size as Verell but has less of a small-city feel to it. It *feels* more like a large village that had no sense of its own size, if that makes sense. But we should find lodgings there and be able to resupply our food. From there it's two days to Little Ford, which is a large town. There's a toll on the bridge there, but it's the safest way to cross Wotlin River, especially this time of year and with all the rain in the mountains raising the rivers. From there, we'll have another seven or eight days to Mistlen, but there should be a town or village to stop in every night, the land is more heavily settled the closer we get to the capital.'

'What about whoever is following us?' Muireann asked, still worried about their stubborn pursuers.

'The land past the mountains is mostly flat and the road leaves the forest in short order and goes through farmland and pasture. They will have a hard time following us or ambushing us through there.'

'We only need to reach the open sections,' Reyleth said. 'And then we should have a better time of it if we are still being pursued.'

'I still wish I knew why we were being harassed like this,' Muireann complained, knowing that no amount of worrying about the issue would change anything.

The two elves exchanged a tense look, then Calla shrugged. 'We will have to try to get some answers to that if it happens again. We can't keep being caught off guard and as well if we know why they are hunting us we can possibly put a stop to it. But we need to consider that there are some confusing factors going on.'

'Such as? Besides the obvious why are they even doing this?' Muireann pressed.

'Such as why is it one organised group, apparently from Donlach, sometimes and other times a very unorganised group with no clear cohesiveness.'

'Yes, that is puzzling,' Muireann said. 'That would be a good place to start looking for answers.'

'It won't be easy to get any answers,' Reyleth said. 'Especially as they melt back into the shadows so quickly and attack so intermittently.'

She didn't like that but couldn't argue it so instead she started seeing what breakfast she could manage out of the venison left from the night before. It was good, better than they would have gotten without Reyleth's assistance, but she found herself missing home-cooked food. Even tavern food, heavier and often greasier, seemed appealing in that moment. She was struck by a sudden longing for the settled life she'd left behind, despite her happiness the night before with her current situation, and she started to wonder if she'd ever be able to settle down again. It would be so easy to dream of living in Strandview with Lee and Reyleth, helping to run the bookshop, walking with Lee along the shoreline. But she had to face the reality that she might spend her lifetime looking for answers about the Aldovanan weapon, or die seeking them. Shaking her head to push away the thoughts she prepared some food for Lee as well and went over to where the selkie was awake, still curled beneath the blankets, her seal skin wrapped around her body. Muireann smiled to see Lee looking relaxed, sitting down next to her wife and offering the plate she'd fixed. The two women ate together in silence, listening to the fire crackling and the soft rain. Whatever the day held, at least it wasn't beginning too badly.

Chapter 6

Every Hand Against Us

It was a slow start that morning, Muireann suspected because everyone was hoping the rain would finally stop before they left. Eventually, though, they couldn't delay any longer, shouldering their packs and heading back out to forge a trail towards the road. The little stream was still swollen into a raging river, and they proceeded along with it, sometimes closer and sometimes further away. As with the previous afternoon they walked with their weapons ready and on alert for another attack, but there was no sign of anyone else around them.

By mid-morning the rain did finally stop, the clouds clearing to reveal a bright blue sky and shining sun. It did little to help the chill in the air, but just being free of the clinging dampness and perpetual rain was cheering. Despite it all they walked a bit faster and with more hope that they'd be free of the entire mess soon.

Muireann was walking towards the front, behind Calla, and so didn't see how it happened but she turned when Tash cried out and watched in helpless horror as the young man fell into the swollen river, sliding down the embankment as his feet slipped on the muddy ground. His leather armour was heavy enough, combined with the pack he was carrying and his wool cloak, to drag him down immediately. Without a ripple he disappeared beneath the churning surface.

Lee and Reyleth both leapt into action before Muireann could take more than a step forward, dropping their packs and preparing to jump into the swirling waters after the human. Rey leapt in first, quickly unclasping his belt and dropping it next to his pack. Lee was not far behind him needing only a few seconds more to throw her things to the ground and pull her sealskin on;

she transformed in mid-air, hitting the water as a grey spotted seal. Muireann and Calla ranged along the edge of the stable area, watching the water racing past, waiting for anyone to re-emerge. An agonizingly long minute later Reyleth resurfaced, struggling to lift Tash's head above the water; he was clearly unconscious. His pack and cloak were gone but even without that it was obviously difficult for Reyleth to manoeuvre him. The two were moving rapidly downstream and Calla and Muireann immediately gave chase on shore. An instant later Lee's head broke the surface, her wide dark seal eyes fixed on the two men. Muireann could see Rey's mouth moving but heard nothing over the roar of the water. Lee disappeared under the surface then popped back up on Tash's other side, one of his limp arms draped across her back. Together the two managed to fight the current to get to the edge of the embankment, where Muireann and Calla scrambled down, struggling not to end up in the river as well, and helped to drag Tash out. Reyleth and Lee followed, Lee removing her sealskin and resuming her human form.

Muireann rolled Tash onto his back, resting a hand on his chest. 'He isn't breathing.'

'Move,' Reyleth said, going down on his knees next to the unconscious young man as Muireann scrambled back. He began chanting in elvish, his hands moving over Tash's body, leaving glowing traces behind that formed a series of arcane symbols. His chanting changed pace, speeding up, his voice seeming to vibrate in the cold air. There was a flash of light, the symbols brightening then plunging into Tash's chest, then the human jerked as if he were having a fit, finally rolling over and opening his mouth to release a large volume of discoloured water onto the ground. He rolled back over, spasmed several more times, his whole body now glowing slightly. Then as suddenly as it had started the spasms stopped and the glow dissipated like mist in the sunlight.

Tash opened his dark eyes, staring in confusion at the worried faces around him, before breaking out in violent shivering. Calla took off her cloak, throwing it over him, then said. 'Muireann, help me get a fire started to warm him. Lee, can you go retrieve your things and Reyleth's?'

'I can go with her to fetch my own things,' Rey said, but his voice sounded strained, cold water dripping from his soaked clothing.

Calla shook her head. 'I'm no mage, mage, but even I know that such magic takes a lot out of a person. Rest for a few minutes and let us take care of Tash from here.'

'I can walk and pick up a bag and my weapons,' Rey stubbornly insisted.

'You'll do us no good if you collapse,' Calla said, as if she were scolding a child. 'Be sensible and stop trying to show off for Muireann.'

'Calla,' Muireann said from her place nearby, as she gathered as much firewood as she could even though everything was soaked.

'What? You're already bedding him; he doesn't need to impress you and this stubbornness will only make a bad situation worse. I swear I forget sometimes how little sense younger elves seem to have.'

'Calla!' Muireann said, fighting the urge to throw a stick at the high elf, mostly because she wasn't sure she wouldn't miss and hit Tash by mistake. He'd already nearly drowned; he didn't need to get smacked in the face with a wet stick on top of that.

'It's alright, Muireann,' Reyleth said, as Lee jogged off alone to retrieve their things. 'She's right that I'm being stubborn, at least. It would be wise for me to sit and rest after that. Besides, without magic that wood will never light.'

Calla nodded slightly but didn't otherwise acknowledge his words, focused on helping Tash stagger to his feet so they could get him out of his wet clothes as Muireann quickly built a rough fire. Reyleth didn't seem bothered by his own wet clothing but nonetheless he stood close by the fire, letting everything dry while he wore it. By the time Lee returned the fire was burning brightly, Tash was huddled in Calla's cloak next to it and Muireann was trying to get his wet clothing arranged on sticks to dry close to the flames. Lee dropped the things she was carrying near Reyleth then met Muireann's eyes. 'I'm going back in to find his pack.'

'Please be careful,' Muireann said, concerned about the risk the selkie was taking. But Lee only smiled and jumped back in the churning water with a wink, leaving Muireann to shake her head.

'Don't worry for her,' Reyleth said, still crouching by the fire. 'Selkies are excellent swimmers and I think she's enjoying herself in the river.'

Muireann started to snap back at him before realising that this was the first time Lee had taken her seal form or been in the water since they'd met. She swallowed her words and went back to work drying Tash's clothes instead.

A short time later the selkie re-emerged with Tash's bag but said his cloak was truly lost. They would have to replace it when they reached Harven and try to manage without it despite the cold weather until then.

At that point there was no sense in pushing on, so Calla called a temporary halt, allowing everyone to rest and eat until Tash felt ready to continue and his clothes had dried out.

Muireann's only small consoling thought as they huddled together on the shore of the flooded area eating their travel rations was that their mysterious pursuers were nowhere to be seen.

They continued on in early afternoon, hoping to at least clear the mountain pass before nightfall. Everyone was quiet and subdued after Tash's mishap and still on edge over any potential attacks. Muireann didn't relish camping out in the open if they were still being followed, even knowing that they planned to set a watch again. In all honesty she was nervous about the idea of being on watch trying to protect a loose encampment of tents, but she knew it was necessary and that she would have to take a turn like everyone else.

The group walked single file through the scrub brush until finally they found the road again, now free of the flooded area as the riverbed turned south while the road stayed east. It was a relief to all of them to see the road and to leave behind the muddy trail and trees they had been walking through.

Muireann had been trying to keep an eye on Tash as they went, worried for the young man after his fall into the river. But as the day wore on he seemed to be recovering well and she slowly drifted back, falling behind Lee until she was walking just ahead of Reyleth. She knew that he must be tired if only because he was trailing the group the way that she had the day before, but he didn't complain and she suspected if she mentioned it to him he'd be offended. So she walked and quietly shifted her attention from Tash to Rey. The space between them and the other three lengthened and she was debating whether to give up all pretence and simply walk next to him so they could talk when she caught a movement, something white, in her peripheral vision.

She turned and searched the area around the sides of the road, an area cluttered with small evergreens and various-sized boulders. Reyleth stopped where he was, a dozen feet behind her, frowning. 'What is it?'

'I don't know,' Muireann said. 'I thought I saw something moving out of the corner of my eye.'

Reyleth drew his sword, his other hand coming up, his fingers moving into strange shapes that she assumed were readying to cast magic. She shifted her bow up, knocking the arrow she held.

Nothing happened.

They stood like that for a full minute, tense, the rest of the group getting further away, until Muireann started to feel foolish. She was just about to apologise when three huge wolves burst from the cover around the road towards Reyleth. They were as big as young cows, their shoulders easily reaching Muireann's chest. Their fur was completely white, as if they'd been formed from snow. Two of them moved together behind Reyleth while the third circled towards the area between where he stood and Muireann.

In the first instant she froze, staring in awe at the gigantic animals. She had read of the Great Wolves who stalked the far northern lands, had even seen drawings of them, but she never dreamed she'd see one alive.

Muireann watched Reyleth cast the spell, the magic coruscating outwards from his hands, catching the two giant animals moving behind him and sending them flying. Before he could turn and take on the third it had already leapt at him, knocking the elf down to the ground hard. His sword flew from his hand, skittering across the hard ground. Everything seemed to slow down, and Muireann was hyper aware of every detail of what was happening. She heard herself yelling his name as if it were someone else doing it. She had the bow raised and aimed before she was consciously thinking to do it, reflex taking over. She let the arrow fly as the Great Wolf snapped at Rey's pack, tearing the fabric. It twisted up then lunged down again this time towards his head. The arrow struck home. The wolf collapsed, falling next to Rey.

Time snapped back to normal. She was running towards him, another arrow already knocked and ready, Lee, Calla and Tash close on her heels. The two wolves he'd used his spell against scrambled to their feet, whining, and then took off running back into the brush; Muireann let them go. She got there and saw the arrow sticking from the downed animal's side, which was deathly still, and set her bow aside, kneeling and reaching instead for Reyleth. 'Rey! Speak to me! Are you injured?'

He groaned, struggling to rise against the weight of his pack and the bulk of the animal so close to his side. Before she could do anything the others were there, Lee reaching down to help him up as Muireann scrambled to her feet. She reached out and started searching his muddy form for wounds, as Lee had done for her yesterday. Lee for her part held his arm, still supporting him where he stood. He swayed slightly on his feet, looking utterly exhausted.

'Are you alright, mage?' Calla asked.

He took several long shuddering breaths, wincing as Muireann felt carefully along his ribs. 'I am mostly uninjured, I think. I've used too much magic today and am tired from the effort, and when the Great Wolf pounced on me and I hit the ground the breath was knocked from me.'

'Are you sure you're alright?' Muireann asked again, still concerned for him.

He spared her a pained smile. 'Thanks to you I will live to spellcast another day.'

'It is a fine day for saving your friends it seems,' Tash said, looking as worried as the others.

Calla looked at the carcass thoughtfully. 'I have never seen or heard of Great Wolves coming this far south.'

'Nor have I,' Reyleth admitted.

'I've never seen them before,' Tash admitted, saying what Muireann was thinking.

Lee shrugged, poking the body with the butt of her spear. 'I've never seen any kind of land wolf before. Why are they called Great Wolves?'

'They are about twice as big as the forest wolves we have here. Great Wolves, like the Snow Bears, are found in the distant north, the parts of Irna where the snow never melts, not even in summer,' Calla said. 'They have huge deer there as well, bigger than horses, which is what these wolves usually eat. I can't imagine what would have compelled them to come this far south.'

Lee made a thoughtful noise. 'For all its size it seems too thin under the fur. If I had to guess I'd say it was starving which may explain why it attacked Reyleth. Desperate animals will do things they would not under normal circumstances.'

'That makes some sense,' Muireann agreed. 'I don't know as much about Great Wolves, but forest wolves don't usually attack humans, they're shy and reclusive animals.'

'I wouldn't describe Great Wolves as either of those things,' Calla said. 'But they rarely attack people because they are smart. Smart enough to know attacking a person only leads to trouble anyway.'

'We don't seem to have any luck today that isn't bad,' Muireann griped, looking from Tash to Reyleth.

'I don't agree,' Tash said quickly. 'It's true things have been difficult, and you could argue that falling into the river was ill chance or that the attack by these poor wolves was, but on the other hand it was great luck that I fell in while travelling with not one but two people capable of diving in to save me with minimal risk to themselves, comparatively, and that Reyleth knows healing spells and was there to revive me. And it was great luck that when the wolves did attack you were there with your bow and quick to shoot – and true with your aim. Despite it all no harm has come to us. If you look at it that way, we have all been very lucky today indeed.'

Muireann smiled at the young man, finding his enthusiasm infectious. 'I suppose that's all true.'

'I don't believe in luck,' Lee said slowly. 'But I do believe that we as a group can and will protect each other. As long as we work together, we can continue to prevail against whatever circumstances we find.'

'As they say, the gods favour those who make their own luck,' Calla said, quoting a common proverb. It was one of those things that the temple-folk hated to hear, believing that the gods were the source of all things good or bad, but that the commonfolk often said. Muireann considered herself reasonably religious – she believed in the seven gods and their power over the world and tried to honour them at the appropriate times – but she thought the commonfolk had the right of this one.

Muireann's introspection was interrupted by Lee pulling her dagger and moving towards the dead animal. She frowned at her wife. 'What are you doing?'

'Taking the pelt for you,' Lee said, as if that should be obvious.

Muireann winced, then shook her head. 'We haven't kept anything from the animals we've hunted so far. And travelling with that will be messy.'

'I can—' Reyleth started, before Muireann cut him off.

'You need to rest before you collapse,' she said with a stern look at the elf. Calla snickered loudly.

Lee made quick work of the hide and held it towards Muireann. 'It's beautiful and it will be very warm, nicer than your cloak. And it's a pity to waste it, especially if it's such a rare animal here. Its death may as well go to something good.'

'It will look nice on you, Muiri,' Calla said, still laughing slightly. 'You will truly look quite the hero in Mistlen with the Dragon Stone around your neck and such a cloak on your shoulders.'

Muireann turned to glare at the high elf who only laughed harder and while she was distracted Rey grabbed the fur and quickly cast his spell on it. By the time she'd turned back and tried to stop him it was done, so that what he held in his hands was thick white fur on one side and soft suede on the other, as fine as if it had been carefully worked by a professional tanner. He swayed on his feet, panting with the effort, and she rushed over to slide herself under his arm, wrapping a hand around his waist to support him. 'You are so stubborn, Reyleth, it's unbelievable.'

He smiled at her. 'It's a little thing, Lennath.'

She felt her cheeks flaming at the elvish word for beloved. 'It could have waited. You've already used too much magic today, you said as much yourself earlier. Major spells take time to recover from, and you used magic for the fire as well after that and to fight the other wolves. I don't want you hurting yourself, and you'll do no one any good if you collapse. Do you want me to have to carry you from here?'

His smile widened. 'I would never miss any opportunity to be in your arms.'

Thoroughly mortified now, she mumbled back. 'You're delirious.'

She wasn't aware they were speaking Elvish – she'd switched subconsciously when he'd called her beloved – until Calla said, for everyone's benefit, 'I didn't realise you spoke any language besides the common tongue, Muiri.'

Reyleth answered for her, proud as always of how well she'd learned, not incidentally from him. 'She speaks several dialects of Elvish, and a few other languages besides. It's important when studying older texts to be familiar with many languages.'

'That's great, Muireann,' Tash said, looking impressed. 'I only speak common. I don't suppose you could teach me Elvish? I've heard some of the knights at the keep practising it and they say it's good to know for speaking to emissaries from the imperial capital or travelling dignitaries.'

'As you get so many of those in Verell,' Calla snorted, teasing them about how admittedly backwater Verell, and all of Lord Arvain's territory, was.

'I will teach you,' Reyleth offered, side-eyeing Calla. 'It may well be useful for you to know.'

'Yes, Reyleth is the one who taught me, he's really an excellent teacher,' Muireann quickly agreed, glad that the two seemed to have become friends. She knew Rey would never have offered unless he genuinely liked Tash, he just wasn't the sort to put himself out for such a thing for a person he wasn't willing to spend tedious hours with.

At her words Reyleth smiled softly then he straightened up so that he wasn't leaning on her any more. She found the large fur pushed into her arms instead. 'Take it and try it on. It should fit you as a cloak would.'

She wanted to lecture him again about whatever magic he'd done to ensure that but she didn't both because she felt like it would be ill grace on her part after he'd put so much effort into it for her and also because she didn't want to give Calla an opening to joke that he made a good tailor as well as cook. Instead, she slid off her wool cloak and handed it to Tash, and pulled the fur around her shoulders. 'It is perfect,' she admitted. 'It fits exactly and it's warmer than I would have believed possible. Warmer than wool.'

The others all admired it until Muireann started to feel self-conscious, so she spoke to Tash. 'You can keep the other cloak. You needed one anyway. It's too short of course but we can get a better one in the next town.'

'Too short is better than freezing without any,' Tash said, putting the cloak on. 'This will do perfectly well until we reach Harven, and I'm sure I can find something there that's a bit longer.'

'Speaking of reaching Harven,' Calla said, pulling back from stroking the new fur cloak with obvious reluctance, 'we should keep moving if we'd like to get anywhere today.'

'We haven't managed to cover much ground,' Muireann said, making a face but setting another arrow to her bow and starting to move again. The group stayed closer together this time, walking single file but all within a few feet of the next person.

'Perhaps not as much as I'd have liked,' Calla admitted, from the front of the group. 'But any progress is better than none.'

'My folk have a saying,' Lee added, walking just ahead of

Muireann in the middle of the line. "Better one fish in a catch than none", I think that applies here nicely. We may not have covered as many miles as we all wanted but we have made some distance and that's better than staying where we were.'

Calla led them down the road around a large cluster of pines; once free of the trees they could all see how much progress they actually had made.

'We're free of the mountains at least,' Calla said, nodding at the foothills and open land that extended before them. They all relaxed as they followed the road down and away from the pass, the air still cold but the weather as pleasant otherwise as anyone could have wished for.

Muireann felt her spirits lifting with every step and when they finally made camp for the night, still in the foothills with the mountains looming above them, her good mood persisted. Despite it all talk around the fire that night was happy, and they fell back into their usual camp routines, excepting only that now they shared guard duty in rotations at night. But the return to even that semi-normalcy was enough for them all to look to the future with hope instead of pessimism.

The difficulties they had just faced had bonded the little group closer together, so that while Reyleth and Lee were still stiffly formal around each other the early awkwardness had melted away, and while Calla still sniped relentlessly at Rey it felt more like teasing now than genuine criticism. Rey and Tash had developed a bond before the incident in the river but that had cemented their friendship. And Muireann found herself more at ease with everyone in general, which made her happy. They felt like a cohesive group now, and while she would never say she was glad for the trials the mountains had imposed, Muireann was excited at the new group dynamic; this was what she'd always imagined being part of such an adventuring group would be like when she read the epic tales. Come to that this was what she'd always imagined having a tightknit group of friends would be like, something she had limited experience of as someone who was usually the odd person out in any group.

Sitting around the fire that night, eating one of the rabbits Lee had caught, listening to Reyleth give Tash his first lesson in Elvish and to Calla and Lee discussing the relative merits of spear fighting versus swords, Muireann felt completely content. They still didn't know who was following them or why, they still had no answers about how to destroy the Aldovanan weapon, but still she was content.

* * *

Harven was exactly as Calla had described it, a sprawling settlement that was large enough to be a town but felt oddly insular for all its size. Muireann liked it. There was no bankers' guild hall here, but Muireann and Calla still had a decent amount of gold on hand so there was no issue getting rooms at the better of the town's two inns, paying for their meals and resupplying the group. It reminded Muireann of the first day in Verell but in a fun way and she had to admit she enjoyed accompanying Calla from merchant to merchant. She'd never been east of the mountains before and was surprised by how different so many things were. There was no seafood to be had here, for any price, which she'd expected but whereas her people had considered goat and sheep staple meats, along with chicken, the eastern part of the kingdom of Lanal was dairy country where beef was as common as fish was in the west. It fascinated Muireann to see a food that was considered a luxury item or something reserved for feast days at home was a part of nearly every dish here. And as well while her people wore darker earth tones primarily the commonfolk here seemed to favour pale greys, tans and orange tones, and lighter weight fabrics for the warmer weather they had. In every shop Muireann watched the people as Calla haggled, fascinated that a week's walk east could mean such drastic changes. Even the common tongue spoken here, while understandable, was clearly accented to Muireann's ears, the vowels and consonants sharper and the words delivered faster.

For their part the people they encountered seemed just as fascinated by the high elf and Muireann as Muireann was with them. Part of that attention was because Muireann was wearing the Great Wolf fur, which stood out not only for its colour but because no one here wore fur cloaks; they were all wool or linen. She felt a bit silly wearing it, knowing people were staring, but couldn't bring herself to put Rey's gift aside. And, of course, Calla used every opportunity to regale people with both the story of the dragon and the tale of the wolf attack, making Muireann sound like an epic hero from the old tales. Muireann wasn't sure how well people believed that given she still looked like her overweight, middle-aged, bespectacled self, but there was the Dragon Stone and wolf cloak as proof.

She supposed she presented quite the puzzle for people used to such epic tales featuring strong handsome young men saving the day and as time wore on her embarrassment at the strange looks while Calla talked transformed into amusement. She started to hope that maybe people would rethink who could feature in those tales and when a group of young girls started following them, whispering quietly, she insisted they stop and made Calla retell the stories just for that audience. She still didn't like the idea of anyone describing her as a hero but seeing the looks on the little girls' faces, seeing the way they stood straighter when they walked away, made her willing to bear it.

As they walked back to the inn with all their purchases, including Tash's new cloak, she said. 'There aren't many female heroes are there?'

'Not nearly enough,' Calla agreed. 'Lucky you came along.'

'I'm not a hero,' Muireann sighed.

'Must we argue about this again?' Calla sighed back,

mimicking Muireann's tone exactly.

Muireann couldn't stop the smile at Calla's teasing. 'I'm not though. You know I regret what I did, and I don't think killing a dragon is a heroic act, no matter how many people do – it's like people who rejoice when any large predator is killed, seeing only one less dangerous animal and not seeing the way the world is poorer for that loss.'

'I know you cried for the dragon,' Calla said more seriously. 'And I know you cried for that wolf as well. You are hard enough to do what has to be done but your heart is still gentle underneath. You are too soft hearted for the life you're living, and to be honest that's one of the things I love about you. You keep that soft heart no matter how cruel the world is to you. But people need heroes, Muiri, they always have, and they always will. You were happy to see those children so delighted at your story, I saw it in your face. They are delighted because they can imagine themselves now growing up to be you, to save the world from dangerous things.'

'Well, I haven't done a good job of that, have I?' Muireann said, bumping her shoulder against Calla's as they walked.

'I beg to differ,' the high elf shot back, bumping Muireann in turn. 'Since so far you – or we – have indeed kept the world safe. And we are going to continue doing so. We will be in Mistlen in a week or so and I'm confident that you will find enough there to either have an answer or know exactly where we need to go next. And honestly, even if it takes longer, we have time. We have money to live on, we have good friends around us, and we are as safe as we can be in this uncertain world. You have two people you love in your bed, me by your side, Tash to study your books with. What more can you ask from life?'

Muireann smiled and put her free arm around Calla's shoulders, balancing the bundles she was carrying against her other hip. 'I don't know what I did to deserve such a good friend as you, Calla.'

'You saved me from a dragon,' the high elf snickered, then sobering slightly she added, 'I will tell you truly, though, I think we would have been friends no matter how we'd met. We get on too well not to be.'

Muireann smiled fondly at that. 'I agree. And however it happened you are well and truly stuck with me now.'

The two women were still laughing when they entered the inn, going their separate ways to their rooms to store what they'd bought. Their talk that afternoon helped Muireann to be less chagrined when Calla stood by the common room's hearth and retold the story of the dragon for everyone. Muireann was sure when Calla was done there wouldn't be a soul in all of Harven who hadn't heard it, but Calla was an excellent storyteller and the whole room was enraptured as she spoke. Even Muireann was able to enjoy it, when she ignored that she was the one Calla was talking about.

As she lay with Lee that night, she started to think that maybe everything was turning in their favour after all.

* * *

Calla didn't want to waste time lingering in Harven so the next morning they set out again, packs noticeably heavier after the high elf's shopping the day before, to walk the two days to Little Ford. Muireann was looking forward to seeing the bridge that crossed the river there, which she'd heard was big enough for four wagons to cross at once side by side. It was hard for her to picture such a thing, when the largest bridge back home barely fit one of the big merchant wagons at once.

The cheer they'd all been feeling since leaving the mountains was still holding and as they walked on the road the second day they chatted, moving aside for the heavy wagons or speeding up around slower foot traffic.

'I think you will all enjoy Little Ford,' Calla said. 'It is a proper town.'

'What constitutes a proper town?' Tash asked, walking just behind her.

'It has a brothel,' Calla shot back immediately, then laughed at Tash's expression. 'What, don't tell me you've never been in a brothel, knight?'

'I'm not a knight yet,' he stuttered, flustered. 'And no I haven't ever been in a brothel. Not that there's anything *wrong* with such work, of course, everyone deserves to earn for their effort and the prostitutes' guild is well respected.'

'More respected than some others,' Muireann agreed.

'Then why haven't you been to one?' Calla pressed, enjoying his discomfort.

'Because I...I...I said there's nothing wrong with it and I believe that, I've known plenty of soldiers who talked fondly of the brothels. But my family were followers of the Rules of Salleth, and I don't know if you know about him, but he preaches that the way to serve the gods best is through chastity and hard work.'

'Oh, I know what he preaches,' Calla said, turning to give Muireann an 'I told you so' look over her shoulder at the mention of one of the strictest of the religious sects.

The road had emptied of other travellers allowing for at least a somewhat private conversation, but Muireann was sure the young man was still having a hard time with the entire topic. Followers of Salleth were often ridiculed for being prudish but Muireann suspected it was more that they were terribly sheltered and taught to feel ashamed of anything sexual in the belief that it would encourage the chastity they preached as a virtue. Feeling sympathetic towards the younger man, Muireann said. 'Tash it doesn't make you uncomfortable, does it? That I'm married but have a lover as well? I think that goes against one of your Guiding Rules.'

Poor Tash looked absolutely mortified at this point, but he

made a valiant effort to answer. 'Oh no! Of course not! You all seem agreeable to it, and I know that's a common way for people to do things. And I'm not really a follower myself. Not anymore. I was just raised in it and sometimes it's hard not to remember...to feel like certain things are wrong...not wrong for others to do but if I did them...oh, I'm making a mess of explaining this.'

'It's alright,' Reyleth said, giving Calla a reproving look. 'There's nothing wrong with monogamy if that's what you prefer and you are very wise if at your age you already realise that different things work for different people.'

Tash looked deeply grateful for that support. Calla, however, was enjoying herself too much to stop teasing. 'Well Muireann tried monogamy and clearly decided multiple lovers is better.'

'Could we please leave Muireann out of this conversation?' the human woman quipped, rolling her eyes. 'My marriage wasn't monogamous, not that I disagree with the practice if the people involved prefer it, but we did as most do and had other lovers as well. That said, though, I happen to agree with Reyleth that people should do what makes them happy, even if it's not what most others do.'

'What or who?' Calla said.

'Calla!' Muireann snapped.

'Look out!' Lee's voice cut through the banter, and Muireann whirled immediately towards the sound of her wife's voice. Despite being on a trade road, despite being in fairly open ground, a group of almost a dozen swordsmen had managed to sneak up on them, taking advantage of the fact they had let their guard down. Muireann pulled an arrow, glad that her bow was ready even if she hadn't been prepared to fight. She let the arrow fly at the closest figure, a woman in rough leather armour, catching her high on the shoulder. The woman fell back, rolling off into the grass at the verge. Muireann pulled a second arrow, but her companions had already engaged the remaining swordsmen and even as good as her aim was she hesitated to shoot and risk hitting one of her friends. Reyleth swung his sword wide, pushing back the two men fighting him to buy time to cast a spell. This time it wasn't a simple defensive spell and as the men surged forward again, he hit them with what looked and sounded like a small burst of lightning, the energy crackling from his hands and lashing into their chests with a small clap of thunder. They both fell back writhing on the hard ground of the road, then lay still. Lee had already taken down two with her spear, injuring them badly enough that they gave up the fight and retreated towards a wooded area a dozen yards from the road – which was where Muireann realised they must have been lying in wait. Lee was fighting two more, but they were clearly reluctant to take on the selkie's wicked spear. Calla disarmed her opponent as Muireann watched and a second later Tash managed to do the same. Routed, the four who were still standing fled, leaving their fallen companions behind.

Muireann watched them go, following them with her bow but unwilling to shoot anyone in the back. Instead, she advanced slowly on the woman she'd hit earlier who was struggling to stand in spite of the arrow transfixing her shoulder and the pool of blood around her. Muireann shook her head to see it, knowing her arrow must have hit an artery and the woman would almost certainly die without help. The two men Rey had struck with his spell lay completely still.

Calla went over and nudged one of the men with her boot. 'It seems you are good for more than cooking and fashioning clothes after all, mage.'

'I'd expect more gratitude, Tinairi,' he snapped back.

Before Muireann could try to intervene between them Calla was laughing easily and slapping Reyleth on the shoulder. 'That was a compliment, mage, take it as it was intended. Fine work to bring them both down with that spell.'

Rey stared at her, brows furrowed, but apparently decided

she was being sincere. 'Then...thank you. It is a difficult spell but effective.'

'I was certainly impressed,' Tash said, smiling at his friend. 'How long will they be out?'

'Several hours at least,' Rey said, shrugging, but Muireann could see the slight smile on his lips and knew he appreciated the acknowledgement.

Calla walked over to join Muireann by the wounded woman, her face hardening. 'Why are you attacking us?'

The stranger looked up, defiant, and spat at the elf. Calla sidestepped it easily before going on. 'You're a mercenary, like me. A sell-sword. Why refuse to tell us who hired you or why? You gain nothing by it.'

The wounded woman's resolve wavered. 'You aren't a mercenary. You dress like a noble.'

'I'm no noble, just a merc who had a turn of good luck and spent it on good clothes and better food.' Calla stepped closer to the woman, holding her hands to each side non-threateningly. 'I can bind that wound up for you. Keep you from bleeding out. Just tell me why you did this.'

The woman looked from the two fallen men to the rest of Muireann's group, her whole demeanour drooping. 'I don't know his name. But he said you have something he needs. We were to take everything you have by any means necessary.'

Calla nodded, flashing Muireann a grim look, before moving to help the wounded woman. Muireann quickly joined her, working with Calla and Tash to get the arrow out and stop the bleeding as best they could. Without a healer she'd still not likely survive long but at least she wasn't in imminent danger of bleeding out and if she could find anyone sympathetic she might be able to ride a wagon to town and get real help.

Reyleth and Lee stood back and watched, Lee looking disapproving and Rey aloof. Muireann could guess easily enough that the selkie thought aiding their enemy was wasted effort and she knew Reyleth well enough to know that he wouldn't risk drawing Calla's attention and being asked for a healing spell; he was undoubtedly tired from the spell he'd already cast and unwilling to waste effort on a woman who had been trying to kill them.

They finished up, the road still miraculously deserted, and left the injured woman and the two still unconscious men, heading back on their way but now on alert. Without a word the group fell into the same habit they'd had in the mountains, walking single file with their weapons at the ready.

The rest of the day passed in uneventful silence.

* * *

They arrived in Little Ford just before sunset, having pushed to travel as fast as possible and skipping a stop for lunch. Calla notably relaxed as they entered the town, bigger and built up more compactly than Harven. Her eyes swept the road behind them one final time before she fully sheathed both her swords, gesturing for Muireann to put up the arrow she was holding.

'We should be safe enough here. Little Ford is a trade town, really almost a small city. Their security is well known, thorough and good quality – it has to be to keep the traders and merchants happy. This town is a hub of several main roads from the Midland Mountain pass, which of course leads to the mountain elf settlement of Ardescir and then on to Lord Arvain's stronghold and eventually Verell or the cities south of that area. North the roads go to either Harven or further east to Brellin and then Port Gray in the north, and south across the river; where we're going there's the road to Mistlen and two others to various larger towns or small cities.'

'So this area really is quite central then?' Tash said, looking around curiously as they walked through the streets. All the buildings here towered three or four storeys, and if this was a place Calla called a town, even a large one, Muireann was a bit afraid of what a city might be like. She'd never imagined a place even as big as this.

'It's one of the main trade towns and a major crossroads, yes,' Calla said. 'Because the bridge here is the only one that can handle heavy wagons for at least a hundred miles along the river. I think the next closest place to cross is in Sternbreg and they don't have a bridge but ferries. So people prefer this way and that's also why they pay the toll to use the bridge.'

'And no doubt the tolls are what keeps the town guard so attentive and the streets so clean,' Reyleth said dryly, obviously unimpressed by the looming buildings or bustling people all around them.

Calla laughed. 'Indeed. And why we have our choice of many fine inns rather than having to pick between one with good food or one with decent beds.'

'Good food and a decent bed?' Reyleth joked, for once matching Calla's mood. 'Such luxury! I don't know how I'll manage it.'

'Are all human towns this hectic?' Lee asked, staring around uncertainly. 'This is nothing like the places we've been before.'

'No, this is a trade town,' Calla said. 'They aren't quite like anything else.'

'Do you really think we can relax here?' Muireann asked, cutting into the banter to press a point she was concerned about. She felt too much like every other time they'd felt safe it had proved false.

Calla nodded. 'Yes, I really do. At least while we are here. Once we leave tomorrow, we will have to be on our guard again, more so than before.'

Calla glanced around the busy street. 'Let's go to the Golden Rose, it's the best inn I know of here. We can discuss this more after we're settled.'

'Over dinner,' Tash said, reminding everyone they had

walked all day and not eaten since breakfast.

Muireann's stomach rumbled in agreement. 'Fine. Lead on, Calla.'

The Golden Rose was by far the nicest place Muireann had ever been in and she marvelled at Calla's ability to keep taking her to places she was forced to say that about. Her and Lee's room was palatial compared to her small expectations, and the bed was so soft and tempting she was almost willing to skip dinner just to stay in it. Almost.

The common room wasn't any bigger than the usual run at least, which was reassuring, but it did have a bard in residence. He was human, perhaps a few years older than Muireann, tan with dark hair, and his sweet baritone voice filled the room. Muireann watched Calla eyeing him and tried not to smile, knowing that she'd undoubtedly share the dragon's story with him and most likely share his bed as well. Muireann could hardly blame her, though, he was handsome and had the charm of any bard.

She settled down into her seat at the table, between Lee and Reyleth and across from Calla and Tash. A moment after they were all seated their server arrived; he was one of the tree-folk and Muireann fought not to stare. She didn't want to be rude, but she'd never seen anyone like him before. He looked for all the world as if he were carved from polished beechwood, his hair like fine leaves, but he moved like flesh and blood. She was so flustered trying not to be awkward that she ordered beef stew automatically and then kicked herself for failing yet again to try anything more interesting. At least the mead they served there was delicious, tangy and with a faint hint of apple, so that she felt a bit adventurous despite the boring food. And the server didn't bat an eye when Lee ordered plain chicken with a bowl of salt, unlike most of the other places they'd stayed at.

Calla waited until they were all eating and the bard had taken a short break to revisit Muireann's question from earlier. 'So now we know that at least one of the groups that's apparently been following and harassing us, the Donlachian one, are hired mercenaries. Hired by who we still don't know.'

'But we know why,' Tash said, leaning forward. 'To steal something we're carrying.'

Muireann exchanged a worried look with Calla, who frowned and took a long drink from her cup. Lee spoke into the tense silence. 'Well they must be after the Dragon Stone, yes?'

Calla looked relieved and even Muireann relaxed, feeling foolish for assuming otherwise. Reyleth nodded. 'That seems the most likely, given that it's no secret we – Muireann that is, has the Stone and it's very valuable.'

'It's priceless,' Calla said dryly. 'So yes, I suppose we could say it's very valuable. But you're right, both of you. I wouldn't think anyone would try to steal such a thing, but to be fair all the others are held by noble families and kept in vaults or trotted out under heavy guard. I don't know what someone would really gain by stealing it, especially as the story of Muireann Dragonslayer spreads across the entire empire, but then again it is the only Dragon Stone anyone could hope to get their hands on.'

The others nodded, unhappy but satisfied by this explanation. Muireann wasn't sure she agreed but also couldn't think of any reasons why. She simply had a nebulous but unwavering feeling that the Dragon Stone wasn't the issue although she couldn't imagine what was since no one beside she and Calla knew about the green stone. Nonetheless, as the conversation drifted to other things she let it go, wanting her friends to enjoy themselves while they could. She was afraid that this pattern of days of quiet followed by an attack when it was least expected was to be their new reality, and it was a hard way to live.

That night Muireann lay curled in Lee's arms in the small bed they were renting, warm beneath the wolf fur and Lee's seal skin. With her passion spent Lee drifted off to sleep, but

Muireann lay awake staring into the darkness, worrying. Everyone, even Calla, felt like the Dragon Stone was the target but for some reason that seemed too easy to Muireann, too unlikely. Yet at the same time who could possibly know about the Aldovanan weapon? They had told no one and it had been lost with the dragon for millennia.

She worried at the problem until exhaustion finally dragged her into sleep, but could find no answers.

* * *

They travelled across the more settled lands towards Mistlen on their guard, wating for another attack, but the journey was almost anticlimactically quiet. There were points where Muireann felt like they were being followed, or thought she saw shadows lurking behind them, but they always melted away and nothing came of it, leaving her feeling tense and exhausted. During the day the hills and farmland rolled by and each night they found lodgings at an inn or tavern, the week of walking passing in a blur. As they set out the final morning towards Mistlen they were all starting to feel as if maybe the attacks were over, and they were free from pursuit.

Midmorning their peace was shattered when the now familiar cloaked figures appeared. This time at least they weren't trying to attack, at least not with swords. The dozen or so figures spread out loosely around them, one man stepping forward slightly towards Muireann and her friends, who were clustered together, weapons at the ready. The other traffic on the road gave the two groups a wide berth.

'We have decided to give you all a chance to redeem yourselves and stop risking your lives to protect the Evil One,' the man said, calmly. His voice was rich, the words rolling out across the open area. Muireann would have bet real gold that he was or had been a bard just by the way he spoke, commanding listeners to pay attention.

'Speak then if you intend to,' Calla said, with all the bored scorn that only an elf could pack into so few words. She held both her swords up and ready, eyeing the group around them.

The man hesitated slightly as if he hadn't expected Calla to speak, then recovered and resumed what Muireann realised must have been a prepared speech. 'You are innocent people, we understand that, and we don't wish to do you any harm. But you are sheltering, protecting someone who has transgressed against the proper order of this world. We are tasked by the greatest of goddesses herself with righting this wrong and avenging the sacrilege that has been done.'

The people arrayed around them muttered ominously, agreeing with the words. Calla's swords lowered slightly. 'You are speaking in riddles. If you mean to give us a message, then do so clearly or stop wasting our time.'

The man extended his hand, his finger pointing directly at Muireann. 'She must die. We will let you all leave freely if you stop protecting her.'

Muireann stared at the man in shock. Her friends looked from her to him then back again, baffled. Lee was the first to recover, bracing her spear and lowering her head belligerently. '*I* will die before I let that happen.'

'She must die!' one of the women yelled, her face twisted with utter fury. 'She is a blasphemer!'

'You're mad,' Tash yelled back, sword out and at the ready. He was eyeing the strangers uneasily, watching as they became more agitated.

'You are aiding a force of great evil!' one of the other cloaked figures yelled, his face as angry as the woman's. 'She murdered the red dragon! She has destroyed that which should not be destroyed!'

Muireann felt as if her whole body had been doused with cold water at his words, her arms dropping. All of her own guilt over what she'd done surged up and for an instant she almost threw herself forward, ready to face the judgement these people were threatening. Then Reyleth was stepping in front of her, his hands moving to call his magic, prepared to attack.

Prepared to defend her.

The man had watched the yelling match calmly but seeing Rey moving forward he held up a single hand. The group immediately fell deathly silent. His eyes fixed on Muireann then her friends, one by one. 'You have been warned. You won't be warned again.'

With that he and the rest of the cloaked group melted back into the fields they'd appeared from. Muireann stood and watched them go, still too stunned to react to any of what had just happened.

When it was clear the group had truly gone Calla and Tash sheathed their swords, Rey relaxed, the subtle magic he'd prepared slipping away, and Lee set the butt of her spear to the earth. Muireann still stood with her bow held slack in one hand, arrow pointed to the ground.

Calla turned and seeing Muireann's face, winced. 'This isn't your fault, Muiri.'

'It pretty clearly is,' Muireann said, still staring into the distance.

'No, it most certainly is not,' Reyleth snapped. 'Those people are Arvethri, dragon worshippers. They mistake the symbols of Erla for the goddess herself and worship the symbol instead of the source. *That* is blasphemy.'

Muireann shifted her shocked gaze to Reyleth, caught off guard by his vehemence, before remembering that Erla was not only the goddess particularly worshipped by elves but also of mages in general, meaning he – as an elf and a mage – probably considered her his main deity. Most people honoured all seven gods equally, but there were those who had special patron deities or those beings who felt strongly connected to a certain deity. Muireann herself wasn't especially devout, and while she acknowledged the gods in a general way she didn't have a particular one she looked to nor did she give extra attention to Calleshen as the god of humanity. It was obvious, though, that Reyleth felt very strongly about the group's uncommon obsession with the dragons, one of the main symbols of Erla.

'They're cultists then,' Calla said, breaking the tense silence that had followed Rey's outburst. 'That explains a lot.'

'I'm sorry,' Muireann said, looking down at the ground, consumed by shame. 'This is all my fault. I've put everyone in terrible danger.'

The other four all talked over each other, trying to contradict her. Finally, Calla spoke loudly enough to silence the rest. 'We are causing a scene, let's move off the road to continue this discussion.'

They all glanced around and quickly realised that indeed the other traffic on the road, sparse as it was, was slowing and watching them. Muireann flushed at the thought and moved off into the open field nearby, the others trailing around her. Lee pulled Muireann into a one-armed hug, leaning her head against the human woman's shoulder. When they were somewhere at least marginally more private Calla continued. 'Muireann this isn't your fault. Those people have no right to act as judge and executioner because you killed a dragon.'

'Don't they?' Muireann shot back. 'They are right that I killed something that wasn't meant to be killed—'

'And if Erla has a problem with it then she herself will set it right,' Calla cut in ruthlessly. 'She could have saved the dragon. She could have revived it, or sent your shot astray or, or made a new dragon, or whatever else it is that goddesses have the power to do. I don't know. But I don't believe that she'd send a bunch of people reviled across all the kingdoms for their perversion of religion after you. This is some bizarre obsessive quest they have set themselves.'

'It's still putting you in danger,' Muireann insisted, stepping away from the others. 'Just like the mercenaries after us are.'

Calla sighed and rubbed a hand across her eyes. 'I'm choosing to be here with you and my job has always meant danger, I don't fear it or blame good people for being targets of bad. Besides, while we think we may have some answers we still don't know for certain that those mercenaries are after you specifically or after the Dragon Stone. And if it comes to it, we could as easily be attacked by highwaymen or robbers just because we look prosperous or they are desperate. We could any of us become the target of someone with a grudge.'

'Calla is right,' Tash said. 'I agreed to go with you as a guard and while I consider us all friends as well now I knew when I joined that there could be danger. Muireann, you warned me yourself it was likely. I'm not afraid to fight for you or any of you.'

'I know what I chose,' Reyleth said simply, not elaborating.

'And, if we are being fully honest,' Calla said slowly. 'You aren't the only one of us with a past that might show back up to put us in danger.'

'It could have been because of me,' Lee blurted out suddenly, causing everyone to turn and stare at her.

'Because of you?' Tash said.

'I was worried they could be chasing me,' Lee admitted, refusing to meet Muireann's eyes.

'Why would anyone be chasing you, Lee?' Calla asked when Muireann couldn't force the question out.

'When Muireann found me,' the selkie said slowly, 'I had come on land because I wanted to see what life is like here, that's true but...my family knew what I wanted to do, and they were against it. They said it was too dangerous. And more that it was wrong for one of the seal-folk to want to live on land. They were very adamant about it and when I said I would go anyway, they...my parents...swore they'd never let me go. That they'd do whatever it took to keep me safe, even if it meant keeping me under guard until I came to my senses.'

'So, you ran away,' Tash said, looking sympathetic.

Lee nodded, her eyes still downcast. Muireann moved to her side and wrapped her up in a fierce embrace. 'Oh, Lee, I'm so sorry that happened to you.'

'You aren't angry with me? For putting you all in danger?'

'We don't know that you did, but even if it's true, it isn't your fault,' Muireann soothed, rubbing the other woman's back. 'You deserve to find happiness even if your family doesn't understand your choices.'

Lee met Muireann's eyes and smiled, the expression tentative but hopeful.

'We don't know for certain that anyone is after Lee or that the selkies would have sent people this far inland for her,' Calla said, frowning.

'We don't but now we can be prepared should that become an issue,' Muireann said. She took a slow step away from Lee. 'I think Calla that we should come clean about everything, with everyone.'

'What does that mean?' Lee said, while Reyleth shot her a worried look.

'They might be after me,' Calla admitted.

'Why?' Muireann said, having been prepared to tell everyone about the green crystal and caught totally off guard by Calla's words.

Calla made a face, looking anywhere but at Muireann. Finally. 'I understand exactly what Lee is talking about, what it feels like to not fit in to the world you were born in...My father is Cylestiallin. I'm the eldest daughter.'

'You're...' Muireann stammered, more flustered than she could ever remember being. 'You're a princess?'

'She's the heir to the High Elven Empire,' Reyleth snapped, his anger ill-concealed. 'Which means her real name is

Cylestiallinia the Second.'

Calla grimaced, physically pulling back from the name. 'I'm right here, you don't need to talk to me like I'm not. And that isn't my name. That's the thing my parents called me, after my father, but it was never me. All of that life was never me; it was just a beautiful cage and I flew from it the first chance I had.'

'Your family is looking for you still,' Reyleth said, relenting and speaking to Calla but obviously still angry.

'Hunting me still, you mean,' she shot back. 'I know. I've managed to dodge bounty hunters and royal guard for, well, probably longer than you've been alive. I'm well aware they are still relentlessly trying to catch me.'

'Calla, you have a right to live your own life, just like Lee,' Muireann said, then, with less vehemence. 'I just don't understand why you didn't tell me this, given everything else. You should know you can trust me with anything at this point.'

The high elf grimaced again, turning pleading eyes to her friend. 'I wasn't trying to deceive you Muiri, truly. Please believe me. It was just too great a risk.'

'I do believe you,' Muireann said. 'And I'm not angry at you. I'm more...sad...that you have carried this secret so long without anyone you can trust.'

'I'm trusting you all now,' Calla said, her eyes sweeping the group. 'As the mage will no doubt be quick enough to tell you there's a substantial reward on my head.'

'For your safe return is how the posters and leaflets phrase it,' Reyleth said, still angry.

'I don't want to return safely or otherwise, ever,' Calla said. 'Why do you think I've gone to such trouble to stay free of them? To work a job, they'd never suspect I'd do, to always keep travelling, to colour my hair?'

'You colour your hair?' Lee asked, looking intrigued at the possibility.

'Yes, it's naturally a dark red,' Calla said, yanking on a strand of her hair. 'Which is a rare colour among my people, but scarlet is very common. So, I lighten it.'

'Alright,' Muireann cut in, rubbing her temples. 'Let's focus. So, some people may be after Lee, and there's a reward for returning Calla unwillingly to Gold Spire. Obviously, there's also at least one group that's after me personally for killing the dragon, and a group of mercenaries that may or may not still be after us to steal something we have.'

'That dragon cult may be the most dangerous,' Reyleth said grimly. 'The others may cause us harm, but their ultimate goal is to take someone or something back with them. They aren't trying to kill us all even if they are willing to if they must. Those cultists, though, mean Muireann's death, and I have no doubt they will kill all of us to achieve it, without hesitating.'

'Fortunate for us they aren't very good fighters,' Calla said, her tone flippant as usual.

'Calla, I don't care how bad they are with swords,' Muireann snapped. 'I don't want any of you hurt for my sake.'

'Well, I'm not going to stand by and see you killed by some dragon worshippers with anger issues,' Calla snapped back.

'You don't owe me protection just because I saved you from the dragon,' Muireann said, knowing it sounded mean but genuinely afraid for all of her friends.

Calla pulled Muireann into a loose embrace. 'I'm not doing it because of that. You're my friend, Muiri, the best friend I've had in a very long time. I will not stand by and see you hurt when I can stop it.'

Reyleth put his hand on Muireann's shoulder. 'I will not abandon you, Lennath, not for anything. If you had killed the emperor himself, I would still stand by you.'

She wanted to roll her eyes at the sheer hyperbole of it, but his words were so sincerely spoken that she couldn't. Lee reached out as well, on her other side. 'I don't pretend to understand all of this, or why anyone would worship a dragon or seek to avenge its death, but you are my wife and a very good wife to me. I will stand by you and protect you as you do for me.'

She smiled at the selkie. 'And I will stand by you. No one is taking you anywhere, including the sea, if you don't want to go there.'

'For my part,' Tash said. 'I will stand with you all because you are my friends, and because I believe you are in the right with this. Muireann, you did an amazing thing by killing that dragon. An impossible thing. Heroes across the ages have aspired to it and I have never heard it spoken of as wrong or evil. No human has the right to decide to judge you for the gods and harm you in their names. That way lies a terrible precedent for all to start killing in the name of what they think the gods want. Calla, if you don't want to rule then you shouldn't. I think for myself you would make a good empress but if I have learned one thing from Muireann's history lessons it's that politics and government are complex and those not suited for it always cause problems for everyone, high and low. If you feel you aren't suited for it, I respect your judgement. And Lee, you should be free to choose your own path in life, as should we all.'

Muireann pulled back from the others, smiling proudly at Tash. 'Very well said indeed. You will make a fine knight one day, Tash.'

'Indeed, a very fine speech,' Calla agreed. 'And now I think we need to get moving again so we can reach the city before nightfall. We will be safer there than on the road.'

'Calla,' Muireann said, shaking her head slightly. 'We have to tell them.'

Calla frowned. 'We agreed—'

'I know what we agreed, but this is all getting too dangerous. Even if nothing that's going on is because of that, if anything happens, they all need to know so it can be protected.'

'What are you talking about?' Tash said, looking from one woman to the other.

'This is what you didn't want to discuss before, isn't it?' Rey said, his eyes searching Muireann's face. 'If it was too dangerous then it may be even more dangerous now.'

'Muireann, we can't,' Calla said.

She shook her head, her fingers clutching the lump in her belt pouch. 'We must.'

Calla opened her mouth to argue then stopped. Finally, she nodded. 'Alright. I don't think it's wise, but alright. Let's share this last secret and then there will be no secrets between any of us.'

The other three all turned expectant faces to Muireann, who took a long deep breath. 'When I killed the dragon, and we, Calla and I, were searching the cave afterwards we found something else. Something dangerous. An old weapon from the First Age, something that has the power to bring almost unimaginable destruction at the will of whoever wields it.'

Reyleth gasped. 'You found the Basglassin? The Green Death?'

Calla and Muireann both gaped at him in open-mouthed shock. Muireann finally managed to stutter. 'How…how do you know about it? What it is?'

Reyleth looked as frightened as she'd ever seen him, reaching up to run a hand over his face. 'I never dreamed… it's so obvious now…asking about the Aldovanan, their magic, enchantments…the dragon's cave…the *red* dragon…'

'Reyleth,' she said, grabbing his arm and trying to get him to meet her eyes. 'How do you know its name? What do you know about it?'

She watched him struggle to steady himself before answering. 'The Green Death and Olcanac, the mage who created and wielded it, are mentioned in several texts. His death is considered one of the triggering events that led to the final fall of the Aldovanan. His death trying to use the stone against the red dragon, Murjergalan, is recorded in the annals and also in several other accounts.'

'Yes, I knew that was the dragon's name, or I figured it out afterwards,' Muireann said, frowning. 'I had read about it in a children's book, a very old one. I should have thought to ask you about the dragon by name. But I was trying to be so careful and circumspect so you wouldn't guess what we had found.'

'It's so obvious now that of course that's the dragon you killed,' he said, grimacing. 'I don't know how I didn't put the pieces together, just from that. And there was speculation in some of the older texts that the weapon had survived, although of course others thought it had been destroyed because dragon fire is magical fire and so able to destroy even that which should be indestructible.'

'It wasn't destroyed,' Muireann confirmed. 'The dragon had added the stone to its hoard and kept it all these millennia. We found it and when I touched it, I had a...vision, I suppose we'd say. A vision of what the stone can do. It was horrific, worse than anything I could ever put into words. I tried to write it in the journal I have for my notes about the dragon, but I just couldn't capture what I saw without making it seem trite. It was...just death. So much death.'

'We took it, safely,' Calla said. 'And are on a mission – a quest – to find some way to render it safe or destroy it.'

'A truly noble quest,' Tash murmured.

'If it couldn't be destroyed by dragon fire, I don't know what it would take,' Reyleth whispered, still looking shocked.

'You said you'd read about it,' Muireann pressed. 'That's what we need. Those books, some place to start to study the stone and learn how to unmake it. I'm so sorry, Reyleth, I should have trusted you with this and you could have been helping us from the start.'

'Don't apologise,' he said, sounding stronger. 'I understand, better than you might think, why you didn't. I almost wish I didn't know the truth even now, to carry such a thing is to be tempted to use it.'

'Absolutely not,' Muireann shuddered.

'Most people would be,' he said.

'We aren't most people,' Calla said with her usual humour. 'We want only to destroy it. But until we can find out how we have to keep it safe.'

'Why not hide it?' Lee said, biting her lip.

'It would be too dangerous, there's too much risk it would be found by chance,' Muireann said.

'On land perhaps, but I could hide it for you in the ocean.'

'You could but there's people in the ocean as well and it isn't only humans that can wield this weapon,' Calla said. 'If it was found by another of the seal-folk or one of the ocean-folk the result would be the same.'

'She's right,' Muireann agreed. 'The only way to keep it safe for now is to keep it and protect it. At least no one else knows we have it.'

'I wouldn't be so certain of that,' Reyleth said grimly. 'If I were a wagering man I would say the Green Death is what those mercenaries are seeking.'

'That's a huge risk for whoever hired them, that they wouldn't find it and keep it themselves,' Calla pointed out.

'We have no idea what exactly he told them,' Rey said. 'He could have said what we had was dangerous or given them strict orders to bring our possessions back to him untouched.'

'How would he even know it existed, never mind that we have it?' Muireann said.

'I'd guess that like myself he's studied the old texts and saw the speculation that it still existed, possibly with the dragon. When word got out that the dragon was dead, he may have gone and sought it himself, and when he found it gone, perhaps he assumed you had taken it.'

'Why assume that and not that it was never there at all?' Muireann said, frustrated.

'Why give up finding it without being certain you hadn't taken it unwittingly?' he said.

'It doesn't matter,' Calla said, shaking her head. 'Not really. But we must assume that is what the mercenaries are after and that they know we have it or at least strongly suspect.'

'They don't know which one of us, though,' Muireann said, locking eyes with Calla.

'No, and that secret we will keep,' Calla said. 'It is the only small advantage we have now. If things go truly badly, we will split up, you and I, Muireann, and hope that gives us a better chance.'

'It hasn't come to that yet,' Lee said.

'No and if fortune favours us, it never will,' Calla said. 'But we must be prepared.'

Silence fell over the group, only the sounds of the wagons rolling by on the road breaking it. Finally, Tash asked, 'Is there anything else to be said?'

'No,' Muireann said, shifting her pack higher on her shoulders. 'Let's get moving.'

'Yes,' Lee agreed, starting towards the road. 'And we'll go on as we have been, watching each other's backs.'

'Except now we know the fate of the very world depends on it,' Reyleth said.

They were all lost in their own worries as they re-joined the small amount of traffic on the road. Muireann was glad that they had come clean with the things they had been keeping secret, but she wasn't sure if it was better or worse to know that the others might also have people pursuing them, and that the existence of the stone might not be a secret any longer.

What she did know for certain was that anyone who would hire mercenaries to murder them for the green crystal would use it for the worst possible things, and that could not be allowed to happen.

* * *

As the day wore on and they drew closer to the city Calla was getting more tense rather than less. Finally she said, 'Alright my friends, I know things have been quiet since this morning but if we are going to be ambushed anywhere it will be in the next mile or so.'

'Why?' Tash asked, drawing his sword.

'I thought we were nearly at the city?' said Lee.

'We are,' Calla said, answering Lee first, then to Tash. 'The road here is about to pass within a few hundred feet of a sheer drop-off. The other side is fairly heavy forest for this area, some kind of hunting reserve for the nobility as I understand it. If it were me planning an ambush that's where I would do it because it will be easy to cut off escape.'

'Is there no other way to reach the city?' Reyleth asked, his hands preparing to spell cast. The whole group was on edge now, as if they expected to be set upon any second.

Calla frowned and shook her head. 'None that wouldn't be worse in different ways. We can backtrack and go down the farmers' path to the lowlands, at the bottom of the cliff we're approaching, but we'll be vulnerable going down and then back up again nearer the city, especially if they have acquired archers. And we could bear west into the woods, but it is much easier to set up an ambush anywhere in there than on the road proper.'

'Our best bet is to continue forward and brace for a possible attack through the area by the cliff?' Muireann said, her bow at the ready.

Calla sighed but nodded. 'If we are lucky we will pass unhindered and all this worry will be for nothing. But in this case, I think it's better to be prepared.'

'Let's keep moving then,' Reyleth said, 'and get this over with.'

They each nodded, their movements sharp, weapons at the ready, then continued down the road. At first things were quiet and normal; an occasional wagon or cart would rumble by, or a rider on a horse, with other foot traffic moving either faster or slower than their own group. The mercenaries travelling with the wagons would always nod curtly to Calla, who would nod back, Tash hastily following suit.

As Calla had predicted within about ten minutes the ground to their left suddenly plummeted down and the trees on their right grew thicker and heavier, a compact wall of oak, beech and ash. The road passed an equal space between these two features, dozens of yards, but Muireann could see a place ahead where things narrowed, the space to each side reduced by half for perhaps a hundred feet. She shifted her bow nervously, knowing that would be the place for trouble if it was going to happen. She suspected this was probably a notorious spot for highwaymen and such, as it was clearly an ideal place to attack anyone on the road.

Even though she was prepared for it, the actual attack took Muireann by surprise. They were in the middle of the narrow stretch of road when what seemed like a flood of people charged from the trees. The other travellers on the road screamed and fled pell-mell, but Muireann and her friends were quickly and efficiently cut off in every direction except the cliffside.

They drew together into a tight group, backs to each other, as the strangers came at them from everywhere. Muireann raised her bow and fired, taking down one of the cloaked figures, and then her mind registered the cloaks which had been the trademark all along of the dragon cultists. Her heart sank.

They tried to stay together but as soon as the fighting started in earnest it became impossible. This time the cultists had a mage of their own and he and Reyleth ended up separated off as they duelled, everyone moving away to avoid being hit by any stray spells. Muireann found herself being pushed back off the road as she dodged swords and fists. She fired several more arrows but there were so many people everywhere, moving, fighting, that she wasn't even sure she'd hit anyone, and she started to fear hitting one of her friends in the melee.

She dodged another sword strike and saw a hand coming at her face. Without thinking she threw her arm up, the bow catching the man in the face. His hood was knocked down and she had a moment to look at his face, perhaps in his thirties, pale, brown hair, a thin moustache, a trickle of blood at his temple where she'd struck him, and then his hands were closing around the bow above and below her own hands. She dropped the arrow she'd been trying to draw, grabbing the shaft of the bow with both hands to keep him from pulling it away from her. The two wrestled that way, amid the screaming swirling mass of the fight, Muireann slowly being forced to step back again and again to keep her balance. She had lost track of the others in the swirl of bodies.

She realised, finally, that he wasn't trying to take the bow from her. He was trying to force her back to the edge of the cliff and using the bow to do it. With dawning horror, she understood – he meant to throw her from the cliff. It was a hundred feet or more to the rocky bottom. No one could survive such a fall. She looked past him and saw Lee fighting fiercely with her spear against a half dozen cultists. Calla and Tash were using their swords to good effect, but the numbers were against them. Reyleth was still locked in battle with the other mage, coloured flames swirling around the two of them. She didn't dare call out for help and distract any of her friends, not when that distraction could get someone killed.

She grappled with the man, fighting desperately not to have the bow ripped from her hands; it would only give him an easy way to knock her senseless and accomplish his goal more easily. Her feet slid across the loose ground as he used the bow to push her back towards the cliff's edge. She focused all of her energy on bracing herself against him, but he was stronger than she was, and she kept sliding inexorably back. She heard yelling, heard her name although she wasn't sure who was calling it.

'We'll both go over!' she said, desperately trying to gain even an inch of solid ground.

'Good!' he shrieked, his eyes wild. 'I will take you with me to Erla's judgement!'

'Please!' she begged, knowing there was no pity in him. 'Don't do this.'

'I know that I will be judged a loyal servant,' he said, his face almost ecstatic now as he forced her back the final small space. 'I will be a hero for ending you!'

And then she was going over, still clutching the bow, the final shove from the man sending them both flying out into empty air. She kicked away from him, but there was no stopping the fall. Air rushed past her body, bitterly cold, and in the few seconds as she fell, she thought how unfair it was that she'd finally found some happiness, a reason to want to live again, only to have it end like this.

Then she hit the ground. There was a flash of pain and a moment when everything went dark, then a jarring moment when her whole world seemed to slip from alignment before righting itself. She lay on the cold ground, waiting for something to happen. Waiting for the world to fade perhaps, or the shock to wear off and the pain to start. But as she lay there and waited, she slowly started to realise that none of that was happening. She shivered eventually from the cold, became aware of various rocks and debris beneath her. But there was no pain.

Slowly she wiggled her toes and fingers, still waiting for the expected agony. Then she grew bolder and moved her legs, her arms, finally opening her eyes. Miraculously her glasses had stayed on her face throughout the fall and landing, and thanks to Rey's spell were completely undamaged. The sky above her was the same cloud drifted blue it had been before, the cliff a wall of stone looming over her.

She sat up. She had landed perhaps a dozen yards from the cliff base, on a stretch of rough rocky ground. Several feet to her left lay the broken body of the cultist who had pushed her from the cliff, clearly and unequivocally dead. Baffled Muireann looked down at herself. Her tunic was torn in several places, probably ruined, and her pants were in a similar condition. The wolf cloak was untouched, probably also thanks to Rey's magic. She quickly felt for her belt pouch, but the green stone remained safe despite everything. Her quiver was still at her hip but most of the arrows were gone; she noticed several of them scattered around the ground near her. Her bow was also gone but when she finally pushed to her feet, she saw it broken a few yards away. Tears sprang to her eyes at the sight of that, the bow she'd had since Gorseview, which she'd practised on until it felt like an extension of herself, the bow she'd killed a dragon with, in pieces across the stony ground.

She went to her knees next to it, crying as she gathered those pieces, feeling as if she'd lost a piece of herself.

Muireann had no idea how long she crouched like that, cradling the broken bow – long enough for the tears to stop and dry on her cheeks – but eventually she heard voices and turned to see her friends stumbling as quickly as possible down a trail that led from above. She hadn't even noticed it, barely a deer path among the rocks. It was steep but it was passable although Tash was trailing behind the others, moving slowly and with obvious fear, his hands flat to the rock wall.

She felt a surge of deep gratitude that they'd come for her, even though they surely believed she was dead.

Muireann stood up and walked towards the base of the cliff where the path met the ground. While the fall didn't seem to have harmed her, sitting on the cold ground had the same effect as it always would have, leaving her feeling stiff and a bit numb. The feeling faded quickly as she moved.

Calla was in the front, Reyleth slightly behind her and Lee a bit further back; the selkie might be agile in the water and a good hunter, but she was not as light on her feet in such treacherous conditions as the elves were. As soon as they reached the bottom Rey surged past Calla, all but knocking her aside, and ran to Muireann, pulling her into his arms. He kissed her far more passionately than she would have expected of him in front of other people, then pulled back enough to whisper. 'I thought you'd been killed.'

'You're crying,' she said softly, shocked to see the tears on his face. She reached up to wipe them away and he grabbed her fingers and kissed those as well. A moment later Calla was by her side, looking as if she were seeing a ghost, and then Lee was flinging herself at Muireann as well so that she was held firmly between both her lovers. Lee kissed her as Reyleth had, then buried her head against Muireann's shoulder and sobbed. She stroked each of their backs helplessly, thoroughly nonplussed by the crying.

'How are you alright?' Calla whispered, walking a full circle around Muireann.

'I don't know,' she said. Tash joined them, looking as unsettled as Calla, tears streaking his cheeks too.

Muireann carefully separated herself from the tangle of Rey's and Lee's arms, stepping back and then holding her hands out and spinning in a circle. 'I don't know how but I'm fine. Not a scratch. My clothes are ruined, though.'

They all stared at her in open-mouthed shock. Finally, hesitantly, Rey reached out again, gently pulling at the rips in her tunic. He muttered to himself. 'There isn't even much blood.'

'What does this mean?' Tash asked, his eyes darting from one person to the next. 'What does this *mean*? No one could survive that fall, it's impossible.'

'Are you all alright? What happened after...after I fell?'

Muireann said, still unsettled by the crying.

'They fled as soon as you went over,' Calla said bitterly. 'The cowards. All they wanted was what they did or thought they did. That must have been their plan all along. None of us were hurt.'

'How are you still alive?' Tash said, finally drawing close enough to reach out and touch her.

'I don't know,' she said again. 'I fell and when I struck the ground there was a moment of pain and then...I'm not sure. But I finally realised I wasn't hurt so I got up and then I saw you all coming down.'

'It's impossible,' Tash said again, still crying.

She looked at their faces, felt terrible that they were all so upset from watching her go over the cliff's edge and thinking she'd died. She looked down, the silence stretching into awkwardness, thinking of everything that had happened since the dragon. The attack where she'd thought her arm was cut but it hadn't seemed injured. The attack where she'd been struck on the head but wasn't hurt. The time she'd been knocked down and Lee had thought she'd seen Muireann stabbed but she'd been fine. She felt her stomach dropping at the implications.

She rolled up one of her ruined sleeves, pushing the fur cloak aside. Then she pulled the small knife at her waist, good for little more than use at meals, and stabbed it directly into her own arm. Or tried to. Before the others could more than gasp and start to cry out the blade had already slid across her skin and aside, despite her aiming for the centre of her forearm. She felt a small flash of pain and watched as the thin cut the knife left behind closed and disappeared as if it had never existed. A few drops of blood beading across her skin were the only indication anything had happened.

'What does this mean?' Tash said again, his voice hushed.

'I think Muireann may be immortal,' Reyleth said, his own words soft.

The words echoed in the silence anyway, or perhaps only in Muireann's heart. She knew, to her core, he was right, and she hated it as much as she was certain it was true. She looked away from them all, unable to bear meeting any of their eyes. 'I think we need to keep moving.'

And so, they did, turning and going slowly to the trail that led back up the cliff, no one speaking. There wasn't much to say.

Chapter 7

Mistlen

They arrived in Mistlen just after sunset, the entire group subdued and grim. Not even the marvel that was the capital city of Lanal, the kingdom Muireann had lived her whole life in, was enough to lift her spirits. She stared dully around at the towering buildings, the cobblestoned streets, the bustling crowds of people made up of nearly every sentient species in Tallan. Not even Reyleth's muttered complaints about how the city had changed, how much bigger it was got her attention. Not even the streetlights – poles along the edge of the street which held magical lights – or the apprentice mages who were going around setting the spells to light them, were enough to snap Muireann out of her daze, even though she'd never seen anything like them anywhere before. As if to echo her mood dark clouds were rolling in and blocking out the stars and rising moon.

Wordlessly Calla led them to an inn called the Blue Star, a multi-story building that sat near the city green and overlooked a large lake. Muireann didn't have the heart to tease the high elf about choosing what was obviously the most ostentatious and grand inn possible. Reyleth's words from earlier echoed in her head over and over, inescapable.

Calla paid for their rooms then led them all upstairs, the others following along like ducklings. Their rooms were all together at the end of the third-floor hallway, and when they reached them, Calla handed out the keys then said. 'Drop your things then meet up in my room.'

Muireann and Lee went into their shared room, Muireann dropping her pack on the floor then throwing her cloak on the bed. She was too upset, even still, to appreciate the absolutely gorgeous room although she noted it in a dull way. She doubted the nobles in Arvain's keep had such luxury. The room even had its own en suite bath, a large copper tub surrounded by a beautifully mosaic tiled floor. Looking away Muireann took the quiver from her belt and dropped it on the floor. Lee gave her a worried look, then crossed the room to take her hand, drawing her along to Calla's room.

Once they were all re-assembled, they stood awkwardly in the open space by the bed, waiting for someone to say something. Finally, Muireann blurted out. 'I broke my bow.'

Calla blinked at her slowly. 'I'll buy you a new one, Muiri.'

She wanted to say that it wouldn't be the same, but she didn't. Instead, she forced a thin smile and nodded slightly.

When she didn't say anything else Lee spoke up. 'Reyleth, you said she was immortal. That seems to be true, at least in that she can't be injured. But the real question is why?'

'I think that when Muireann killed the dragon, or more precisely the moment that it actually died, it was touching her,' Reyleth said, staring at the floor, unable to meet her eyes. 'You said the claw struck you and you passed out, yes?'

'Yes,' she admitted, trying not to think about it. 'But I don't know if that was when it died, I don't remember any of that part clearly.'

'I understand but nonetheless, I think that's what happened,' he said. 'It was touching you at the moment that it died and somehow its essence, its magic, was transferred into you.'

'I don't believe that,' Muireann said stubbornly. 'I'm not possessed by a dragon's spirit. I'm still myself.'

'True,' he agreed, the others looking on with obvious concern. 'But there's no other explanation for you surviving that fall. Not only surviving it but walking away completely unharmed. And then what you did to your arm…'

'No,' she said, shaking her head. 'Dragons are pure magic, certainly, but they are protected from injury by their scales, not their magic.'

'Their scales are the first line of defence,' Reyleth agreed, 'but not the only one. I have heard of those who tried to crush them in rockslides, used catapults, nets to drag them under the sea... and always the dragon survived unharmed. Uninjured as far as observers could tell. That's why it is so rare that they are killed and always under exceptional, even miraculous circumstances.'

'I killed one and it wasn't miraculous, nor did the dragon's magic protect it,' she insisted, refusing to mention the poison even though she realised that may have qualified as an exceptional circumstance. 'And I'm not full of some dragon's spirit. I can't breathe fire, or fly, I'm not impervious to magic—'

'You may be,' Reyleth said, frowning now. 'Not the first two, obviously, but impervious to magic...you might be. Dragons cannot be affected by most weapons nor by any magic we have now, so if it's true that you absorbed the dragon's protection against wounds then you may have that aspect of the dragon's power against magic as well. We'd have to test it.'

'How?' Lee asked, frowning.

'I could try to cast some simple, harmless enchantments on Muireann and see what happened. If they don't have any effect, we could work up to seeing if she truly seems impervious to magic.'

'You mean she might actually be magic-proof?' Calla breathed, sounding awed at the idea.

'No,' Muireann said, her voice cutting through the stunned silence. 'No, I don't want this. I don't want any of this.'

'Muireann,' Calla started to say, her voice unusually gentle, but the human woman wouldn't let her finish.

'No! This is...this is so unfair,' Muireann said, flinching away from her friends' worried looks.

'Most people would see immortality as a gift,' Tash said, his own voice conflicted.

'Most people don't have to live with it,' she shot back, feeling tears filling her eyes despite the anger in her voice. 'Look at me! I still can't see without my glasses. I'm not stronger, faster, I'm not any different than I was before, except apparently, I'm as hard to kill as a dragon now. Isn't that some irony?'

'Muireann,' Lee started, looking as upset as Muireann felt.

She shook her head. 'This isn't a gift, this is a punishment. For killing something that shouldn't be killed.'

'Muireann,' Reyleth tried to interject. She wouldn't hear it, though, not from anyone. Outside it began to rain, the sound loud on the roof and windows. She wondered when the storm had blown in.

'No,' she said. 'I can't talk about this right now. I don't want to even think about it. It's too immense. Just…just everyone leave me alone. We'll figure out what to do about the other problem in the morning. But I can't do this right now.'

She turned and fled without another word, seeking the only sanctuary that was available, her room across the hall.

No one followed her and she was grateful for that.

* * *

Later that night, after Muireann had missed dinner and spent far too long staring listlessly out at the rain, there was a knock at the door. Reyleth stood there uncertainly until she gestured him in.

'I wanted to check on you,' he said, reaching out awkwardly to set a hand on her shoulder as if he wasn't sure what else to do. 'To make sure you were alright. Everyone else is together in the common room, but I was worried that you still hadn't come down.'

'You've always known me well,' she said softly, then closed the distance between them, kissing him with as much passion as he had kissed her at the bottom of the cliff. She still wanted to be alone but she also wanted the comfort of physical intimacy, the two urges warring within her. After hours of her mind running in circles, she found that she didn't want to think for a while, not about anything vital. She just wanted to feel alive. He gave her what she needed and then the two sat together on the bed in that grand rented room, the fire crackling cheerfully in the hearth, the rain a softer sound against the windows and roof.

She curled up in his arms watching the rain, her heart full of too many things to name but glad that she wasn't alone. She was the one who had pushed everyone away but now the idea of being by herself seemed terrible. He stroked her back gently, sensitive to her mood and trying to give her the space she needed and the intimacy she was also craving.

Finally, she tried to breach the silence with a joke. 'Well, I guess our positions have reversed.'

He shifted next to her, his hand still tracing soothing patterns on her skin. 'How so?'

'You said that you wanted to be with me even though my life would be so short, but now I'm the one looking at facing an eternity of living where your life won't be as long.' She looked down, reaching out to take his other hand in hers. 'I don't think I like it.'

'It's an adjustment, Lennath, but I'll live a thousand years. We have plenty of time together.'

She smiled slightly, still looking down. 'That's how I felt before when it was me that was the short lived one. Being on this side feels very different.'

He sighed. 'It is a problem for many, many tomorrows from now. If you want to worry about this, worry about Lee. Selkies are not as long lived as elves, and you will have to say goodbye to her first.'

She almost moved away from him then, unsure if he meant that as a joke or was trying to get her to stop talking about his dying, a subject elves were notoriously not fond of. But she didn't move away, she snuggled closer, pressing into his warmth. 'I don't even know if I can have children now, but if we had a child and they were human we'd both have to watch them grow old and die.'

He sighed, pulling her closer. 'We may never have to face that fear, but we could as likely have a child and they could be born an elf.'

'I'd still have to watch them grow old and die,' she said softly. 'I'll have to watch you do that, you know.'

'You are talking about worries of things that haven't even happened yet and may never happen, or things that are a very long time off,' he said gently. 'I cannot tell you that you won't have to see people you care about die, you know that, even were you mortal still that would be true. But you don't have to mourn your friends while they still live. You don't have to mourn me when I'm right here.'

'Will I forget them?' she said, her voice so soft it was barely a whisper.

'Who? Lee and—'

'No,' she cut him off, turning to bury her face against his chest. 'My children. My children with Edren. Will I forget them? I'm only 38, I can't imagine a hundred years from now or a thousand or an age. It's so very long...I'm afraid I'll forget about them and that scares me more than anything.'

'Oh Muireann,' he murmured, kissing her temple then pulling her closer. 'I can't tell you for certain that you won't. I can't tell you that you won't forget all of us eventually. But I believe that as long as you think of those you've lost regularly you will remember some part of them. Perhaps not the details, those fade with time, but the heart of them you'll remember.'

She sniffled slightly, fighting tears. He stroked her hair, the silence stretching between them until he said. 'Perhaps you could write about them, your children, the way you did about the red dragon. Record as much as you can remember now, so that you can always read it when you feel like they are slipping away.'

Muireann straightened, pulling away from him, unable to hide her excitement. 'Yes! I can make a memory book. What a brilliant idea. I can write about my children and about Lee and you and everyone. And you can enchant it for me, can't you? Like my glasses so that it can't be ruined?'

He hesitated slightly at the request but quickly relented. 'If it would please you, yes. I can find a way to do that.'

'It would, yes, please,' she said, stumbling over her words. Even the small hope he was offering soothed her in the face of an eternity without everyone she loved.

Lee slipped quietly into the room, her eyes on Muireann's face. She didn't speak but the question in her eyes was enough. Muireann held her arms out to the selkie, wrapping her into a tight embrace as Rey edged back slightly. She suspected the elf would probably have left if he could have, but since he was up against the wall there wasn't any way for him to leave that wouldn't be more awkward than staying. She was selfishly glad about it; she knew the two only tolerated each other for her sake but at the moment she needed them both with her.

* * *

When she had regained some of her equilibrium she left, with Rey now sleeping in her bed and Lee reading by the fireplace, to go find Calla. It was the high elf who found her, though, as she was peering around the common room – much larger and fuller than any of the others they'd stayed in. Calla came up behind her, arm in arm with a stranger who Muireann would have bet her Dragon Stone was nobility.

The high elf turned to the man and smiled, leaning over to kiss him before patting his ass and telling him to go wait for her at their table. To Muireann's surprise he smiled back and went without complaint at being so summarily dismissed. She couldn't resist saying, 'You definitely have a certain type you prefer, don't you?'

Still smiling Calla took Muireann's elbow and guided her out of a side door. 'I know what I like and how to find it. And you can hardly talk as it's pretty clear what your type is.'

Muireann shook her head. 'I don't know what you mean. Reyleth and Lee are very different people.'

'Mmmhmm,' the high elf snickered, 'if you say so, my clearly-water-obsessed-friend.'

'Anyway, that's not what I wanted to talk to you about,' Muireann said, shaking her head slightly. 'Walk with me for a minute.'

Calla followed the human woman out into the night silently, the two walking under the narrow overhang that edged the building to keep clear of the rain. Once they were away from the crowd enough that they couldn't be easily overheard, Calla stopped.

'How are you doing, Muiri?' she asked, resting one hand on Muireann's shoulder.

'Honestly, I don't know. I'm angry more than anything but I also feel as if this is a punishment for what I did and I deserve it.'

'Most people would see this as a gift,' the high elf pointed out gently, repeating what had been said earlier.

'Most people are fools,' Muireann shot back, feeling some of that anger bubbling near the surface. She fought it back and took a long steadying breath. 'But that isn't why I wanted to talk to you either.'

'At some point, my friend, you do need to talk about this, about how you're feeling.'

'I know that,' Muireann said, wincing at the thought. 'But not now.'

She reached into her belt pouch and took out the battered compact that held the Aldovanan weapon. 'You need to be the one to carry this now.'

Calla took it with obvious reluctance, slipping it into her own belt pouch. 'Why?'

'Because, firstly, the ones who are hunting us to get it have almost certainly figured out I'm the one carrying it. I know we thought that they might be focusing on me when they attack because I'm the weakest fighter or the one who was alone but the more I've thought about it the more I think it's because they know I have it. Maybe because I have the Dragon Stone and so they assume I must have the other as well.' She paused to take another deep breath. 'And I'm fine with bearing that risk – honestly I feel terrible passing it off to you – but secondly and more importantly, it's too dangerous for me to have that stone now.'

'Why?' Calla asked again, glancing around to be sure no one was eavesdropping.

'Calla, if Reyleth is right, and I believe he is, and I'm basically immortal now the way the dragons are then the absolute worst-case scenario would be me touching that stone again and being seduced by its power. I could have been last time and if it weren't for you, I might have been. Bad enough to have that happen to anyone but a human or elf can be killed, if necessary, no matter how hard the stone would make doing that. If I can't be killed and I get that stone, it would take the gods themselves to stop me. And we all know how disinclined the gods seem to be to interfere with anything directly. I can't live with that risk.'

Calla nodded, as solemn as Muireann had ever seen her. 'But the dragon was exempt from the crystal's influence, if everything Reyleth suggested is true then maybe you will be as well.'

Muireann shook her head. 'The risk is too great. I was already influenced by it once even after killing the dragon. We cannot take that chance.'

Calla looked down, her hand tracing the shapes in her belt

pouch. 'And if I am corrupted by it, you would be the only one who could stop me.'

Muireann pulled the elf into a loose hug. 'It won't come to that.'

'If it did—'

'If it did, I'd do what I had to, but it won't. I've been carrying it safely all this time. As long as it's contained, you'll be fine as well.'

Calla sighed, returning the embrace for a moment before pulling back. 'Alright. That does make sense.'

'One more thing,' Muireann said, bracing herself. 'I want to tell you how I killed the dragon, how I really did it. But you have to swear to me – swear to me, Calla, on your life – that you won't tell anyone else or try it on another dragon.'

'So, you didn't kill it with an arrow?' the elf said, looking interested.

'I did, but there was more to it than that. Promise me.'

'I promise I won't repeat it.'

'Or use what I tell you except against me if you must.'

'Muiri!'

'Promise. Me.'

Calla glared at her friend. 'This is why you're bringing this to me and not Reyleth, isn't it?'

Muireann nodded. 'I can't be sure he'd do it if he had to. The same with Lee. They'd let emotions cloud things, I think. I trust you to do what has to be done, if it comes to that.'

'That's a lot for me to live with.'

'I know. I'm sorry,' Muireann said, meaning it. 'But someone needs to know, someone I trust not to misuse the information.'

'You trust me that much?'

'With my life and my death,' Muireann said, her voice low.

'Then I promise I will prove worthy of your trust,' Calla said solemnly, then pulled the other woman into a tight hug. 'But gods grant that I never have to.'

Muireann leaned close against her friend's shoulder, whispering into her ear and hoping anyone who saw them would misread the situation. When she'd told Calla everything she finally pulled away, trembling. 'Alright. I've said my piece. You go and find that man and have your way with him.'

Calla smiled, although it didn't quite reach her eyes. 'I will very thoroughly do so, don't worry. And you go and find what joy you can with your loves.'

Muireann nodded, not bothering to share how she'd already spent her evening. 'I will. We have to find joy when we can, don't we?'

Now the smile did reach the high elf's eyes. 'We do indeed, my friend, unless things start chafing then we need to take a break.'

Muireann was surprised into a laugh, even knowing Calla's bawdy sense of humour she somehow hadn't expected that. 'Goodnight, Calla.'

'Goodnight, Muiri.'

Muireann jogged up the stairs to her room, feeling more cheerful than she had all day.

* * *

The next morning, after she'd found quite a bit of joy with Lee so that they missed breakfast, she asked the selkie to accompany her to the library to do her research, offering to buy her breakfast on the way to make up for delaying her in the morning. Not that Lee had complained about the delay. The other three had their own things to attend to that day: Reyleth was going with Calla into the elven section of the city to hunt for some obscure books he thought could be helpful – and which Calla could afford to buy where he never could – and Tash had volunteered to guard their rooms and keep an eye out for anyone asking around about them.

After stopping to eat at a street stand Muireann and Lee moved deeper into the city, following a map Muireann had of Mistlen that looked like it should lead them easily to the library, one of the treasures of the city, famed even on the north-west shore among Muireann's people.

In a better mood, mostly due to deciding to ignore the revelations of the day before, Muireann indulged in some crowd watching as they walked. She'd never been anywhere nearly as large as the capital city, and it was fascinating to see the hustle and bustle of urban life in contrast to her small village or even Strandview. The streets were thronged with every walk of life, from beggars and rag sellers to the lesser nobility. Many of the buildings they passed in that area of the city were storefronts, usually with the owners living above the store, but the sidewalk was also full of street vendors and people selling directly from carts. She saw the expected range of humans, most dressed in the lighter and brighter clothing she'd come to expect in the eastern part of the country although she also saw some who were clearly from one of the other kingdoms. There were also many of the other sentient species in Tallan, excepting only the selkies and ocean-folk who rarely came so far inland. They passed a group of half-a-dozen tree-folk near a fountain, their leaf green hair moving in the slight breeze and the sun making their golden polished-oakwood skin glow slightly. The colour of it reminded Muireann slightly of Calla's and a moment after she thought it several high elves passed on horseback, the familiar tawny skin and fire-coloured hair – in this group ranging from flame red to orange to marigold yellow – catching Muireann's eye. They were chatting among themselves in elvish but Muireann overhead enough to gather they were members of the weavers' guild going to some sort of meeting. Beyond them she saw a meadow elf woman hurrying by with a child in her arms, her green clothing only slightly darker than her moss-coloured skin, her dark green hair covering her to her knees like a cloak. They passed a group of dwarves near a blacksmith's shopfront, the dozen or so men talking and laughing among themselves. The tallest was just under Lee's height, and they all wore armour that made them seem heavier than they probably were. Muireann tried not to stare at the intricately looped and woven braids in their beards and hair, impressed by the time she knew it took to do such work. A block further down a dark-skinned mountain elf stood at a street stall, selling small magical charms, his purple tunic and belt indicating he was a mage with one of the local magic schools. It was a fascinating and dizzying array of cultures and species to Muireann, who felt her own past experience was very parochial compared to city life.

When they were within sight of the library Muireann remembered something else she'd seen on the city map and suddenly made up her mind to handle an errand she'd been putting off for too long.

'Lee, I have a little thing I'd like to do first, is that alright?' Muireann asked, already nervous about what she planned to do.

The selkie looked curious but didn't directly ask. 'Of course.'

Muireann nodded and reached out to take Lee's hand, leading her through the streets slightly west of the looming library building. They wove through foot traffic which gradually thinned out as they left the busier sections of the city. A few streets later they arrived at the temple.

It covered a full city block, its walls two storeys high and fine marble. It was far, far more impressive than anything Muireann had ever seen before but the main gate featured the intricately carved double door of any temple showing the symbols of the seven gods. The sign over the gate was in bronze rather than the wood of the temples she'd grown up with, but the words were the same: 'Beginning to End; The seven are All'.

She hesitated at the doors, trying to get the courage to enter. Sensing her fear Lee asked. 'Is everything alright?'

Muireann let out a long shaky sigh. 'I meant to do this in Verell but then everything got so complicated so quickly. But now – maybe especially now – I think I have to.'

'Do you want me to wait out here?' Lee asked, squeezing Muireann's hand gently.

She shook her head. 'I want you with me, if that's alright.'

'I'm always here when you need me,' Lee said. Then when Muireann continued to stand without moving, she added, 'Are you afraid to go in?'

'Yes,' she admitted, looking down. 'I don't know what I'm afraid of exactly. But I am afraid.'

'Do you think the gods might strike you down for killing the dragon? Because you must know that's silly. They wouldn't have waited for you to come to a temple just to do that.'

Muireann laughed at that, some of her tension easing. 'I suppose you're right.'

Lee squeezed her hand again. 'Let's go in.'

Muireann nodded and reached out to knock on the gate pillar as custom demanded, to announce her entry to the spirits. Then she carefully pushed the ornate doors open, leading Lee into the temple proper.

It was shockingly quiet inside, as if the sounds of the city were not allowed to intrude here. As with any temple the gate opened into a large open-air courtyard with the shrines of the seven ranged in covered alcoves around the edges of the open space. The rain had stopped late the night before but while the city streets were still damp and puddled everything in here was pristine and dry.

Immediately to Muireann's right was a smaller door which she knew led to the priests' and priestesses' living quarters. Directly along the right-side wall were shrines to Vorren, god of the sea and travellers, Ostilla, goddess of wilderness and animals, and Ven, god of mischief, thieves and luck. On the left side were shrines for Incha, goddess of weather, Calleshen, god of the harvest and of war, and Erla, goddess of magic and healing. Straight ahead was Alva's shrine, larger than the other six because she was the goddess of creation, giver of all inspiration and skill. To the right of her shrine grew a gnarled ancient yew and to the left was the door to the inner temple. A single priestess, clad in the grey robes of a dedicant to Incha, was sweeping the open space; she ignored the two women completely.

Muireann took a deep breath and headed into the centre of the courtyard, looking from shrine to shrine. 'I haven't been in a temple in almost year.'

She turned and looked at Lee's curious face before going on. 'Not since the last festival before...before my family was killed.'

'I'm sorry, Muireann,' Lee said, and as always Muireann appreciated the sincerity in the selkie's words.

'It feels strange to be standing here now,' she admitted. 'I didn't think I'd ever set foot in a temple again.'

'Why not?'

'Because I was very angry, afterwards,' Muireann admitted, feeling that knot of anger easing slightly in her chest. 'I know the gods are real but losing all my children together like that...I was just so bitter and angry and...'

'It's alright,' Lee said, reaching up to rub her back soothingly.

'It's really not. All of that is what led me to do what I did, and I shouldn't have.'

'If you hadn't, we'd never have met,' Lee pointed out, startling Muireann into meeting her eyes. 'And I'd be stuck in a marriage by force to a man I didn't want and could never find any happiness with.'

'That's true, and I'd never want that for you, not ever,' Muireann said, meaning it.

'So, you see some good has come from what you did,' Lee said, smiling gently. Then she leaned forward and kissed Muireann before stepping away. 'I need to make an offering to Vorren, father of all seal-folk, and pray to him a bit about my choice to travel and leave the sea. I suppose I have my own peace to make there. I think perhaps you need to do this part alone, but if you can't I will be back and help you soon.'

Muireann nodded, digging into her belt pouch to hand Lee a coin. 'I think you're right, you are definitely an immensely good thing in my life. Here, take this to offer.'

Lee took the coin, then gave Muireann an encouraging look before setting off towards Vorren's shrine. Bracing herself and feeling braver after talking with Lee, Muireann turned and walked towards Erla's shrine. It sat in a recess just deep enough to provide a person with privacy to pray. The side walls were wood-panelled in a deep oak, bare of all decoration except for paired wall sconces where oil lamps hung, their flickering light visible even in the sunlight. At the back of the space was the shrine itself, a long low table covered in offerings in front of a carved relief of the goddess, her form shifting between woman and smoke. To one side a unicorn reared up, its body neither horse nor goat but reminiscent of both, its horn like a twisted dagger jutting from its forehead. And on the other side in a mirroring position was a dragon breathing fire to match the shape of the unicorn's horn.

Muireann stood at the edge of the shrine staring at the carved dragon for a very long time, feeling again the grief she'd felt standing next to the red dragon's corpse. The overwhelming feeling that she'd murdered something magical and irreplaceable. She wished from the depths of her soul that she had failed in what she'd tried, that the dragon had killed her or at least that the dragon worshippers could make an end of things for her.

She found herself moving forward without thinking to do it, fear slicing through her self-loathing when she realised she had no control over her own movements. She fell to her knees before the offering table, only that uncanny power keeping her from flinging herself onto it and to the mercy of Erla herself.

She waited for the goddess's wrath to fall fully onto her.

Instead, she was overwhelmed with a sense of comfort and the very visceral memory of her grandmother's arms around her when she was a child. She broke and sobbed without restraint, giving herself over to that presence which reassured her without words as she let all of her anger, grief – over her family and the dragon – fear and misery pour out. Everything she'd spent more than six months holding inside, hiding from everyone, even those closest to her. All of her tangled feelings about her newfound immortality. She laid her soul bare before Erla, embracing that sense of presence until the catharsis was done and she had no more tears.

She had assumed the experience would end there but it didn't. It was nothing like the myths and stories of people talking to a deity, nor of what she'd have imagined such an experience would be like. The sense of presence remained strongly with her, and she found herself simply knowing things without understanding exactly how she knew them. Reyleth was right that the dragon touching her in the moment it died was pivotal. The magic that had been in the dragon was now contained in her. This was unique, because always before when Erla's creatures were killed their magic was simply lost to the living world, returning to the goddess. The world was lessened by this, each time, to Erla's regret, but the world followed rules set down at the founding of it and she must follow them to keep the balance of the seven. This meant that when her creatures died it was understood as part of their fate and the great weaving of the world, at the will of Alva, just as balance required all things to have their limitations and weaknesses. Muireann was unique now, a container for this magic that had not been fashioned by Erla herself at the birth of the world. This too was seen as the will of Alva, part of the great weaving. Now Muireann was like the unicorns, like the dragons, a being of pure magic in a physical form. She would serve the goddess as these beings did, by being a beacon of living magic in the created world who anchored Erla's presence there. Muireann tried to focus her thoughts, to communicate back, to express her fear about outliving everyone she loved, her worry about forgetting herself. This was met by confusion. She had a vague sense that the goddess didn't understand these things. She would live as long as magic existed and know many people. Didn't living creatures often lose those they loved? Wasn't that natural? She was herself, she would always be herself, how could that be lost? Muireann gave up in the face of this, unsure how to explain to a literal deity that she wasn't made for such time scales.

For an instant the presence flooded into her more strongly, filling her to a point that was somewhere between agony and ecstasy. She knew without knowing how she knew that Erla was finishing what had begun at the dragon's death. She felt pain flare through the scar on her cheek as if it were being cut anew, then a burning in her eyes, then immediately after that a wave of terrible dizziness.

She woke up in an uncomfortable position on the floor, curled over her legs with her chin almost against her knees, something that she was not nearly thin enough to do. Lee was standing several feet away, calling her name anxiously, and she realised that was what had woken her. Grunting she pushed herself up, turning her head to look back at Lee only to find the selkie was standing with the priestess she'd seen earlier, both looking almost frantic. Wincing she staggered to her feet and stepped away from the shrine. 'It's alright, Lee, I'm alright.'

The selkie still looked worried but nodded at the reassurance. The priestess, however, was still extremely upset. 'What happened, ma'am? Did you come here for healing? Because anyone seeking healing from Erla is to go through the mediator of a priest or priestess, and it will be done in the inner temple.'

Lee gave the woman an annoyed look, for which Muireann felt inexplicably grateful. Stepping fully out of the space she tried to look reassuring. 'No. That's not why I'm here. I honestly don't know why I passed out but perhaps I simply haven't eaten enough today.'

The woman looked dubious; Muireann ignored her, turning to Lee. 'I think we should leave now.'

'Yes, I agree,' Lee said, quickly going to Muireann's side and walking out with her. The priestess hesitated behind them, but Muireann didn't give her a chance to say anything else, hurrying out as fast as she could without running.

When they reached the street, they turned and started walking towards the library, still keeping a fast pace. It wasn't until they were several blocks away, almost back to the library, when Muireann finally slowed. Lee laid a hand on her arm. 'Are you alright? Truly?'

'I'm not sure,' Muireann admitted, then thinking of the pain she'd felt in her scar. 'Does my cheek look any different to you? Where my scar is?'

They stopped walking, backing up against a wall to let people pass them by while they talked. Lee leaned forward and carefully examined her cheek. 'No, I don't see anything different – Oh!'

'What?' Muireann said, swallowing hard. When Lee didn't say anything else she started to panic. 'What is it?'

'Can you take your glasses off for a moment?' Lee said softly.

Muireann made a face, hating to feel so vulnerable on the street but she did as Lee asked, her world reduced to colourful blurs as soon as the frames slid off. Lee leaned in close enough that her face was clear to Muireann, hovering inches away, then said slowly. 'Oh...my.'

'What? Please, Lee, you're scaring me.'

'I wish I had a mirror, this would be easier to show you than to explain,' the selkie said. 'But your eyes...your eyes are two colours now. Green like they were before on the outside but the inner part, by the pupil, is kind of orange-red now.'

'Red?' Muireann gasped, horrified at the thought of it. 'My eyes are red now?'

'Only the inner part,' Lee repeated, trying to sound soothing. 'It matches your hair actually, sort of a copper colour.'

Muireann shook her head slowly, trying to understand what that could possibly mean. Then she had a flash of the dragon's eye, wide and dead and staring and *orange-red*. 'I don't understand,' she whispered. 'Why would the goddess do this?'

'Do what?' Lee said, and then. 'What goddess? Erla?'

Muireann took a slow deep breath, sliding her glasses back on. 'Yes. Blast it, she could have given me perfect vision if she was going to mess with my eyes.'

Lee was looking at her in wide-eyed shock and so Muireann told her what had happened in the shrine, as much as she could remember and put into words at least. By the end the selkie was shaking her head, looking awed. 'You're dedicated to the goddess now? Like a priestess?'

'No,' Muireann was quick to say. 'It's not like that. It's more like, like I'm taking the dragon's place in the world. Which I suppose is only fair considering I killed it.'

Lee still looked unduly impressed, so Muireann shook her head. 'Never mind. I'll have to explain to everyone tonight anyway and we can talk about it all then. For now, we'd better get to the library. Reyleth gave me a general idea of where to look but this is still likely to be tedious.'

Lee nodded but Muireann was already moving, heading towards the huge stone edifice. It was an impressive building, massive and all in granite it almost looked as if the entire thing had been carved from an existing mountain. The walls extended up three storeys, spotted frequently with windows. The main entrance was a set of bronze-fitted oak doors, closed against the noise and bustle of the city outside. There was something about it that strongly reminded Muireann of the temple and she shivered slightly at the thought, Erla's presence still fresh in her mind.

They entered the library, finding that the other side of the massive doors opened up into a large foyer. There were two guards, in chainmail and leather armour, standing just inside the door; they stepped forward as soon as the two women entered.

'No weapons allowed in the library,' the first said, his tone painfully neutral.

Lee frowned. 'Where am I to leave my spear then?'

'If you set it here against the wall, we will watch it for you,' the second one said.

Lee didn't want to, that was plain, so Muireann set a hand on her arm and leaned into her ear. 'It's alright. It's their job to make sure there's no blood spilt in here. We're safe enough with them guarding the door and your spear will be here when we leave.'

Lee still didn't look happy about it but grudgingly set the spear against the wall by the door. The two guards nodded then stood back, ignoring them.

Muireann finally turned and looked around at the inside of the Great Library. Separating that area from the actual bookshelves there was a wooden railing and desk, which Muireann had never seen in a library before, so that anyone coming in would have to go by the desk, and the woman sitting at it, to be admitted into the library proper. There were bookshelves beyond that as far as the eye could see, crowding even the large space that was the Great Library of Mistlen. And Muireann knew there were two more floors.

She stood and gaped at the space, not having ever conceived of so many books existing in the whole world. If someone had tried to describe this to her, she'd not have believed it.

The woman behind the desk cleared her throat loudly giving

the two woman a condescending look. 'May I help you?'

Her tone made it clear she very much wanted to help them right back out of the door. She was younger than Muireann but probably not by too much, her dark brown hair twisted up into a complex hairstyle of curls and braids. Her dress was drably coloured and modestly cut but of the finest silk. Even Muireann could see that she was either from the nobility or made exceptionally good money working there.

Trying to pull herself together and look less like a tourist who'd just arrived in the city – even if that's what she was – Muireann advanced on the desk, glad she had chosen to wear her nicest clothes for this. The emerald green tunic and dark brown pants weren't the dress of a noblewoman but they were expensive materials and clearly finely made, and the wolf fur if nothing else was rare and unusual. The messenger bag she wore across one shoulder to carry her notebook and writing supplies was old and battered, since it was the same one she'd taken from the dragon, but it had been excellent workmanship when it was new. Lee, of course, was dressed as usual in a loosely flowing light blue dress, her seal skin around her shoulders. Muireann put on her best 'dealing with the mayor' face, smiling and ignoring the woman's attitude. 'I hope that you may help us. I'm a travelling scholar and would like to do some research here. I have heard that you have a particularly fine collection of older works.'

The woman sniffed slightly, eyeing the furs Lee and Muireann were wearing. 'And you are from...?'

'Strandview, originally.'

'I've never heard of it,' she said, starting to turn away.

Muireann held her temper carefully, thinking of what Calla might do in this situation. 'The library takes donations, yes?'

The woman paused, looking down her nose at them. 'It does. We appreciate patrons of the arts who are willing to support our work here. I don't think *you*, however—'

The officious woman was interrupted by the arrival of another woman, appearing behind the first. 'What is the difficulty here, Crellia?'

The second woman looked much like the first except she was older, and her hair was a washed out blonde. Sensing that whatever happened next would make or break her chance to get in and feeling desperately sure that she had to get inside, Muireann seized the brief distraction to slip the Dragon Stone out of her tunic so that it lay, swirling red, against her chest.

'Nothing you need worry about, my lady,' the desk worker simpered.

Muireann cut in quickly. 'I was just asking how one would go about making a donation.'

The first woman turned back to give her an annoyed glare which changed to a gasp when she caught sight of the stone. The second woman walked over to the desk, her eyes flicking over Lee and Muireann appraisingly. She didn't gasp when she saw the stone, but her eyes did widen and her voice was noticeably sweeter when she spoke again. 'The library is always grateful for any donations we receive, Miss…?'

'Muireann,' she said then still trying to do as she thought Calla would. 'Muireann Dragonslayer of Strandview.'

Both women were rendered speechless at this, which made Muireann keenly uncomfortable. She grabbed her belt pouch, holding the green crystal in its case through the leather, and poured coins out onto the desk without looking. 'Is this a sufficient donation do you think? I was hoping to be able to do some research here.'

The younger woman now looked very much as if she'd swallowed a live frog. The older one smiled eagerly, moving around the desk to open the gate in the railing and let Muireann and Lee pass. 'Of course, my lady, your generosity is enormously appreciated. If you'd follow me?'

As Muireann and Lee moved to enter, the blonde looked

back at the woman behind the desk. 'Crellia, be a dear and put that into the vault, will you?'

'This, this has to be at least fifty gold coins,' the younger woman stammered.

Feeling almost giddy now at the absurdity of it, Muireann waved a hand. 'It's nothing I'm sure, compared to all your many donations from dedicated patrons. But since I am here visiting of course I want to help in some small way.'

'Of course, my lady,' the older woman said again, looking dazzled now. 'We truly appreciate it. Truly. If you'd follow me?'

Muireann and Lee proceeded into the library, their guide chattering on about its history and prestige as she toured them around. '...and this is the section on mythology and folklore. We have one of the premiere collections in all the kingdoms. Back through there is a small sitting room where we offer a selection of food for patrons...at the rear of each floor are the lavatories... upstairs the second-floor houses all of our history books, not only history of the human kingdoms you know but the empire itself and every one of the sentient species, as well as epic works of poetry and literature...'

Muireann interrupted at that point, glancing up the stairs. 'Do you have much on the Aldovanan? I'm quite interested in researching their history, especially the more obscure material.'

Their guide smiled warmly, leading them up the stairs. 'But, of course. We have several very rare works, including an original edition of Ghellonan's Complete History of the Aldovanan, which I'm sure a discerning patron such as yourself can appreciate is practically one of a kind.'

'Excellent,' Muireann agreed, resisting the urge to tell the woman to leave them alone. It would be too rude and while she might be able to get away with it she knew she could very easily end up needing assistance later and it would be foolish to alienate anyone here without good reason.

'And what is on the third floor?' Lee asked, peering curiously at all the shelved books.

The woman gave her an uncertain look, her eyes flicking between the two, but her voice retained its cheer when she answered. 'The third floor is a collection of medical and healing texts, magical treatises and a small restricted section that's reserved for a handful of specialised scholars.'

'Why are any books here restricted?' Lee asked, still looking around at the shelves.

'My, your guard is quite inquisitive, isn't she?' the woman asked, laughing nervously.

Lee frowned at that, but Muireann forced a reassuring smile. 'It's her job to keep me safe, after all.'

The woman laughed again, obviously uncomfortable. 'Well there's certainly no danger to you here. Feel free to browse at your leisure. You'll find the Aldovanan books in this section here. My name is Sallenia, please let me know if you need anything else – there's a red rope just there by the stairs; if you pull it a bell will notify me or Crellia that you need something and we will help you or send one of the novices – you can also ask any of them for assistance if you see them in the stacks. They wear light blue tunics, very distinctive. There are of course many other scholars and mages who come here to research or study but you'll find they prefer not to be disturbed with idyl conversation. There are writing desks on every floor equipped with paper and quills if you'd like to take any notes. We can of course provide a novice to take notes for you if you'd prefer. Otherwise, you are free to read as much as you would like while you are here. We provide food throughout the day, although we prefer you eat downstairs in the sitting room. You understand?'

'Of course,' Muireann murmured, already thinking of where she should get started. 'Thank you for your help.'

The woman, Sallenia, nodded and dropped into a curtesy before hurrying back down the stairs.

Lee and Muireann watched her go; Lee still frowning,

Muireann bemused. She felt ridiculous throwing that much money around, and she'd have to stop by the bankers' guild hall to get more travelling money, but it was almost worth it for the look on that desk clerk's snobby face.

When they were alone, Sallenia's footsteps fading away below, Lee turned to her. 'I'm your guard, am I?'

The selkie was clearly annoyed but Muireann giggled. 'Well, you do protect me, don't you? Without my bow I'm practically helpless.'

Lee snorted at that and then started laughing as well. 'Helpless isn't a word I'd ever call you, *my lady*. If I remember correctly, you're fairly fierce with your fists too.'

Muireann giggled harder, putting a hand over her mouth to smother the noise. 'What's wrong, Lee? You don't want to be my bodyguard?'

Lee pressed close to her, walking her back until they were deep in the stacks, away from the stairs, Muireann giggling the whole way. 'There's a lot of things I want to do with your body.'

Muireann struggled to stop laughing, even as Lee started kissing her neck. 'Lee! Someone will hear us.'

'Then you'd better be quiet.'

'We'll get kicked out,' Muireann said, kissing her back.

'Then you'd better be *very* quiet,' the selkie purred back.

Muireann knew she should put her foot down, that she'd just spent more money than anyone in her village would see in a lifetime just to get into this library. That it was very important they find out what the books here said about the Aldovanan. But with Lee's hands and mouth distracting her it was easy to forget, and after the events at the temple she craved the distraction.

Sometime later they got to work doing what they'd actually come there to do. Since they hadn't been summarily thrown out Muireann assumed that they'd either managed to be quiet enough or that the money she'd donated earned them more than just entry and a guided tour. Either way, given the frustrating way the rest of the day went, with none of the books she managed to get through helping at all, she was glad they'd had a little bit of fun at least.

When they left just before dinner-time, Lee stopping to get her spear from the door guards, Muireann made sure to let the young man who was working the desk (an unknown face to her but who had obviously been told she was there as he was as differential as the women had been) that they'd be back the next day.

She had a feeling she'd be seeing a lot of the Great Library.

* * *

When the group was gathered again for dinner Muireann found herself recapping the events at the temple for everyone before getting into the frustrating day searching the library stacks. There wasn't much to tell there anyway, and she left out her and Lee's personal adventure, despite knowing Calla would undoubtedly appreciate hearing about it.

Everyone was fascinated by what had happened in the temple, particularly Reyleth, which she should have anticipated since it was his patron goddess. He asked her an exhausting array of questions as they ate, leaned over and studied her eyes carefully, then asked more questions after they were done eating. Eventually she held a hand up to stop the steady stream. 'Reyleth, please. I've told you everything three times over now. I can't give you any more details than I already have, and I don't know what else to say about it that I haven't already said. All that really matters here is that Erla seems to be using me as a vessel for the dragon's magic – or I became that by coincidence, and she's accepted it. The only practical change that means besides my eyes being two colours now is that I am, as you already guessed, immortal. At least as much so as the dragons are which clearly isn't truly immortal.'

'Close enough,' Tash said. He was still acting odd around Muireann, uncomfortable with her in an overawed sort of way. She really hoped that would change soon.

'Well, besides that I'm still me. Still can't see without my glasses, can't sword fight, slowest runner in the group me. And we've talked more than enough about me,' Muireann said. 'Let's move on to how everyone else's day went.'

The others had not made much more progress than Muireann had. Reyleth had found several books he'd been looking for, but the texts were obscure and hard to read, even for him. 'I'm sure there's useful material in here, but it may take me weeks, if not months to read through everything and find the bits we specifically need.'

Calla nodded at his words. 'I'm glad we found anything useful at all, but between that and hearing about your progress, Muireann—'

'Or lack of it,' Muireann muttered.

Calla ignored her. 'We may be in Mistlen for a while. So, I propose a new plan. Reyleth can hunker down in his room and work through the books we found today. Lee and Tash can alternate going with Muireann to the library while the other one stays here to keep a look out for anyone that may be hunting us. Since I know the city best and have contacts with the mercenaries' guild and a few others I'll start subtly asking around, listening for gossip, anything that might give us a hint as to who hired the mercs who attacked us on the road. We'll have to be on our guard as much as possible because the longer we stay in any one place, the greater the risk whoever is still pursuing us will find us. But we need to find out as much as we can here about the object we're researching and use this time to try to turn the tables on whoever is after us and maybe get an idea of who they really are. How does that sound?'

None of them were exactly happy about it, but Muireann had known at the start it might take a long time to get any answers.

She just hadn't expected to be actively hunted while trying to get them. They all slowly nodded.

'Excellent,' Calla said. 'Then I'm off to mingle around the room. I'll share the dragon story, but I'll also keep an ear out for any useful information.'

Tash ran a hand over his face then yawned. 'I think I'm for bed. It's been a long day. Muireann, I'll go with you tomorrow, alright?'

'Sure,' she said, looking forward to the chance to spend some time with him and hopefully get him to thaw a bit towards her. 'I'll meet you in the morning after breakfast if that suits.'

'I'm going to head up to my room,' Reyleth said, frowning. 'I want to start going through the material I have and taking some notes. Muireann, when you get back tomorrow, I'd like to talk with you and compare what we've found, see if we have a preliminary direction to go in yet.'

'Sounds like a good plan.'

With that the other three each drifted off, Rey and Tash walking upstairs together talking quietly, Calla disappearing into the crowded room. Muireann turned to look at Lee, surprised the selkie had been so quiet only to find the other woman's eyes fixed on a table across the room.

Muireann looked past Lee, to where she was looking. A very well-dressed young woman sat alone at a table against the opposite wall, her blonde hair in a fashionable coiffe, her pink dress in a cut that Muireann didn't recognise but which she suspected was the current trend and almost certainly silk. *Now there's someone who pink looks good on*, she thought to herself. She glanced at Lee and saw the selkie looking down but throwing glances back at the woman. She smiled softly. 'She very pretty isn't she, Lee?'

Lee looked up, surprised, then smiled back. 'She is.'

'She's watching you,' Muireann said, trying not to stare at the other woman. 'I think she'd like you to join her.'

Lee glanced back at the woman then down then at Muireann. 'Do you really think so?'

'I do,' Muireann said, trying to sound encouraging. 'If you want to, you should go. At least see if she needs some company.'

'What about you?'

Muireann shrugged. 'I was just about to go back to our room. I thought I might read for a bit. But I may stay down here for a while and read before going up.'

'Are you sure?' Lee pressed, and Muireann knew she wasn't talking about staying up to read.

'If it would make you happy then I'm sure, of course,' Muireann said. 'You can meet me in our room later.'

'I may be back sooner rather than later if she doesn't want my company,' Lee said, smiling nervously.

'I can't imagine anyone not wanting your company.'

The selkie gave her a fond look, then stood, stepping close to Muireann's chair. Muireann was puzzled and asked. 'What is it? Don't tell me you want a kiss for luck because that might confuse your new admirer.'

Lee giggled and shook her head. 'As much as I always want your kisses, no, it wasn't that.'

She reached up and slipped the seal skin from its accustomed place around her shoulders, bundling the fur up and holding it out to Muireann. 'Please watch this for me? It's safer with you, if I mean to do this.'

Muireann felt her cheeks colouring and reached out to take the seal skin, the most precious thing to Lee. She pressed the fur against her chest. 'I'll guard it with all care and keep it safely for you until you return.'

'I know you will,' Lee said, reaching out to squeeze Muireann's hand before turning and heading across the room. Muireann watched her go, her heart full of joy for Lee's happiness and also that her wife trusted her so much. She settled into her seat, the seal skin safely in her lap, pulling out her journal and starting to pore over the notes she'd taken that day. She hadn't found anything that seemed useful but perhaps giving it all a second look would help. She'd ordered another mead and was half through her notes when Rey joined her.

'Decided you wanted some company?'

He shrugged slightly. 'I had thought we could compare notes now if you were still up and when I knocked at your door, and no one answered I came down here.'

She smiled, sliding her journal towards him. 'Would you like to go over all the nothing I found today?'

He laughed slightly at that, but took her notes and started reading anyway, passing her one of the books he'd found. She watched out of the corner of her eye as Lee and the woman in pink left the common room, going up the stairs. Smiling, she sipped her mead, then opened Reyleth's book, finding it just as obscure and difficult as he'd said it would be.

She hoped that the next day of research would prove more fruitful.

Chapter 8

The Library

When Muireann woke early the next morning Lee was still curled up asleep under the blankets, her sealskin as always wrapped around her body. Muireann reached out and stroked the soft fur but didn't wake the sleeping woman. She thought that Lee deserved to get some extra rest while she could. Instead, she slipped from their shared bed and dressed quickly in the still dark room, the glowing coals of the hearth fire the only small light.

Since she was planning to go back to the library and understood a little better now what sort of place it was, and more since she'd have to stop by the bankers' guild hall, she took the time to rummage through her things until she found her best clothes. She'd thought Calla was being silly when she'd picked out the dark blue silk knee-length dress, with its fancy side laces, long tight sleeves and embroidered square neckline. It was unlike anything Muireann had ever owned or could imagine herself wearing but she guessed it would be perfect for the elitist library and she had to admit that she didn't look terrible in it. Because she didn't have any skirts to wear with it, she matched it with a pair of dark leggings, deciding if anyone commented on the odd look, she'd claim it was some new western fashion. How would they know anyway?

Trying to get into the dress was more of a production than she'd expected, and she finally took off her glasses which were getting in the way of the tightly tailored fabric. She dressed by feel from there, getting the dress on and mostly in place, lacing up the sides and pulling on the leggings. Glasses back in place she quickly brushed and re-braided her unruly hair, tied her belt around her waist and pushed her feet into her boots.

Ready to face the day she threw a final glance at Lee's sleeping form, wrote out a quick note so the selkie wouldn't worry, then slipped out into the hallway.

She wasn't entirely surprised to find Tash already in the common room eating some porridge and reading. The room was nearly empty, only a few other people sitting and eating, and they were all obviously merchants preparing to leave the city. She slid into a seat across from Tash, trying to catch the eye of the young woman serving tables.

'Good morning, Muireann,' Tash said, his tone overly formal.

She sighed. 'Tash, can we talk for a minute?'

He nodded, not meeting her eyes. She sighed again, convinced it was too early in the morning for this but unable to bear the thought of an entire day of it either. 'Tash. I know things are strange right now but I'm still the same person I was when you met me.'

He made a face. 'I suppose that's true but it's hard not to think of you differently now. You're…you're…'

'I'm still me,' she said again. 'I'm the exact same person you've always known me as. The one who's been helping you study. The one who you taught to camp properly. Your friend.'

'Muireann, I know you are but…you died,' he whispered it, leaning forward. 'I saw you die. But you aren't dead. I'm glad you aren't but watching you go over that cliff and walking down to get your body and finding you alive and totally unharmed. I can't get my head around it. I'm trying but I can't.'

She leaned forward too, reaching out to take his hands in hers. 'I didn't die, Tash. I know I fell but it isn't like I fell and died and came back to life. It isn't even like I was healed from grievous injuries with magic. I didn't die. I didn't get hurt. I'm sure I *can* still be killed but it's just much harder now than before. And that's something I have to come to terms with myself.'

'It's an amazing blessing,' he said.

She shook her head. 'To be truthful with you, I think it's a curse.'

'Why would you say that?'

'Because it's what I think,' she said. 'I think it's my punishment for what I did. I killed the dragon and now I have to take its place, which is going to mean outliving everyone I love. I've already lost my children once, now I have to face the reality that if I have any more children – if I even can – I'd inevitably watch them grow old and die. Even if I had a child with Reyleth and the child was elven and lived a thousand years I'd still watch them die. I'll have to watch Lee die, Calla and Reyleth. You. Everyone around me will age and die following the natural cycle – except me. How can I see that as anything except a punishment? It's unimaginably cruel. Dragons have existed since the world was made, they don't age as far as anyone knows and they are almost impossible to kill.'

'You killed one,' he said, his voice subdued now.

'I did, but after my...experience...with Erla I'd be afraid to, well, let's just say do the same thing to myself. Or try to. I'm not sure that she'd allow it and I don't know how much actual influence she has on me now.'

'Muireann!' he gasped, clearly horrified by her words. 'That's not what I meant. I'd never suggest such a thing!'

'I'm sorry, Tash, I didn't mean to upset you. But it is something I've thought about and staring down millennia slowly losing everyone I love over and over again.' She closed her eyes and took a deep breath. 'I buried my children less than a year ago. I haven't even really come to terms with that. I'm not sure I ever will. And now there's this. It's just...a lot.'

'I'm sorry,' he said softly, squeezing her hands where they held his.

She looked down at their joined hands, his dark ones clasping her pale ones, shaking her head. She knew that everything she'd said was true, but she was trying very hard not to think too much about it, and she certainly hadn't discussed it with anyone else.

She didn't know why she'd spoken so freely to Tash. 'I didn't mean to burden you with all of that. I was just trying to talk to you and show you I'm still the same person. Still your friend.'

He smiled slightly, then nodded. 'I know you are, Muireann, it's just an adjustment for me, I guess. And I still stand by everything I said before, about being glad I'm with you, all of you, and being willing to face this risk. That's truer now actually knowing what's really at stake. I am more certain now than ever that I want to be a knight and no true knight could turn from such a thing.'

Muireann thought he was being more than a bit naïve and romantic with that but since he was talking to her like normal again, she let it pass. If he wanted to imagine he was on some great quest to save the world she didn't see the harm in it, and he was certainly closer to the truth than she had been when she'd set out to kill the dragon without any thought as to what that would actually mean, what would happen afterwards.

He sat and chatted with her while she ate, talking about his thoughts of the city and of their travels so far. She had to admit that it was refreshing to see his enthusiasm and optimism when she herself had been so consumed by pessimism of late. It reminded her that there was something worth fighting for, if people like Tash were in the world.

Finally, she pushed her bowl away and stood. 'Let's get on with this. It's a bit of a walk to the library from here and I'm afraid you're in for a rather boring day.'

He stood, his sword already at his side, and gave her fancy clothes a sidelong look. 'Should I change into my formal wear?'

She laughed slightly. 'If you'd like to feel free, but you don't need to. Yesterday we found out that the library isn't like the ones we have, it's not exactly open to the public. They seem to expect a rather more, ah, "refined" sort of person to be in there.'

'What sort of library isn't open to the public?' he asked, baffled at the thought.

'This one,' she said, shrugging as they walked out into the brisk morning air. 'I gather they cater to scholars, mages and the wealthy. I basically paid to get in, not that it was that obvious, but I had to make a significant donation before they'd let us pass the door. I thought going back today, it would help to dress the part more.'

'So let me guess then,' he said, nodding along. 'That makes me...your bodyguard?'

'Exactly so,' she said. 'There are guards at the door, and you'll have to leave your sword when we go in, but you stay with me all day as I work.'

'How am I to protect you if we are attacked without my sword?' he worried, frowning.

'Tash, you are a good fighter, with or without your sword.'

He smiled looking down, obviously a bit embarrassed by the praise. 'Well, Calla has been showing me some unarmed fighting moves. And they'll let me keep my daggers, won't they?'

She nodded briskly, weaving through the city foot traffic. 'They will.'

'Then I'm confident I can protect you even without a sword,' he said, following slightly behind her.

She didn't bother pointing out that he didn't have to worry about her getting hurt, since she didn't want to remind him of that now that things were more normal between them. She also didn't bother pointing out that the real dangers were more likely to be in coming and going from the library, not in it. As much as she believed that they were relatively safe at this point, they'd been attacked so many times when they'd thought they were safe or had let their guard down that she thought it was better for him to worry than assume a safety that might not be there, no matter how secure the library seemed.

* * *

When they returned to the inn after a second frustrating day of little headway, Muireann left Tash in the common room and went up to find Lee, to let the selkie know she was back. Their room was empty, though, and after some searching she found a note from Lee where she'd left hers in the morning, saying that she and Calla had gone to the blacksmiths where Lee wanted to look at their selection of spears. Muireann shrugged and set the note down. She contemplated a bath in the fancy tub, then thought of reading and taking more notes. But she found herself too restless to settle down to anything like that, not after a day of pointless tedium in the library. As much as she loved reading and research and having access to such a huge array of texts, she was starting to feel like she'd never find anything helpful to their purpose and it was depressing. She knew it might take time, knew that it was only just the beginning, but two solid days of pouring through the stacks without even a hint of anything, not even a single book that mentioned either the green crystal or Olcanac, was disheartening.

Finally, she settled on going to Reyleth's room to see if he was there and in the mood to talk. He had mentioned wanting to compare their progress and, quite frankly, she missed him.

His room was next to Muireann's so it was a short walk then she was knocking softly on his door, feeling slightly foolish. She started to second guess herself, unsure if he was doing something he wouldn't want interrupted when the door opened. Reyleth smiled warmly when he saw her and that made her feel better about going to his room.

'I was wondering if I could come in?' she said, too blunt as always with him. 'If you'd like some company?'

He smiled at her, pulling her into the room and into his arms. 'I always want your company, Lennath.'

She let herself be folded against his body, sighing slightly. She loved Lee and the time they had together, which was always frequent, but she loved Reyleth as well and enjoyed this intimacy, which was somewhat less frequent. All of her nebulous plans to discuss their mission with him or her frustration with the library melted away as he kissed her, and she found that talking was actually the last thing she wanted to do.

They stood wrapped in each other, kissing for a long time until she grew restless again. She slid free of his grasp and moved over to the bed, unclasping her belt then pulling off her fancy dress, huffing at the time it took to unlace the sides and squirm free of the clinging material. He stood close by, shedding his own clothes with far more ease.

'Muireann,' Rey said, his voice so soft and shocked that she froze. His hands reached out, tracing along her back. 'Please don't overreact but your eyes aren't the only thing Erla changed.'

'Please explain that before I start screaming,' Muireann said in a voice so calm she surprised herself, turning her head to squint at him over her shoulder. 'Because my eyes are still weak and I'm still chubby and I certainly can't breathe fire.'

'No, of course not,' he said, his fingers still tracing across her skin. 'It's nothing like that. You have a dragon on your back.'

'I have a what?' she repeated, unable to make sense of the words.

'Have you ever seen the tattoos some people have? Ink under skin?' When she nodded, he went on. 'It reminds me of that but it's far more realistic than any drawing could ever hope to be.'

'I have the image of a dragon on my back?' she repeated, starting to get upset.

'It's beautiful,' he breathed, sounding awed. Then his mouth replaced his hands, his lips tracing her skin.

She shivered, enjoying it, but then moved away. 'How much does it cover?'

He reached out, seemingly unable to stop touching her. His fingers grazed the top of her left shoulder. 'From here, this is the head.' His touch traced across her back and moved down to her waist, to the top of her leggings. 'The body and wings cover your back and trail off below here.'

She squirmed quickly out of her remaining clothes, standing with her back still to him. 'How far down?'

'See for yourself,' he said, kneeling and touching her right ankle.

She bent over and looked down, gasping at the sight of a distinctive red dragon's tail coiling languidly around her right leg, from her hip to just above her foot. He was right that it was beautiful, as if the red dragon itself with all its jewel tones was imprinted on her flesh.

He looked up at her, eyes shining. 'You hadn't noticed this?'

Flushing, she shook her head, the movement sharp. 'No, I... it's been so hectic since the temple yesterday. Last night Lee and I slept together but only sleep. And when I changed clothes last night she wasn't in the room, and this morning she was still asleep. And you know my eyes are so bad I can't see my own leg without my glasses on and I wasn't thinking to *look* at my leg either- '

'Shhh, it's alright,' he soothed.

'This is not alright,' she whispered, feeling on the verge of tears. *But maybe,* she thought to herself, *this is exactly the punishment you deserve. Forever marked for what you did, truly embodying the dragon now and inescapably reminded of it.*

'It's beautiful. You're beautiful,' he kissed her again, working his way up her body, his passion clear.

She didn't know how to get him to understand how she felt, as if she'd been branded without her knowledge, permanently marked with the sign of her deepest personal shame. Her eyes changing colour were bad enough, but at least that was only a small change and some of her own green remained. This was so massive and so overwhelming she didn't know how to begin processing it. The only thing she did know was that Erla had surely done this for a reason, but what that reason was eluded Muireann.

As Reyleth stood, his mouth finally finding hers, she held him close and kissed him back fiercely, her emotions swinging like a pendulum from fear back to passion. She wanted to feel like she was still herself, to feel grounded in her own body. To feel as beautiful as he said she was.

And as always, he gave her what she wanted.

* * *

She found Lee later when the selkie returned with her new spear and explained about the dragon mark, then ended up showing her. Lee's reaction was surprisingly similar to Reyleth's and Muireann started to worry that there was some layer here to the mark that inspired lust in people.

It was reassuring when she told Calla and Tash at dinner and showed them what she could of it by pulling the back of her tunic down and then baring her lower leg that while they were both fascinated neither seemed to find it or Muireann unexpectedly alluring.

'Argue as you will, Muiri,' Calla said, looking deeply amused. 'but you truly are the image of a great hero now.'

'Calla,' Muireann sighed, rolling her pant leg back down. 'My eyes have a red ring in them. If that's the image of anything it isn't heroic.'

Calla started listing things off on her fingers. 'You wear a Dragon Stone from a dragon you killed. You have a white fur cloak from a rare, dangerous northern predator, which you killed yourself. And now you have the mark of Erla on you, a dragon's image that could never have been fashioned by any living hand.'

Lee, Tash and Reyleth were watching this exchange with varying degrees of amusement, but all wisely chose to stay out of it, eating their meals and silently observing. Muireann leaned forward, reaching out and slowly folding Calla's fingers back down one at time. 'I regret killing the dragon and the wolf. Killing an animal doesn't make a person a hero. This mark isn't a reward.'

Calla was openly struggling not to laugh now as she raised each finger again, saying, 'You saved my life when you killed the dragon. You saved Reyleth from the wolf. That mark is gorgeous and no one who sees it will think otherwise.'

Before Muireann could think of good rebuttals, Lee added, 'And you saved me from that awful man.'

Calla raised a fourth finger and Muireann gave up, sitting back melodramatically and rolling her eyes. 'You simply won't rest until you convince me of this, will you?'

'No, I've made it my life's mission,' Calla shot back, laughing. 'You are a hero whether you like it or not and honestly I find your humility – well annoying to be frank – but besides that I find it refreshing. The world is full of people far less deserving of the title who insist on claiming it.'

'We aren't going to agree on this.'

'Tell me, Muiri, why keep the fur cloak if you don't agree it's a symbol of what you did?'

Muireann shot a guilty look at Rey and Lee. 'It's warm and better quality than anything else I'd get. And…it was a gift. From Lee who took the skin and from Reyleth who fashioned it.'

Both Lee and Reyleth looked flattered at her words, and Muireann felt her cheeks flushing. Calla just sighed. 'You are so sentimental. Alright then, have it as you will. But we all know I'm right and deep down you know I am as well.'

Their good-natured squabbling was interrupted by the arrival of a stranger at their table. He was a dwarf, his long, fair beard elaborately braided in a way that matched his hair, almost as tall as Lee but where she was soft curves, he was all muscle and bulk, giving him a much heftier look. His eyes were a clear grey. Muireann had met only a few dwarves in her life, usually traders, but where they all ubiquitously wore leather and wool, he was wearing silk and velvet, albeit still in the earth tones she'd have expected.

To Muireann's surprise Calla rose gracefully to her feet and bowed slightly. 'Good evening, sir bard. To what do we owe the honour of your presence?'

Muireann knew from that greeting that he was not only a bard but the highest rank of such, the sort that usually served a lord directly and taught others. She wondered why he was in Mistlen, but then again it was the capital of the kingdom, it could be that his liege was here negotiating a treaty or even that he served Queen Felecia here, although dwarves were usually insular, reclusive folk. Muireann had long thought that if they didn't need others to buy the crafts they made, especially the metal work they were renowned for, they might have retreated into their mountain homes entirely and cut themselves off from the other species. As it was, though, their work was considered the best metalwork in all of Tallan and their skill at crafting undisputed and much sought after.

He bowed slightly at Calla's acknowledgement. 'Good evening to you as well. I hope I am not disturbing your meal, but I have heard much of your tale and would like to get the story of the dragon directly from the source.'

'Not at all,' Calla said then stepped forward and slid her arm into his. 'And I would be more than pleased to tell you the tale in full.'

He glanced at Muireann, his heavy brows furrowing slightly and Calla quickly added. 'I was captured by the dragon and was a first-hand witness to the events. It has been my honour to share the tale across the land as we have travelled, although I cannot hope to do it as much justice as you yourself will, of course.'

Obviously flattered the dwarf smiled and patted Calla's arm where it was joined with his, now allowing himself to be led away. 'I am sure that you tell a very thrilling version of the events my dear. I was thinking, though, to make an epic poem of it...'

As soon as the pair were out of earshot Muireann started giggling and the rest of the table soon joined in. Tash took a swig of his ale, shaking his head slightly. 'She certainly enjoys telling that story.'

'I won't complain,' Muireann said, finishing the last of her own drink. 'It saves me from having to deal with all the curious people.'

'Fortunate since your version of events would be something along the lines of "I shot it with my bow,"' Reyleth said, and the whole group burst out laughing at what was only the plain truth.

'Calla's the better storyteller, certainly, and I don't begrudge her the fun she has telling it,' Muireann said. 'When she first told me her plan to spread the story, I thought it was a bad idea, but I have to admit with everything else going on I've changed my mind. It may very well be better that the truth of it is told so that no one else can muddle the facts, or at least not easily.'

'You say that even with the Arvethri hunting you?' Rey asked, frowning at the table top.

'Yes,' Muireann said. 'I think they'd have found me either way and at least this way they aren't murdering random people foolishly trying to claim credit for the dragon's death. I did it and they know I did it and if that means facing their anger then so be it.'

'You talk like you deserve what they are trying to do to you,' Lee said, reaching out for Muireann's hand. 'You don't.'

'Perhaps not, but I'd still rather they aim it at me than kill innocent people,' Muireann said, squeezing Lee's hand. 'And besides, they can't actually hurt me. I only worry that one of you will be hurt for my sake and that I don't want.'

'Well, if we are lucky, they have stopped pursuing you because they think they already succeeded,' Tash said.

'True,' Muireann agreed, and then she stood and stretched. 'Well today has been long and strange and tiring so I think I'll head to bed early.'

'I'll come with you,' Lee said quickly, even though her drink was still half full.

'No, love, you stay here and enjoy yourself,' Muireann insisted. 'I'm just going straight to bed, I think. There's no reason for everyone to cut their own fun short for my sake.'

Tash nodded. 'Stay, Lee and finish your drink. I'd like to talk to you about a few things if you don't mind.'

Lee looked intrigued by that and settled back into her seat. Reyleth had just ordered more wine, so Muireann knew he intended to stay for a bit. She smiled at the trio, wished them a good night again and headed up to her room

It was nice and quiet there, peaceful, and even though she'd said she meant to go straight to bed she found herself taking out the journal she had been writing about the dragon in, now expanded to include her personal memories as well, and started writing about her friends, starting with Calla.

She lost track of time as she wrote, compressing the time she'd known the high elf into words that captured her personality without sounding trite was harder than she'd expected, when there was a knock at the door. She hesitated a moment before reluctantly putting the book aside and going to answer it.

Calla was standing there holding a bow in one hand, the other arm behind her back. Muireann looked from the weapon to the woman then gestured for her to enter the room.

'I suppose this seems like an odd time for this, all things considered,' Calla said. 'But I ordered you a new bow when Reyleth and I were out yesterday, and I picked it up today. I wanted to give it to you, so you'd have a weapon at hand.'

'It seems a bit late, I'd have thought this could wait until tomorrow...and that you'd be busy with that bard.'

'Mmm, I do like bards,' Calla smirked, 'and I fully intend to be very *busy* with him shortly. But while he relaxes in my room I wanted to run over and give you this.'

'It couldn't wait?' Muireann said again, amused.

'No,' Calla said simply, pushing the new bow into Muireann's hands. 'I don't like thinking of you without your best weapon. I meant to give it to you earlier, but I forgot and then you were busy yourself and then...well, at dinner didn't seem the appropriate place. I know this isn't your old bow, which can't be replaced. But this is the finest of elven work and no one makes bows as well as the elves, if I do say so myself.'

'Thank you, Calla,' Muireann said, sliding her hands along the smoothly polished wood. It really was an exquisitely made weapon, combining beauty and function as only the elves could do.

The high elf relaxed slightly and brought her other hand forward, holding out a new quiver full of arrows for her human friend. 'This too.'

Muireann took the quiver, finely tooled leather covered in a pattern of leaves and birds. 'Were you afraid I'd refuse the bow?'

'It had occurred to me that you might,' Calla admitted. 'Because you are such a humble person and also because I know how upset you were over the loss of your other one.'

'I wouldn't refuse a gift from you, Calla,' Muireann said, giving her friend an awkward hug, the quiver and bow still in her hands.

'Well now that I've given it, I have to get back to my room before Þerroð gets bored and wanders off,' Calla said with a wink.

Muireann shook her head and laughed, doing her best to push Calla out with her full hands. 'Go on then. Just don't get too loud. Some of us plan on getting some sleep.'

'I promise nothing,' Calla said, pulling the door shut behind herself.

Still shaking her head slightly at her friend interrupting a tryst to walk over and deliver a gift, she went and set the bow down carefully along with the new quiver. Her old quiver was still lying on the floor where she'd dropped it when they'd first arrived, and she picked it up slowly. It was simple work, shaped birchbark with a leather strap to attach it to her belt. She'd lost all but a couple of arrows when she'd fallen and she pulled them out, running her hands along the shafts. She'd made those herself, practising over and over last winter. She looked from the old quiver to the arrows for several minutes and then carefully added the two old arrows to the new quiver. The old one she carried to the fireplace of the room, a stone enclosure where a small fire burned cheerfully, just big enough to provide some light and heat in the space. She crouched down and watched the flames for a bit then before she could lose her nerve, she cast the old quiver in, landing it precariously on top of one of the burning logs.

She grabbed the fire poker to adjust it but when that only caused the now burning quiver to slide forward, she reflexively reached out to push it back. She poked it fast, yanking her hand back, before remembering that the fire wouldn't do her any harm. Feeling braver she reached in again, expecting a flash of pain but not worried about actually hurting herself. She moved the quiver to a better position so that it burned safely among the logs, but there was no pain. It was a pleasant sensation, warm and fluid, as if she were immersing her hand in warm water. It reminded her of the hot springs actually. Fascinated she moved her hand back and forth in the fire, watching the flames lick harmlessly around her fingers. It distracted her from the quiver so that when she finally tore her attention away all that remained of that was ash and the brass fixtures that had been on the leather.

She sat back staring at the ash, feeling like she'd finally let the last piece of the old Muireann go. She'd expected to feel sad, but she didn't in that moment. She looked down at her hand again, the one that had been in the fire, and frowned, deciding not to mention that to anyone just yet. Like the dragon mark or her eye colour she wasn't sure what it meant but it also didn't seem to actually do anything helpful.

Standing, she decided that she'd had enough for one day, of everything, and changed to go to sleep. Another long day at the library awaited her and she suspected it would be only one of many to come.

* * *

The next several weeks passed in a blur of mind-numbing research fatigue for Muireann. The weather warmed as spring transitioned to early summer. Muireann learned the names of all the servers, cleaning staff, bartenders and the owners at the Blue Star and her room became as familiar to her as the one she'd had at her brother's house. Their group fell into a new routine, somewhat similar to their camp one. Muireann and Reyleth worked on finding out anything they could about the green crystal, the mage who had made it, or the red dragon, making slow headway at piecing together the story. Calla continued to spend her time looking for answers about who was pursuing them, and Tash and Lee alternated between staying with Muireann at the library or hanging around the inn to keep an eye out for anyone looking for them. Muireann kept in practice with her bow by going down to the lake in the early mornings and shooting where she safely could. In the evenings they met back up for a shared dinner and discussed the day. Muireann continued to tutor Tash, taking turns with Reyleth, who was still teaching him Elvish. Calla and Lee sweet-talked the innkeeper into letting them use the area behind the inn to spar at night, often joined by others staying there who wanted to practise sword fighting or hand-to-hand combat. When Muireann found out Lee was growing bored as the days dragged on the two explored various options until they stumbled upon knitting, a past chore Muireann had always disliked but which Lee found soothing and peaceful, giving the usually very physically active selkie something to do to relax while Muireann was reading. And Muireann found a balance between nights with her wife in their room and nights with Reyleth in his, finding joy with each of them; often when Muireann was with Reyleth, Lee would find her own company to pass the evening with, giving Muireann the sealskin to guard.

It was a comfortable routine to fall into, but with every passing day Muireann grew more frustrated with their lack of real progress. She was working her way through every book the Great Library had on the Aldovanan, having tried skimming several before realising there was nothing for it but to read them all until she found something helpful. She knew more than she'd ever wanted to about the history of the First Age and the wars that had ended it but had found only single line references to Olcanac, and nothing so far like what Reyleth had mentioned. For his part he was still painstakingly going through the texts he'd acquired, making notes about the Aldovanan magic as he went. He didn't seem the least bit bothered by the slow pace of their research and seemed amused by Muireann's growing impatience, but she couldn't shake the gnawing certainty that they needed to find a solution soon before their fragile security was shattered.

Whoever might still be hunting them had disappeared into the shadows and each week wore on with no sign of anything strange or of any danger. After a full month had gone Muireann started to wonder if maybe she was being paranoid and they were finally safe, at least as long as they remained in Mistlen. She couldn't help but remember, though, that every other time they'd let their guard down their enemy had re-emerged, and she worried that staying in one place and having such a set routine might work against them.

That morning they all lingered over breakfast, enjoying the seasonal berries that were on offer that day.

'I'll be going to the trade market today,' Calla said, sighing and leaning back in her chair. 'We're hitting the start of the busy season for merchants which means multiple large caravans going through every day. If there's any good gossip to be found that's the most likely place.'

'I'm here today,' Lee said, shrugging. 'I'll stay down in the common room and knit, see if I overhear anything interesting.'

Reyleth sighed. 'I'm going to go back to the bookshop where I found several of the texts I've been studying and see if they have any dictionaries or glossaries of older elvish. There are some obscure passages that I am just unable to translate.'

'I'm sorry, that must be so frustrating,' Muireann said sympathetically.

He sighed. 'It's...yes, let's just say frustrating. How about yourself? Back into the stacks?'

She nodded. 'Tash and I will be at the library today, as usual. I suspect that the book we need, the history annal that you mentioned that discusses Olcanac at more length, is in their restricted section.'

'Have they agreed to let you access it?' Calla asked, knowing that Muireann had been trying to get in there for the past week.

'Not yet, but if I can't get in one way, I'll try another.'

'You realise if they catch you sneaking in when they've denied you permission they may ban you from the building,' Reyleth said, looking amused.

'Oh, I'm aware,' she said archly. 'But at this point I haven't found anything remotely useful in any of the history books in the main section, so why not?'

'Have you tried any of the other sections?' Calla asked, spearing a berry with her fork.

'No, why would I? We need information on the Aldovanan,

that's history.'

'Sure, but didn't you say you'd learned the dragon's name from a children's book?' Calla said, talking and chewing. 'Why not look there too?'

Muireann stared at her friend in shock. 'Calla! That's brilliant!'

'What is?' Tash said.

'I've had tunnel vision with all of this, narrowed down on just history because I was thinking we needed to find out as much as we could about the First Age. But you're exactly right. I learned more from that old children's story book than I have in a month going through history texts,' Muireann said, feeling re-inspired. 'I'll try looking in the mythology and folklore section today.'

'So, you won't try to get into the restricted section?' Reyleth pressed.

She wasn't sure if he was worried for her safety or worried about the absolute scandal of her getting barred from a library, but she could tell he was genuinely worried. 'Well...I'm not saying I won't no. But I might save that for later.'

He sighed as if he was being very much put upon but smiled when he said. 'Alright then, I don't suppose anyone can stop you if you've set your mind on this, probably including the library staff.'

'Let's hope but first things first, I'll check through the other books and be sure there's nothing there that may help.'

He nodded and with breakfast finished the group broke up to their own ventures for the day. Muireann and Tash walked the now familiar route to the library quickly, greeting the door guards by name. Today a young man named Cayvin was working the front desk, but he knew Muireann and Tash on sight and let them in with a cheerful 'good morning'.

Unlike usual, however, Muireann didn't head straight for the second floor, instead moving into the first-floor stacks, searching for the folklore section. Tash was in the habit now of reading while Muireann worked and found a book that caught his interest while she considered and discarded multiple choices. Ignoring the young man as he leaned against a wall and read, Muireann worked her way methodically through every book that seemed like a possibility. She was surprised to find several that did include stories of Murjergalan killing Olcanac, although neither was called by name. They were all children's tales with titles like 'The Mage and Dragon' or 'The Great Beast and the Wizard', but the story was clearly the one she was looking for. She scribbled several pages of notes based on these tales, not sure which details might be useful.

At mid-day they stopped, Muireann putting her books back and tapping Tash on the shoulder to get his attention. 'Lunch time.'

He put his book up and then stretched. 'I have to admit I like this change of pace. I think I've studied so much history I can practically recite every event from the First Age through Felecia's coronation.'

She smiled at him as they walked back to the small sitting room the library had for its patrons to eat in. 'Well then, you are well on your way to a solid education. But you know you can always read something from whatever section you like, you don't have to stick with history just because that's where I am.'

He sobered slightly, glancing around. 'I think it's better I stay with you. Just in case,'

She started to tell him he didn't need to, but then stopped and just nodded. The library seemed safe enough, but he was right that they shouldn't assume anything. Silent now they entered the little sitting room, heading for the small table that held a buffet of food options. Mostly finger foods but enough to tide them over until they returned to the inn for dinner. They filled their plates and then went to sit in a back corner. Muireann nodded a greeting to a man sitting at a table in the middle of the room who was a frequent sight both in the library and the sitting room. Salevil was a mage attached to the largest school of magic in Mistlen, although he seemed to spend most of his time in the library. As usual he was sitting with one of the books he wasn't supposed to have around the food, his narrow shoulders hunched over and his long black hair obscuring half his face. He nodded back to Muireann but quickly returned to his reading, absentmindedly stuffing some sort of flaky pastry into his mouth every few minutes.

Muireann sat and ate as quickly as she could without seeming totally uncouth, eager to get back to work. The only other person in the room was another man sitting in the opposite corner. She didn't know his name but had seen him a handful of times around the library and assumed he was most likely a scholar, although his clothes were fine enough he could have been one of the lesser nobility, she supposed. It was difficult for Muireann to get a clear read on the man – she guessed he was around her own age, but he could have been a decade older or younger. His hair was a sandy brown, his skin a light tan, his eyes an unremarkable hazel. Everything about him was anonymously bland but instead of finding him easily forgettable Muireann thought of him as a puzzle. By his appearance and the cut of his clothes she'd guess he might be Donlachian, but she didn't know enough about the other kingdoms to be certain of even that. Despite her curiosity, though, she had never found an excuse to speak to the stranger.

When they were done eating, they returned to the children's books, Muireann continuing to hunt around for any clues. By late afternoon she'd grown frustrated again and turned to Tash. 'I think I've gotten as much from here as we're likely to. Before we leave, I'd like to take a tour of the third floor.'

'Are you sure?' he asked, looking back at the desk where Cayvin still sat.

'I'm sure. I know we might not be able to get into the

restricted section, but I'd like to at least see it.'

'Lead the way then,' Tash agreed, setting the book he'd been reading aside.

Muireann walked slowly up to the second floor and then around to the stairs for the third floor. They walked up and then paused, Muireann listening for anyone who might be following them. Everything was quiet so she continued on. This floor was initially rows of medical and herbal text. They walked through those into rows of shelves filled with magical books. Muireann hesitated there, realising that this might be another area worth checking out. But that could wait so she led them further until they reached the final area, in the very back of the third floor.

She had feared that the restricted section would be a separate room which would be a considerable problem for them, but it wasn't. As with the entrance there was a chest-high railing and a gate behind which were perhaps a dozen floor to ceiling shelves. She stepped closer, leaning forward to inspect the gate.

'Why isn't there a guard?' Tash asked.

'I suspect there are magical wards on this rail and doorway,' Muireann said. 'If I had to guess, which I would be since I'm not a mage, they probably give a special talisman to anyone with permission to enter that negates them, otherwise you either can't get in or it sets off an alarm of some sort.'

'So how do you get in?'

'I'm not sure yet,' Muireann said, slowly. 'I have an idea, but I need to talk to Reyleth first. I definitely need to get in there, though.'

'Why?' he asked, although he sounded resigned to the inevitability of it.

'Because I can see the book I need, the one Rey mentioned reading a long time ago with the full story in it. It's on a shelf close to the gate.'

Tash sighed. 'Well, that's that then.'

She smiled and gave him an affectionate pat on the shoulder.

'That's a problem for tomorrow. Let's head back and get some dinner.'

'Now that sounds like a good plan,' Tash said, perking up.

Shaking her head in amusement at his eagerness for the same food they'd been eating for the last month, which she was thoroughly bored with, she led the way back towards the stairs. Of course, part of her boredom was that she'd fallen into such a habit of ordering stew on the road that she'd continued it when they'd arrived in Mistlen and by the time she realised and worked up the nerve to try something different the servers were so accustomed to her order being the same they didn't even ask anymore. And she was too polite – and embarrassed – to say anything. At least her other meals were more diverse.

She stepped out from the stacks but found a man standing there, blocking them. She hadn't heard anyone come up and was startled to see him there now. It was the nondescript stranger, the one whose name she didn't know. She tensed and stepped closer to Tash, feeling oddly unsettled by his sudden appearance. 'Excuse us, sir, we were just heading back down.'

'Didn't find what you were looking for?' he said, smiling slightly as if it were a personal joke.

She liked that even less than him popping up on the third floor. 'I suppose we didn't. If you'll excuse us.'

'Actually, I won't,' the man said, his voice more pleasant than the words.

Next to her Tash tensed, hand reaching for a sword he didn't have. 'And why will you not?'

'I'd like to speak to you for a moment, in private,' he said, still blocking their way.

'Alright,' Muireann said, standing her ground but nervous about this entire encounter.

'My name is Ghellin,' he said, and when they didn't introduce themselves went on. 'And you, young sir, are Tash, a new sell-sword. And you, my lady, are Muireann Dragonslayer.'

Muireann's unease was growing quickly, but she simply nodded at him. 'As you say. Would you like to speak to us of more than just our names?'

He actually smiled at that. 'You are bold. I admire that, although I shouldn't be surprised that the woman who killed Murjergalan would be bold.'

Tash threw Muireann a desperate look, wanting some direction on how to handle the man. Muireann sighed and crossed her arms. 'So you're the one who hired the mercenaries that have been pursuing us then.'

Tash gasped slightly at her words and Ghellin looked genuinely surprised for an instant before recovering. 'Bold and clever. I should have expected that as well. Good, if you are so clever then perhaps you'll listen to reason.'

'You've tried to kill us several times,' Muireann pointed out. 'I'm more likely to expect a dagger in the back from you than any reason.'

His eyes narrowed at that, his carefully bland mask slipping for just an instant before returning. 'We have a different understanding of the situation. I never ordered anyone to kill you, nor would I be so...direct. If the people I hired were too rough in their methods, well, that is one problem with mercenaries, isn't it?'

She arched an eyebrow, trying to imitate the way Calla could look bored and condescending at once. 'Let me see if I can continue to be *clever*. So, the people you hired before we arrived here failed to rob us before we got here. Repeatedly. Now we are here but we're also very high profile. Staying in a well-known inn, patronising the Great Library. I imagine that makes it difficult to find anyone else willing to go after us, at least anyone who wouldn't be a risk to you, shall we say taking what you want for themselves.'

His eyes hardened and she knew she'd guessed correctly. But when he spoke his voice was still conversationally pleasant.

'Perhaps. But I have quite a bit of money to throw around and for the right price these things can still be arranged. Having such a high-profile cuts both ways, Muireann. You may think it protects you, but it also makes you very, very easy to find.'

He spread his hands out as if to show the truth of his words. She kept her face impassive. 'What do you want?'

'I want the stone, of course.'

She feigned surprise then reached in and pulled the Dragon Stone from her tunic. 'It would be fairly obvious who you stole it from.'

For a moment she could see his confusion, could see him trying to decide if she really believed that was the stone he was after. When he spoke this time, his anger was not as well concealed. 'Now you are trying my patience. You know that isn't what I was talking about.'

'Do I?'

'Give me the other stone, the Basglassin,' he said, stepping forward.

Tash moved in front of Muireann, and Ghellin immediately stopped, putting his hands out to his sides. When he spoke again the pleasant tone was back. 'I asked you to listen to reason, will you?'

'Say what you intend to say,' Muireann said, knowing she wasn't going to want to hear it.

'Give me the stone, the one you found,' he said. 'The one that you took from the dragon's cave. You don't understand what it is, what it can do, but I do understand. I've been looking for it for decades. Trying to find a way to get it from that cave.'

She shook her head. 'I know what it is.'

'You don't,' he insisted. 'You can't, not really, or you wouldn't be in here every day researching it. You have no idea what it can do.'

'I know it's a weapon the likes of which this world hasn't seen in an age.'

He faltered slightly at her words, as if he had truly believed she couldn't know that much. 'It is the most powerful relic in existence. It can be used to change this world.'

'The only change it would bring is death,' she said sadly.

'Don't you see?' he said, his voice pleading but his eyes hard. 'That is exactly what we need to make Tallan what it should be. We live in a world where humans are the most common but least powerful of all the species. Look around you. Humans farm, work the land, provide food and provide soldiers for kings and emperors. But the elves rule everything, they hold all the real power. Dwarves are the craftsmen, giving humans no chance to flourish there, making human made items seem cheap. The selkies and ocean-folk rule the seas. The tree-folk control the wild places. And every other people have magic where human mages are rare and less skilled. The shortest lived, the least magical, humans are reduced to farming and fighting, as if we were good for nothing else. With that weapon we can change everything. We can end the elven empire and put humans in power where they should be.'

'The nine kingdoms are ruled by humans,' Tash said defiantly, and Muireann felt a surge of gratitude that he wasn't being swayed by the man's words. 'Human kings and queens over the kingdoms, ruling across the land.'

'Puppet rulers,' the man sneered. 'Who answer always to the elven throne. You haven't been to Gold Spire, you haven't seen the decadence they live in, apart from the people they rule.'

'Do you really think a human empire would be any different?' Muireann asked, knowing that ultimately kings and empires would always be what they were, some better and others worse but none ideal. The elven empire was as fairly ruled as any she'd ever read about, rarely interfering directly in the nine kingdoms and serving mostly to keep the wider peace and make sure the rule of law was equal across the land and upheld. Yes, they taxed the people and she was sure they lived in a luxury that the common people could only dream of, but to overthrow them just because they were elves would mean setting the world into chaos and returning them to the time before the empire, when kingdoms endlessly battled each other and the law was whatever each lord and petty ruler declared it to be. 'Do you think humans would rule better?'

'With the elves gone and humans free to grow into their own power, yes,' he said, edging forward again.

Muireann gasped as the implication hit her. 'You intend to annihilate them all. All the elves. Gone, murdered with this weapon?'

'No,' Tash whispered, too horrified to say anything else.

'Yes,' Ghellin said calmly. 'It's the only logical solution. With the elves gone humans can flourish. *We* can flourish.'

'You can't mean this,' Muireann said, remembering the terrible visions the stone had given her and knowing that if he got the green crystal, he might be able to do what he was saying. Not all at once but eventually he could make his vision real. 'A world without elves is a world without balance.'

'A world without elves is a world dominated by humans,' he said. 'And otherwise, they would just seize power again, one way or another. I can't allow that.'

'And what then?' Tash asked, looking sick. 'You remove the dwarves as well? The selkies? The tree-folk? Every non-human people until only humans are left?'

'This world should belong to humans,' he said. 'And I will make it so.'

'No,' Muireann said, shaking her head. 'You can't do this. Every sentient species has its own place in the world, every one exists as part of the wider balance. Yes, humans have less magic, but we have the most skill with farming and agriculture, children of Calleshen that we are. We are the best strategists and creative thinkers, the most able to adapt to change of all the species.'

'Exactly!' he said, leaning forward. 'Where would the others be without us producing crops, feeding everyone? Where would they be without humans innovating new ways to do things? And yet we do not rule as we should.'

'Of course not,' Muireann said. 'We live in *balance* with the others. We have things we do best as they have things they do. We all need each other.'

He frowned. 'I should have known a woman who married a selkie and spreads her legs for an elf wouldn't care about doing what's best for humans.'

Muireann jerked back at his words, not because she was insulted, which she wasn't, but because he knew such personal details. Her marriage to Lee wasn't a secret but very few people knew about her and Reyleth; he wasn't demonstrably affectionate in public with her and when they bedded each other it was always in his room, never anywhere else, at least not since they'd arrived in Mistlen, and even on the road it hadn't been anywhere they could have been seen.

Ghellin misread her reaction, relaxing slightly and forcing a friendlier tone. 'I see you do have some shame left at least about these...unsavoury dalliances of yours—'

'Don't speak to her that way,' Tash cut in, angry on Muireann's behalf.

Ghellin held up a hand. 'No, young man, this is good. There's hope yet if she knows in her heart what she's doing is wrong. Listen to me, Muireann, I'm a reasonable man. I don't want to make things messy, but I will if I have to. Give me the stone. You know it's the right thing to do.'

Muireann said nothing, scrambling to think of any way to respond that wouldn't make it clear she didn't have the stone, which might implicate Calla. Especially since he seemed to know so many personal details about them all. Tash turned and looked at her over his shoulder, his face questioning her silence.

Again Ghellin misread her. He nodded. 'I see you need time

to consider my words. Never let it be said I am not a generous man. I will give you three days to consider what I've said, then you can meet me back here to do what you know is right. I know you don't need money, but I can pay you if you want me to, just name the price. Or you can give it to me freely because you know that everything I've said is true, that the Second Age is coming to an end, the time of the other so-called sentient species. It's time for humans to ascend to the dominance we deserve. You can do what's right for *your* people. You can hand me that weapon and help me to remake the world and erase all of them from it.'

Muireann's eyes flicked up to meet Ghellin's, speechless in the face of what he was saying as if all her clever words had evaporated under such unrestrained hate. He relaxed slightly, but went on. 'Of course, in fairness I should tell you that I would be remiss not to be sure that the city gates are watched, in case you try to flee, but I'm sure you realise that your chances on the road, well…as I said I don't want this to get messy but it is much easier to find people willing to go after a small group on the road. I'm sure you understand. It's your choice, Muireann, to be a hero who ushers humanity into a new age…or not.'

Muireann nodded, then said softly. 'Three days. Here.'

He smiled. 'I see we understand each other.'

'I understand you,' Muireann said, her voice flat with shock.

He inclined his head slightly at both of them. 'Good night, my friends. I look forward to our next meeting.'

And then he was gone, his footsteps echoing down the stairway.

'Muireann—' Tash started, obviously very upset, but she held up a hand and then put a finger to her lips to tell him to be silent. They stood there as the minutes dragged out and the sound of Ghellin's steps died away. Only when Muireann heard the faint sound of the front doors of the library opening and closing – grateful that they were so heavy and loud – did she gesture for Tash to follow her as she jogged down the stairs.

'We have to tell the others,' she said. 'But keep on your guard all the way back. I don't put it past him to have set up an ambush, all his words about time to think to the contrary.'

Tash nodded, his lips set in a grim line.

Chapter 9

A New Plan

The walk back to the inn was one of the longest of Muireann's life, every sound and shadow making her wish for her bow and her quiver at her hip.

They burst into the common room of the Blue Star, walking quickly to the other three already sitting at their usual table. Muireann glanced around the room, seeing every face as a potential spy, then leaned over the table pitching her voice low. 'Calla's room. Now.'

Perplexed and alarmed the others followed her up the stairs. Calla unlocked the room and they shuffled in, but as soon as the door was closed Muireann pulled Lee and Reyleth into a loose embrace, shaking as the aftermath of the confrontation hit her.

'What is it, Muiri? What happened?' Calla said, looking from her to Tash in real concern.

'We met the man who hired the mercenaries,' Tash said.

'What?' the other three spoke over each other in their agitation.

'He found us, to be more precise, at the library,' Muireann said, still clinging to Rey and Lee. 'He's been watching us there. Not that we knew that until now, but I mean I've seen him there a few times before. I didn't think anything of it because there are regulars who go there. But tonight this man, Ghellin, waited until we went to the third floor to look at the restricted area and he confronted us when we were leaving. Probably because the third floor is pretty quiet. He admitted he hired the mercenaries and that he wants the green crystal.'

'And he told us why,' Tash said, looking ill at the memory.

'What did he say?' Calla asked.

'It's worse than anything I could ever have imagined,'

Muireann whispered, holding tighter to Lee and Rey.

'What is it, Muireann?' Reyleth said gently. 'What's his plan?'

'He means to use the crystal to kill every non-human on Tallan,' Tash said.

There was silence for a moment then Calla said. 'That's impossible. Everyone who isn't human in the entire world? Just kill them all?'

'Yes,' Tash and Muireann said together.

'That's impossible,' Calla said again, but Muireann could see the fear in her and knew the high elf understood that it was far too possible with this weapon. She watched Calla's hand move to her belt pouch, as Muireann had been in a habit of doing when she carried the stone, and knew the other woman was reassuring herself it was still safe.

'Whatever happens, under no circumstances can Ghellin get the crystal,' Muireann said, her voice shaking. Next to her, Tash nodded.

'But how are we to keep it safe?' Calla asked, fingers tightening around the pouch she clutched.

'I don't know yet,' Muireann admitted. 'But I think there's a book in the library that may help give us some direction.'

'It's in the restricted section,' Tash said, looking as frustrated as Muireann felt. 'You have to have a special pass to enter that area and they won't give it to you, Muireann.'

'We'll need a plan to sneak you in, Muiri,' Calla said, her eyes narrowing as she thought over the problem.

'Yes, and I think I may have an idea, but first we have several other problems,' Muireann said.

'He knows a great deal about us,' Tash said.

'He must have someone spying on us,' Muireann said, still agitated. 'There's no other way he can know what he does. Our names, that Tash was a new mercenary. That we had enough money that we couldn't be bought off. That I was married to Lee and sleeping with Reyleth.'

Calla whistled. 'That is a *lot* of information for him to have.'

'He's probably paying someone here to tell him things,' Reyleth said, frowning and holding tighter to Muireann. 'All this time we've been looking out for strangers asking questions about us but none of us thought to worry about the staff at the inn.'

Calla frowned and started pacing. 'Yes, that was sloppy. I apologise, my friends, I should have known better.'

'We've all gotten too comfortable here,' Lee said softly.

'We'll have to move to another inn and be more careful,' Calla said, still pacing. 'Someplace obscure—'

'Not necessarily obscure,' Muireann corrected her, remembering other things Ghellin had said. 'He had said something else about part of why the attacks stopped when we arrived here was that he couldn't find anyone willing to go after us so publicly when we were so well known.'

'Ha!' Calla smiled at that. 'So, you see the advantage of my spreading your story everywhere.'

'What he said was that it was harder to find people willing to do it,' Tash said. 'Not that it was impossible.'

'Still, it's been a month and he's been forced to confront us directly,' Calla said. 'Which means he either can't afford the people he'd need for the job, or he knows it would be traced back to him.'

Muireann finally moved away from her lovers, who predictably stepped away from each other as soon as she was gone. She went to stand closer to Calla's window. 'He chose his time carefully I think, when it was just me and Tash. I really believe he thought he could convince us that what he was trying to do was right.'

'He's mad then,' Calla said, shaking her head. 'And for all his spying he knows you not at all.'

'What else did he say?' Reyleth asked.

'He wants us to give him the crystal, voluntarily, and he

really seemed to think he'd persuaded us, or at least me. He's convinced I can give the crystal to him. Or he implied he'd take it by force, and blast the consequences,' Muireann said, trying to remember the entire conversation. 'That I was to meet him back there in three days with it. And that he was having all the gates out of Mistlen watched.'

Calla shrugged. 'I'd assume that's been true since we arrived. He must have a great deal of money to throw at this pet project of his. He might be a noble, or from one of the old, wealthy merchant families.'

'So then, what are our options?' Tash said. 'If we move someplace new it may warn him we intend to fight back. But if we stay here we have no idea who is relaying information back to him.'

'Do we trust him to really wait three days for Muireann to go to him, after he's revealed his plan?' Lee asked.

'Oddly enough, I do trust that,' Muireann said. 'I think he genuinely believes that what he wants to do is reasonable and should appeal to all humans and I'll join him willingly.'

'You think he has convinced himself you mean to give him the crystal?' Reyleth said, looking uneasy.

'I think he assumes that since I have the Dragon Stone, I have the green crystal and the power to hand it over to him if I choose to,' Muireann said, thinking as she talked. 'Which is why he reached out to me. The fact I'm human probably plays a role too, given his obvious prejudice against others. He believes that given a few days to think about what he said I'll agree with him, despite – how did he say it? – my "unsavoury dalliances".'

Reyleth frowned, looking very unhappy at that. She met his eyes and smiled softly. 'He's a fool several times over if he thinks you are either a dalliance or anyone I would ever betray. Even if it wasn't more than just your fate – or Lee or Calla's at stake.' She turned and met the eyes of the other two as well before going on. 'I would never hand a weapon to anyone's hand knowing it would be used against you. Nor would I be part of annihilating entire species.'

Rey's face softened, but he still looked concerned. 'I know that, of course. But that he is so convinced humans in general would side with him...is concerning.'

'I would never,' Tash said forcefully. 'What he's suggesting is abhorrent. There may be some humans who would side with him, there are always evil men to be found, but I believe that most people would see his plan for the horror it is.'

Muireann nodded. 'There are those who don't like elves, hate them even, but Tash is right. I have to believe he is. Most wouldn't side with Ghellin. Otherwise, why bother with this quest for the crystal? Why not just raise an army? He said it himself, humans outnumber the other species.'

'This is getting philosophical, and I don't know that we have time for it.' Calla stopped pacing near the fire, the flames making her golden skin look amber. 'For now, we stay here, but we say nothing outside our rooms or when anyone except our own group is around. Assume everyone around us could be a spy. We have three days until he expects to meet with Muireann, which means we have three days to keep up appearances that nothing has changed while we come up with a plan to get the book we need and get out of Mistlen.'

'I have an idea about getting the book, but I need to work out some details,' Muireann said. 'Let's do this, tomorrow we act as usual. I'll try to work out the details of my idea. Lee goes with me tomorrow and I don't think I'll see Ghellin. I suspect he's been avoiding days when Lee's with me.'

'Perhaps so, but we can't assume everyone at the library isn't also a spy for him,' Calla said, frowning. 'Speaking of what we do and don't know, I'll see what I can find out about this "Ghellin" tomorrow. I know how to ask without raising too many alarms with people. And I'll see about ways to get out of the city that don't involve the main gates.'

'There are ways out that aren't guarded?' Muireann said, having assumed Mistlen was too well run for that.

'Oh, my dear sweet naïve friend,' Calla smirked at her. 'Mistlen is a city, and any city has its illegal trade, and any illegal trade has its own ways in and out.'

'What should Tash and I do?' Reyleth asked, frowning.

'Tash can stay here and keep guard on our rooms,' Calla said. 'Maybe he'll see who among the staff seems particularly interested in us. As to you, best to get any supplies you may need when we leave the city or possibly for dealing with the crystal. It may be that when we go, we'll have to go quickly.'

'Before we wrap this up, I do think we need a better way of hiding the green crystal,' Muireann said. 'If Ghellin knows we have it, then there's always a chance he'll try a more direct approach to getting it.'

'Our solution up to this point has been effective,' Calla pointed out.

'True, but up to this point we didn't know for certain anyone was trying to get it or knew we had it,' Muireann said.

'I thought we agreed hiding it was a bad idea?' Lee said. 'What other option is there besides carrying it on one of us?'

'Which is what we've been doing, but in a way that all things considered may be too vulnerable. Alright, well, it's a smaller stone, smaller than the Dragon Stone, and I wear that one,' Muireann said, thinking quickly. 'What if we turn it into a jewellery piece, something Calla could wear but where the entire stone would be covered, hidden. We could...put it in a locket. The kind that ladies wear to carry tokens from lovers. But we could seal it closed.'

She watched Lee, Tash and Rey glance at Calla in unison and realised that she'd just let slip who had the crystal, but there was no taking it back. She sighed, then admitted. 'Calla has had the crystal since we entered Mistlen. I decided it was too dangerous for me to carry, all things considered.'

'And it would be just as dangerous for us to trade it around between us,' Calla said, frowning. 'I've been thinking about that too—'

'I don't want it,' Reyleth cut in, looking alarmed. 'I'm sorry, I will do anything I can to keep it safe, but not that. It's too dangerous for a mage to risk touching it, I think.'

Tash nodded grimly. 'If I had to, I would do my part to carry it, but I'd rather not chance it.'

'It's not an issue,' Muireann said before Lee could jump in as well. 'Calla and I found it and ultimately it's my responsibility for killing the dragon that was guarding it. But as it's too dangerous for me to have it, Calla has agreed to carry it now.'

'I like the idea of wearing it, hidden in plain sight,' Calla said, smiling slowly. 'No one can see what it really is and no one, including me, can touch it, but it will be safer than in a belt pouch.'

'Exactly,' Muireann said. 'It wouldn't look like anything exceptional, and you'd have it with you all the time.'

'Hmmm,' Reyleth said. 'I can see the wisdom, but it may look suspicious if Calla suddenly starts wearing such a thing. We know Ghellin is watching us closely, we must assume he'll notice.'

'So...all four of you will start wearing something similar,' Muireann said. 'I'll get some gold from my account at the bankers guildhall, and I can also get an emerald I have there which is a close match for the green crystal. That gives us a fake in case we need one. Then I'll go to a jeweller and commission four lockets. I can make a show of giving them to you all over dinner, say something about how they are a token of our friendship, something like that.'

Lee looked excited, Tash thoughtful, Reyleth decidedly resigned. She doubted he liked the idea of wearing such an ostentatious pendant but when he didn't say anything knew he'd play along. Calla nodded with enthusiasm. 'I like it. But when you go to the jeweller make a point of ordering a special case as well. Something that could hold the real crystal. Make a point of being vague about it, act suspicious. If Ghellin does get word of this, hopefully he'll assume it was all a ruse to get that to store the crystal and ignore the pendants.'

'Hopefully,' Muireann agreed. 'And we can put the emerald in the new case so if he does try anything or order us to be attacked, they'll be looking for the fake in the case.'

Reyleth still looked unhappy, but he nodded. Calla's eyes swept the group. 'Alright, well let us head back down to eat before our absence seems too strange, since we've established some very predictable patterns.'

'I'll be down shortly,' Muireann said to Calla then, 'Reyleth, can you wait a moment?'

He did, of course, waiting until the others had left and the door was shut to ask, 'What is it?'

'Let's go to my room – no actually, let's go to yours,' she said.

He looked even more puzzled but led the way over to his room. She went over and stood next to the fire, contemplating the flames. 'I'm glad we know who exactly is behind this now, but I wanted to ask you about something you'd mentioned a while ago, back when we first found out I have some of the dragon's imperviousness.'

'Alright?' he said, looking curious now.

'You said that I might be impervious to magic as well, but at the time I didn't want to talk about it.'

'I remember,' he said, his voice gentle.

'Well, I've come to terms a bit better with things now and more than that I think I – we – need to know if you were right.'

'You want me to see if I can affect you with magic?' he sounded hesitant, which surprised her.

'It was your idea,' she reminded him again.

'Why do you want to know this, Muireann?' he asked.

'Because it's important,' she said. 'If we know I can't be influenced or harmed with magic then that gives us an advantage. If I still can be then that's something we need to know as well.'

He still hesitated, his eyes searching her face. She was confused by the sudden reticence. 'Why don't you want to do this? It *was* your idea.'

'I'm willing to do it, but I don't want you doing anything foolish if I was wrong.'

'I already tried and succeeded in killing a dragon,' she said wryly. 'Pretty sure I can't get more foolish than that.'

He closed the distance between them, reaching out to stroke her cheek. 'I know. That's' what frightens me.'

'I don't understand.'

'I know that when you fought the dragon you didn't mean to walk away from it,' he said, his voice barely a whisper.

'Rey...' she trailed off, not sure what to say, but also unsurprised that he'd guessed as much as he had. She'd always known if anyone would see her true motives in what she'd done, it would be him.

'Lennath, please,' he said, letting her see the pain that thought gave him. 'I've known you too long and I love you too dearly not to have realised what you were actually intending. And I know why you see this immortality as a curse instead of a blessing.'

'It is!'

'For someone who doesn't want to live I imagine it feels that way.'

'Rey!' Muireann gasped that he'd said it so bluntly. 'No, please, don't think that. It's not like that anymore. Yes, I admit you are right, when I faced the dragon I didn't think I'd walk away from it. I just wanted to...I don't even know anymore. To make a grand gesture for my children. But I didn't die and so much has changed since then. I'm still grieving, part of me may always be grieving, but I don't feel immersed in it anymore. I have you and Lee, I have Calla, Tash, and we have this important thing to do.'

He was still searching her face, still looking anguished and it hurt her to see it. She reached up and took his hands in hers. 'Reyleth, I swear to you I want to live. And I intend to do so.'

'I don't want you testing this in order to try to find a way to change that,' he said.

'I'm not, I *swear* it. I honestly believe you are right anyway, and I don't think Erla, goddess of magic, would have magic as a way that her creatures could be killed. Which is why it doesn't work on dragons or unicorns.'

He let out a shaking breath, but nodded. 'I've gotten rather used to the idea of having you around for the rest of my life, you know.'

'You don't think I'll end up annoying you in another couple of hundred years?' She tried to joke to lighten the mood.

'No,' he said simply.

She giggled but tried to look serious. 'You're so stubborn.'

'Yes,' he agreed, smiling now.

'Alright, well I still would like you to do what you can to check and see if magic might affect me, please,' she said before they could become too side-tracked with each other. 'Firstly, because I think we need to know before we get into another fight, but secondly because if it doesn't then I think I may be able to get past the wards and into the restricted section of the library.'

He stepped back, letting her hands go reluctantly. 'I see. You would just walk in past the wards. That is not a bad idea at all, but you realise there is almost certainly a spell to ensure no books are taken out as well?'

'I had a thought about that too, but I don't think you're going to like it.'

'Dare I ask?' he sounded amused at least, rather than

annoyed, which gave her some hope they'd moved past the uncomfortable soul baring of earlier.

'It involves windows,' she said slowly.

'You mean to throw a priceless centuries old book out of a window?' he said, sounding as if the mere idea caused him physical pain.

'Not exactly.'

He stared at her until she went on. 'I was thinking more of, well, jumping out of the window with the book.'

'Muireann!'

'What?' she said, trying and failing to look innocent. 'It won't hurt me, and the book would be safe.'

'You are an absolute menace, do you realise that?' he said, shaking his head in disbelief.

'Says the person who just swore he wanted me around for the next 800 years,' she pointed out.

He tried not to laugh and failed, pulling her into his arms. 'Clearly I have no choice but to stay with you as long as possible to keep you out of trouble.'

'Oh clearly,' she agreed, laughing with him. 'Now come on and test whether I'm magic-proof or not so we can go eat.'

He rolled his eyes at that but dutifully stepped back. 'I'll start small, let me know if you feel anything.'

He steadied himself for a moment, then chanted something quickly. She felt something nebulous, but she couldn't describe it. When he looked at her expectantly, she shrugged.

He hesitated, frowned then tried again. His fingers formed shapes and he chanted softly, the motion and words familiar enough that she suspected it was his basic self-defence spell. She felt something, as if a slight breeze was swirling around her, then nothing. She shrugged again.

His serious expression broke under a smile. 'Nothing at all? Then I suspect I was correct, if that didn't even register with you.'

'I felt like a breeze was blowing but nothing serious or even alarming,' she said. 'If I hadn't known you were trying something I probably wouldn't have noticed at all.'

He nodded. 'Alright, let me try one more thing. It's a bit more extreme, but if this doesn't do anything then I would be reasonably confident that I was right.'

'Let's prove you right then,' she said, smiling.

He braced himself, chanted and looked sharply at her; she felt a slight stirring of something that reminded her a bit of the air in very dry weather. Again, she shrugged and this time his smile was wide and he was very obviously pleased. 'That was the small lightning spell I used on the mercenaries. If you didn't feel that at all then I don't think magic can affect you in a noticeable way.'

'Could you try one more thing?' she asked, smiling with him. Reyleth had always enjoyed it when his personal theories could be shown to be true.

He nodded but looked less happy. 'I can, but I must admit I am a bit fatigued after that. I can't manage a stronger spell without preparing further or resting first.'

'I don't want you to do anything stronger, just set a basic ward so we can see if I can pass through it.'

'Not a bad idea, actually, if you mean to follow through with your idea,' he admitted. He stepped over to the area where his bathtub was, using the tiles to demarcate the border of the ward. After a few minutes of pouring out a powder from a pouch at his belt and chanting softly he nodded to her. 'Go on and try then.'

She walked over, suddenly nervous that this out of everything would still affect her, when her nebulous plan depended on her being able to walk into an area that no one should be able to enter. But when she reached the tile, she stepped across and walked to the tub without missing a step. As with the other spells, she didn't even really notice anything except a faint tingle when she walked across the line, and she wasn't totally sure that wasn't her imagination.

She turned back to him, smiling now as he had been earlier, meeting his equally pleased face. 'I suppose that answers that question then.'

'Indeed, it does,' he agreed. 'Fascinating. You stepped through the ward but didn't disrupt it or break it. I wonder... well, no matter. I can speculate later. You've proven your own theory holds, so you will proceed with your plan?'

'At this point my plan is to get some dinner and after all that magic you must be starving,' she said. 'I'll work out what I'm going to do for certain tomorrow.'

He looked for a moment as if he were going to say something more, then shook his head and went to the door. 'Let us go to dinner then.'

'Let's,' she agreed. She had a lot of details to work out by tomorrow but after everything that had transpired that day, she didn't want to think of anything more complex than what food to order. For once she was going to let tomorrow worry about itself.

* * *

Muireann's first stop the next morning was the bankers' hall, where she withdrew some gold and also, surreptitiously, the emerald she thought was similar to the green crystal. She and Lee then went to a jeweller and she made a show of picking out four lockets, trying to find things she thought the others would actually wear, as well as a small flat metal case that could hold the emerald. That she made sure to fuss quite a bit about, asking all sorts of questions about how strong it was and how sturdy the clasp and hinges were. She was fairly sure if she wasn't spending such an obscene amount of money they'd probably have kicked her out, but she was confident that Ghellin would hear about it all, which made it worthwhile.

As Muireann and Lee headed for the library after that she had to admit she still didn't have a much better plan than the tentative one she'd told Reyleth about. And she'd be the first to admit that plan had some serious issues, including the fact that it would advertise her invulnerability or at the very least raise questions about it to people she very much didn't want to have that information.

As they wove their way through the familiar streets she caught herself watching the people around her as if she suspected they were all agents of Ghellin's and winced. Lee reached out and took her hand. 'What's wrong, love?'

'This whole situation,' Muireann said, sighing. 'I almost liked it better when we didn't know about Ghellin or his plan, when we didn't know he was spying on us here.'

'Why?' Lee said, baffled. 'I much prefer knowing the truth and having our enemy exposed, to thinking we were safe when we weren't.'

'Yes, of course that makes sense,' Muireann agreed. 'I just...I find myself jumping at shadows now, looking at every face around me and wondering who his informants are. And I don't like it.'

Lee squeezed Muireann's fingers. 'That is a terrible way to live. But we only have to get through a few more days and then one way or another it will change.'

'Hopefully for the better,' Muireann said, squeezing Lee's fingers back. Her relationship with the selkie was still new and in many ways they were still getting to know each other, but she had already come to rely on the other woman's presence in her life. Lee was a constant comfort and also a source of joy even when they were facing seemingly impossible odds. She pulled the other woman to a halt just outside the library. 'Lee. I just wanted to tell you...that I am very grateful to have you in my life and that I love you. I don't think I could have gotten through a lot of things these last few weeks without you there.'

Lee smiled shyly, her dark eyes bright. 'I love you as well, Muireann. I told you when we met that I thought we'd suit each other and we do, very well. We protect each other and we make each other happy – isn't that what wives should do?'

'Yes, I think it is,' Muireann agreed, remembering that awkward, wonderful first day with Lee. It was hard for her to believe that had been slightly less than two months ago. She leaned forward and kissed the selkie, then stepped away. 'Now on to the next difficult thing.'

'I'm right here with you.'

'I know.'

They walked in and greeted the guards by name, Lee setting her spear by the wall and asking the tall, fair guard how his wife was doing. While they made small talk Muireann took a moment to look around. The library was empty, but it was still early; the scholars and mages generally didn't show until late morning. Crellia was working the desk, as she had been the first day Muireann had gone to the Great Library, but unlike the first day this time the woman smiled and greeted Muireann with a friendly 'good morning, my lady'. Muireann forced a return smile and absently made another library donation, not paying any attention to how much she was giving but knowing the gesture would further the reputation she'd gained as a kind of dilettante scholar and keep Crellia from asking any real questions, even to make small talk. It also went no small way to easing Muireann's conscience over what she was about to do.

She walked over to the second-floor stairway and noticed a young woman, perhaps 17 and dressed as an apprentice mage in a loose purple tunic and leggings, lounging against one of the shelves, reading. Any other day Muireann would have ignored her but now that she was on high alert, she noticed the way the girl was watching her over the top of the book she was pretending to read – quite obviously pretending since the book was upside down. Muireann's shoulders tightened under the scrutiny, and she struggled not to stare back. She jogged as quickly as she could up the stairs, scanning the second floor for a similar spy but found it empty. It was a quiet day in the library without the usual apprentices, novices and scholars bustling around and Muireann was grateful for it.

When Lee came up behind her, she held a finger to her lips and gestured back towards the middle of the shelves. Only when they were buried in the stacks and she was sure they were alone did she dare whisper. 'We're being watched.'

Lee tensed, eyes cutting around the silent space. 'Who?'

'At the bottom of the stairs, a young woman in an apprentice mage's clothes. She was watching me, I'm sure of it.'

Lee nodded, trusting Muireann's word. 'Ghellin has made sure to keep an eye on you here when he is absent.'

'So, it seems,' Muireann agreed.

'Do you have a plan?' Lee said, her eyes still carefully roving over the area.

Muireann hesitated, not wanting to admit that she didn't. Her original idea seemed more and more ludicrous, especially since it would mean forcing Lee to make her own way out of the library – if she had Lee leave before she took the book it would be enormously suspicious since she had a long-established habit of only coming and going with a guard, but if she broke the window with Lee still in the building the selkie might be trapped inside by the door guards. Finally, she shrugged. 'For the moment we should act as we normally would and do research. Or pretend to. We'll have lunch as usual and then wait until later this afternoon to act. If we were to leave early, it would definitely be suspicious.'

Lee nodded, looking more confident than Muireann felt and took out her knitting to occupy herself. Muireann knew she should make the most of the time, but the truth was she'd gone through nearly every book on that floor by now and she couldn't bear the thought of even pretending to re-read any of them. She settled down at one of the small work tables instead and worked on the memory section of her journal, writing more about the journey her friends had made through the mountains.

Lunch was a stiff, quiet affair with neither Lee nor Muireann in the mood to talk. Muireann didn't miss the young woman who was watching them sliding into the sitting room and getting herself some food. Even as she ate, she was still watching, and it killed Muireann's appetite. She sat and ignored her food, waiting for Lee to finish eating but couldn't resist stealing occasional glances at the girl in purple. She was surprised to see the gloating smirk on the woman's face as time went on and couldn't puzzle it out until Lee got up to put her plate and utensils back and the spy smirked, glancing between the two women. *Oh, I see,* Muireann thought, fixing her eyes on her own mostly full plate. *She thinks we aren't getting along, and it pleases her. That's actually not a bad idea. If Ghellin is given the impression I'm at odds with Lee, or better Lee and Reyleth, he'll feel more confident that I'm being swayed by his words.*

With that in mind she waited until Lee sat back down and then stood abruptly, going to return her own plate and then leaving the room so that the selkie was forced to catch up. She walked quickly back to the stairs, then up to the relative privacy of the second floor and plunged into the stacks. Lee caught up with her there, obviously annoyed. 'Muireann, what's wrong?'

'I'm sorry, there wasn't any way to explain first,' Muireann said, pulling Lee into a loose hug. 'I saw that girl watching us and realised it would be good if she thought we were fighting.'

'Hmph,' the selkie said. 'I suppose that makes sense, but I didn't enjoy it.'

'I know, I'm sorry, truly,' Muireann said. 'But if you really thought I was being rude then I'm sure she believed it as well.'

'I'll be glad when all of this is over,' Lee said, leaning into Muireann's shoulder.

'I will as well,' Muireann said. 'And then we can just relax and spend some time together without the weight of the world on us. But you know there's an advantage to this besides possibly making Ghellin think I'm taking his offer seriously. We can leave early now without it looking odd, if we play it like we've had a fight.'

Lee perked up at that. 'What do we do now?'

'I'm going to the third floor. Wait for me by the bottom of the stairs. If anyone is there, I'll grab a book and come back down. If it's empty, I'll come to the top of the stairs and signal you. Then you can act as a guard at the bottom of the stairs – if anyone comes, just start talking to me as if I'd told you to stay away from me or something.'

'So, it won't look suspicious that we're apart.'

'Right,' Muireann said. 'And meanwhile I'll get the book.'

'And then we leave,' Lee said happily.

'Yes, but we'll have to play at arguing on the way out for it to be believable.'

'Right,' Lee said, nodding seriously.

Muireann kissed Lee quickly. 'For luck.'

The third floor proved as empty as the second and Muireann hoped that meant luck really was with them. After checking the whole floor, she went to the stairs to signal all clear to Lee then moved back to the restricted section.

She stepped through the gate easily, without any hint she'd set anything off. Still, she listened carefully for Lee warning her of anyone approaching, unsure if she'd know if she had somehow tripped these wards. She and Reyleth had only experimented with a few things after all, and she couldn't really be sure their conclusion was entirely correct. But when the sound of running footsteps didn't appear she dared hope it had worked.

She stepped over to the shelf she needed and pulled out the book, Annals of the Aldovanan, cradling it in her hands. It was old, far older than any book she'd ever touched before. The binding was leather, so worn it was flaking slightly, and the pages were vellum. If not for the magic used to preserve it she doubted it would have survived this long, except in fragments.

She bit her lip, feeling bad about her idea to go out of the window with it now. Even with her holding it to protect it she wasn't sure it would survive, not as fragile as it was. Wincing she looked around the restricted section, trying to come up with a new idea on the fly and painfully aware that she needed to hurry.

What finally came to her was an idea so outlandish she knew she was truly desperate. Nonetheless she set the book down and pulled her heavy braid around over one shoulder, then took out her small dagger. She had tried to use it on her arm to no effect, to prove she couldn't be harmed by blades, and now she tried the same thing on her hair. She pulled the sharp little blade across a section of braid, wincing, but as she'd half hoped and half feared nothing happened. She closed her eyes for a moment, overwhelmed again by the extent of this change. *Well,* she thought, putting the blade back in its sheath, *I guess I better get used to my hair at this length. Forever.* She glanced at her fingernails and was glad she'd cut them right before taking on the dragon. *It shows how little attention I've been paying to anything including myself that I hadn't even noticed my nails haven't grown in all this time.*

She quickly unbraided her hair, the copper-red waves falling like a heavy curtain to her waist. She walked over to the gate and leaned forward, letting her hair fall across the threshold. Nothing happened. Again, she thought that she might not know if something were going to happen, though, and her stomach clenched. But if the theory held that her hair couldn't be cut because it was part of her and she was filled with the dragon's magic then it followed that her hair, like the rest of her, was also magic-proof.

She picked up the book and carefully wrapped it up in her

hair, covering it as thoroughly as she could. It took several minutes of arranging and moving the book against her body before she felt confident enough to risk moving forward and even then her heart pounded in her ears as she approached the gate. She had no idea exactly what magic was on it or the book.

Taking a deep steadying breath, she stepped across the threshold.

Nothing happened.

She stood there on the other side for an instant, heart still racing, then moved away from the restricted section, waiting until she was well clear of it to risk fumbling the stolen book free of her hair. She set it carefully in her messenger bag behind her personal journal and the small notebook she was using for her Aldovanan research. Closing the leather bag, she tied it securely and then walked back to the stairs. Lee was waiting, her head swivelling around towards Muireann as she jogged down the stairs. 'Let's go.'

'Why is your hair down?' Lee whispered, and only then did Muireann remember she'd unbraided it.

'Blast! Hold on, let me fix it,' she muttered, stopping so she could twist the hair back into its ubiquitous braid. 'Thank you for noticing, that would definitely have looked odd.'

'Maybe they'd just have assumed we were having fun up here by ourselves again,' Lee giggled, reminding Muireann of how she'd spent her first day at the Great Library.

Muireann felt her cheeks flaming but she couldn't fight a smile in return. 'Probably, but that would hardly make them think we were fighting now, would it?'

Lee sighed melodramatically. 'I suppose not, but it would be fun.'

'Well, we can have fun later, for now let's get out of here,' Muireann said. 'Let me go down first like I'm rushing, and you follow. We'll just act like we're at odds, alright?'

'What should I say?'

'I'm not sure but anything that makes sense in the moment as long as it makes it seem like we aren't getting along.'

Lee nodded and Muireann hurried across to the first-floor stairs and then down. She was about halfway to the door when she heard Lee behind her, speaking in a quarrelsome way that was very at odds with the selkie's cheerful personality. 'I am your guard, *my lady*, you should let me do my job.'

Taking her cue Muireann snapped back. 'You're supposed to guard me, not hover around me incessantly. How can I think when you never leave me alone?'

They had made it to the desk now, and Muireann dared glance back to see both Crellia and the spy staring in wide-eyed surprise at the scene unfolding before them. The stolen book banged against her hip with every step.

'I don't remember you asking for space,' Lee whined.

'I shouldn't have to, you should just know when you're being annoying,' Muireann said.

'I don't seem to annoy you as long as I'm serving your *whims*, do I, *my lady*?' Lee huffed. The implication in that was very clear and the two guards, who they were quickly approaching, looked embarrassed, although Muireann wasn't sure if that was for themselves or for Lee, who they were fond of.

'Well, if you're too dense to understand what does and doesn't please me, maybe I should find a guard who will!' Muireann said loudly, just shy of yelling, then flew through the heavy doors.

Before they slammed behind her, she just heard one of the guards saying to Lee. 'Don't fret, she'll change her mind, nobility are always like this—'

She smothered laughter, not wanting to ruin the act and stomped slowly down the street. Lee wasn't too long behind her, spear now clutched in her hand, face still angry. She risked meeting the selkie's eyes and caught the wink Lee threw her, feeling the tightness in her chest easing slightly. Turning she kept her chin up and did her best to imitate her mother in a really fine snit the rest of the way back to the inn, which was more exhausting than she expected.

Only when they were back in their own room did she fall into Lee's arms, kissing her thoroughly. 'Oh, that was brilliant! I half believed you myself.'

'That was really fun,' Lee said, giggling and kissing Muireann in return. 'The looks on their faces! I thought that woman at the desk was going to faint.'

'I doubt they get many melodramatic fights between lovers there,' Muireann snickered. 'That was an especially nice touch by the way. I don't think anyone wanted to intercede once you said that bit.'

'Who would dare?' Lee said, still giggling. 'A fight between an employer and employee who are also bedding each other? The scandal!'

'The drama!' Muireann said. 'Although they do know we're married, but still. Definitely were not expecting that nonsense.'

They laughed together until they were practically crying, and Muireann knew half of their reaction was releasing the sheer tension of what they'd done. Finally, she pulled herself together. 'I have the book, now I need to read it. We're back early and I'm sure Tash is beside himself wanting to know what happened—'

'Oh, I'll be happy to tell him,' Lee said, eyes shining. 'I can play it in the hall like I want a sympathetic ear then get him in his room and tell him the truth of it all.'

'Good,' Muireann said. 'That should make it even more believable for anyone relaying information to Ghellin. Meanwhile, I'll stay here and read, and you can tell everyone to meet up here later.'

'I may play that as well, as if I want assistance confronting you,' Lee said, still looking thoroughly amused.

'Feel free, if it pleases you,' Muireann agreed, carefully

removing the stolen book from her bag. 'We may as well have what fun we can with this situation.'

Lee took a moment to compose herself, managing to look upset again before she left the room. Muireann shook her head slightly at the selkie's enthusiasm for their charade, then settled down on the bed to read.

* * *

She had lost track of time when the door opened again, and one by one Lee and the others filed in. She watched until the door was safely shut against eavesdroppers then jumped right to discussing what she'd read without preamble

'This is fascinating,' Muireann said, putting down the stolen book. 'It's a copy of a copy of a translation of one of the final books from the Aldovanan, a record of the final years of their empire. It mentions Olcanac at some length because his death against the dragon broke a stalemate that had preserved the status quo of their civil war and triggered the series of events that ended with the empire itself falling completely and the end of the First Age.'

'So, you were right, this is exactly what we needed,' Calla said, leaning back against the wall by the fireplace.

'It's lucky that Reyleth remembered as much about it as he did,' Muireann said. 'To point us in the direction of looking for it.'

'Fortunate indeed considering I read it a century ago,' Rey said dryly. 'So now that you've tried to protect my ego, what have you found in there that I had forgotten?'

Muireann looked down, fighting a smile that he'd seen through her so easily. 'There is a lot more to the story, or I should say the history, than what Reyleth remembered, it's true. Olcanac was wielding the green crystal when he died and he did die trying to kill the dragon, believing in his arrogance that the weapon was powerful enough to kill even a magical being. He had used it to gain ground for his faction in the civil war and had unwittingly created a balance of power between himself and the leading mage in the opposing faction who also had a powerful weapon. The two were equally matched and neither could overcome the other. His death created a chain reaction that ultimately brought an end to the entire Aldovanan empire and ultimately the Frist Age.'

'How does that help us?' Tash asked.

'Be patient and let me explain it,' Muireann said. 'Because I think it's important to see the full picture. What I've just covered is what we mostly already knew. What the book also tells us, which we didn't know, is that the green crystal was originally made by someone else.'

'So Olcanac wasn't the creator of the Green Death?' Reyleth said, looking thoughtful.

'No, according to this his teacher was, a woman named Brethen. She intended it to be used purely for defensive purposes but after she died, he inherited it, or took it...the text is unclear on that, and he used it to attack instead of defend.'

'But the crystal is too dangerous, you said.' Lee was frowning now. 'It would tempt anyone who holds it to use it.'

'I thought that after touching it, yes,' Muireann admitted. 'But I think the crystal is like any deadly weapon; it's not the weapon itself that's the danger, it's the person who holds it and what they intend to use it for.'

'What does that mean?' Rey was frowning now as well.

'The real question might be the one we've all been overlooking: who can safely wield the weapon?' Muireann said.

Calla frowned hard. 'It can't be safely wielded, you said that yourself.'

'I said that people who held it would be tempted by its power, which they will be, if they have any inclination towards ambition or desire for vengeance, anything like that. That's what happened to Olcanac, he wanted to be the greatest mage-general of his time and he used the crystal to that end. But what the book is saying is that someone who has no desire to use the stone can safely possess it, that was how Brethen held it for her lifetime, safely. She only wanted to protect people, not conquer them. You can't be tempted to use a weapon when you have no interest in destroying anything.'

'Most people who do terrible things believe they are doing good, at least for a small group of people,' Calla said.

'That's true, but there are some genuinely good, selfless people in the world,' Muireann said. 'So, as I see it, we can keep on as we've been, hiding the crystal and trying to protect it or we can have someone without any dangerous ambition, anger or urge to conquer take it. If I'm reading this correctly then that person could hold the crystal, could touch it, safely.'

They all looked uneasily at each other. Finally, Calla spoke again. 'What if the person who had it was tempted by it?'

'You won't be,' Muireann said confidently.

'Me? Why me?' Calla said, stepping away from the wall, looking alarmed. 'Why not you?'

'Calla, of all of us you are the only one who had basically unlimited power and chose to walk away from it,' Muireann said, leaning forward. 'You've already faced all of that temptation. If you take the stone, own it, then it can't be taken from you while you live.'

'I don't like the part where I risk being tempted to destroy the world,' Calla said, frowning.

'I still think you could wield it safely, Calla, but I understand if you don't want to risk it,' Muireann said. 'We can keep hiding it until we find a way to destroy it, if you don't want the risk of wielding it. I'll keep studying the book and see what else I can learn.'

'I don't want to risk finding out I don't live up to your faith in me, no,' Calla said, giving Muireann a lopsided smile. 'Or that whole destroying the world thing. I imagine it's much the same way you feel about the risk of you trying to take it.'

'Ultimately it doesn't matter who is carrying it, if Ghellin keeps hunting us for it and we don't intend to use it,' Reyleth cut in. 'He may believe Muireann has it now, but he'll work out that she doesn't sooner or later, and he'll go through each of us seeking it. Which is why I won't suggest we split up and flee separately because it will only make it easier for him to target each of us and quickly narrow down who does have it.'

'Should we flee, though?' Tash asked, frowning. 'Aren't we safer here?'

'I doubt we're safe anywhere at this point,' Calla said. 'If we stay in Mistlen we're just giving Ghellin time to plot against us and think of the best ways to get at us, especially as we're so predictable. If we change our routines, we warn him we plan to fight back. Yet if we flee, he's sure to pursue us as he has been since Verell, and we may be more vulnerable on the road or in a smaller town.'

'Then what do we do?' Lee asked. 'What do we do until Muireann finds a way to unmake the crystal?'

'I'll keep it as safe as I can,' Calla said. 'But at some point, we will have to confront Ghellin somehow. I don't see how we can avoid it, as otherwise he'll simply hunt us for the crystal until he gets it, and with his resources we will be hard pressed to evade him for long, despite our own considerable dragon-provided money.'

'He won't pursue us if he doesn't think we have it,' Muireann said.

'And the plan grows more complex,' Reyleth murmured.

'Listen, right now Ghellin knows we have the stone, but I don't think he knows what it looks like, beyond that it's green and a crystal,' Muireann said. 'How could he? Only Calla and I have seen it and the old texts describe it but only in general terms.'

'If we offered him a substitute, he'd know it wasn't real,' Lee pointed out. 'As soon as he touched it, he'd know.'

'If we offered him one, yes,' Muireann agreed. 'But not if we made him think we'd gotten rid of the original or hidden it where we thought he couldn't find it.'

'Go on,' Calla said.

'Lee had offered before to hide it under the sea, but we thought the risk too great at the time, with the real stone,' Muireann said. 'What if we kept the real stone, left it with Calla to keep safe, but made him think we were fleeing to the sea to hide it? But instead, we hide the fake we've made, the emerald in the jewellery case. He should already know about the case and think it's likely where we're keeping the crystal anyway. He'll waste a long time finding the decoy.'

'We'd be vulnerable on the road, though, between here and the shore,' Tash pointed out.

'We would,' Calla said slowly. 'But I know that road well and if we can get even a few hours head start on him and go straight to the shore we should be able to make it. And we'll know he's behind us and be anticipating his attack. We'd just have to make sure we stayed far enough ahead to get to the shore before he could catch up to us, then make a show of hiding the decoy.'

'We'd have to be quite convincing,' Reyleth said, looking thoughtful. It gave her hope he wasn't dismissing the idea out of hand. 'And it would be dangerous for Lee. If they thought she had the real stone they'd stop at nothing to kill her for it.'

'I'm willing to accept the risk,' Lee said gravely. 'I think this is a good plan. They can't easily follow me and will waste years – decades perhaps – trying to search the ocean for it.'

'And if Ghellin and his mercenaries think it's in the ocean so will anyone else seeking it, if there is anyone else,' Tash said.

'Right,' Muireann said. 'We lead him to the shore and convince him we've sent the stone to the sea bottom. Then we flee. And we can keep working to unmake the stone or destroy it but without the worry of Ghellin chasing us.'

'At least for a while,' Lee agreed.

'He's human,' Tash said. 'He has to be about middle age. Even if he eventually figures out that we still have the stone he'd be an old man by then.'

'He may tell others,' Reyleth said, frowning. 'We can't assume the secret of the stone's existence would die with him.'

'Come to that if we have a chance, we should try to kill him,' Calla said. 'It may sound ruthless but, well, let me tell you what I've learned of him today.'

The others all nodded, and Calla settled back against the wall again. 'Our new friend Ghellin is a cousin to the king of Donlach. He's not especially well placed in the royal family, but he is royalty, and has the money and resources that provides. The reason he isn't well placed is because he has a reputation for his prejudice against non-humans that makes him a political nightmare and had tried once about twenty years ago to lead a coup against his uncle, although from what I heard there wasn't enough proof to convict him for it. Nonetheless he has lived in Lanal since then.'

Tash whistled softly. 'That explains the Donlachian mercenaries.'

'According to my sources he's been obsessively studying dragons for the last decade or so and was paying several people to keep track of the red dragon's movements.'

'So, he certainly figured out that the red dragon had the stone,' Reyleth said.

'And he must have known very quickly that it had been killed, but still how could he have set the mercenaries on us so fast?' Tash said.

'Because he only arrived in Mistlen shortly before we did; he's been living in Lord Arvain's keep as a guest of the lord,' Calla said. 'I've no doubt he was at the dragon's cave very shortly after it died, possibly within days of us, Muireann. He may well have been in Verell before we left.'

Tash looked truly shocked at that. 'I don't remember ever seeing the man before or hearing talk of a noble guest.'

'He is a rather forgettable looking man,' Muireann said, making a face. 'And if he had been there before you started your term, perhaps people just treated him as a facet of the place?'

'You think he's been there since his exile?' Reyleth asked.

'I think if I were obsessed with obtaining that crystal I'd stay as close as I could but somewhere that seemed safe,' Muireann said. 'Arvain's keep is both fairly close and also the safest possible option. In fact I wouldn't be surprised at all if Ghellin is why we kept having knights and would-be heroes throwing their lives away attacking the dragon every few years.'

'It makes sense,' Calla agreed. 'He can't hire anyone to try to kill it because not even a noble's coffers could pay enough for that, but if he's charismatic enough he could get young knights and such fired up enough to believe they could try and succeed.'

'Well, it seems he was charismatic enough to stir up a rebellion and avoid the noose for it, so I'd guess he probably had an easy time inspiring people to throw their lives away on a dragon for him,' Muireann said.

'That also explains why he thought he could persuade Muireann,' Lee said.

'If that is his best attempt at a persuasive speech then I am unimpressed by his charisma,' Tash said flatly.

Muireann smiled at that. 'I don't think we received his best work to be honest. That whole encounter seemed unplanned on his part. If anything I'd guess he'd grown frustrated after so many weeks of watching us but getting no closer to his goal.'

'Yes, and on that note,' Calla said, 'now that we have the book and some semblance of a plan, I think we should get out of Mistlen immediately. Tonight.'

'I assume you have a plan for that?' Muireann said, as the others all turned to Calla expectantly.

'I do, but for now just pack everything up and then as soon as the inn quiets down for the night, we'll make our way out.'

'If we're being watched—' Tash started.

Calla held up a hand. 'I doubt he wastes money having anyone watch us sleep, and at this point I hope our predictability will have lulled him into some sense of trust in assuming he knows what we'll do. But even if he is alerted quickly all we need is some small head start since we need him following us anyway.'

'We can pack after dinner,' Muireann said. 'I have the pendants for everyone, and we still need to do that as publicly as we can.'

'Alright,' Calla agreed. 'After dinner we pack. When it's clear we sneak out and head to the shore as quickly as we can. Then we work to mislead him.'

'This is less a plan than a vague idea,' Reyleth complained, looking worried again.

'It's all we have,' Calla said. 'If we stay here, he'll come for us eventually. We can't trust the stone to anyone else, nor risk hiding it here or making him think we've done so. Our only hope at this point is to get him to follow us and convince him we've hidden the stone where he can get it if he tries long enough, the ocean. Once we don't have it, or he thinks we don't, he has no reason to keep pursuing us.'

'We hope,' Rey said.

'Hope is better at this point than nothing,' Muireann said. 'Unless anyone thinks of any better ideas that won't get us – you – killed. And at least on the road we have more of a chance to fight back – I'd rather an honest fight than a knife in the back here. Especially if Ghellin decides picking you off one by one may persuade me to give him what he wants.'

The others were all silent, unable to argue or make any better suggestions.

They went down to the common room, pretending they weren't getting along, which wasn't difficult for Muireann who was distracted by the tension of it all. She found herself trying to pick Ghellin's spies from the crowd in the room, trying to see if the serving woman was lingering too long by their table. It was exhausting. They ate in a stiff silence that was at odds with their usual cheer and had to be noticeable to anyone who was watching them.

When the food was being cleared away Calla caught Muireann's eye and nodded slightly. Clearing her throat and keenly aware of the serving woman's presence Muireann made a show of pulling out the pendants she'd bought. 'I know things right now are a bit tense between us all but I got these for everyone, and I still want you all to have them.'

She was at a loss as to how to hand them out that would fit the act they were selling so she defaulted to just shoving each one towards the person it was meant for without another word. It was abrupt and not in line with any sort of appropriate gift giving, but she caught the server watching the exchange and was glad for the show she was putting on. Even if the woman wasn't Ghellin's spy, the story would still spread.

Tash took his and admired it openly, turning the gold locket over in his hands and tracing the eagle engraved on it with a slight smile. Calla took hers with a shrug and pulled it on without a closer look; it sat just under her collarbone, the small rubies on the front glittering in the firelight. Lee took hers slowly, face blank, as she examined the jewellery. Reyleth frowned at his. 'Isn't this a woman's locket?'

'I thought it was pretty,' Muireann said, defensively. 'It has a wolf on it.'

'Because river elves are known to be so fond of wolves,' he said, the sarcasm so sharp the eavesdropping server, who was clearing the table as slowly as possible now, gasped slightly.

Muireann threw a genuinely worried look at the elf, relieved when she saw the slight glint in his eye and the way his fingers were caressing the locket. He'd played his part so well it had even fooled her for an instant despite her certainty when she'd chosen it that he'd understand what the wolf meant. She forced a pout onto her face. 'It's a gift. I thought you'd appreciate it because I gave it to you.'

He made a show of rolling his eyes and sighing as he put the pendant on, slipping it into his tunic. 'There I'm wearing it, are you satisfied?'

She pushed up from the table standing so suddenly she nearly knocked the serving woman down. 'I don't know why I bother with any of you.'

She started to storm off but her dramatic exit was stopped by Calla grabbing her wrist and loudly whispering. 'But you got what we really needed, right? At the jewellers?'

'Yes,' Muireann said loudly, pulling her arm free. 'Since that's all you care about. Yes, I got it.'

Muireann pulled out the small, gaudy case she'd bought and threw it at Calla before fleeing the room. She ran up the stairs to her own room, hoping she looked adequately upset given that really she was trying not to laugh. The whole situation was so absurd. In a way it was fun to play-act like this, but it was also nerve wracking to know what was at stake with it all.

Once back in her room Muireann started packing her things, surprised by how scattered they'd become. After a month in the room, she and Lee had both become comfortable there and started to treat it like an actual home rather than a rented room. It wasn't as if Muireann had a lot of possessions but she had bought a few more outfits, things that would blend in better at the library, as well as a dozen new books, several more journals…she stared at it all after she'd piled it on the bed and started to doubt she could fit it in her bag.

When Lee joined her Muireann was trying to decide what to keep and what to leave. Lee stared at the two piles curiously, prompting Muireann to say. 'I can't fit it all.'

'I suppose we have bought a few things while we were here,'

Lee agreed, although she was far less of a clothes horse than Muireann and had only bought herself a few small things even including the knitting supplies; she had no trouble packing. It was odd for Muireann to stare at the pile of things she couldn't fit and realise how easily she'd grown used to having money to spend. A year ago the thought of abandoning a book she'd bought and enjoyed reading would have pained her but now she knew she could replace it. She wasn't sure she liked this feeling, the way that formerly precious things suddenly seemed disposable.

Shaking the thoughts away she crammed what she could into her bag, attached her quiver to her hip, readied her bow and waited for Calla.

'I really do like the necklace, you know,' Lee said suddenly, breaking the tense silence. Muireann looked at her in surprise, and she went on. 'I know you only got it as part of this ruse, but I do like it. It's beautiful.'

Muireann dropped her bag and went over to join Lee sitting on the bed. 'I chose it because I thought it suited you.'

She lifted the locket from the selkie's chest, her fingers brushing across the tiny sapphires set in a starburst shape. 'It reminded me of you. Bright and beautiful.'

Lee smiled shyly, taking Muireann's hand so that the locket dropped back into its place between her breasts. 'I love it even more now. I thought you just chose something random because you had to.'

'No, I chose what I thought you might like,' Muireann admitted. 'You don't wear any jewellery, so I wasn't sure what you'd think of it, but it is a real gift, for all the theatre around its presentation.'

'Would you have gotten it for me if it wasn't part of our plan?'

'If I knew you wanted jewellery I would have.'

Lee's smile widened. 'I've never had any before but having

this now I am glad for it.'

They kissed, softly at first then with more passion, stopping when someone knocked on the door. Muireann sighed and let go of Lee reluctantly, going to the door to see who it was.

Tash was there, looking as nervous as she'd ever seen him. 'Calla said it's time.'

'I thought she wanted to wait until later?' Muireann said, glancing back at Lee who was already standing and shouldering her pack.

'She said now's good because everyone is distracted,' Tash said, shrugging.

'Alright, hang on a minute.'

Muireann went back into the room, put on her fur cloak, shouldered her pack and grabbed her bow then she and Lee slipped from the room. Tash was alone in the deserted hallway. 'Follow me.'

They did, although Muireann was very curious now about where the others were and why they were leaving early. Tash led them down the back stairway the servants used and through several twists and turns in back hallways, finally emerging near the stables. Waiting next to the building was a heavy wagon, the top and back covered by canvas. Calla was standing in the shadows of the barn talking to a dwarf – not the bard they'd met but a merchant. His hair and beard were dark, his clothes the leather and heavy canvas of a brewer. Catching sight of them Calla waved them over. 'Birgir, these are my friends, the ones I was telling you about.'

The dwarf turned and looked them over, his grey eyes critical. Finally, he grunted, then said. 'Yeah, I can fit them with you and the other elf in the wagon. It'll be tight, though.'

Calla smiled widely and slapped him on the shoulder. 'We can deal with close quarters, and we won't complain.'

'Well then get in and we'll start moving. Remember, if the guard does find you, ask for Lerrin and pay him what I said to.'

'I remember,' Calla said, going to the back of the wagon and lowering the gate. She turned to Tash, who was closest, and gestured him up. 'Get in and move to the back, behind the crates.'

Tash and Lee dutifully climbed up, but Muireann hesitated with a hand on the wagon frame, leaning towards Calla. 'Who's this?'

'An old friend,' Calla said, shrugging. 'He brings merchandise from the closest dwarven outpost, Steinfoss, into Mistlen several times a month. The guards know him and know he'll slip them a bit of silver to let him through without checking the wagon.'

'He's a smuggler?' Muireann said, keeping her voice low.

'He's a creative businessman,' Calla said. 'Who knows that dwarven fire mead is illegal here but very popular and that the taxes to export certain herbs out of Mistlen really are unfairly high, especially for the dwarves.'

'I see,' Muireann said, peering into the wagon, which smelled of oak and alcohol and was piled with heavy wooden crates.

'Good,' Calla said. 'Then get in, we need to get moving before he decides to ask for more gold than I've already paid him.'

Muireann clambered into the wagon, working around the piled boxes which took up the space from floor to canvas top, excepting only a small narrow aisle on the right. It was hard to navigate with the bulky pack and her bow, in a space that she would have found narrow without either of those things, but she managed to squeeze through. She felt her way back in the darkness until a hand reached out and took hers. She fought the reflex to scream but jerked back sharply until Reyleth's voice emerged from the depths of the wagon. 'Step a bit to your left. Tash is in the corner, we'll help you over next to him.'

Relaxing at the sound she let herself be guided back, recognising Lee's touch when the selkie reached out and helped her as well. She worked her way back until she bumped into Tash, turning to stand with her back against the wagon frame.

She heard shuffling and then Lee and Reyleth moved closer against her, pressing her closer to Tash. Calla's voice whispered in the stifling darkness. 'Birgir will take us out through the soldier's gate. Once we're a few miles clear of the city he'll stop and let us out. From now until then we need to be silent, so we don't raise any suspicion.'

'Won't it look odd that he's leaving at night?' Tash asked.

'No, the dwarves prefer to travel at night when they can,' Calla said. 'Their eyes are very sensitive to the light because they live mostly under the earth, in their mountain cities. It's a full moon tonight and many of the dwarves will be on the roads.'

Muireann braced herself as the wagon suddenly lurched into motion, setting one hand on the crates in front of her and the other sliding between herself and Tash to grab the wagon behind her. She strained her ears to listen as the wagon rolled along but it was impossible to be sure how much ground they were covering or what was going on outside. They would stop and start seemingly at random, although she assumed it was traffic on the city roads. When the wagon turned, she was thrown either into Tash on her right or Lee on her left, the bulky pack making it painfully hard to balance in the bouncing wagon.

Finally they stopped and she distinctly heard laughter and men speaking loudly although she couldn't make out the words. A torch lit up the canvas near her, the light shining through even the heavy material. She tensed, feeling as if the air in the small space had thickened as the wagon back was lowered and the light shone in, breaking through the cracks between the crates and down the narrow aisle; Muireann could see Calla pressed tight against Reyleth just out of the track of light. Muireann held her breath waiting for the guard to call them out. Seconds passed agonizingly slow.

Then the light was retreating, the wagon back was relocked, and she let her breath out as quietly as she could. Still her heart pounded in her ears and she stood as tense as ever until the wagon finally started moving again. It felt like they were going downhill, Muireann having to struggle anew to find her balance, but she was glad for it; downhill meant they were out of the city through the gate Calla had mentioned, heading south now along the main trade road. The ride was unpleasant, but she could bear it if it had bought them even a small head start on Ghellin.

Some indeterminate time later the wagon stopped again and a minute later the back was lowered, but this time it was Birgir's gruff voice that reached them. 'All clear then, Calla, time to get out.'

Calla moved quickly to slide out of the confining space, with Reyleth and Lee close behind. Muireann followed more slowly, stumbling slightly. The moonlight provided some illumination, and it was a great relief compared to the cramped wagon space, but Muireann still couldn't see very clearly so she was very careful climbing down. Tash following behind her leapt from the wagon with an ease that Muireann flatly envied, even though she knew he was eighteen years younger than she was.

The dwarf gave them a final long look then closed the wagon up before heading back to the front. Muireann assumed he was going to leave like that, but after he climbed back into the driver's seat and had taken up the reins, he turned back one final time, looking at Calla, and said, 'Don't know and don't want to know what this was all about, but whatever it was, I wish you luck with it.'

'Thanks, my friend,' Calla said, shouldering her pack. 'We're going to need it.'

* * *

It was their second night on the road after fleeing Mistlen, and Muireann sat by the fireside, thinking. She rolled her sleeve up and stretched her hand towards the crackling fire. Reyleth was in the stream nearby, swimming, Lee was hunting and Calla was inside her tent, Muireann assumed getting her things arranged as she liked them. Tash walked up and dropped firewood near her then stood, watching her as she moved her hand and forearm back and forth through the flames. Catching him staring she said. 'It doesn't hurt at all. Other things there's always this moment of pain and then nothing but the fire...it almost feels pleasant. Soft, like a warm breeze over my skin or water. Not painful or burning at all. That's strange, isn't it?'

'Not that strange, all things considered,' he said, sitting down close to her but further from the fire than she was. 'Although I must admit it's unnerving to watch.'

'I'm sorry,' she said, pulling her hand back. 'I didn't mean to make you uncomfortable. I was just thinking, and I started doing it without realising.'

'Don't stop on my account,' he said, trying to smile.

'No,' she insisted, rolling her sleeve down. 'I'm sorry, I shouldn't have done that.'

'Muireann—' he started, before they were interrupted by Lee running back into camp.

'Hurry! They are almost upon us!' the selkie called to them all, clearly agitated.

'They? Who? Ghellin's men?' Muireann yelped, grabbing her bow. Calla emerged from her tent, having heard Lee's warning, and a moment later Reyleth appeared as well, his hair still dripping from the river.

Before Lee could explain cloaked figures started to pour from the trees around the clearing, filling the field between the trees and the small camp.

'The Arvethri,' Calla said, frustrated. 'Blast that cult! They would choose the worst possible time to show back up.'

'They must have heard rumours Muireann was still alive,' Lee said, holding her spear tighter as the cult members fanned out around them.

'We don't want to harm you,' their leader spoke loudly, his sonorous voice carrying easily. 'Just give us the Evil One and we will let you pass unharmed.'

Muireann watched as more and more cloaked figures kept filing out of the woods and she knew they were in real trouble this time. There were already easily a hundred cultists and more were coming. Her friends had made it clear they wouldn't abandon her even if the cultists couldn't actually kill her, but these odds were overwhelming. No matter how much more martially skilled the little group might be the numbers against them and zealousness made up for their enemies' lack with weapons. Muireann only had twenty arrows, once she'd fired them all she'd be helpless amid the fighting.

Rey straightened up, pitching his voice to carry. 'You can't kill her, that would be true blasphemy.'

And impossible, Muireann thought, but since they were so badly outnumbered, she was willing to see where the elf was going with this.

'She killed the dragon,' one of the men in front said, his voice equal parts outrage and pain. Muireann winced as he added, 'She deserves to die for her blasphemy.'

'She is the dragon,' Reyleth said, as calmly as if they were discussing the weather.

The cult's leader laughed in a nasty way. 'That is impossible. I saw the body myself, the great Murjergalan laid low and rotting. Because of her.'

'Her arrow took the dragon down, that is true,' Rey said, still utterly calm. 'But in the moment it died its essence transferred into her. She is the dragon now, its spirit in this form, blessed by Erla. How else do you explain her surviving the fall from the cliff?'

The cultists shifted uncomfortably behind their leader, muttering to themselves. His eyes had fixed on Muireann, his expression impossible to read. 'What proof can you give us that you speak the truth?'

Reyleth hesitated a moment, then turned to Muireann. 'Show them.'

She shook her head slightly, still so conflicted about all of it. It felt like being asked to lay bare the depth of her shame to these strangers. Rey met her eyes, his love and fear plain on his face. 'You have to show them.'

She turned to the hostile group, these people who had been chasing them across so many months and miles.

'You don't have to do this,' Lee said from behind her, spear still at the ready.

Muireann didn't answer, stepping forward towards their camp fire which was still burning. She knew that Reyleth was right, she did have to do this, because if it came to a fight her friends would be the ones suffering, not her. And she couldn't let that happen.

The cultists watched her as if she were a poisonous snake about to strike. She took off her boots and socks, her belt, cast aside the wolf fur cloak, everything but her smallclothes and undershirt to save as much as she could.

Then she stepped into the fire.

The flames quickly caught in her clothes, climbing up and dancing around her body. The light was dazzling and obscured everything outside it, but she could hear the gasps and cries of the people in front of her. She waited until she knew she must look like a human torch and then stepped forward out of the ring of stones that contained the fire. Her clothes still burned, although the cloth was falling away now as it disintegrated. Only her glasses were untouched by the conflagration, thanks to Reyleth's enchantment. She paused for a moment to give the cultists a moment to grasp that she was truly unhurt by the fire then turned, pulling her braid forward over her shoulder, letting them see the red dragon that wove across her back and leg. She had no way to know that in the fire the image of the dragon was shining as if lit from within, the subtle colours on the scales illuminated and gleaming just as the living dragon had.

She briefly met Tash's eyes, a sea of awe, and then closed hers, not wanting to see it, especially from him. Behind her she heard gasps and cries, people sobbing. Chaos.

Muireann turned back to the crowd then held up a hand and silence fell across the space, making her cringe. 'You need to leave.'

And they did, turning and walking away immediately, even their leader going without a word of complaint. Muireann was glad to see them go but the way they did what she said so unquestioningly, these people who minutes before meant her death, made her feel ill. As soon as the last cultist had faded from sight Muireann turned on Reyleth, not making any effort to hide her anger.

'Why did you do that?' Muireann hissed. 'Why convince them I'm the dragon?'

'They were trying to kill you and they were not going to stop,' Rey said, pleading with her.

'They weren't going to succeed either,' she pointed out, hating the way Tash wouldn't quite look at her; she hoped because of her nudity and not the show she'd just put on. She'd worked too hard already to get him to treat her normally to see it all undone. 'And now instead of a dragon worshipping cult trying to kill me I have a dragon worshipping cult worshipping *me* because they think I'm a dragon, which I'm not.'

'You said that except for fire anything else that should hurt you does still cause you pain, just not damage,' he said. 'You don't deserve to suffer even if it won't kill you.'

'Maybe I do deserve it for what I did,' she snapped.

'We'll all be safer now, though,' Lee said gently, stepping up and wrapping Muireann in her sealskin. 'If they stop pursuing you, they stop pursuing us as well.'

Rey nodded. 'Yes, the selkie is right. This makes us all safer – if you don't care about that for yourself, care about it for our sakes. We'd have died fighting to keep them from taking you, and now we are all safe.'

Muireann felt suddenly ashamed of losing her temper towards him and of the way she'd only been looking at how this all affected her. Especially since she knew he was right and had been thinking much the same thing herself, had even stepped willingly into the fire. It was only seeing the reactions to the mark that made her angry, and she'd turned that anger on him. She bowed her head, cuddling into the reassurance of Lee's arms. 'That is a good point. And you are right, it was worth doing just for that. I wouldn't ever forgive myself if you came to harm because of me.'

'I'd have fought for you, Muiri,' Calla said. 'But with those odds I can't say I'm unhappy that it didn't come to that.'

'I understand,' Muireann said. She'd been thinking much the same thing about the odds against them earlier.

'Tash, you come with me, and we'll follow them for a bit just to be certain they are actually leaving,' Calla said, keeping her swords ready. Tash nodded, giving Muireann a reassuring look before jogging after Calla.

Rey picked up her discarded clothes and held them out to her, like a peace offering, and she felt even worse for being so angry before. She took the clothes, holding them against her chest. 'I'm sorry, Reyleth, for what I said before. You did the right thing, and I know that.'

'It's alright,' he said softly. 'I know that what I asked you to do was difficult.'

'Not as difficult as watching you all die or even get hurt would have been,' Muireann said, Lee's arms still warm around her. 'I was being very selfish.'

'No, you weren't,' Lee said. 'It's your choice to show people the dragon mark or allow them to see some of what you can do now. No one should force you to reveal anything you aren't comfortable showing.'

She glared at Reyleth when she said it, Rey for his part returning the hostile look, and Muireann winced afraid that the tentative peace between the two was fracturing under this stress. 'Hey, please don't fight with each other over this. I need you both more than ever right now. Lee, I love that you are so protective of me and that you won't let anyone force me into anything, but he didn't. He just told me what I already knew, that the only way to stop that without violence was to show them something they'd consider miraculous. Reyleth, you were right but so is Lee in that I didn't want to do that – I had to, and I did because my feelings aren't more important than your lives – but that didn't make it any easier or less traumatic.'

Lee leaned her head against Muireann's shoulder. 'I'm sorry it came to that.'

'As am I,' Reyleth said, his voice uncertain. She smiled tentatively at him, hoping he could see that she wasn't upset with him, just with the entire situation.

'I need to get dressed,' she said, moving away from both of them towards her tent. She didn't let herself look back to see their faces and they didn't follow her.

As she dressed, she hoped that the rest of the journey would be less eventful.

Chapter 10

To the Sea

They travelled for a week south to the shore, walking as far as they could every day and camping at night. Unlike the last time they'd made a long journey they avoided towns and cities as much as possible, going into a civilised area only when they had to for supplies or when there was no way to avoid it. While they knew they might be safer in the settled areas they were all worried about word of their presence spreading, especially after the confrontation with the cultists. Their plan, such as it was, hinged on Ghellin following them or sending people after them, but it was also essential they make it to the shoreline as safely as possible and walking the fine line between those two things was more challenging than Muireann had anticipated.

Calla was confident that once they reached the shore word would spread and they had only to arrange everything and wait for Ghellin or his men to show, but Muireann wasn't so sure it would be that easy. Always before he'd managed to get the drop on them usually when they were most confident they were safe. It meant that the whole week as they walked Muireann fretted constantly, jumping at shadows and watching for signs of pursuit. Even her new bow in her hands and the weight of her new quiver at her hip didn't reassure her; the cult's attack had shown that the small group could be easily outnumbered, and she only had a couple of dozen arrows. The others all seemed to be in good spirits, though, glad that the Arvethri weren't a threat any longer and that there was hope that soon Ghellin wouldn't be either. Even if their plan was as much wishful thinking as actual strategy.

The final night before they'd reach the coast they made camp following their usual routines, but after dinner as everyone else chatted and relaxed Muireann noticed Lee slipping quietly into their tent. Curious and a bit worried that the selkie seemed withdrawn she followed, finding Lee sitting on their blankets holding her current knitting work in her hands, but staring at her feet motionless. She set her bow and quiver down and moved to join her wife, sitting next to her but ready to get up again if Lee wanted to be alone. 'Mind if I join you?'

'If you'd like,' Lee said. 'I don't think I'll be very good company.'

Muireann reached out, stroking a hand down Lee's back. 'What's wrong?'

'It's nothing,' the other woman said, trying to put on a brave face.

'Lee, you can talk to me, whatever it is,' Muireann said, worried now. She wrapped Lee in a loose hug.

'I know I can,' Lee said, setting down the knitting and turning in Muireann's arms so that they were face to face. 'I suppose I just feel foolish worrying about it when we have so much else going on.'

'Are you afraid of what you're going to do?' Muireann said, caressing the selkie's hair. 'Because if you don't want to go through with it—'

'No, no, of course not,' Lee rushed to reassure her. 'I want to help to do my part. Everyone else has already taken on so much risk I'd feel terrible if I shirked now.'

'I don't want anything to happen to you,' Muireann said, leaning her forehead against Lee's.

The selkie smiled, her eyes soft. 'Then I'll just have to stay safe, won't I?'

'Yes, you will,' Muireann said, kissing her. Lee reciprocated with feeling, her hand coming up to tangle in the mess of Muireann's red curls. Muireann pulled back, though, after a moment. 'So then, what is bothering you, my love?'

Lee sighed, lingering close. 'Returning to the ocean. I'm not sure what might happen. My folk are north-west of this coast but if they've spread word to the other clans to watch for me... it could be trouble.'

'I won't let anyone take you Lee, not against your will,' Muireann said with more confidence than she felt. In truth much like the rest of their plan she didn't know how she would actually pull it off if it came to that.

'I know you won't,' Lee said, smiling again. 'I knew when you saved me from that man that you would be good to me and that you would never force me to do anything against my will. That's what made me want to marry you. And the more I got to know you after that the more I loved you, because you are such a good person, and you treat me so well.'

Muireann felt her cheeks flaming at the compliments. She kissed Lee again. 'And the fact that we can't keep our hands off each other doesn't hurt either.'

Lee laughed, the sound happy and light. 'That as well. We are good together.'

'We are,' Muireann agreed. 'So, try not to worry too much about what may happen tomorrow or when we are near the water. We'll protect each other and you know none of our friends will stand by and let you be taken away.'

'I know,' Lee said. 'I suppose I just feel selfish for worrying about this when what really matters is making sure the weapon is safe until we can destroy it.'

Muireann shifted slightly where she was sitting, reminded of an idea she'd had while they were walking. 'That is what matters, but you matter too. It's not selfish to be worried or afraid now that we're so much closer to doing this.'

'I don't want to let you down,' Lee said.

'I don't want to let you down either,' Muireann said, hugging the selkie closer. 'But I know that we are all doing our best and all we can do at this point is keep trying as we have been.'

'I suppose that's true,' Lee agreed. She sighed, snuggling

closer to Muireann.

'It is true, and Lee, really everything will be alright in the end as long as we stick together and fight for each other.'

'I know,' the selkie said, sighing softly. 'I think I just need a little bit of time alone right now, if that's alright?'

'Of course,' Muireann said, getting up. 'I just wanted to see how you were doing and let you know we won't abandon you. But you take the time you need. I'll be back later when it's time to get some sleep.'

'Thanks, Muireann,' Lee said, smiling uncertainly and picking her work back up.

Muireann slipped out of their tent and went to find Reyleth, wanting to talk to him about something before they reached the shore or had any run-ins with Ghellin or his people. Talking with Lee had reminded her of an idea that she'd had; she suspected Rey wouldn't like it but despite that she was going to suggest it anyway. Reaching his tent she waited outside until he let her in. Once he did, though, she jumped right into what she wanted to talk about.

'I think you can channel magic through me, the way a mage could with a relic or talisman.'

'You're a person, not an object,' he snapped, frowning.

'You know what I mean,' she said, walking further into the small space and flopping down on his bedroll.

He sighed but went to sit next to her. 'What you're talking about could be very dangerous.'

'You can't kill me,' she said, shrugging. 'And this could give us a real advantage in another fight. It would mean you can use more spells and more powerful spells.'

'We don't know that I can't kill you,' he said sharply, getting up and pacing away from her, agitated. 'We don't truly know the limits of any of it. And if you are carrying the dragon's magic then one possible way you could be killed might be to have all that magic drained.'

She stood and stopped his anxious movements, grabbing his hands. 'I trust you, Reyleth. I don't believe that you would do anything to harm me or that you can or would perform any spell that could possibly drain that much magic from me. Not a dragon's worth.'

He didn't look convinced, and she reached up and stroked his cheek. 'Let's experiment. We can start small and if it makes me feel odd or bad, we'll stop. But even I know a mage is limited by how much magic he possesses or can draw from smaller outside sources. If this does work and it's safe for both of us you could potentially cast major spells, things that others only dream of. Even the lesser things would be made so much easier.'

'This sort of thing isn't done and I'm afraid that if we prove it can be done to you safely or otherwise it would be very dangerous for you,' he said.

'What do you mean?'

'In the First Age mages knew how to access deeper magics, deeper sources, perhaps even directly connect to and pull from Erla herself,' he said carefully. 'That was all lost when the Aldovanan fell, but for all the millennia since people have tried to recapture that knowledge. Magic now is so much more limited than what we know – think we know – the Aldovanan could do. Our greatest spells today are a shadow of what magic once was, and to get even remotely close to the old results mages either have to work in groups or use very unethical sources, including murder. Those darker magics are forbidden but that doesn't stop some people from pursuing them. And those people if they found out that magic could be pulled from you would stop at nothing – and I mean nothing, Lennath – to get access to that power.'

She thought about what he'd said for several minutes, turning his words over carefully in her mind. She was keenly aware of how very vulnerable she could be, and yet... 'I understand what you are saying, Reyleth. I truly do. And I don't want to be pursued by power hungry mages or open to that sort of manipulation. But if this gives us a significant strategic advantage that ends up being the deciding factor between success or Ghellin getting the weapon, I don't think we can risk not using it. Not with this much at stake. I think we must use this if we can. I think you must see if you can use this power in me if you can.'

'You are not an object,' he repeated, obviously agonised at the thought of treating her as such.

'We are partners,' she soothed. 'Think of it that way.'

Still, he hesitated, refusing to meet her eyes. She reached up and pulled his head to hers, kissing him softly. 'Start small. Just see if it can be done. You don't have to make use of it if you don't want but if we know you can do it then in a truly dire situation it may save us. All of us.'

'Alright,' he said but with obvious reluctance. 'Only to see if it's possible.'

She stepped back, smiling. 'Good. Let me know if I need to do anything to help.'

He sighed, then shook his head. 'Just be still, but let me know immediately if you feel strangely, alright?'

'Of course,' Muireann said dutifully. She thought he was being overly cautious and that his concern was unwarranted but could see how nervous he was and wanted to reassure him. He walked around her, frowning and still looking uncertain; she struggled to stay patient, wanting him to start but knowing that he had a lot of reservations about all of this.

After several slow minutes went by he finally stopped, standing in front of her. She met his eyes correctly, reading the fear in their blue depths and reached out to take his hands, squeezing slightly. 'Why don't you start with the light spell you did when we were in the caves?'

He licked his lips, then nodded. 'Alright. That's a very minor spell, it should be simple enough to cast and you may not even notice anything.'

'I'll let you know if I do,' she said.

He nodded again, but still didn't do anything. As the silence dragged out, she said, 'Reyleth, please, just try. One small spell won't do anything dire.'

'I know that,' he snapped, with a bit of his usual spirit. Then his blue-ish white cheeks flushed slightly pink as he admitted, 'I'm not sure how to start.'

'How would you start if you were pulling from a talisman or ley line?' she said, hoping to help him see the problem from a different angle.

His eyes darkened and she held up a hand to forestall the argument. 'I'm not a thing, yes, agreed. But theoretically, how would you start pulling from a non-living source?'

He sighed. 'I'd try to connect to the object on an energetic level, then use that connection to draw the energy from it.'

She smirked, letting her eyes fall below his face. 'That shouldn't be too hard then. We've *connected* pretty thoroughly, at least enough that you should be able to feel what joins us, yes?'

To her real shock at what she'd thought was a very tame bit of teasing the colour in his cheeks darkened, the red mixing with the blue in his complexion to give his face a purple tint. She couldn't hold back a laugh. 'Are you *blushing*? You, the always serious elven mage?'

He swallowed hard. 'You are an absolute menace, Lennath.'

'You've said that before.'

'Because it's true.'

'Well, it's also true that we're pretty thoroughly connected,' she said. 'Repeatedly even. So, you shouldn't find this too difficult. Just focus on that and pull the energy from that place.'

He closed his eyes, his cheeks still faintly coloured, but this time she could tell he was making some kind of effort. A moment later a ball of light appeared above their heads, illuminating the shadowy tent far better than the single candle he'd had burning.

It seemed brighter to her than the one he'd cast in the caves, but her memory of that time was admittedly clouded by the emotions attached to the experience, which painted it in her mind in gentle soft tones.

He opened his eyes, his gaze cutting immediately to her face, but Muireann just shrugged. 'I didn't feel anything.'

He frowned, looking thoughtful, then nodded. 'It's a minor spell which wouldn't take a noticeable amount of energy from me either. Let us try something slightly larger.'

'Let's,' she agreed, glad that he was willing to continue.

He thought for a moment. 'I'm going to try a spell to create a mirror, or at least the illusion of one – it's not a permanent physical object.'

'That sounds useful, especially while travelling.'

'It is,' he said, relaxing slightly as they talked. 'It's also something I use often, so I'm very familiar with the spell, and it takes a noticeable amount of energy but not a significant amount.'

She nodded agreeably and he turned slightly to the side, chanting and tracing a two-foot oval in the air. A moment later the shimmering image of a gilt mirror appeared suspended in the air, solidifying into what seemed like a very real object. She leaned forward, marvelling at how real it seemed; she and Reyleth were perfectly reflected in the surface.

'Anything?' he asked, breaking her concentration.

She straightened up. 'I noticed something slight. It's hard to put into words.'

He frowned slightly. 'Can you try?'

She shook her head. 'It's too nebulous and vague really. Why don't you try something a bit stronger, and I'll tell you how that feels?'

'I'll try a more complex illusion,' he said, waving his hand so that the mirror disappeared. When she signalled she was ready he closed his eyes and chanted again, this time something more flowing and complex; the words were almost familiar and she suspected the language was a form of ancient elvish.

The space around them rippled and changed, from a simple tent to a grand bedroom; the walls became deep blue silk hangings, the bedroll a sturdy dark wood canopy bed, draped with the same silk and covered with silk sheets. A moment later she smelled incense, heavy and sweet, on the air, and could faintly hear music although she couldn't quite place what kind. Muireann stared around the changed space, dazzled by the luxury of it all. 'Wow. Can I touch it? Would it feel real?'

Rey opened his eyes, smiling at the changed room. 'Try it and see.'

Feeling both foolish and excited Muireann moved to the illusory bed, reaching out and running her hands along the silk; it was as soft and smooth as any real silk she'd ever touched, if not finer. She turned back to Reyleth, not trying to hide her delight. 'This is amazing. Could I sit on the bed?'

'You should be able to,' he said, walking over to join her.

She sat down tentatively, then when the bed proved as solid as if it were real, she climbed eagerly onto it. 'Oh, this is amazing. I had no idea you could do anything like this.'

'I can't usually,' he admitted, joining her on the bed. 'This is far more detailed and substantial than I've ever achieved before.'

'Because you were pulling from me?' she asked, curious, still obsessively running her hands over the silk.

'I must believe so,' he said. 'And to the important question at hand – what did you feel?'

'I noticed something this time,' she said carefully. 'Nothing bad or concerning, but as if I could feel that we were connected, and something was passing between us. It's still a bit difficult to describe, but it was almost pleasant.'

'Pleasant?' he said, looking sceptical.

'Yes,' she said, lying back on the soft mattress. It felt as real as the feather bed in the Blue Rose; she was utterly fascinated by it, and by the realisation that when given free rein to create any illusion he went for what she'd least expect from him, pure luxury. 'As I said, it's hard to properly explain. But as if I could feel something going out from me and the sensation was enjoyable.'

'Are you tired? Do you feel dizzy at all?' he pressed.

She shook her head quickly. 'I feel fine. Actually, I feel pretty good and a bit hyper, but I'm not sure if that's from the energy going through me or because this is exciting.'

He thought for a minute then said. 'Let's go outside.'

'We may gain an audience,' she pointed out.

'Perhaps, but I want to try one more thing and I think it's safer outside.'

She got up with great reluctance; once they were both standing, he chanted again and the illusion dissipated like smoke, the interior of the tent returning to normal. The little ball of light remained, though, and followed them as they went outside; she was grateful for that because the heavy clouds looming above them meant it was fairly dark. Reyleth led her just beyond the edge of their camp, near a dead tree. It had lost most of its limbs, but the weathered bark-less trunk still stood. She looked from the tree to Rey curiously.

'I want to try my small lightning spell,' he said. 'I think it will be a good test because it is a more powerful spell, one that usually tires me greatly to use, but I don't think it would be dangerous for us to test now. Also, since you've seen me use it before you are somewhat familiar with it, and how you react to my using it should be very telling.'

'Sounds good to me,' she said amicably.

He stood a bit in front of her, closer to the dead tree, and took up a more combative stance. She waited, trying to see what she felt as he chanted, noting the same subtle feeling of flow and pleasure.

Then the world exploded in light and sound, everything bleaching white as thunder peeled through the space and the scent of ozone clogged her nose. Reyleth fell backwards, knocking her down with him so that they landed in a pile of tangled limbs.

For the first instant she lay stunned, Reyleth mostly on top of her, her vision a field of white, her ears ringing. Distantly she heard voices, then Rey was being pulled off of her and Calla was looking anxiously into her face. When she spoke the words sounded oddly distant. 'Are you alright? Say something if you are alright.'

'Where's Reyleth?' Muireann said, looking around for the elf, still blinking away streaks of light. She quickly saw him standing, half supported by Tash nearby. Lee was standing, looking stunned, a few feet further back. 'What happened?'

'I think there was a lightning strike,' Tash said.

'Bad luck to have lightning without rain but very fortunate it didn't directly hit either of you,' Calla said, now looking at the smoking ruin that was all that remained of the dead tree. Muireann stared at it in open-mouthed shock.

Reyleth finally pushed away from Tash, moving anxiously back to Muireann's side. 'Are you alright? Are you hurt?'

'I was going to ask you that,' she quipped, but he didn't look either amused or soothed by her words.

'Muireann, be serious for a moment,' he snapped. 'Are you alright?'

'Of course, I'm alright,' she said. 'I'm basically immortal. An actual lighting strike wouldn't kill me, probably, and a magical one definitely not. Are you alright, though?'

'I'm fine, that was just…not what I expected,' he muttered.

Calla's eyes sharpened. 'Magical? What did you two do?'

When Rey hesitated Muireann jumped in to answer. 'I had a theory that Reyleth might be able to channel magic through me, and that it could give him more to work with, make casting spells easier for him.'

'Well, it definitely seems to have given him more to work with,' Calla repeated dryly, her eyes flicking to the smoking tree stump. 'So, you did this, mage? Why would you risk a lightning spell this close to camp?'

'It wasn't supposed to be a lightning spell,' Reyleth said, still staring anxiously at Muireann. 'It was the same spell I used on the mercenaries when they attacked us, it should have been enough to knock an adult unconscious not to cause an actual lightning strike.'

Calla looked even more concerned, then thoughtful. 'Interesting. So channelling magic through her gives you a significant power increase.'

'So it would seem and without noticeably tiring me,' he agreed. 'But it's clearly too dangerous to use.'

'It clearly isn't,' Muireann cut in, finally able to see and hear normally as the after effects of the lightning wore off. 'I agree it isn't something to use lightly or even often. But in an emergency, something like that is a distinct advantage. And if pulling magic through me has an amplifying effect on all your magic, think of how that could apply to something like healing.'

At that he did hesitate, considering her words. 'We'd need to experiment more.'

'Clearly,' Calla said, arching an eyebrow. 'But I'm on Muireann's side with this one. It may need some serious fine tuning but the strategic advantages here are staggering. And I for one am in favour of calling down lightning on one's enemies.'

'Calla!' Muireann snorted.

'Under certain circumstances,' Calla amended, grinning. 'You'll have to keep practising until you can control how much power you pull and not accidently blow us all up, though. Muireann may survive it but the rest of us wouldn't.'

Rey hesitated, but finally nodded unhappily. 'It will require recalibration, certainly. I admit I've only occasionally worked with charged talismans, and they tend to empty quickly, and ley lines are...very different. Like trying to take water from a river by hand. This is like being able to direct the river and have it go where you choose.'

'Very poetic,' Calla said, yawning. 'I assume that translates to, "yes, Calla, we need to practise so we don't accidently blow everyone up".'

He glared at her, so Muireann stepped in. 'We'll keep practising. But further from camp and not tonight.'

'I wouldn't count on any of this being useful in time to help us with our current situation,' Reyleth said. 'This may take some time to work out and the risk of using it without that finesse is too great.'

'Well, either way that's enough excitement for tonight,' Calla said, gesturing for the group to head back towards the tents. 'Muireann, you're on watch next, why don't you go grab your bow and quiver?'

'Sure,' she agreed.

'We should be extra cautious tonight,' Tash said, peering into the dark night, the moon still hidden behind heavy clouds. 'That lightning may well have drawn attention to us.'

'Yes, it was far from subtle,' Reyleth said.

Muireann grimaced at that but jogged back to her tent to get her things. That had certainly not gone as she'd expected but she was more convinced than ever that she was right and Reyleth channelling magic from her was useful. She was equally sure that after that disaster of a test he'd be even more reluctant to actually use it.

Sighing she attached the quiver to her hip and set off to patrol, hoping that tonight at least would be quiet. She knew that they were running out of time, one way or another.

* * *

The next morning the little group closed the last distance between themselves and the shoreline, reaching the coast just past mid-day. Both Tash and Lee had reported seeing shadows behind them throughout the morning, hints of figures that melted away before they could be clearly seen, and everyone was on edge waiting for an attack that never came.

When they finally crested a hill and came in sight of the shore Muireann stood staring at the waves, her heart full with the sight and sound. She had not even realised how much she missed it all until that moment, even the seagulls wheeling overhead a welcome sight, where she usually found them annoying. Lee came up next to her, taking her hand. 'I can taste the salt in the air.'

'It's beautiful,' Muireann said, closing her eyes and letting the scent wash over her, salt and seaweed and that bitter smell of low tide. Her heart ached with it.

Lee squeezed her hand, a silent communication they'd both fallen into to express support. 'I didn't realise you missed it so much.'

'I feel like part of me is missing when I'm away from the ocean,' Muireann admitted. 'Like I don't know how to properly be myself without it.'

'I understand,' Lee said, her voice soft and slightly anguished.

Muireann looked at her sharply, remembering exactly who she was talking to and regretting being so open. 'I'm sorry Lee––'

'No,' Lee cut her off, squeezing her hand again. 'Don't. Don't try to lessen yourself to keep me comfortable. I want to see this side of you and to support you when you are struggling the way you support me. And Muireann, I do understand what you are saying. I don't regret anything I've done or being with you and I'd change none of it, but even living my dream to explore the world on land, to live among the shore-folk, there's always that part of me that knows I can't truly leave the ocean behind. It's part of who I am, and that's alright.'

'Do you want to go in the water?' Reyleth, who was standing slightly to their left, asked carefully.

Lee hesitated for an agonizingly long moment then shook her head. 'No. Not yet. When the time comes I'll be ready but not yet.'

Reyleth started to say something, looking unhappy, then shut his mouth and simply nodded. Slightly behind them Calla and Tash were equally silent, solemn as they looked at the water. It occurred to Muireann that this was it, they had reached their destination and all that remained was to set their final plan in motion – and that everything was about to get very, very dangerous for all of them.

'What now?' she asked softly, unsure who she was even asking.

Calla answered, her hand clasping the locket that hung above her heart and held the green crystal. 'Now we go down to the strand and reconnoitre the area, finalise our plans, and then we wait.'

'I doubt we'll have long to wait,' Tash said, his gaze behind them on the road inland.

'Well, better they attack now, when we've made it this far than they had attacked before,' Muireann said, trying to sound reasonable and not scared, which she was. She didn't want to be attacked at all and knowing it was inevitably coming was worse in a way than the terrible uncertainty they'd dealt with before.

Much subdued the group continued the last small distance to the water, stopping where sea grass gave way to sand. They stood together and watched the waves roll in for several minutes until Calla shook herself slightly. 'Alright, Lee the plan hinges on you taking the jewellery case into the water to hide it. Does this seem like a good place, or should we seek a different area?'

Lee moved closer to the water, then looked up and down the coast, her brow furrowed. 'I think a rockier area would be better. Let's move a bit north and try to find a place that is more challenging for others to go into.'

'Ah yes, I see,' Calla agreed, starting to walk north along the beach. 'Some place that's less inviting and more off putting. That's a good idea.'

'And will offer a landmark we can use to find it again,' Reyleth suggested.

'Another good point,' Calla agreed.

They moved along the sandy area, Lee walking slightly in front looking for something in the waterline that the others couldn't see. The beach curved in and jutted out, went from sand to rock and back again as they walked. Lee was focused on whatever it was she was looking for, but Muireann saw Calla quietly pull her swords, and she reached for an arrow, aware of the shapes in the heavy grass around them.

'Lee—' she stared to say, and then the grass and reeds parted, a heavily armed group of selkies emerging from all sides. They wore their sealskins as cloaks, much like Lee, but were otherwise naked and they wielded spears made of white polished wood, the tips sharpened to efficient points. Muireann moved ahead of her wife, arrow at the ready, as their other friends also moved to protect Lee by circling around her.

They were surrounded quickly and Muireann was reminded, perforce, that selkies were faster than humans and stronger. There were, perhaps, a dozen of them, led by a dark-haired man who was taller than the rest. His eyes swept their group, finding Lee even though she was standing behind the other four who were trying to shield her. 'Come forth, Coralee, we are here to rescue you from those who have taken you by force from your kin.'

'We didn't take her anywhere,' Calla said, swords up and ready. 'She is with us freely.'

'Return her to us!' the tall selkie said, shifting his spear forward. 'She doesn't belong with you.'

'Yes, she does,' Muireann said. 'She's my wife.'

The selkies faces reflected their fury at these words, but again it was the leader who spoke. 'You stole her sealskin?'

'No,' Muireann said, looking back at Lee who as always had the fur draped over her shoulders.

Lee stepped forward, pushing through the protective barrier of her friends, back straightening. 'She didn't steal anything from me. She defended me from a man who would have taken my sealskin and won it back for me. And then I chose to go with her, as her wife.'

The gathered faces showed confusion now, and when their leader spoke again it wasn't as belligerently. 'That isn't what we were told by your kin. They would have it that you were compelled from the sea, not by the old laws of marriage but by darker manipulations.'

'My kin didn't want me to go on land,' Lee said, chin still up although Muireann could see the fine trembling in her hands. 'I wanted to know what it was like to experience more of life than what they could offer. I left them when they threatened to imprison me themselves. I chose to leave the waves and stay with Muireann, to go where she goes.'

The gathered selkies looked uncertain now, but much less hostile. One of the women among them spoke out. 'Is she good to you?'

'She is,' Lee said. 'She is very good to me, and we protect each other as it should be. That is why we have come to this shore, because we are being pursued by a terrible man who wants to steal something we have, a dangerous magical weapon.'

Muireann and Calla both tensed, sharing a nervous look at Lee's words. The selkies, though, relaxed visibly, moving their spearpoints down. The leader spoke again this time. 'And you are seeking refuge in the sea? All of you?'

'No,' Lee said. 'We are planning to hide what he seeks where he will never find it, then head north over-land.'

'You mean to hide it in the ocean,' the leader said, nodding slightly. 'I will tell you this then, Coralee, daughter of Shannen, your kin are spreading the tale that you were taken by force and need rescuing. We made clear we would not interfere if you had lost your sealskin, because that law is as old as the waves and binds us all as surely as the law that a selkie may take a human into the sea if they weep in the water and wish for it. We will not interfere now if you have truly chosen this fate freely – others may disagree with a person repudiating their kin, but we believe that all should walk the path that Vorren sets them. I am glad to know that you live by choice in this, only remember that you would always have a place with us should you want it. I will tell you this as well, the shore to the north of here is our domain but from this beach south belongs to no one for two dozen leagues, until the territory of the sea-folk begins. If you intend to hide a thing this would be the location to set out from.'

Lee bowed her head respectfully to the other selkie. 'Thank you for this advice and for your offer.'

His eyes swept their group, then settled back on Lee. 'My name is Tonntren. If you decide to return to your people but not your kin, come to our borders and ask to speak to me.'

Lee smiled, but her face was sad. 'Thank you, Tonntren. I will do so should the situation ever arise.'

Slowly the gathered selkies dispersed, disappearing back into the waves. Silence consumed the group of friends, who stood with the sea breeze pulling at their hair and clothes.

Muireann looked at Lee, who was staring at her feet. Not knowing what else to say she said. 'Your name is Coralee?'

Startled Lee looked up, then made a face. 'I prefer Lee.'

'I'm rather fond of Lee too,' Muireann said, earning a smile from the selkie. 'I just wasn't sure if you'd given us a short name because you were trying to hide or something.'

'No, nothing like that,' Lee said. 'I just like Lee better. I thought it suited me more, especially for my new life on land.'

'Then we'll keep calling you Lee,' Calla said calmly, finally sheathing her swords. 'I'm sorry you had to go through that but at least now we know you can venture into the water here safely, or relatively so.'

Lee nodded, taking a deep breath and finally lowering her spear. 'I'm glad for that. I know you all may not have understood everything that was just said, not the nuances of it, but Tonntren was saying that he disagreed with my family and what they tried to do, and that he'd welcome me here even if I'm...not like other selkies.'

'You could have a home here if you wanted one,' Tash said.

'My home is with Muireann, but yes,' Lee said, smiling at Tash. 'It's a relief to know that not all my people are against me.'

'I can imagine,' Calla said, her voice subdued, then shaking herself slightly. 'Well at the moment we have pressing problems to deal with and while I appreciate how useful this confrontation ultimately was, we can't let it distract us. If Tash and Lee were right that we are being followed now, and I don't doubt it, we must assume it's likely Ghellin's men or spies and that he won't be far behind.'

'And we cannot go further north than this,' Reyleth said, his eyes on the land behind them. 'So, we must go back and find a suitable place in what shoreline we've already covered.'

'I have a couple of ideas,' Lee said. 'I was looking for somewhere ideal, but we have passed several places that would be suitable I think or at least I can make them work.'

'Let's retrace our steps then,' Calla said, eyes still on the sea.

'Calla,' Tash started, but she was quick to interrupt.

'I know, Tash, I saw them too,' the high elf said.

'Saw who?' Muireann asked, uneasy.

'Our recent discussion with the selkies wasn't a private one,' Calla said. 'Let's turn back and try to find a better spot. I suspect we don't have much time left.'

'If Ghellin thinks we are about to hide the stone here he will surely attack quickly,' Reyleth said, pulling his sword again.

'Most likely,' Calla agreed as Lee led them south again. 'But so far he has rarely done exactly what we expected him to do. At this point I won't assume anything.'

Rey looked annoyed at the implication he was assuming something, but he let the moment pass, trailing the group. Watching him let an opportunity to needle Calla pass by made Muireann nervous and showed her how very serious everyone was taking the situation. It was starting to really sink in that the final step of their plan was about to happen and Muireann was keenly aware of how many ways this could all go wrong. *If only we knew how to destroy it,* she lamented to herself, *all of this drama and risk would be unnecessary.*

Lee led them back to one of the rockier sections of shore they'd passed, an area where the land extended out into the water to form a short narrow peninsula. Slightly beyond the breakwater Muireann could see a series of rocks breaking the surface. Even though she wasn't a sailor herself she'd grown up along the coast and knew this would be bad water for boats or ships which wouldn't be able to safely navigate the hidden rocks. She nodded to Lee. 'I think I see why you picked this.'

Lee smiled. 'I'll have to explore underwater a bit, but I think I'll be able to find a perfect hiding place that won't be easy for any shore-folk to access.'

Tash cast his eyes upwards at the heavy clouds that still lingered and to the horizon. 'We only have an hour or so until sunset.'

'What should we do?' Muireann said to Calla.

For once the high elf looked uncertain, and when she spoke, she kept her voice low. 'I suppose this part of the plan is a bit nebulous. We want him to come at us while he still thinks we have the stone but since he hasn't taken the bait so far there's no telling when he'll attack.'

'Why not just hide it now and let him worry about finding

it?' Tash asked.

'Because,' Calla said with a sigh, 'if he doesn't see us hide it, and isn't certain we've done so, he will still be after us on the chance we have it or to force us to tell him where we hid it. This only works if he thinks we don't have it anymore and thinks he knows exactly where to look for it.'

'Won't it look odd that we're hanging around here but not doing anything?' Reyleth worried.

'Possibly, but what else can we do?' Calla said. 'We must be sure he's fallen for the trick or there's no point doing it.'

'This was never a plan,' Reyleth complained. 'Just a vague idea. We've had all this time to think of something better or work out details and here we are on a beach with no idea what to do if he hasn't taken our bait.'

'Well, I didn't see you suggesting anything better, mage,' Calla snapped.

'There was nothing to suggest, Tinairi,' he snapped back. 'Except to keep running and hiding as we had been.'

'Which would never have worked in the long run,' Calla argued.

'Which is why we need an actual plan!'

'It's a bit late for that now, isn't it?' Calla said, crossing her arms over her chest. 'Ghellin's spies are all around us, for all we know he could attack at any moment!'

'Enough,' Muireann cut in. 'This isn't helping anything. We've come this far, however good or bad this plan is, it's all we have right now. If he doesn't follow through then we can head north, maybe seek shelter with Tonntren's people while we think of something new. But right now, we should see this through.'

They all stood unhappily, silent after her outburst, unsure what to do.

'Let's keep walking within a mile or so of this section,' Calla said finally. 'Lee, you can go into the water and scout around but be ready to return quickly if needed.'

Lee nodded and Muireann could see when the selkie looked at the water that her deep sadness was gone. It was a small thing, but Muireann was glad for it anyway and the knowledge that whatever happened Lee could have a home here if she wanted one.

They walked up and down the same mile of beach for the next few hours, as the sun dipped lower and lower, waiting for Ghellin to make his move. As the hours crawled by and nothing happened, Muireann started to wonder if he meant to wait but could see no logic in him risking them following through with hiding the stone where he'd be unable to locate it. Finally, Calla signalled them all to gather together. 'It's getting late, and we need to make camp. I doubt he'll attack at night, but we'll work in pairs to guard camp tonight and be ready before dawn. If nothing happens then we'll head north tomorrow.'

They each nodded, exhausted but aware of how much danger remained.

For all their preparation they were woefully caught off guard when the attack finally came. If Ghellin had planned it that way it was masterfully done, giving them just enough time to start to think he meant to wait until the next day. As they moved to start setting up camp at the top of the sand where it met the sea grass, the sounds of marching feet reached them. They scrambled to regroup, Calla swearing loudly. Several dozen mercenaries marched over the crest of the nearby hill, fanning out to surround the five friends, the superior force giving them few options. Behind the soldiers Ghellin walked as casually as if he were out for a twilight stroll. Next to him was a tall white-haired man in a mage's formal robes, the purple dull in the growing gloom.

As the ranks of organised mercenaries circled around them, Muireann dropped her heavy pack and cloak, wanting to be unhindered in the fight to come. The others did the same, dropping their things into a pile and edging away from it. They stood back-to-back facing their enemy.

'Give me the stone,' Ghellin said calmly from behind the shelter of his hired swordsmen. 'You cannot win in a fight, and I will kill you all if I have to.'

'We won't give it to you,' Muireann said, watching the others bracing themselves around her. 'Whatever happens we won't hand it over to you.'

'You don't have a choice,' Ghellin said, then, smiling. 'Well, you have a choice between giving it to me freely or having me take it from your corpse. That's your choice.'

'You will never get it,' she said with more strength than she felt.

'You are a clever woman, Muireann,' he said, still calm. 'Look around you. There's no escape. You can't possibly think you have a chance to fight and win.'

'How do you know we haven't already hidden the stone?' she bluffed.

'I'm disappointed,' he said, shaking his head. 'I told you I'd be generous and have given you all of this time to make the right choice.'

'I did make the right choice,' she said.

'I know you still have the stone, Muireann,' he said, still smiling slightly. 'I've been watching you, everything you've done. I let you slip from the city, it was my decision to allow that – I told you it's so much easier to find people to go after a group on the road, didn't I? Even that illusionary pageantry with those Arvethri – and that was clever, I'll give you that, letting your mage fool them with charlatan's tricks into thinking you could walk through fire. Overly dramatic, but impressive. You see I could have taken the stone anytime, but I wanted to let you come around to giving it to me. I know you will because you understand how important the stone is, even if you don't understand its awesome power. All this back and forth today by the water, but you don't trust anyone enough to give them the stone. I know you haven't, I'd have seen it the moment you started to hand anything like the Basglassin to any of these others, and my mage would have struck you down. And I know why you haven't.'

'You know nothing,' Muireann said, unnerved nonetheless about what he was saying, how much he knew and had seen.

'I know that deep down you know I'm right,' he said casually. 'You want to give me the stone.'

'We are going to hide the stone where you will never find it,' she said. She watched his eyes narrow and then dart to the water and Lee.

'She'll be dead before she can reach the first wave,' he said coldly. 'I may hesitate to waste a human life, but I will not so much as blink over killing a selkie. Move to give the stone to her and she dies where she stands.'

So, he really does think I have it, that wasn't bluffing on his part, Muireann thought before saying. 'Whatever happens here, Ghellin, you will not get the stone. If Lee can't get into the water, someone else will.'

'I'm disappointed, Muireann, I really thought you understood,' Ghellin said, actually managing to sound disappointed. 'I thought you'd choose the side of humanity.'

'I understand what you want to do, that's why I'm trying to stop you,' she said, the bow string taut against her fingers.

'If you truly understood you'd be helping me, but like these others standing with you, you see only the obvious and miss the deeper possibilities.'

'I can't let you do this,' she repeated, starting to understand that he really did believe she'd give him the stone, that he could convince her. It was unnerving to think he was so certain.

'You can't stop me,' Ghellin said, his mercenaries edging forward. 'The Second Age ends and the Third Age, the Age of Humanity, begins.'

'We have the weapon, what makes you so sure we won't use it against you?' she bluffed, desperately seeking any opening for Lee to get to the water's edge. Their nebulous plan was falling apart so quickly.

He laughed without humour. 'You don't understand the Basglassin or how to use it. Why else would you have been so frantically researching it? Why else flee Mistlen when you knew I was hunting you? No, you have it but have no idea how to activate it.'

'I know how to use it,' Muireann said, remembering the vision the stone had given her.

'Then use it now, mighty Dragonslayer,' he said mockingly.

'My lord,' the mage next to him said, frowning. 'Don't tempt her to try, the consequences-'

'Silence, Laertan,' Ghellin snapped, waving a hand. 'I pay you for your magic not your opinions.'

He turned his attention back to Muireann, continuing to ignore the others. 'Give me the stone.'

'No,' she said, lifting her chin and trying to look braver than she felt in that moment.

He let out a long, annoyed breath, as if losing patience with a recalcitrant child, then waved his hand. 'Kill them all.'

The mercenaries were on them in moments and utter chaos broke. The mage cast a spell, knocking Reyleth off his feet, his power obviously greater than the elf's. Calla and Tash disappeared in a flurry of blades. Lee stood swinging her spear at the half dozen swordsmen trying to get under her guard. Muireann released the arrow she'd prepared, aiming for Ghellin but striking a swordsman in the melee instead. She reached to draw another arrow.

A sword struck her on the side of the head. There was the familiar flash of pain as she fell, knocked off balance by the force of the blow. Her glasses flew from her face. Everything around her was reduced to blurring motion and noise as she desperately crawled amid the stomping feet, trying to find her glasses, her bow clutched in one hand. Someone stepped on her arm, another flash of pain, and then her fingers closed on the familiar metal frame. Another foot came down on her hand, now holding the glasses, and she was forced to wait until they stepped away to pull her hand back. Glasses back in place she struggled to stand; another swordsman came at her, and she drew an arrow and fired at almost point-blank range. He fell screaming, clutching the feathered shaft barely protruding from his chest.

Back on her feet she ducked another sword, felt a blade stab her side and ignored it, trying to get a sense of events. Calla was nearby, fighting furiously. Remembering that the high elf still had the jewellery case that was holding the fake crystal, she worked her way through the fighting towards her. This was yet another flaw in their plan, and Muireann realised that they had been far too overconfident in thinking that it would be simple to mislead Ghellin and get away clean. She lost count of how many times she was hit, intentionally or accidentally, by swords. Reaching Calla she ducked another flurry of blades, grabbing the pouch at the elf's waist.

'What are you doing?' Calla yelled, trying to keep fighting with Muireann in the way.

'Getting the stone to Lee,' Muireann said, breathless. The next moment the silver case was in her hand, and she was stumbling away, still taking blow after blow from the swordsmen. At some point her bow was ripped from her hands, but she pushed on heedlessly. She didn't even try to defend herself, focusing on getting to Lee's side. Once there she shoved the case at Lee, who dropped her spear to take it. The nearest mercenary saw them, saw what they were doing, and moved to block them. Lee was helpless in the fight without her spear and all Muireann could do was physically put herself between the other woman and harm.

'Reyleth! Cast the spell! Now!' Muireann shouted across the space separating them, desperately trying to wrestle the man away from Lee so she could run.

'It's too dangerous!' he yelled back, his own sword a blur as he fought.

Muireann managed, finally, to throw the heavier man down. She met her wife's eyes for a split second amid the chaos. 'Run, Lee.'

The selkie ran, dodging fighters, the jewellery case clutched in her hand. Over it all Muireann heard Ghellin yelling for his men to stop Lee, but the selkie was agile and fast, weaving through the chaos. She ran towards the waves, and Ghellin screamed in frustration.

'Kill her! Laertan, now! Kill her before she goes too far,' Ghellin ordered the mage. Muireann saw the mage's eyes shifting from Reyleth, who he'd been watching battle against the mercenaries, towards the water. She knew that whatever he was about to do Lee would be helpless against it.

'Reyleth! The spell, now,' she yelled over the din of the ongoing battle, running towards Laertan, thinking that if all else failed she could physically throw herself in front of the spell.

'It's too dangerous,' he said again.

'There's no choice,' she turned, still running, and her eyes met his, pleading. Ghellin's mage had started chanting, his voice low and terrible, but she was still a dozen yards away.

Reyleth downed the man he was fighting, stepped back and started chanting. Muireann felt that sense of flow, from herself to him, that vague pleasurable warmth as the magic moved within her.

Muireann was closing the distance now, but was still too far to block him. Laertan raised his hands, pointing at Lee as she crossed the last few feet to the water. Reyleth finished his chant. Magic vibrated in the air.

The world exploded in white light and sound.

Muireann woke up on her back in the sand, staring up at the churning clouds overhead. For an instant she couldn't make sense of what had happened. Then she smelled the ozone and something worse, and the memory came. She rolled to her knees, staring around at what had, moments before, been a raging battle. The two mercenaries who had been closest to Muireann were dead. Many of the others were down, some moving slowly, others climbing to their feet and leaving as quickly as they could. They had all clearly decided they weren't being paid enough to risk what had just happened. Reyleth was standing, staring around at the scene in wide-eyed shock. Tash and Calla were also down but moving. Lee had disappeared into the water. Muireann turned and looked the other way.

Ghellin lay a few yards from her, his entire body smoking. The stench was unimaginable. Slightly past him, Laertan also lay, not smoking but completely still. Where Ghellin had been standing was a blackened circle in the sand.

Muireann staggered to her feet, covering her mouth at the smell and backing away from what was left of Ghellin. Reyleth's hands on her shoulders startled her and she jerked away, then realising it was him, threw herself into his arms. 'Are you alright?'

'Am I? You were struck by lightning,' he said, his hands on her body shaking. 'Your clothes are all but rags and there's blood everywhere.'

She winced. 'That's not from the spell, that was before. In the fighting. I'm fine, though, you know I'm fine as always.' She glanced back at the body. 'Ghellin is definitely not fine.'

Reyleth was still shaking, his hands running over her as if he really thought she could be hurt. She reached up, stroking his hair. 'Is it just me or was that a bit...more...than last time we tried that spell?'

'More than a bit more,' he quipped, but he was still shaking when he said it. 'I was rushing and wasn't as focused as I should have been. I wasn't thinking to control the flow, just to cast the spell before the other mage could cast his.'

'It's alright, Reyleth.'

'I could easily have killed all of us,' he said, shaking his head. 'That is not alright.'

'You didn't,' she pointed out, watching more of the mercenaries leave. 'And the fight is definitely over now. Ghellin is dead. The stone is safe. Despite that disaster of a plan I think we actually won, because of you.'

'I need help,' Tash said, his voice low and desperate and only then did Muireann look over, past Reyleth, near the waves where Lee had disappeared. Tash was on his knees next to Calla, a pool of blood spreading across the sand.

Muireann and Reyleth ran to them, ignoring the few mercenaries that still moved on the ground and jumping over or dodging the bodies of those who weren't moving. Tash was crouched over Calla, holding pressure against a gaping wound in her side. She lay completely still, her chest barely moving as she breathed.

Muireann fell to her knees next to her friend, then looked up at Reyleth. 'You have to heal her.'

'I can't, this is a mortal wound—'

'You can if I help you!'

'Lennath please, I can't control the flow of it,' he said, looking around at the destruction that surrounded them.

'You can,' she insisted, watching the blood spreading across the ground, soaking into the knees of her pants. 'I know you can. I trust you even if you don't trust yourself.'

He hesitated, still looking around. Tash pressed harder against Calla's side. 'Please, Reyleth, she's dying. Please try.'

He finally looked back at Calla, then knelt down next to Muireann, one hand on her shoulder, one on Calla's. 'I don't suppose I can hurt her if I try.'

'Please,' Muireann repeated, understanding why he felt so conflicted but afraid his hesitancy would cost Calla any chance of surviving.

He lowered his head and a moment later she felt the now familiar flow of magic between them, felt her worry being washed away under the warmth of it. She had meant to keep her eyes on Calla, but as the energy moved through her she found her eyes closing against her will, an almost euphoric feeling overwhelming her. She knew somehow that Reyleth was pulling more than he ever had before, more even than for the recent disastrous lighting strike. But it felt good. It felt right.

When he stopped it was so abrupt that Muireann gasped at the loss of the feeling, her eyes snapping open. Calla was looking up at her, amused despite it all. 'Do you need a private moment, Muiri?'

Muireann felt her cheeks flaming at the implication but was too overjoyed at hearing Calla speak to care. 'You're alive!'

'Or she's just too stubborn to admit she's dead,' Reyleth said, but she could hear the happiness in his voice too.

'You'd miss me if I died, mage,' Calla said, sitting up. She turned and pulled Tash into a hug. 'Don't think I don't know that you helped save me, knight.'

'I'm not a knight yet,' Tash shot back automatically, but he was smiling so hard Muireann thought his cheeks would hurt later.

'You are, you just don't realise it,' Calla said, letting him go. Her smile finally fell away as she examined the gaping hole in her corset and shirt. 'Blast it, I really loved this corset.'

'You should wear armour,' Tash said.

'I don't look this sexy in armour,' Calla said, with her usual smirk and suddenly they were all laughing, relief washing over them.

'Why are we laughing?' Lee asked, joining them, naked

except for the sealskin, her hair dripping salt water.

'Because Calla is ridiculous,' Muireann said, 'and still alive.'

'I'm not ridiculous. I just know where my priorities are.'

'I'll buy you new clothes,' Muireann said. 'When we get to the next town.'

'I'll buy us all a feast,' Calla said, pushing them all away so she could stand. 'But speaking of all of that, I assume we've won the day?'

'Ghellin is dead,' Muireann confirmed.

'And the item is hidden in the rocks,' Lee added, her eyes now taking in the scene on shore. Ghellin's body was still smoking slightly. Besides the mage there were another five bodies down and not moving; Muireann assumed they were dead. Another three wounded mercenaries were still struggling on the ground, abandoned by the others.

'Are we all unharmed?' Tash asked, cleaning his sword reflexively.

'You know I am,' Muireann said, forcing a smile. Reyleth had not exaggerated the state of her clothing; she was covered in blood and her tunic and pants were torn to rags. Even her leather corset was ruined.

'And you know I am, thanks to Reyleth,' Calla said, running her hands absently over the large hole in her clothing. The flesh underneath was perfect and unmarked.

'I am well enough,' Reyleth said. 'What small wounds I had seem to have also been healed with the spell I cast on Calla.'

'I'm fine,' Lee confirmed, then jogged off.

Before Muireann could call out to the selkie to ask where she was going, Tash was speaking again. 'I am not gravely injured, but Reyleth, if you could manage another healing spell—'

'Where are you hurt, my friend?' the elf asked, quickly going to the young human's side.

Tash looked embarrassed and grateful in equal measure. 'It's nothing dire. But I took a blow to my arm.'

Muireann pressed close as Reyleth pulled away the rough bandage Tash had fashioned to reveal a long bloody gash in his arm. Rey turned to Muireann. 'Can you do more today, do you think?'

'Reyleth, I've told you, you channelling magic through me doesn't tire me,' she said, nodding. 'If you are able to do more today than I am certainly here to help.'

He flushed. 'Normally I'd be far beyond my usual limits, but things are different when you help.'

'Then let's get this done,' she said gently.

He nodded then focused on Tash. This time she could tell that he connected faster, the magic feeling almost eager to go to him. It was an odd sensation on top of all the other things she felt when he did this, but not bad. And as with every other time she didn't feel at all ill or drained, but rather felt excited. She realised that all of her exhaustion, all the physical and emotional weight of the stress from the day was gone. She felt as good as if she'd just gotten up from a long rest.

A moment later it ended, and Rey stepped back. Tash's wound was healed without a scar, and the young man smiled, flexing his arm. 'Thank you.'

'Thank you,' Reyleth said, resting his hand on Tash's shoulder for a moment. 'If you hadn't gone to Calla's aid when she was down, she would have died before I could heal her.'

Tash smiled shyly. 'The advantage of being a healer's son, I know more than I ever meant to learn about such things.'

'And it has stood you in good stead,' Reyleth said.

'Speaking of armour, I'll have to get you a better set,' Calla said, smiling at Tash. 'To thank you for what you did for me. Don't get any ideas, mage, I'm not getting you anything, that's what you have Muireann for.'

'Calla!' Muireann snorted, too glad her friend was alright to be very annoyed.

Even Reyleth looked amused. 'That isn't what I have

Muireann for, if we could even say that I have her, but rest assured I don't want anything from you.'

'Oh, I'm pretty sure we can say that you have her fairly often—' Calla started, but the rest of her teasing was cut off by Lee's return.

The selkie had her spear back in her hand and had redressed, the flowing material billowing in the sea breeze. She interrupted Calla, either heedlessly or, perhaps having heard enough of what she was saying, intentionally. 'Muireann, I have your bow for you.'

Lee handed the bow to Muireann, who smiled. 'Thank you. I was afraid it was broken in the fighting.'

For a moment they all stood in silence, Muireann inspecting the bow, the waves loud around them. Then Calla sighed. 'I suppose it's too far to walk to any town now, with the sun all but down. Still, I'm not camping here among corpses nor am I cleaning up this mess. Let's get our things and look for a better place to set up away from all of this and tomorrow we can find an adequate town and really celebrate.'

They walked over to their packs, picking up their things and chatting animatedly now that the moment of solemness was broken.

'I can hunt us a fine dinner tonight,' Lee said. 'Some decent fish.'

'We don't all like fish the way you do,' Calla said.

'It will be a good change of pace,' Tash said, smiling at Lee's enthusiasm.

'I have mead in my pack, which will be a nice change of pace,' Calla said, patting her bag. The locket Muireann had given her swung above her ruined corset, reflecting the fading light.

'Come on, Lennath,' Reyleth said, turning back to Muireann who was lingering behind the others as the group started walking north again.

'I'll be right there,' she said, nodding for him to go on.

Muireann stood for a moment after the others had turned away, staring out over the water, her fingers tracing the scar on her cheek. The Arvethri were still out there somewhere but at least now they weren't trying to kill her, although she still didn't think the alternative was much better and she doubted they'd seen the last of the dragon worshippers. Ghellin was dead and with him his ambition to wield the weapon and destroy anyone who wasn't human. They, and their world, were safe.

But the weapon still existed and their solution was a temporary one, even if temporary meant they didn't have to worry about it for hundreds of years. The others were all in a mood to celebrate and part of her wanted that as well, but she felt a lingering worry that until they unmade the green crystal they wouldn't be truly safe. She reached down and felt the bulk of the stolen book in her bag, somewhat reassured that at least with that she might be able to eventually figure out how to destroy the crystal. *If I can kill a dragon with a single note in the margins of a book then I can solve this problem too, with the right book and enough time,* Muireann thought. *And at this point I have all the time in the world.*

'Muireann?' Lee called to her, slowing down and waiting for Muireann to catch up.

Pushing the worries away Muireann turned and adjusted her pack on her shoulders, setting her bow and quiver in place, before moving to re-join the group. Calla and Tash were still talking about food, now in an animated debate about what did or didn't qualify as a feast. Listening to them Muireann slid her hand into Lee's and then reached out for Reyleth on the other side.

They had won that day, against all odds without any causalities, and bought the time they needed to find a better solution. The world was safe. Feeling happy at that thought at least, she said, 'Let's go and make our own party for tonight and you can both have whatever feast you want tomorrow.'

'That's the plan, Muiri, that's the plan,' Calla said, grinning back at her.

They had won for the day, and that was enough reason to celebrate.

FANTASY, SCI-FI, HORROR & PARANORMAL

If you prefer to spend your nights with Vampires and Werewolves rather than the mundane then we publish the books for you. If your preference is for Dragons and Faeries or Angels and Demons – we should be your first stop. Perhaps your perfect partner has artificial skin or comes from another planet – step right this way. If your passion is Fantasy (including magical realism and spiritual fantasy), Metaphysical Cosmology, Horror or Science Fiction (including Steampunk), Cosmic Egg books will feed your hunger. Our curiosity shop contains treasures you will enjoy unearthing. If you have enjoyed this book, why not tell other readers by posting a review on your preferred book site.

Recent bestsellers from Cosmic Egg Books are:

The Zombie Rule Book
A Zombie Apocalypse Survival Guide
Tony Newton
The book the living-dead don't want you to have!
Paperback: 978-1-78279-334-2 ebook: 978-1-78279-333-5

Cryptogram
Because the Past is Never Past
Michael Tobert
Welcome to the dystopian world of 2050, where three lovers are
haunted by echoes from eight-hundred years ago.
Paperback: 978-1-78279-681-7 ebook: 978-1-78279-680-0

Purefinder
Ben Gwalchmai
London, 1858. A child is dead; a man is blamed and dragged
through hell in this Dantean tale of loss, mystery and fraternity.
Paperback: 978-1-78279-098-3 ebook: 978-1-78279-097-6

600ppm
A Novel of Climate Change
Clarke W. Owens
Nature is collapsing. The government doesn't want you to know
why. Welcome to 2051 and 600ppm.
Paperback: 978-1-78279-992-4 ebook: 978-1-78279-993-1

Creations
William Mitchell
Earth 2040 is on the brink of disaster. Can Max Lowrie stop the
self-replicating machines before it's too late?
Paperback: 978-1-78279-186-7 ebook: 978-1-78279-161-4

The Gawain Legacy
Jon Mackley
If you try to control every secret, secrets may end up controlling
you.
Paperback: 978-1-78279-485-1 ebook: 978-1-78279-484-4

Readers of ebooks can buy or view any of these bestsellers by
clicking on the live link in the title. Most titles are published
in paperback and as an ebook. Paperbacks are available in
traditional bookshops. Both print and ebook formats are
available online.
Find more titles and sign up to our readers' newsletter at
http://www.johnhuntpublishing.com/fiction
Follow us on Facebook at https://www.facebook.com/JHPfiction
and Twitter at https://twitter.com/JHPFiction